DON'T KNOW WHERE, DON'T KNOW WHEN

Also by Annette Laing
A Different Day, A Different Destiny

For Athena Katherine —
+
I am deaf. 🙂

DON'T KNOW WHERE,
DON'T KNOW WHEN

Cheers!

🙂

By
Annette Laing

Annette Laing

2014

CONFUSION
PRESS
Statesboro, Georgia

For My Grandmother, May Simpson, and All the
British Ladies of Two World Wars
Who Enlivened My Childhood, With Much Love.

Library of Congress Control Number: 2007901732
ISBN 10: 0-9794769-4-1
ISBN 13: 978-0-9794769-4-5

Printed in the U.S.A.

Cover design: Deborah Harvey
Inside design: Kelley Callaway

Author website: www.AnnetteLaing.com

Contents

FOREWORD

by Dr. K.D.G. Harrower, Snipesville State College

Dear Reader:

Don't read this if you don't want to. The last thing I want to do is to bore you silly, especially because I'm not the author of this fine book. I am just the person writing the introduction, or Foreword. So if you feel your eyelids starting to droop, or if drool is beginning to trickle from the corner of your mouth, flip to the real start of the story, which you'll find on page 1. Honestly, I don't mind.

If you have foolishly decided to read this introduction, I promise I will try not to sound like a history teacher who is trying out for the next United States Olympic Boring Team.

There two very important things I must tell you:
I am an historian.
This is not a history book.

But because much of this book takes place in Britain during World War I and World War II, the author believes you will find it helpful if I tell you a little bit about the history. I hope she's right. I shall try to keep it short and silly, rather like the author herself. That's a joke, by the way. She is an old friend, so I'm sure she won't mind.

I should first explain that Britain is one country made up of three smaller countries: England, Scotland, and Wales. It's not hard to understand if you think about it. It's just like how the United States of America is composed of fifty states. See? Now you can impress your parents by explaining this to them.

• **World War I started in 1914. Nobody was quite sure why. It ended in 1918 because everyone was fed up of it.** The First World War was a disaster. Millions of young men were killed or injured for no good reason. But in 1915, a year that we will visit in this book, the terrible truth was only beginning to dawn on most people. Soldiers, of course, were the first to know how badly things were going on the battlefield.

• **World War II (1939-45) was the sequel to World War I. But it was a very different kind of war.** The Second World War began on September 1, 1939, when Germany invaded Poland. Too many Germans had lost their minds in the 1930s and decided that Adolf Hitler was their ideal leader. Hitler was a nasty little man with a silly moustache, who spent a lot of his time and energy hating people he didn't know, and thinking of ways to kill them. But I bet you already knew that.

• **By summer, 1940, Germany was winning World War II, and Britain was almost its only undefeated opponent.** Britain's leader, Prime Minister Winston Churchill, hinted to the United States that although the Americans had arrived late for the First World War, it would be very, very nice if they could show up promptly for this one. But Americans remembered what a waste of time and people World War One had been. And so, although American President Franklin D. Roosevelt wanted to help Britain, he was unable to convince his people to send soldiers. Still, America sent weapons and food to the besieged Brits. Indeed, America sent *lots* of food, even if it was mostly dried eggs and Spam.

• **In fall, 1940, Germany was preparing to invade Britain.** To pave the way for the invasion, Hitler launched a massive bombing attack on British cities, especially London. The bombs killed thousands, and destroyed much of that fine old city. The British nicknamed this attack the Blitz. Thousands of children were evacuated from the cities to escape the bombing, and were known as evacuees. Most evacuees were sent to live with strangers.

• **Britain unleashed a secret weapon during World War II.** It wasn't a bomb or a plane, but a civilian army of tough, brave, take-no-nonsense women. Prime Minister Churchill probably should have sent these women to deal with Hitler. Had he done so, the war might have ended much sooner.*

Alright. That's it for the history lesson. After all, this isn't a history book, and I should know, because I am an historian.

This is the story of Alex, Brandon, and Hannah, who are three twenty-first century American kids. They are much like any other kids of their age, perhaps including you, except for one thing: They are time travelers. They have lived through the history I have just described, and much more. To them, indeed, it is not history at all.

You are about to read their first adventure, which took place long before they were born. I do hope you will enjoy reliving the journey with them, just as I enjoyed watching them live through it the first time.

Sincerely,

K.D.G. Harrower, Ph.D.
Dr. K.D.G. Harrower
Department of History
Snipesville State College
Snipesville, Georgia

[*]These women were amazing. One of them actually did visit Hitler in Germany, three years before the war began. Dame Irene Ward was an enormous woman who wore enormous hats and carried enormous handbags. In 1931, she was one of the first women elected as a Member of Parliament, or M.P., in the House of Commons (sort of like the House of Representatives, but with more power and very bad manners.)

In 1936, Dame Irene was among a group of British M.P.s attending a polite party with Htiler in Germany. Suddenly, as sometimes happens at adult parties, the room fell silent, and everyone clearly heard her tell Hitler off: "What absolute bosh you are talking!" she said. She was probably the only person ever to scold this ruthless dictator, and live to tell about it. You see what I mean about those women…

DON'T KNOW WHERE, DON'T KNOW WHEN

PROLOGUE

I am sorry to interrupt this book, but it's me again, Professor Harrower, the person who wrote the Foreword you have skipped over. I just want to warn you that this story begins in different places, and at different times. I told the author that you might find it helpful to be introduced to the people, places, and times of this tale. So here they are. KDGH

Balesworth, England: July 11, 1915

The First World War was almost a year old, and would have more than three years still to go. Rain was falling yet again on the High Street in the sleepy English town of Balesworth, thirty-five miles and a world away from London. A balding Scotsman in his forties stood on the covered front porch of his large two-story brick row house, which was also where he practised his profession as a dentist. With him were his nephew, a small boy of only seven, and his handsome young son of twenty-one, who was dressed in the uniform of a second lieutenant of the British army.

"Send me a postcard from France, Cousin James," said the little boy eagerly.

"With a bit of luck, Oliver," the young man replied, laughing and roughing up the boy's hair, "I'll send you more than one." He turned to his father. "Aren't Mother and Peggy coming out to say goodbye?"

Mr. Gordon looked uncomfortable. "War is difficult for women, James. You know that."

Nothing more on the subject was said.

"All the best, then, James," said his father, awkwardly shaking his hand, and trying not to look as anxious as he felt. "And keep your head down."

Balesworth, England: September 11, 1940

It was a year since World War Two had begun, and now, Britain stood alone in the fight against Germany. Rain tapped on the windows, and a coal fire glowed brightly in the two-story cottage on a road on the very edge of Balesworth, a growing town north of London. On three sides of the house were open fields. A small boy with dark hair, wearing the short grey trousers, white shirt, and grey woolen vest of his school uniform, was lying on the floor. He was playing noisily with a paper airplane that he had just made, his half-drunk mug of cocoa sitting forgotten on the small table nearby.

The tall, grey-haired woman sitting at the desk was busily writing with an ink pen in a small notebook with a marbled cardboard cover. A black Labrador lay sprawled at her feet, while a tiny red and white spaniel was taking advantage of her absence to curl up in the armchair by the fire.

Finally, as she always did, Mrs. Devenish finished by writing out the date of the following day's entry, September 12, 1940. She took off her reading glasses, put down her pen, replaced the diary in the desk drawer, then rubbed her eyes, and stifled a yawn.

Noticing the empty bucket next to the fire, she said to the small boy, "Eric? Would you please go and fetch more coal? It's almost time to listen to the wireless. The prime minister is to address the nation about the German bomb attacks on London."

"Sure fing, Mrs. D.," he said, and scrambled to his feet.

She looked askance at him, and said wearily, "Eric, the letters "T" and "H" both appear in the word "thing" but, to my recollection, the letter "F" does not."

He smiled to himself as he picked up the bucket and left the room. He was used to her constantly correcting his London accent, and he really didn't mind.

Snipesville, Georgia: Today

It was another hot day in the small, tumbledown town of Snipesville, Georgia, an hour inland from Savannah and the Atlantic Ocean. The temperature was already in the high eighties, and the humidity was even higher. It was only ten in the morning. Inside the small old whitewashed clapboard house, the air conditioning churned noisily. The screen door opened. A short-haired black boy, wearing a T-shirt and shorts, stepped outside, and grimaced as he felt the heat. Carrying a handful of change, Brandon walked down the street to the convenience store, and slotted the coins one after the other into the Coke machine outside the entrance. The soda can came clattering down, and he leaned down and collected it from the slot below.

"You doin' alright there, Brandon?" asked a kindly older man, a friend of his father's, who stopped on his way into the store.

"Yes, sir, Mr. Dixon. How 'bout you?"

"Jes' fine, thank you."

It was the exact same conversation Brandon always had with Mr. Dixon, in fact, with most adults come to that, every single time they met. Short, sweet, and exactly the same.

San Francisco, California: Today

The girl with long brown hair was packing the last of her stuff into a box in the apartment in the Mission District. She threw in a teddy bear, and then began to clear the photos from the top of her dresser. There was one of her with her brother, Alex, at Disneyland. Another photo showed her with her dad, on a cable car in San Francisco. Yet another image captured a visit with her grandparents at a winery in Napa Valley. Finally, she picked up the last picture, and hesitated.

Here was the photo of her mother at the Golden Gate Bridge, taken years before Hannah was born. Her mom was giving a crooked smile into the camera lens, and the teeth of a strong San Francisco Bay wind. Her chestnut brown hair was held down by a burgundy scarf so it wouldn't fly away, and she was pulling her thick black wool coat around her, her hands in the pockets. She looked so young and so beautiful. Stifling a sob, Hannah thought how, now, she always would.

"You okay?" It was Alex, who had appeared in the doorway.

She wiped at the tear that had trickled down her nose. "I just can't believe we're actually leaving California. I looked up this place in Georgia on the web, and it looks soooo boring."

"Hey, c'mon Hannah, it'll be an adventure! Anyway, you're always saying how bored you are here, so what difference does it make where we are?"

She scowled at him. "You can be so annoying, dork."

Balesworth, England: Today

There is a library in Balesworth, a growing English city that is separated only by a few precious acres of farmland here and there from the growing sprawl of London. The library is in a building made of concrete, glass and steel. Once upon a time, after World War Two, this building style was called modern. Now, as it grows old and grey, it's known simply as ugly.

The young librarian stopped the cart, and picked up the small notebook with its bent corners and marbled cardboard cover. She placed it on the heavy oak table in front of the Professor. "That woman's diary from World War Two you were asking about? We found it, finally," she said.

"Thanks very much for hunting it down," said the Professor with a smile.

"Well, I knew you'd be happy to have it before you fly back to America tomorrow. Here's the volume for 1940. Just let me know if you want me to get any of it photocopied for you." The Professor thanked her again, and she moved on to make more deliveries to other researchers in the room.

The Professor opened the notebook, and began to read the neat handwritten entries. She often thought to herself that one of the great pleasures of being an historian was that she got to read other people's letters and journals, without anybody thinking she was weird.

Twenty minutes went by. The only sounds in the small archive were those of turning pages and clicking keyboards, as researchers tapped notes into their laptops. If any of the people present had looked up from their books, old documents, or computers, they would have seen the Professor suddenly sit up straight, exhale sharply, slump back in her seat, and rub her eyes. If they were good at lip-reading, they would have also seen her say silently to herself, "Oh, no, not again."

You cannot be an historian without traveling in time. But the Professor is different. Time travel is not something she can end simply by closing a book or filing away a manuscript. It is real.

Chapter 1:
SNIPESVILLE

Hannah Dias looked around at the packing boxes in her room, frowned, sighed, and tossed back her hair. It was all so totally unfair.

She hated Snipesville from the moment the car crested the only hill in the whole of South Georgia, and she first clapped eyes on the town. It was all billboards, decrepit houses, mobile homes, and subdivisions. Oh, yes, and trees. Her brother Alex had talked constantly, all the way from Savannah Airport, about how many pine trees there were in Georgia. Yes, said Hannah, lots and lots. Big whoop.

Before they left California, Dad, Hannah, and Alex had visited Grandma and Grandpa in Sacramento for a farewell dinner. The grandparents' house was brick, with little fake turrets, like a castle, and an arch that created a small courtyard next to the front door. When she was little, Hannah had liked to pretend it was a cottage from a fairytale, like Little Red Riding Hood.

That makes sense, she thought now, because Grandma is a bit like a wolf. Not that she looks like one, of course: She is as beautiful as an old lady can be, but she is also clever and sly. It wouldn't have surprised Hannah if she had had sharp teeth to eat people with. Hannah felt ugly and dumb most of the time these days. Although she usually enjoyed her grandmother's company, there were days she would have given anything to have a fat, plain, dimwitted Grandma who orbited around her, offering lots of sympathy and home-made chocolate chip cookies.

But no. Grandma was the first woman high school principal in the city, and she was the most stylish, smart, and scary old lady Hannah had ever known. She always wore clothes with expensive designer labels, and colorful, hip jewelry from the Sacramento Artists' Collective. Hannah had never seen her Grandma with a single grey hair or without makeup. Her dad had once muttered a snarky comment about Grandma having had a facelift, but since Hannah had figured out that there was no love lost between her dad and his mother-in-law, she kind of doubted it.

Grandma threw open the door and her arms to Hannah: "Sweetheart! It's so great to see you!" Hannah hugged her awkwardly, before pulling free, dashing past, and throwing her arms round Grandpa, who was a good foot taller than his wife.

"So are you practising your Scarlett O'Hara routine yet?" he asked with a chuckle.

Hannah looked up at him. "Scarlett say what?"

"Never mind." He kissed the top of her head. "It's from a movie about the South your grandma and I saw back in the day, sometime around the late seventeenth century. Right, Ellen?" Grandma rolled her eyes, and playfully slapped Grandpa on the arm.

That was the last light moment. Afterwards, the evening descended unstoppably into disaster.

Grandma ordered the farewell dinner from a Mexican restaurant, because she refused to believe that they would have real Mexican food in Georgia. But the food took over an hour and a half to arrive, and meanwhile, everyone grew hungrier and hungrier, and grumpier and grumpier.

Grandma was the grumpiest of all. Her mood did not improve with the arrival of the limp, lukewarm food. During dinner, Grandma needled her son-in-law about the move to Georgia: Schools, the library, the politics, the weather, how often they could visit their grandchildren, the food, the arts scene (not that there would be one to speak of, she muttered), how often their grandchildren could visit California, and lots besides. She never seemed pleased with Dad's answers.

Grandpa contented himself with cracking jokes about the Deep South, which was, Hannah knew, his way of telling her Dad that he was unhappy, too. He rubbed his hands together and said "So what's first on the agenda, Bill? You gonna change your name to Billy Bob, or invite the neighbors round for a cross-burning?" Then he laughed loudly at his own joke.

Shooting him a warning look, Grandma said, "Don't scare the kids, Fred."

Like she hasn't been scaring me for the past two hours with her stupid questions, Hannah thought angrily.

Looking directly at Hannah, Grandma said, in a knowing tone, "Your grandpa thinks the South is as bad as it was fifty years ago."

Hannah had been getting madder and madder, and now her head exploded.

She jumped up at the table, and yelled, "You do too. That's why you're asking Dad all these retarded questions." She picked up her napkin and threw it at Grandma, landing it squarely on her head. Everyone at table paused, stunned. Alex sat with his mouth open.

Grandma slowly plucked off the napkin, and folded it. In a soothing voice that made Hannah madder than ever, she said "Hannah, perhaps you should go into the living room, and calm down."

Hannah had expected someone to yell at her, and "young lady" her a lot, but Dad just looked depressed, Alex looked embarrassed, and even Grandpa was uncomfortably quiet. Hannah sat down in silence at the table, and tried not to look at her grandmother again.

Later, when Hannah was in the den with Alex, watching TV, she overheard Grandma and Dad talking in the kitchen. She overheard her name, and words like "self-esteem," "counseling," and "issues." Hannah was always being told that she had "issues," and she had begun to explain her own behavior to herself and adults in terms of "issues," too. Adults seemed to like it when she talked about "issues," and it got them off her case. Too bad that it always made her squirm a little.

When they said goodbye, Grandma hugged Hannah tightly, and apologized for upsetting her, which both pleased and annoyed her granddaughter. Grandpa told Hannah that she was just like her mother, and there were tears in his eyes. Both of them told Dad to look after Hannah and Alex, and himself. On the way home, nobody in the car said anything at all.

Brandon Clark lived in Snipesville, Georgia, in a ramshackle old whitewashed wooden house that belonged to his parents. His great-great-grandparents had built it, when they were among the first black homeowners in West Snipesville, back in 1899.

Most of the house was neat and normal. Brandon's older brother Jonathan's sports trophies took pride of place in the family room, next to the new flatscreen TV. Photos lined the white beadboard walls: Brandon's parents' wedding, Brandon as a toddler, Jonathan in Little League, Brandon's grandparents' 45th wedding anniversary, and Jonathan's wedding.

Then there was Brandon's room. A dusty three-dimensional model of the solar system floated from a hanger. Little glow-in-the-dark stickers in the shapes of stars and moons were glued to the ceiling, and some were falling off. An old, disintegrating bookcase was crammed two deep with books. There were dusty books on the floor. Books were piled on the nightstand by Brandon's unmade bed.

A few were the sort of books you get from well-meaning but clueless family members or the school library, like *Nature's Wonders: Our Friend, The Frog*, *Timmy TooGood Celebrates Our Nation's Heritage*, *Puppy and Kitty Find a Ball and Play With It*, and *A Kid's Guide to Success Through Appropriate Behavior*.

Most were books that Brandon had bought for himself from online bookstores, using his allowance, and the gift certificates he begged from every family member every Christmas and birthday. There were books of science fiction, comic books, funny books in which all the jokes were about poop and toilets, and books about history. Brandon especially liked historical picture books. He could imagine walking through the camera lens and into those faraway, lost worlds.

A dust-speckled baseball bat, deflated football, and saggy basketball sat in a corner of the room.

Brandon's grandparents had founded the family business that was now known as Clark and Sons Home of Eternal Rest, Inc. His father and uncle owned the funeral home, together with his mom's sister, his aunt Marcia. She worked the front desk, and dealt with grieving customers. She was almost never known to smile, although Brandon's dad swore he had heard her laugh for a full half minute in 1981, when she saw a neighbor's cat run over by a car. Brandon and his dad had secretly nicknamed her Morticia, until his mom overheard them one day, and put a stop to it. Well, kind of. They still called her Morticia when they were sure Mom was well out of earshot.

Brandon's dad also worked as an insurance broker, and more and more of his attention went to that business, while Brandon's uncle and auntie kept up the funeral home. Two years ago, Mr. Clark had opened a new office, close by the tiny Snipesville Mall, which was known to everyone as the Small. With more and more people retiring to Snipesville, Brandon's dad had explained, he could expand what he called his "customer base" out of West Snipesville: "White folks still don't like being buried by a black man, but these days, some of them will buy insurance from one," he said. And so, Gordon Clark and Son Insurance of Snipesville was born.

Brandon had a horrible feeling that he was the "Son" in the title: Nobody had consulted him, but there were no other likely candidates. He had a frightening vision of the future he was sure his parents had planned for him. He would get a degree in business from Snipesville College, followed by a partnership in either the funeral home or the insurance agency, or, most likely, both. And he would marry some girl he probably already knew at the Authentic Original First African Baptist Church of Snipesville (so named in 1967, to distinguish it from the Original First African Baptist Church, after there was a big split in the First African Baptist Church over some terrible controversy. Nobody now could remember what the fuss was about.)

Brandon wasn't sure what he wanted out of life, but this sure wasn't it. Two years ago, he had met his second cousin Franklin at the family reunion at the church hall. Franklin was a Big Shot, one of many Big Shots who had left black Snipesville to find careers they couldn't have in town, where white Snipesville controlled most of the jobs. Big Shots were lawyers, businesspeople, professors, and, as in Franklin's case, doctors, all across America.

Brandon liked Franklin, and was impressed by the enormous respect everyone showed to the young man. What excited him most were Franklin's tales of life in Boston, and all the traveling he had done while he was a college student.

This was the kind of life Brandon wanted, but he kept very quiet about it. He was too afraid that somebody would say no—and especially his mom, who scared everyone, including his dad.

At Alex and Hannah's new house in Snipesville, the silence was deafening, broken only briefly when Alex came back in from the yard, carrying two huge pinecones. "I love this place! You seen these? They're awesome."

Hannah looked at him as though he was the saddest person she had ever known. "You need a life. Big pine cones? That's pitiful."

"No, it's not," Alex shot back. "It's too cool to have a big yard, and a big house. I mean, this is way better than California. You know, I saw an actual woodpecker this morning."

Hannah gave an exaggerated yawn. "This place is, like, the boredom capital of America."

Hannah still didn't believe her dad's story about why they had left California. He had told her and Alex that the bank was transferring him to Georgia, and he had no choice. Hannah had begged him to look for another job, but he said it wasn't that easy, and, anyway, it would be fun to live in a small town, with clean air and less crime. And, he said, they would be able to afford a big house, because Georgia was so much cheaper than California.

That part had been true, Hannah thought resentfully. They had a big house, alright, with a bathroom for each of them, plus one more… in Nowheresville, USA. The house wasn't even in Snipesville, where she could at least have gone shopping at the tiny mall, or hung out at the college.

Instead, they were living in Magnolia Acres, "an exclusive luxury community," according to the sign at the gate, that was surrounded by cotton fields. There were no parks, no shops, no buses, and almost nobody under the age of 60. And it was too far from town for Hannah and Alex to walk or ride their bikes.

When Hannah complained, her dad promised to check into summer programs at the college. Remembering that conversation, Hannah sighed heavily. Now Alex was signed up for baseball camp—even though he hated baseball—and she was registered for creative writing camp, which she thought sounded a little too forced, kind of like calling a camp "mandatory fun."

Hannah was just staring blankly at the big pile of boxes, when the doorbell rang. Through the frosted glass front door, she could see someone with long blonde hair. When she opened the door, the visitor flashed a big smile at Hannah, who disliked her on sight: Blonde *and* perky, Hannah thought. I *hate* perky. I *hate* blonde.

"Hi, I'm Kimberly?" Hannah also hated girls who said everything like it was a question, and who carried prissy purses—which Kimberly was doing, of course. Hannah stared at her, but Kimberly plowed on. "Your dad sent me?"

"You're the babysitter, yeah?"

"Um, yeah, that's right. You guys ready?"

Hannah shrugged, and yelled "Alex?" over her shoulder. She did not invite Kimberly inside.

Kimberly drove a huge SUV, and she looked, Hannah thought, like a Barbie doll driving a tank. They traveled the short distance into Snipesville while Alex played on his GameBoy, and Hannah looked out of the window. The first things she saw coming into Snipesville were the billboards, most of them for local businesses. Hannah read them all, fascinated by how amazingly tacky they were:

Peanut Pines Inn: Classy Elegance with Southern Sass! announced one.

Another: *Mama Fred's BBQ and Gifts.* Hannah tried to picture Mama Fred, and imagined a big bearded guy, wearing a pink housedress and fluffy slippers. She smirked.

Kimberly took Hannah's superior smile as a sign of approval: "Snipesville is such a beautiful place, isn't it?" she said. Hannah looked at her as if she was mad, thinking, is this chick blind or just stupid?

They passed *Casey's Mobile Home's: Luxury Living. Easy Credit. Se Habla Espanol,* which was an overgrown field lined with identical white trailers. Next to it was *Sluggett's Motel: Modern Facility, Old-Fashion Southern Hospitality,* an establishment that looked as though it was built in 1950 and had not had a coat of paint since. Hannah thought it would make a great setting for a horror movie.

Suddenly, there was a break in all the tattered bill boards, tatty old motels, trailer parks, and used car lots that littered the edge of Snipesville. Two handsome brick pillars marked the entrance to Snipesville State College, and Kimberly turned onto the road that ran between them. "Okay, y'all, I'll drop off Hannah first, because the baseball fields are round the other side of campus. Cool?"

"Whatever," muttered Hannah. Alex frowned anxiously at her, embarrassed that she was being so rude. Trying to make amends, he said brightly to Kimberly, "Yeah, that's cool. Thanks, Kimberly."

Hannah made a sucking-up face at him, which he ignored.

They pulled up outside a building that looked just like a large version of the mobile homes they had seen all over Snipes County.

"Do you want me to walk in with you?" Kimberly sang.

"No," said Hannah abruptly, as she opened the passenger door and slid from the seat. "Ciao, Alex," she said with a backward wave.

Walking through the darkened, empty, echoing halls, past deserted, windowless classrooms, Hannah started to think uneasily that this wasn't where she wanted to spend the next week. Soon, she realized how quiet the building was, and it struck her that she might be in the wrong place.

Hearing voices from the hallway ahead, Hannah followed the sounds into an office. A girl of college age was sitting at a computer, idly playing on the keyboard. Sitting sideways in front of the desk, slumped in a chair, was a man in a baseball cap, who, Hannah guessed from the awkward silence, was the boyfriend.

The girl looked both bored and irritated when Hannah presented herself. "Can I hep yew?" she asked, in a way that managed to be both polite and discouraging, all at once.

That *accent*, Hannah thought. Why can't people here learn to talk normally, like they do in California?

"Yeah, I'm here for the writing camp."

"Rahttin' camp?"

"Uh-huh." Hannah said.

The girl shrugged. "Not here."

Hannah sighed impatiently. "Do you know where it is, then?"

But the girl was eager to get rid of her, and her eyes turned back to the monitor. "Try the Union. It's next door." She gestured vaguely to the left.

The writing camp wasn't in the Union, either. On the bulletin boards, Hannah saw signs for a beauty pageant for kids, a seminar on leadership, and a foreign film series, but no writing camp. Then suddenly, a green and white sign caught her eye, and she felt the warm rush of recognizing a familiar place. She pushed through the glass door and stepped into the campus Starbucks. Huge, colorful abstract murals lined the walls, and jazz was playing quietly.

Hannah's Grandma liked to take her to Starbucks. Grandma would order a macchiato, and Hannah would order a hot chocolate or, her favorite, a Strawberries and Crème Frappuccino.

Now, walking in was just like walking into California. A smiling, hip-looking young man with a goatee, wearing the uniform green apron and cap, asked her what drink he could get started for her, while a girl with red hair rang up her sale, and fetched her a peanut butter cookie, popping it into a brown bag.

It was all so comfortable, like putting on pajamas, and Hannah felt very grown up to be there by herself. She was soon curled up in a squashy armchair with her drink, a cookie, and a magazine that somebody had left behind. She hoped that she looked like a college student, or at least like a very smart kid.

Hannah paid no attention to the middle-aged woman who was sitting in another corner of Starbucks, sipping her coffee. But the woman was paying very close attention to Hannah. For the next several minutes, she sat silently in a chair by the window, watching her with interest, and as discreetly as she could. Then she quietly dropped her empty cup in the trash, and left the coffeehouse through the main doors. Hannah, who had had her back to the woman the whole time, never even saw her leave.

Alex, meanwhile, had happily accepted Kimberly's offer to accompany him to registration for baseball camp. Now he watched with dismay as athletic-looking kids tossed balls to each other. The registration line was long, and Alex found himself listening to the conversation going on behind him. A black mother was talking nonstop at her son, a short kid, who looked as nervous as Alex felt.

"Don't forget, I'll be at the church women's council, so daddy will fetch you and take you to Bible study." She didn't notice, but Alex did, when the boy rolled his eyes. The mother continued: "Tomorrow, I'll be at the hospital, so Ivory will pick you up and take you to the library. Don't forget, now, I want you to get math and science books, too, not just all those fun books you've been reading. You have to keep up your math if you're going to major in business." The boy caught Alex's eye, and pulled a face like he was choking. His mother continued, oblivious. "Brandon, don't forget to listen to what Coach says, now, and pay attention in practice. You'll never get on any travel teams the way you're going."

When registration had ended, a large white man with a fat stomach crammed into a baseball uniform introduced himself as Coach Mike.

"Okay, guys, we're gonna start with a detailed assessment of your fundamentals."

"Sounds painful," Brandon muttered to Alex, who burst into giggles.

Coach Mike looked suspiciously at them. "Everything okay there, boys?"

"Yes, sir," said Brandon, while Alex nodded and tried to keep his face straight. Coach Mike didn't look like he believed them.

The assessment was a disaster. Alex had hardly ever played baseball before. His pitch dropped about three feet in front of him. When the ball was thrown to him at bat, he swung helplessly at it. He could see Brandon with the older boys on the other side of the field, doing no better.

The coaches made unconvincingly encouraging comments to Alex, while the other boys smirked at each other. They also laughed at Brandon—he could hit the ball, but only when he was paying attention, which wasn't most of the time. When Coach Mike told all the boys to run a lap around the field, Brandon was left behind as he stared into space, until one of younger coaches ran back to remind him to move.

"What a dork!" said one boy, shaking his head. "Do you know that kid?"

"Yeah," puffed another, "He thinks he knows everythin'. They call him the Professor. He don't know baseball, though."

By late morning, the assessment was done, and Coach Mike told the boys to follow the assistant coaches to the Union for lunch. Brandon and Alex trailed at the back, talking first about how much they hated baseball, then sports generally, and finally about things they did like, such as comic books with toilet jokes, and science of all kinds.

One of the assistant coaches was walking behind them when his cell phone rang. He answered it, and shouted ahead to the other coaches that he would be gone for a few minutes. Then he turned back in the direction of the field house.

"So, you're not from round here, right?" Brandon asked Alex, who told him about the move from California, then asked Brandon if he was from Snipesville.

"Yep, right here," said Brandon with a heavy sigh. "And as soon as I get out of high school, I'm outta here. My parents want me to stay close and go to college at Snipesville State, or maybe University of Georgia. I want to go to Boston or New York. I know I can do it. I get all 'A's, but my mom's always hassling me about my grades. Is your mom like that?"

"No," said Alex quietly. "My mom died in a car accident."

"Man, I'm sorry," Brandon said. There was an awkward silence. Alex looked through the windows of the Union as they approached the building, and he suddenly pointed excitedly.

"Hey, that's my sister! What's she doing there?"

The boys slowed down and stopped at the doors to Starbucks, while the rest of the kids disappeared ahead of them around the corner to the building's main entrance.

Hannah definitely was not thrilled to see Alex. "What are you doing? You're supposed to be at baseball camp!"

Alex slumped into the armchair next to her. "Yeah, well, you're supposed to be at writing camp."

Hannah shrugged and sipped on her straw. "I couldn't find it."

"You could have asked someone."

"I did, and she didn't know. Anyway, who's this?" She jerked her head at Brandon, who was awkwardly waiting to be introduced.

"This is Brandon," Alex said without explanation.

Hannah raised her eyebrows, which was as close as she felt like saying hello to this dorky boy her brother had dragged in. Brandon nodded in reply, and sat in the third armchair.

"So, sis, do you mind if we hide out here with you?" Alex asked.

"Yes," retorted Hannah.

"Too bad," her brother said.

Hannah ordered a second Strawberries and Crème Frappuccino, while Alex and Brandon, with money borrowed from a reluctant Hannah, bought milks and a chocolate chip cookie to share.

When they were done, Hannah decided they should find something to do for the afternoon. "Do you guys want to check out the library? We might be able to play on the computers."

"Are we allowed in the library?" Alex asked.

"I guess," Brandon said, and added as evidence, "Our class took a field trip there once."

"Okay, then," said Hannah, throwing her bag over her shoulder. "Let's go."

But Alex looked worried. "What about camp?"

Hannah pulled out her cell phone, and dialed. She waited for the voice-mail.

"Hi, Kimberly? It's Hannah. We're gonna be done a little early, so I'll meet up with Alex, and we'll meet you where you dropped me off this morning. Oh, and Kimberly? Thank you *so* much for dropping me at the wrong building. See ya."

She hung up.

Alex looked at Brandon. "But what about you?"

Brandon shrugged. "I'll tell Dad that it was awful, and I quit early. He won't mind—so long as my mom doesn't know."

Alex was still worried. "But won't the camps tell our parents?"

Hannah tossed back her hair. "Chill, Alex. Just try to live a little, okay? Dad will understand. He's too busy with his new job to worry about our stuff anyway."

The library was three stories of grim grey cement, surrounded on every floor with ugly, creepy breezeway balconies. As they approached the double doors, Hannah said, "Look serious, and like you know where you're going, but don't run." When they entered the lobby, they were hit by the musty old-book smell that always put Hannah to sleep in libraries.

She spotted a small group of computers ahead. However, they were right in front of the reference desk, which was staffed by a sour-looking, lanky, grey-haired man who wore his glasses on the end of his nose. He looked up from his computer and peered suspiciously at them. Hannah turned to the boys and nodded toward the elevator ahead of them. "Let's go upstairs," she said.

They emerged on the third floor, and the first thing they saw was a wall of books. Alex and Hannah immediately set off in search of computers, but Brandon paused, catching sight of one of the titles on the shelf in front of him: *World War II.*

"Hey, y'all, wait up!" he called, but Hannah and Alex were already out of earshot. Brandon figured he would catch up with them easily enough. He reached up on tiptoes, plucked the book off the shelf, and opened it up. Its spine creaked, as though it had never been opened before. Flipping through it, he was disappointed to find that there were no pictures. The print was tiny, and the first sentence Brandon tried to read made very little sense to him.

If this is what college is like, he thought, I'll give it a pass. He put the book back where he had found it, and looked farther upward. On the very top shelf, he spotted another promising book, one with a scarlet red cover on which was printed in gold type, *Children in Wartime Britain, 1939-1945.* But it was well out of reach. Looking around, Brandon spotted a round, mushroom-like step-stool nearby, and he dragged it over.

Retrieving the book, he opened it up while still standing on the stool. He flipped to the middle, and found a black and white photo of white boys in old-fashioned caps and short pants. Each boy wore a label hanging from his jacket with string, and a small box, also threaded with string, hung from each boy's shoulder. The boys looked back at the camera with serious faces. Brandon remembered seeing a TV documentary about children like these, sent out of British cities for safety's sake when bombs started to fall during World War II.

Suddenly, something fell from the book. Brandon tried to catch it, but he missed, and it spiraled to the floor. It was a grey and blue cardboard booklet, about the size of an ordinary photograph.

Jumping down, he picked up the card, and flipped it over. It read, "NATIONAL REGISTRATION IDENTITY CARD." Above the words was a drawing of a lion and a unicorn standing on their hind legs, supporting a crown.

Brandon opened up the booklet. It belonged to someone called George Braithwaite. Puzzled but curious, he shoved it in his pocket, before hurrying off to catch up with the others.

The library floor was quiet, and much of it was taken up by rows of computers. Alex and Hannah quickly realized that they had it to themselves, and Alex suddenly threw the baseball he was carrying to Hannah, who pitched it back. Soon, all three of them were laughing and playing catch in the center of the third floor of the library.

Brandon waved his arms at Alex, calling "Hey, over here!" Alex tossed the ball to him, he pitched it to Hannah, and Hannah returned it to Alex. Alex, getting faster with confidence, threw a high pitch. It went right over Brandon's head, and rolled under the computers, disappearing out of sight.

Brandon had taken only a few steps in pursuit, when suddenly a woman's voice rang out loudly, calling "Over here."

All three kids froze, startled. There was a hand, held up from behind the computer stations. It reminded Brandon of King Arthur's Lady of the Lake, only, instead a sword, she was holding the baseball. Cautiously, he followed Alex and Hannah, who were already making their way in the direction of the hand.

Chapter 2
THE PROFESSOR

The woman behind the hand was sitting patiently at the computer terminal. "Yours, I believe?" She smiled as she handed the ball to Hannah.

Hannah guessed that she was in her fifties. She was small and slim, with a heart-shaped face, high cheekbones, and grey hair. She was dressed in a flowing silk grey suit. Hannah was reminded of a cat. She didn't like cats much.

"We thought we were on our own," Hannah said accusingly, as if the woman had been spying on them.

"Not to worry. You're not really disturbing me. In fact, you're a pleasant distraction from this nonsense." She nodded at the screen, but all Hannah could see on it was some densely-packed text. The woman's accent was distinctly unusual for Georgia.

"Are you from England?" Alex asked.

"A lot of people think that," laughed the woman. "Anyway, what are you guys doing inside on such a lovely day?"

Hannah noticed that she hadn't really answered Alex's question, but she let it go. "It's not a lovely day," she said. "It's gross out there."

"Excuse me, ma'am?" Brandon interrupted. The woman looked at him, and her piercing blue eyes unnerved him so much that he almost forgot his question. "Are you a professor?"

"Yes, I am. I'm an historian."

"Awesome. Look, I found this." Brandon fumbled in his pocket, and produced the card he had found in the library book. She took it and examined it carefully, running her finger across the cover. "It fell out of an old book," Brandon explained. "Do you know what it is?"

"Hmm," she said, opening it up. "Indeed I do."

There was a silence, and Hannah grew impatient. "So what is it?"

"Oh, it's a national identity card, of course."

"You think?" said Hannah sarcastically, glancing pointedly at the title on the cover.

The Professor gave her a tight smile. "It's from England, during World War Two. The law said everyone had to carry one. It was supposed to make it easier to identify German spies."

Hannah stepped behind the Professor, and looked over her shoulder at the inside of the card.

"No photo?" she asked, puzzled.

"No," the Professor shook her head. "Odd, isn't it? That's one reason I don't suppose it was much use for its intended purpose." She looked back at Hannah. "But, you see, the British didn't want photo IDs. They didn't want a tightly-controlled society. That reminded them too much of Hitler and the Nazis. I suppose this was an odd compromise: An identification card with no photo."

Alex piped up: "Why do you think it was in a library book?"

She looked thoughtful. "I can't imagine," she said. Then she seemed struck by an idea. "Perhaps the owner emigrated after the war, and now lives in Snipesville? He may have used it as a bookmark, and then forgotten all about it. You kids could do some research and find out." She gave them all a sunny smile, and handed back the card to Brandon.

Brandon smiled happily, Alex smiled politely, and Hannah scowled, muttering "Whatever" under her breath. *Like we don't get enough busy work in school,* she thought.

The Professor wished them a good day, and returned to her work while the boys followed Hannah back to the elevator.

"What now?" Brandon asked. "I thought we were going to play on the computers?"

Hannah shook her head. "I don't know. She gives me the creeps. Let's get out of here." Then she had a sudden inspiration. "Why don't we go see if there's a computer lab back in the Union?"

As the elevator reached the first floor, the doors opened, and the three stepped out.

Hannah immediately noticed a peculiar smell and a sharp, rapid tapping sound.

"What *is* that?" she asked Brandon.

He shrugged. "I dunno…" Then he snapped his fingers. "You know what? It sounds like my grandma's old typewriter." Hannah looked skeptically at him before glancing back at the reference desk.

"Hey!" she exclaimed. "The computers have gone!"

Brandon and Alex looked to where she was pointing, and she was right.

Only one computer remained, sitting on the reference desk, but the librarian who was now stationed there, a thin woman in a dress who wore her hair in a tight bun, wasn't using it. Instead, she was tapping on a noisy old-fashioned typewriter.

That, Brandon thought, *explains the smell.* It was carbon paper, like his grandma used.

"Weird," Brandon said. "They must have removed all the computers while we were upstairs. Maybe they're being replaced with state-of-the-art stuff?"

"Wow, that was fast, though, huh?" said Alex.

Hearing them, the librarian suddenly looked up and glared.

"What are you children doing in here?" she called across the lobby. "And especially you?" She pointed to Brandon, to everyone's confusion.

Alarmed, the kids began to walk quickly to the door. "Just leaving, ma'am," Brandon called back. As he fled, he distinctly heard her say, "You know your kind isn't allowed in here." In his confused retreat, he failed to notice that the computer on her desk had simply disappeared.

"Our kind?" Hannah blustered, outside. "What does that mean? How totally rude. And why did she have it in for you? Have you gotten in trouble here before?" Bewildered, Brandon shook his head.

Trotting down the steps, he spied a rack filled with copies of the campus newspaper. He grabbed one as he passed, and scanned the front page as he followed Alex and Hannah.

Seconds later, Hannah realized that she and Alex were walking alone. She looked back to see Brandon rooted to the spot outside the library, and yelled to him, "Come on, let's go! She might call campus security or something." But Brandon did not move or answer. He was staring at the newspaper in shock.

Alex ran to him, and Hannah reluctantly followed her brother. "Look at this," Brandon said quietly, and he turned the front page so Alex and Hannah could see it. "Check out the date."

Hannah peered closer, and read: September 11, 1940.

She gave an exaggerated sigh. "It's a joke. What, you think we just travelled back in time, or something?"

Brandon said nothing.

"Man, you are so weird. My brother can really pick 'em. Look, I bet they didn't have *those* in 1940. Happy?"

Brandon's eyes followed to where she was pointing, and he was relieved to see that it was a Hummer in the parking lot.

"Hey," said Hannah, "do you guys remember where the Union is?"

The boys followed her along the path that led to the oldest part of the college. Had they turned and looked behind them, they would have seen the Hummer gradually fade, and vanish into nothingness. But they didn't.

They emerged onto the great lawn that was surrounded by century-old brick buildings. Pecan trees and live oaks draped with Spanish moss lined the paths. Alex thought how odd it was that the trees seemed to have shrunk since he had seen them from Kimberly's car that morning. Or was his imagination running away with him?

Brandon gestured ahead to the corner of one of the buildings, and said, "I'm pretty sure we turn left there."

Following him, Alex and Hannah found themselves, not in front of the Union as they expected, but on a quiet country road on the edge of the campus. It was lined with trees and high hedgerows, which were spotted with tiny bright yellow and purple wildflowers. Some of the trees reached across the lane, formed an arch, and cast areas ahead into virtual darkness. It seemed to have been raining: A slippery mush of brown and golden leaves had formed a thin lacy layer on the road's wet surface, and collected in dank-smelling heaps along its sides.

"Cool!" Alex said, transfixed. Then suddenly, he took off running down the middle of the road, turning at a sharp left bend, and disappearing out of sight.

"Watch out for cars, you moron!" Hannah yelled, racing after him.

Only Brandon hung back, confused. He felt a chill running up his back. "This isn't right," he mumbled to himself. "This isn't right...."

He called after Hannah and Alex to stop, but they did not. He ran after them for about a hundred yards, and then, on impulse, turned to look behind him, but all he could see was the road. There was no sign of the buildings they had just left behind.

Brandon's mind was racing. Perhaps this was just an area of the college he had never seen? After all, he didn't visit this part of Snipesville too often. Maybe, he thought, this was a new road, cut through the countryside, because, after all, someone was always building in Snipesville. But there was something about it that struck Brandon as peculiar. If only he could figure out what it was...

Hannah had caught up with Alex, who was examining a spiky green object he had picked up from among the hundreds littering the road. It was about the size of a ping-pong ball, and was attached to a large three-pronged leaf. Alex handled his find gingerly, and began to pick at a crack in the skin. Pulling apart the thick, pithy, spiny shell, he revealed what looked like a glossy brown nut.

"What's this?" he asked Hannah.

"No clue. You don't know? Ask your dorky little friend. Must be a Georgia thing."

Alex held up the nut for Brandon's inspection, but Brandon raised his eyebrows and shook his head.

"Must be pretty rare, huh," Alex said, happily pocketing his discovery.

Alex had noticed several strong smells along the hedgerow. Some were sweet and sugary, while others smelled sour. One in particular reminded him strongly of cat's pee. He thought at first that it *was* cat's pee, until he identified the source as a clump of tiny white flowers. Hannah was less interested in the plant life around them than she was in the fact that the air had cooled down drastically. The stifling humidity had completely disappeared, and there was a damp chill in the air. She shivered, and rubbed her arms. Overhead, she could see dark gray clouds rapidly gathering.

Alex and Brandon were examining a tall plant lined with jagged-edged leaves of varying sizes and Brandon extended his hand toward the leaves. "I've never seen these before either…OWWW!!!"

He jumped back, and rubbed his fingers on his shirt. "Man, that really hurts. What the heck are those things? There's no spikes, but they totally sting." He held his hand out for Alex to look at, but neither of them could see any damage.

"You don't know much about your hometown, do you?" Hannah said dryly.

As soon as she had spoken, a loud noise pierced the quiet. It sounded like a single-engine plane, putt-putting its way across the sky. The kids looked up automatically, and Brandon gave a sharp intake of breath. This was not just because the plane was flying very low, although it was. It was also because he could clearly see red, white, and blue targets painted on its wings.

"Spitfire!" gasped Brandon. The word had no sooner left his lips when a clunky-looking black car suddenly appeared around a corner of the road, and the three of them jumped even further to the side of the lane to avoid being run over. The driver pushed his horn, which sounded not like "honk" or "beep," but "harr-oo-uh."

There was a stunned silence. And then all three kids spoke at once.

"Okay," Alex said wonderingly, "Now I'm freaked."

"No waaay," murmured Brandon, still looking at the sky in disbelief. "It's a Spitfire…. Yeah, that's freaky."

"It's just an old plane and car, that's all," said Hannah. "What's the big deal?"

Brandon turned to her excitedly. "Listen, I know my trains, planes and automobiles, and those were both from World War Two England."

"Cool!" Alex said. "There must be an old-time air and car show going on. Let's go check it out!"

But then Hannah spoke, in a voice that was hoarse and trembling. "Look… Alex, look at your clothes."

Alex glanced down, figuring he must have got mud all over his baseball pants.

What he saw staggered him: His clothes were morphing. There was no other way to describe what was happening. He watched as a shimmering gray wave traveled slowly down the length of his body.

Brandon and Hannah were now looking at themselves, too, and at each other, as waves of change overtook them both. Within seconds, Alex and Brandon were dressed alike, wearing short, heavy grey wool pants that ended well above their knees, and grey V-necked sweaters over stiff white shirts. Brandon's neck felt tight, as though someone was very politely trying to strangle him, and that's when he realized he was wearing a tie.

Alex put his hands to his head, seeing Brandon do the same, and he pulled off a small woolen peaked cap. Brandon was now rummaging in his pants pocket, from which he drew out a handful of coins. He gazed at them in amazement. "Look at these," he said quietly. He held them out for Alex to see: Some were small and silver, while others were large, bronze, and very heavy.

Hannah was gripping her hair in two hands, carefully examining what had, just a minute before, been long, loose tresses. Her light brown hair was now tightly braided into two plaits, one on either side of her head. She was wearing a knee-length skirt, something she hadn't worn since she had gone to her cousin's wedding in third grade. Then she realized that it was actually a kind of pinafore dress, with a bib in navy blue. She was also wearing a tie, just like the boys, knee-length white socks, and a thick jacket. She dug a hand into the jacket pocket and brought out a small red coin purse.

As Brandon and Alex examined the coins Brandon had found in his pocket, Hannah opened the purse, and drew out a large folded piece of paper. She opened it up, and saw that it was a small certificate. At first, it was a little difficult to read the words. They were printed in a fancy font on a blue and beige background. But then she made out what it said: *Bank of England promise to pay the Bearer on Demand the sum of One Pound.* It wasn't a certificate after all. It was...

"English money," said Brandon. He flipped over a silver coin about the size of a quarter, and studied what he guessed was a picture of the king on one side. The back of the coin told him that he was holding *One Shilling.* The date on the coin was 1940, but it was as shiny as if it were brand new.

"Who was the king of England in 1940?" Alex asked Hannah, speaking slowly as though he were in a daze.

"I don't know," Hannah said vaguely. Then, suddenly she jerked to attention, as if she had just awoken from sleepwalking. "Are you totally stupid?" she snapped at him. "Who cares? Where ARE we? And why am I wearing these butt-ugly clothes?" She shivered again as a chill gust of wind brushed against her knees, and she began to feel a wave of panic expanding through her body. She consciously forced it back to a dull ache in her stomach.

"Okay, this is totally weird," she said as calmly as she could. "But do you guys really think we just walked into a time warp, and traveled all the way to

World War Two England?" The two boys nodded hard, but she continued. "Maybe there were chemicals in the library. That's it…we're hallucinating!"

"Yeah?" Brandon retorted. "If you're so smart, how come we're all seeing the same thing? Like those. Don't tell me you can't see them." He pointed behind Hannah to three small brown cases stacked on the road. Atop them sat three small beige cardboard boxes, each with a long piece of string to be used as a carrying strap. Alex leaned down, and looked at the label on one of the suitcases.

"It says Braithwaite," he said. "Isn't that the guy's name on the card you found?"

Dumbfounded, Brandon nodded. Without really knowing why he was doing it, he picked up the case and the box labeled *Braithwaite*. As he did so, he noticed a thin piece of card twirling on a string from the front of his jacket. Catching it between his thumb and forefinger, he read *George Braithwaite* and some printed words that made no sense to him. Hannah and Alex were also now wearing the same labels. Their first names were given correctly, but instead of Dias, the last name on the labels was Day. The word *Day* was also scrawled on both the remaining suitcases.

Silently, Hannah handed Alex a case, and one of the smaller boxes which he immediately opened. He pulled out a gas mask.

"I think everyone was supposed to carry those," explained Brandon.

"Everyone? Who is 'everyone'?" asked Hannah.

"Everyone in England," said Brandon, hesitating under Hannah's stare. "You know…During World War Two."

Chapter 3
CHANGES

They retraced their steps, but Alex and Hannah soon found out that Brandon was right: The college had simply disappeared.

Alex could think of only one possible explanation: "It's magic."

Hannah stared disgustedly at her brother. "Thank you, Harry Potter. You wanna get out your wand now, or should we wait on Dumbledore?"

Alex ignored her, and said, "I think we should just wait and see what happens."

Brandon sighed. "Right now, I don't think we have much of a choice."

But then Alex pointed to something ahead of them. "Well, here's one choice."

It was a sign, a tall wooden post, with arrows pointing in two different directions: One straight ahead, and one to the right. But someone had painted out the place names. "Why would anyone do something that dumb?" Alex asked.

"It wasn't a prank," Brandon said excitedly. "I saw this once on TV. English people removed road signs so if the Nazis invaded, they would get lost. But I guess the only people who got lost were other English people."

"Smart," said Hannah sarcastically. She stood on tiptoe and peered up. "They did a lousy job, because I can still read it. It says someplace called Balesworth, and I'm guessing the number means it's 1/4 mile ahead."

They began to tramp up the road.

Ten minutes later, the kids could no longer deny where and when they were. The street before them was strange and old. Really old. The buildings mostly were of red brick, mostly with red slate roofs, and mostly joined to their neighbors. But they were otherwise a hodgepodge of styles and colors, very few of them with the rigid lines of modern buildings. A roof suspended over one passageway between two houses seemed in danger of falling down. The windows were oddly arranged, and they were crooked, too. A half-timbered cottage had warped beams, and a brick pub's windows were cut in small diamonds. Next to it stood a smart new three-story white building, with perfectly rectangular picture windows spaced at regular intervals. Brandon thought that one stately two-story brick building looked like the pictures he had seen of colonial America. Next to it there squatted a tiny and ancient shop, with potbellied bay windows.

Further down the street, they passed a row of nineteenth-century houses, each with its own small front yard bounded by a low brick wall. Affixed to the wall in front of one of these houses was a tarnished brass plaque that Brandon read. It said *R. Gordon, D.D.S., Dental Surgery*. Next door, a newly-painted sign proudly advertised *Miss Violet Bates, Piano Lessons*.

The people on the street were no more familiar to the kids than were the buildings. Their clothes, their expressions, their way of walking, and, indeed, everything about them seemed strange. Most of them were middle-aged women who were striding purposefully on various errands. All of them appeared more or less the same. Most were dressed in small neat hats and long woollen coats. Some wore small round eyeglasses, and all carried wicker shopping baskets. An old man, wearing a suit, tie, and flat cap, was smoking a pipe on a park bench, as a small dog slept at his feet. A young man in greasy brown overalls was tinkering under the hood of a car that looked very much like the one that had passed the kids on the country lane. The kids now noticed how very few cars had passed them by, even though this was a street lined with shops.

Brandon paused in front of one brick building. Its first floor windows were frosted, and the borders of the glass were swirled in elaborate patterns. A hanging board outside, illustrated by a complicated coat of arms featuring horses, lions, and fancy flourishes, announced that this was *The Balesworth Arms*. Over the front door a small handpainted notice proclaimed *Ernest Arthur Tarrant, Prop., Licenced to Sell Beer, Wine, and Spirits*.

"I guess we could go in there and ask somebody where we are," suggested Brandon doubtfully.

"No," said Hannah. "It's a pub, yeah? Kids aren't allowed in pubs, just like bars. I've got a better idea." She marched off without explanation in the direction of a side street, looking about her as she walked. The boys glanced at each other, then trailed after her.

Finally, in a tiny alley, Hannah found what she had been looking for. It was a long, crooked, and very old whitewashed building. A checkerboard pattern was worked into the plaster on the second story. On the first floor, set back down a short narrow passageway, stood a door with a four-paned window, in which was hung a sign reading *Open*. As Hannah moved to the entrance, Brandon hesitated.

"What's this?" he asked Hannah. Wordlessly, she pointed above the door. There hung a black and white sign: *The Tudor Tea Rooms*.

As the door clattered open, a high-pitched bell tinkled, announcing the kids' arrival. Alex, last in, carefully closed the door with a thunk of wood, accompanied by more jingling of the bell, and the rattling of the Open sign. They turned right, and immediately felt large and awkward: They were in a tiny room, crammed with rickety wooden chairs and eight small tables, each of them draped with a white tablecloth.

Crooked beams snaked across the ceiling. On the walls hung watercolors and oil paintings of country landscapes, flowers, and bowls of fruit. Three cake stands sat atop a large heavy dark wood buffet by the wall. They held a modest assortment of plain, unfrosted pastries and cakes. Brandon identified a sponge with red filling, a fruit cake, and something that looked to him like plain muffins. Tucked in a corner of the room was a narrow staircase, while a door in the back wall apparently led to a kitchen.

Even more than the appearance of the place, the kids were struck by its smell. It was very odd. Delicious sweet and buttery scents hung richly in the air. But so did a slightly sour, slightly acidy nostril-pinching smell, not unpleasant, which Brandon recognized from when his mom brewed sweet iced Southern tea. And there was a mustiness that probably came from the building itself, or perhaps it was sour milk? The room smelled not so much like a restaurant, as it did like a house that had not been cleaned in a very long time. And overlaying all the smells was the overpowering stench of cigarettes.

All three kids wrinkled their noses. Hannah frantically waved her hand in front of her face, and said very loudly for all to hear, "Yuk. They allow smoking in restaurants? That is so gross."

Startled, several customers looked over at her. One in particular, a man with thinning grey hair and a moustache, put down his newspaper to stare disapprovingly at her. He then focused his gaze on Brandon, and glared even more sourly at him.

At that moment, the kitchen door opened, and a woman bustled in, wearing a black dress, white apron, and white lace cap. She carried a tiny dustpan and brush, which she used to sweep the crumbs vigorously from one of the tables. The kids waited for her to show them a table, but she ignored them.

"Excuse me?" called Hannah loudly. "We want a table in the non-smoking section." Brandon tapped her arm urgently and whispered, "I don't think they know what that means…"

The waitress glanced upward. Looking annoyed, she straightened up, and said, "Give me a minute. Can't you see I'm busy?" Then she returned to brushing at the tablecloth.

Hannah glowered at her, and then, with enormous dignity, simply marched forward and chose a table by the window, as far from the smokers as possible. The boys followed awkwardly, pulling out the wooden chairs with loud scraping noises. Hannah perched sideways on her chair, positioning herself so she could stare accusingly at the waitress. The two boys slumped in their seats.

Keenly aware that he was the only black person in the room, Brandon fiddled nervously with the edge of the tablecloth. Two old ladies who had been quietly chatting over tea glanced at the children, and one of them tutted. Hannah raised an eyebrow at her, as if to say "You have a problem?" and she quickly looked away again.

Meanwhile, the waitress had disappeared into the kitchen, but she soon returned, and approached their table. "What are you lot having, then?" she said sharply. They looked at each other helplessly, and the waitress let out a deep sigh. "Don't waste my time. Like I told you, I'm busy. Either you lot make up your minds, or you can hop it!"

Hannah said, "A menu would be nice."

"There isn't one," the waitress snapped. "This ain't the Ritz, is it?"

Hannah wasn't easily deterred. "Well, what do you have to eat, then?"

"Sweet or savory?" was the response.

Brandon, hungry, decided he would prefer something savory, and was offered a choice of sardines on toast or Marmite sandwich. "Meat pie is off," the waitress added mysteriously. The boys both opted for the sandwiches, especially after Alex told Brandon that sardines were little fish, eaten whole, possibly with eyeballs still intact. Brandon didn't know what a Marmite sandwich might be, but it sounded better than crunchy eyeball fish, and Alex had ordered it so confidently that he felt reassured.

Hannah asked for the choices in sweets.

"We got currant loaf, Victoria sponge, scones, and toasted teacakes," said the waitress.

"What's a Victoria sponge?" asked Hannah.

"None of your lip," warned the waitress, huffing that she didn't believe for a minute that Hannah wasn't giving her trouble. "Fancy saying you don't know what it is," she grumbled. Hannah looked at her crossly, then ordered a scone as the only item she recognized by name.

"Jam?" the waitress spat. Hannah nodded.

"It's thruppence extra." Hannah guessed that she was being charged more for jam. "And you'll want tea, I suppose?" the waitress groused, walking away without waiting for an answer.

"Yeah, well, I'm guessing a Caramel Frappuccino ain't happening..." Hannah said to her retreating back.

The waitress soon returned with two metal tea pots, one tall and thin, the other short and squat.

"What's the second pot for?" asked Hannah.

"Hot water, of course," she snapped. " 'Aven't you never 'ad tea before, neither?"

She bustled off again, returning this time with a tray laden with cups and saucers, and their food. Hannah's small round scone was served with a knife, a pat of margarine, and a bright red splodge of jam alongside.

Hannah started to pour the tea, only to watch in horror as tea leaves cascaded into the cup. It was then she realized the point of the tiny sieve lying on the table, and she balanced it over the lip of the cup before trying once more.

Brandon and Alex looked glumly at the tiny plain sandwiches with which they had been served.

"Alex, what exactly is Marmite?" Brandon asked.

"I don't know." Alex said. "It just sounds good."

Hannah suggested, unhelpfully, "Isn't it some kind of small furry animal?"

Brandon gulped.

"No," Alex corrected his sister. "You mean a mar*mot*. A marmot's a groundhog."

Brandon picked up a sandwich, and carefully opened it. Peering inside at the thin dark brown smear of filling, he said, "Well, this stuff looks like it might be from a marmot's butt."

All the same, he closed up the sandwich and took a large bite. He immediately pulled a horrified face, clutched his throat, and grasped around the table for a napkin, but the waitress hadn't brought any. When he managed to gasp the word "napkin," Hannah called out, "Hey, could we get some napkins over here?"

The waitress looked more offended than ever. "Hoity-toity!" she spat. "In case you 'aven't heard, there is a war on, you know."

Hannah, thinking quickly, pushed a steaming cup of tea toward Brandon, who sipped from it gratefully. Even so, he grimaced after he drank it. "Yuck! No sugar, and this stuff is *strong*!"

Hannah tasted hers, and had to agree. It was like drinking stewed weeds which, she thought, was basically what tea was. And where was the sugar, anyway?

"Do you think there might be another place in town where we could get burgers and Cokes?" Hannah asked Brandon. Both boys gave her a skeptical look.

The man reading his newspaper and smoking in the corner of the tea room suddenly stubbed out his cigarette, folded his newspaper in half, threw it on the table, and got to his feet. Approaching the waitress, he said, "Are these kids bothering you?" Without waiting for her answer, he walked up to Hannah, Brandon and Alex, and stood over them.

"You evacuees?"

Hannah sensed that "yes" would be the best answer, but she didn't like his tone one bit. Instead, she said stonily, "No. We're time travelers from the twenty-first century."

His eyes widened, and he stabbed a long finger at her. "I'll have none of your cheek, my girl…"

Brandon interrupted hurriedly, "Yes, we're evacuees."

The man glowered briefly at Hannah before turning to Brandon.

"Oh, you are, are you? Well, let me tell you who I am. My name is Mr. Smedley, and I'm with the Ministry of Health in London. Now you lot, I don't know what the devil you think you're playing at, but you finish up your tea right now, then I'm marching the three of you down the parish hall. We have enough on our plate today without you playing silly beggars."

With that, he turned on his heel, returned to his table, and opened his paper, giving it a good shake. He glanced at the kids before taking a big bite from a buttered scone.

Chapter 4
EVACUATION

Hannah whispered urgently to Brandon, "Evacuees? Say what?"

"Yeah. I read about this," Brandon said eagerly. "Most of the kids in the cities in England were sent to live out in the country when World War Two started in 1939, so they wouldn't get killed when the Germans dropped bombs. They had the stuff we have, you know, like the cases and the gas masks and stuff? So whoever sent us here, sent us as evacuees."

"Whoever sent us?" said Hannah, alarmed.

Alex interrupted, "Didn't their parents go with them?"

"Uh-uh," Brandon said. "They went all by themselves."

Hannah pointed to the calendar on the wall behind Brandon, which clearly said *September, 1940*.

At first, Brandon was puzzled by the date, but then he had an idea. "I bet this is when the Blitz started." He turned to Alex. "That was when Hitler dropped bombs on London every night for months. Lots more kids left the cities then."

Alex nodded, interested, but Hannah said, in a voice laden with scorn, "Thanks for the history lesson…. Hey, look out. That guy's coming back."

Smedley had returned, and was standing over them. "Come on, now, you lot, finish your tea like I told you. We can't waste good food in a war, but I want you done in one minute flat. And no funny business, or else."

Hannah scowled at him and thought about asking "Or else, what?" but looking at Smedley's hard face, she thought better of it.

"And that'll be two and six for your teas," added the waitress, leaning round Smedley's shoulder. Alex and Hannah looked blankly at her. Only Brandon realized she wanted to be paid.

Rummaging in his pockets, Brandon quickly handed her the largest silver coin he could find, a half crown, which seemed to do the trick. "Thank you," said the waitress primly, as he pressed the coin into her hand.

"Don't I get change?" asked Brandon.

"And 'ow exactly," she asked, as if he was the most stupid person she'd ever served, "am I supposed to give you change out of two and six?"

Smedley continued to stand next to the table, waiting impatiently for them to finish their snacks. Brandon looked apprehensively at the uneaten Marmite sandwich, appalled at the idea of putting in his mouth again. Alex was giving his sandwich a nervous exploratory sniff. Just as the situation seemed desperate, a woman in a dark green dress and beret suddenly popped her head out from behind Smedley, startling him.

"May I be of assistance?" she asked with a bright smile. The woman wore wire-rimmed glasses with small round lenses. Propped on her carefully waved brown hair was a green beret, on the front of which was sewn a patch bearing the letters WVS. An identical patch was on the front pocket of her plain dark green dress.

She smiled warmly at Smedley and extended a hand for him to shake. Hannah took full advantage of the moment, and reached out her hand to deftly sweep the boys' sandwiches off the table. The food tumbled onto the floor next to the window.

"Miss Tatchell, WVS," the woman was saying to Smedley.

"Oh, right." Smedley said, nodding at her. "I'm Mr. Smedley, Ministry of Health. He jerked his head at the kids. "Do you know anything about these children?"

"I don't know them myself, but I should say they are evacuees, although what they're doing here, I couldn't say. I'm quite certain they're meant to be with us." She added, with authority, "I shall accompany them to the church hall."

Smedley gave a wan smile. "Well, then, Miss…Tatchell was it?… I should be much obliged to you. If it wouldn't be too much trouble."

She assured him that it would not, and then looked at him expectantly, until he took the hint, and scurried back to his table.

"Now," she said, turning to the children, "If you're quite finished, we shall proceed."

Alex quietly asked Brandon, "Do you think we should go with her?"

"Got any better ideas?" Brandon shot back.

Miss Tatchell walked quickly, and the children hurried behind her, as a drizzling rain began to fall from the overcast skies. The kids struggled to keep up as they were drawn to pause and stare, fascinated by the shops and houses they passed. Dead rabbits, their furry ears dangling, hung alongside birds in full feather outside one shop, whose brightly painted, but grimy, sign identified it as *Donald Askew, Family Butcher and High Class Provisions*. In the window, strings of plump pale pink sausages lay on metal trays, together with a rather dried-up piece of roasting beef, garnished with a few small sprigs of parsley. Huge black flies buzzed around the meat, to Hannah's disgust. Next door, at *G.H. Foster, Greengrocer and Fruiterer*, a man in a tie and buttoned-up long white coat, just like a doctor's, was standing outside. He was carefully arranging apples in a shallow wooden box propped on a table in front of the window, next to another box that was filled with green cabbages.

"Got no bananas, then?" asked Brandon with a quick grin as he passed.

The shopkeeper turned and shook his fist at Brandon's departing back, "Blinkin' cheek you've got," he yelled.

Hannah asked, "What was that about?'

Brandon chuckled. "The Brits couldn't get bananas during World War Two. It was too hard to bring them from other countries because German submarines were sinking the ships, and I guess it's too cold to grow 'em here."

"Smartass," Hannah said, but she smiled.

Ahead of them was a church, although it certainly wasn't what Hannah had in mind when she thought of English churches: Built from brick, it looked brand new. It had no steeple or stained glass windows, and only the high-pitched roof gave away that it was a church. If the roof had been blue, Hannah thought, she might have mistaken the church for a pancake house. A large rectangular painted wooden sign stuck on two poles in the small churchyard announced that this was *St. Mark's Parish Church, Balesworth. Vicar: Rev. T.E.S. Roberts, Curate: Rev. R.J.H. Pattinson.*

Attached to the church was the church hall, an even squatter brick building, with a doorway on the side. The entance door was propped open, and as the children crossed the road with Miss Tatchell to the front of the church, a red double-decker bus pulled up. Kids began to tumble out of the door at the front of the bus, and the open corner platform at its back. They all carried gas mask boxes and small cases, and they wore labels like those worn by Alex, Brandon, and Hannah, attached to their coats on pieces of string.

A short man with a moustache and horn-rimmed glasses was stationed at the hall entrance. He was smoking a pipe and holding a pencil and clipboard, making a quick checkmark every time a child passed before him. Some kids were excited, laughing and poking at each other. Others looked weary and nervous. Hannah felt sad when she saw a small boy clutching a teddy bear tightly as he trailed forlornly after the crowd stampeding into the hall.

By the time Alex, Brandon, Hannah, and Miss Tatchell arrived at the door, the last of the children had entered the building, followed by the official, and the bus was pulling away.

Miss Tatchell turned and urged the kids to hurry. They passed into a tiny vestibule. Covering much of one wall was a notice board, lined with green felt, and tacked with small brightly colored posters. Hannah paused to read a flyer that urged mothers to leave their evacuated children in the countryside, while a drawing of a ghostly Hitler tried to persuade an anxious-looking woman to send them back to the bombed city in the distance.

Passing into the hall itself, the kids were immediately hit by the smells of hot tea, wet wool, and wax polish, as well as a babble of noise from the children, who were chattering excitedly. The official with the moustache was now sitting at a table next to the vestibule, adding up numbers from his clipboard.

Miss Tatchell coughed, and he looked up. "I'm Miss Tatchell, WVS. These children need to be found billets."

The man looked at his clipboard, and ran his finger down the list, then removed his pipe from between his teeth. "And which school are they with?"

Hannah immediately felt nervous, but Miss Tatchell, to her surprise, had an answer for them. "They're late arrivals from St. Sebastian's in Cricklewood, so you won't find them on your list. Their schoolmates have already been billeted near Hitchin, but we're scrambling to find room there, so it was decided to send them here."

Before he could ask for more explanation, she added, "I'm afraid I must leave you to deal with them. I need to be at the station shortly, if I'm to catch my train back to London." She turned to the kids and said quickly, "Goodbye, children, and good luck. I'm sure you'll be well taken care of."

Hannah took a good look at Miss Tatchell for the first time, and felt a glimmer of recognition. "Have we met?" she asked.

Miss Tatchell smiled. "Perhaps, my dear. And perhaps we'll meet again. Goodbye, now."

The official was getting to his feet, saying, "Hang on a minute, Miss..." But she had already hurried from the hall.

Hannah stared into the space Miss Tatchell had left behind, furiously trying to remember where she had seen her face before. And then it came to her. The hair and the accent were definitely different, the glasses and uniform fit perfectly in 1940, but the smile was a dead giveaway. Miss Tatchell was the Professor.

Chapter 5
LOST

"What's your name, then, sonny? Let me have a look." The official leaned forward and flipped over the luggage label dangling from Alex's coat. On it was printed *CRICKLEWOOD, St. Sebastian's C of E Primary School,* and, in a handwritten scrawl… "Alexander Day," the official read aloud, before putting his pipe back between his teeth.

Alex corrected him. "Actually, my name's Dias, not Day." But the man ignored him and turned to Hannah. "And you will be?"

"Hannah Day," she said firmly, as Alex gawked at her.

Brandon was looking thoughtfully at his nametag, and after only the slightest hesitation, announced that he was George Braithwaite. When Hannah looked questioningly at him, he raised his eyebrows, as if to say, "What else can I tell him when I'm wearing this?"

A large cloud of pipe tobacco smoke wafted over the children, and Hannah waved at it with both hands. "Excuse me?" she said to the official, who was still writing down "George's" name. "Would you mind not smoking in here?"

The man looked astonished. "Cheeky girl, aren't you?" He returned his attention to his papers, and waved the kids away. "Alright, the three of you cut along now and take a seat with the others."

As they traipsed over to three empty chairs, an exasperated Brandon said to Hannah, "I wish you wouldn't keep drawing attention to us like that. When are you going to figure out that these people have no problem with smoking?"

"Whatever," Hannah said. "I have a problem with it. They must be totally ignorant if they don't know that smoking kills people."

Brandon sighed, "Yes, they are. Nobody in the whole world has that figured out yet. And haven't you ever heard about 'when in Rome'?"

"No," said Hannah crossly, although of course she had.

"Why has our name been changed to Day?" asked Alex, fiddling with his label.

Hannah shrugged. "I guess because Dias would be too strange for these people….It's Portuguese, they're English." Suddenly, remembering what she wanted to tell the boys, she sat up straight.

"Guys, you know the lady who brought us here?"

"Miss…Something," said Brandon without interest, as he glanced around the bustling room.

"It was *her.* That professor woman we met in the library."

Now both boys looked at her in amazement.

"Maybe she's a witch!" said Alex, excitedly.

"Cool it, Harry," Hannah said, but she was unnerved.

Brandon said, "Well, at least now we know she's got something to do with us being here."

Hannah gazed at him coolly. "You think?"

But Brandon was really fed up with Hannah now. "Yeah, I do. And I think, maybe, she could help us get home….Anyway, why do you always throw an attitude every time you open your big mouth?"

Hannah glared at him, but Brandon glared right back and got to his feet. "I'm going to find the restroom," he said huffily.

As he approached the back of the hall, he spotted the moustached official talking with an unpleasantly familiar figure, Mr. Smedley from the tea room. Brandon tried to dash past the two men, but Smedley spotted him, and summoned him over.

"Now take this one," Smedley said, pointing at an anxious Brandon. "You'll have a hard time finding people round here willing to take this one, I'm telling you." He stared thoughtfully at Brandon. "Look, tell you what, why don't I take him with me? I'm going back to London this afternoon, and I can put him on a train to North Wales. That's where we take a lot of the colored evacuees from Liverpool."

"I'm not leaving my friends," Brandon protested.

"Hold your tongue, boy," Smedley growled. "There's a war on, and we don't always get to do what we want. And after seeing what you three get up to together, I think it's high time you went your separate ways. Troublemakers, that's what you are."

Brandon looked at Smedley, and then at the official, who, judging by the expression on his face, was uncomfortable. However, Brandon realized, he wasn't showing any sign that he would overrule Smedley.

Suddenly, Brandon's legs made a decision for him. He sprang forward, straight between the two men, and hurtled through the door. Emerging onto the street, he looked about him quickly, then sprinted down the sidewalk to his right. Swearing under his breath, Smedley gave chase, but he slowed to a halt as he saw Brandon dashing down Church Lane, a narrow road behind the High Street.

"Off you go then, Sunny Jim," he muttered, panting. "But a colored boy won't get far round here." He smiled thinly to himself, lit a cigarette, and returned to the church hall.

Alex and Hannah, sitting with their backs to the door in the busy hall, never saw any of this drama. They waited in silence, expecting Brandon's return at any moment, as the clock ticked by.

After about half an hour, a tall, grey-haired woman approached them. Hannah immediately thought to herself that the lady would probably look quite a bit younger if she wore makeup, dyed her hair, and got her wrinkles ironed out with Botox. Actually, a complete facelift wouldn't hurt, and she might want to consider getting her teeth straightened and bleached, too…

Like Miss Tatchell, this woman was wearing some kind of uniform, with a patch on her sleeve and a pin on her hat that both read *WVS*. Hannah thought that whatever WVS meant, this version of its uniform was much less frumpy than Miss Tatchell's dress. It was a green skirt suit, with a burgundy shirt buttoned up to the throat. The woman's brimmed grey-green hat was rather stylish, too.

"Nice outfit," Hannah said. "Who's the designer?"

The woman looked taken aback, and then mildly amused. "Mr. Norman Hartnell," she said, "Her Majesty the Queen's dressmaker. He designed this uniform for us. I trust that it meets with your approval?"

"Way cool," said Hannah admiringly. "Much cooler than that dress that other lady from your group was wearing. That kind of looked like a sack…"

The woman's expression instantly turned frosty. "That will do," she said sharply. "It is extremely rude of you to criticize someone else's appearance, and especially that of a grown-up. Now, come and have something to eat, both of you."

She escorted the kids to a long table, on which sat an enormous metal tea urn that was piping steam, and a large jug from which she poured them glasses of something that looked like punch, but which she called orange squash. She offered them sausage rolls, which seemed to be thin slivers of grey meat wrapped thickly in pie crust, and "currant buns", which resembled small bread rolls studded with raisins. Hannah refused the food with a shake of her head. The WVS lady asked if she was unwell, but Hannah told her bluntly that she just didn't want any.

"Don't be fussy," the woman chided. "You'll go hungry, and it's not just a sin, but a crime to waste food. And where on earth are your manners, young woman?"

"I'll never be that hungry," Hannah muttered to Alex as she sat down. The woman had insisted she take a glass of squash and a sausage roll, both of which she now passed off to her brother.

He took a bite, and chewed thoughtfully. "It's pretty good," he said through a mouthful of crumbs. "Just kind of heavy. This crust would bounce if I tossed it at the wall."

"You can say that again," said a thin blonde girl sitting behind them. Hannah and Alex turned around in their seats to look at her. "My mum says she reckons they've started putting sawdust in the pastry since the war started. Where are you two from, then?" she asked brightly.

Before Hannah could shush him, Alex piped up, "California."

The girl looked puzzled.

"In the United States," Alex added helpfully.

Now she looked dubious. "How come you don't sound like they do in Hollywood films, then?"

Alex and Hannah glanced at each other, then looked back at her. Hannah said quickly, "Oh, we only lived there for a short while. And we've been living in…in London for years."

"Whereabouts in London?"

"Oh, nowhere you would know, I'm guessing."

But the girl said, "It says Cricklewood on your label. I know where that is."

Hannah changed the subject. "Is there a restroom in here somewhere?" The girl gestured to the back of the hall. Alex saw that Hannah looked surprised by her answer, but he couldn't imagine why. As Hannah got up, she motioned to Alex to follow her.

Once they were near the back of the hall, Hannah whispered urgently to her brother, "Did you notice? She doesn't think we have American accents. And she understood when I said restroom."

"So?" asked Alex. "I don't understand."

"Alex, the English don't say the word *restroom*. That's one thing I remember Mom telling me one time, when we used to watch all those British shows on PBS. They say toilet, or loo, or something. It's like everything we say here is going through some kind of filter so they can understand us. Too bad it doesn't work the other way, because I feel like they're not even speaking English to us half the time."

"Hey, you know what I've noticed?" Alex said.

"What?"

"Everyone here is white except Brandon. I wonder if they can see that he's black? And anyway, where the heck is Brandon?"

At that moment, a large middle-aged woman in a hat and long coat with a folded umbrella, together with a heavily-built older man in a moustache, suit, and brimmed black homburg hat, carrying a raincoat still dripping with rain, paused in front of Alex and Hannah. "Are you two together?" the woman asked.

Brandon, rain dripping through his hair, into his eyes, down his nose, and in a small trickle along his spine, watched the door of the parish hall from the corner of a row of shops across the street. He had been stationed there for an hour.

Running off may have been a bad idea, he thought. He had realized that he stood out as probably the only black kid in town. And where was he going to go? He didn't dare risk being separated from Hannah and Alex. He felt in his jacket pocket, and his fingers closed around his identity card. He pulled it out, and read it again. What had happened to the real George Braithwaite, he wondered? And why was he taking his place, if that was what was happening to him? Did George Braithwaite even exist?

Brandon replaced the card in his damp jacket pocket, and returned to his vigil, monitoring the doorway of the church hall. For some time, a parade of adults had arrived at the hall on foot. After a short while, each left again with a kid or two in tow. But there was no sign of Alex and Hannah. Brandon knew, however, that they would eventually emerge, and then he could follow them home, because none of the adults seemed to have cars. Maybe, he thought in a burst of optimism, he could get their foster family to take him in, too.

The latest adult arrivals, a stout couple, walked briskly into the hall, the man pulling off his raincoat, and the woman closing her umbrella.

As they crossed the threshold, Smedley brushed past them on his way out. He paused, lit a cigarette, and tossed the match into the gutter. He crossed the street almost at a run, but he didn't spot Brandon, who pressed himself against the wall to avoid being seen.

After a few minutes, Brandon heard voices from the direction of the church hall, and he peered cautiously around the corner. The heavy couple he had spied earlier had returned outside, and the man was putting on his hat. They were trailed by Alex and Hannah, who were carrying their cases, and looking around desperately, as if searching for Brandon.

As Brandon saw them all turn a corner and out of sight, he realized he would have to take a chance and follow. He poked his head out to check the coast was clear, and all he saw was an old man pushing an old bike up the street, an old dog with grey whiskers walking alongside him.

Quickly, Brandon jogged down the street, in the direction of Alex and Hannah. He did not spot Smedley emerging from the newsagents' shop with his cigarettes and newspaper, but Smedley immediately caught sight of him.

"Oi, you!" he yelled. Brandon, startled, looked back, saw him, and immediately took off at a run. But this time, Smedley gave serious chase, and he moved much faster than Brandon would have expected from a man of his age. He was gaining on him.

Desperately, Brandon ran down an alley, and, in the most amazing athletic feat of his life, jumped the first fence he saw into a back yard. He looked around frantically for somewhere to hide, but almost the whole garden was planted with vegetables. Just then, he caught sight of a small, steep grass-covered hill in the middle of the vegetable patch, and he dashed for it as fast as he had ever run. Rounding the front of the hill, he recognized it. "It's an air raid shelter!" he gasped to himself as he saw the corrugated iron front. Immediately, he hurled himself through the small piece of sacking covering the entrance. Inside were two sets of bunkbeds, a tiny table, and little else. Silently, he climbed into an upper bunk, and prepared to wait out Smedley.

Smedley had lost sight of Brandon, but he knew the boy could not have got far on a dead-end street, and this time, he was determined to catch him. He walked slowly up and down the lane. Spotting a woman wearing a headscarf and apron who was weeding her garden, he cleared his throat. She looked up.

"Can I help you?"

"Yes, madam. My name's Smedley, Ministry of Health. I'm looking for a runaway, a small colored boy, just ran past here."

"Colored boy, you say?" she said with surprise. "Don't get many colored people round here."

"Yes, madam. A Negro. Boy's an evacuee from London."

She was just shaking her head when Smedley heard someone whistle from behind him. A second woman, also with her hair wrapped in a headscarf, was leaning from an open upstairs window, a few houses back, near the entrance to the alley. As he came closer, she stabbed a finger at the air raid shelter and mouthed clearly, "*In There.*" Smedley acknowledged her help with a wave, and quickly put his finger to his lips.

Quietly, he retraced his steps, carefully levered himself over the back gate, and slowly padded through the rows of carrots and cabbages to the front of the shelter. Leaning down, he called inside, "All right, Braithwaite, out you come."

Brandon sat up suddenly, dinging his head on the shelter's ceiling. He hadn't hurt himself badly, but rubbing at his head gave him time to think of a strategy. Perhaps, he thought desperately, he could make another run for it. Smedley had straightened up, and the curtain had dropped back into place over the shelter entrance. Brandon tried to estimate the height of the step up from the shelter door to the garden. As quietly as he could, he lowered himself to the ground, bent down, looked again at the entrance and then charged head first. But he had miscalculated: As he tried to jump through, he tripped on the step up, and fell flat on his face.

Smedley, who had been standing to one side of the entrance, grabbed him by the arm and hauled him to his feet. He drew back his free hand, and clouted Brandon hard across the back of the head. Now Brandon's ears really began to ring.

"Don't you play bloody games with me, sonny," Smedley spat, as he grabbed a dazed Brandon by the ear, and marched him toward the back gate. "I don't know how you managed to run off the first time, but I'd better not catch you doing it again."

Chapter 6

LEAVING

Mr. and Mrs. Archer were heavy, but they didn't waddle or show any lack of energy. In fact, Alex and Hannah struggled to keep pace with the adults as they strode purposefully down the sidewalk. They showed no sign of stopping.

"Where's your car? Is it far?" asked Alex, puffing.

Mr. Archer laughed. "Car? Whatever gave you that idea?" Then he turned back to the children, and asked curiously, "Does your father have a car?"

"Yes," said Alex, "and so did my mom." He almost added, *when she was alive*, but, as usual, he found it too hard to say.

"Goodness," Mrs. Archer said with astonishment. "Did you hear that, Geoffrey? Two cars." Then, to the kids, "Your family must be very well-to-do." Neither Alex nor Hannah knew what to say, so they let it pass.

Hannah quickened her pace to draw even with the Archers. "Our friend that we mentioned," she said. "Can you help us find him? Please?"

"We'll do what we can, dear," Mr. Archer said. "I'm sure you'll see him at school."

"I guess," Hannah said, "But it's so, like, weird that he just took off like that. Something must have scared him. He never said anything to us, we just thought he was going to use the…loo."

Hannah had used a British word for toilet that she remembered from the British sitcoms on PBS she had watched with her mom. She was quite proud to have used a word in a foreign language, but the Archers looked slightly shocked.

"That's a rather common expression," Mrs. Archer said. "Do your parents approve of you saying that?"

Hannah didn't know how to answer, and a silence fell. She didn't remember "loo" being a shocking word for the English, but apparently it was. Or maybe it just was in 1940?

Now they arrived at a small wooden gate, between two hedges. Behind the hedges sat a house that was joined to its identical neighbor by a common wall. The first floor was of brick, but the upper story was whitewashed, with oak beams crisscrossing it. "This house must be really old!" exclaimed Alex.

"Not at all, young fellow," said Mr. Archer. "It was only built two years ago. It's what we call Mock Tudor. It looks old, but it's very modern indeed."

"So the Tudor Tea Room, is that new too?"

"Oh, no," said Mr. Archer as he unlocked the door. "That's the real McCoy. You can tell by the crooked beams, you see. You notice that ours are rather straighter."

"What are the white lines on the windows?" asked Alex.

"Surely you know what that is? It's tape, in case of a bomb blast," said Mr. Archer. "It would stop shattered glass from coming in the house. At least I hope it would. Luckily, I don't think the Germans are terribly interested in bombing Balesworth. It's London they're after. But we still have to have blackout curtains, just in case their pilots see our lights at night, and decide to have a go at us." He gestured upward, and Alex now noticed that this and every house had at least some of its windows blacked out with paint, drapes, or some other material.

As soon as they entered, Hannah asked to use the restroom. "The lavatory is upstairs, the first door on the right," Mrs. Archer told her. Hannah found the bathroom, locked the door, and sat on the toilet with a sigh. She began to pull toilet paper from the roll. Suddenly, she stopped, and stared at the crinkly paper in her hand. It looked and felt like wax paper. "*What*," she said aloud in disgust, "am I supposed to do with *this*?" And it took her six tries pulling on the long chain that hung from the high-up cistern to get the toilet to flush. Even then, some of the paper floated.

Smedley, with his briefcase in one hand and two tiny thick cardboard railway tickets in the other, stood on the platform at Balesworth Station with Brandon at his side, as the London train, puffing and hissing in a cloud of coal smoke, pulled up in front of them. The train stopped, and let out a terrific burst of steam. Smedley pushed Brandon ahead of him toward a carriage with the word SMOKING painted in the window.

After the departing passengers had disembarked from the compartment, Smedley and Brandon climbed aboard. Brandon noticed that the only doors were the one through which they had entered, and another facing it on the other side. There was no access from the compartment to the rest of the train, and so, Brandon thought, it was a good thing he didn't need to use the restroom. Two long seats ran across the compartment, and there were luggage racks overhead. As another man boarded and settled into a seat, Smedley removed his newspaper from his briefcase. He threw his briefcase, raincoat and Brandon's case into a rack, before sitting down next to the window. He pointed gravely to the seat opposite him, and Brandon sat down.

Smedley reached into his jacket pocket, and pulled out cigarettes and matches. As the last few carriage doors banged shut, the guard's whistle sounded sharply from the platform. The engine began to chuff, and a cloud of dark coal smoke floated past the carriage windows. Brandon could smell it, even though the window was closed. Although the smell was acrid, he quite liked it. He could not say the same for the cloud of smoke that was coming from Smedley.

Brandon coughed, stood up and tried to open the window.

"Sit down!" barked Smedley.

"I just need some fresh…"

"…and be quiet," Smedley growled with the cigarette between his lips, returning to his newspaper.

"I have asthma." Brandon said flatly. Actually, it was his brother who had asthma, but it was the best excuse he could think of. Smedley looked at him over his paper, and Brandon added quickly, "If I get an attack, I could pass out."

"It's all in your head," Smedley grumbled.

But then the other passenger in the compartment, a suited man in his mid-thirties, wearing horn-rimmed glasses, who was himself smoking a pipe, said quietly to Smedley, "I really wouldn't object if the boy opened the window a little." He tapped out his pipe.

Smedley glowered at Brandon, then jerked his head toward the window. But when Brandon tried to pull it up, no matter how hard he tugged, it wouldn't budge. The kindly man rose to his feet and came to the rescue, pulling the window downward by a few inches. He smiled at Brandon and said, "Not been on a lot of trains, eh?"

"Evacuee," interjected Smedley, as if that explained everything.

"I beg your pardon?" the man said.

"This one," Smedley said loudly, as if the man was deaf. "He's an evacuee."

"Isn't he going in the wrong direction, in that case?" The man gave a half-smile.

Smedley blew out a puff of smoke. "Bit of a trouble-maker, sir. I'm just taking him to a hostel for tonight, then up north tomorrow. See if I can find a place that will take him."

"What's your name, lad?" the man asked gently.

"Br…Braithwaite. George Braithwaite."

"Well, that's a good Yorkshire name. Are you from Yorkshire?"

Brandon agreed that he was.

"Whereabouts?"

"Excuse me?" Brandon stammered.

"Whereabouts in Yorkshire?"

Brandon paused, panicked, and then took a wild guess. "Um…York?"

The man seemed satisfied with the answer. "Now that's interesting. Your father, was he from the West Indies?" Again, agreeing with the man seemed the easiest thing to do. It's amazing, Brandon thought, how often adults will answer their own questions if you hesitate long enough.

But the man seemed disappointed with Brandon's answer. He hesitated for a second, before appearing to come to a decision. He addressed the back of Smedley's newspaper. "I might be able to help. My name's Healdstone. Dr. Arthur Healdstone." He pronounced it "Heeldstun."

Smedley lowered his newspaper when he heard the title. "Doctor, eh?"

"Just a country doctor, I'm afraid," the man answered modestly. "Look, my wife and I live in Balesworth, and I'm sure our son would be happy of the company of another boy. I'd have to speak to my wife, of course, but I'm sure she'd be willing to consider it. What with the present situation."

"Well, that would be very obliging of you, sir. All the same…" He looked doubtfully at Brandon.

"That would be awesome!" Brandon whooped, and the doctor laughed. "Steady on, chum. I wouldn't go that far if I were you."

Brandon's enthusiasm seemed to have the reverse effect upon Smedley. "We'll have to see, sir. I'll have to make a full report on this lad, and we'll need to take your particulars on the official form before we can proceed. And, as you say, it might be best if you were first to consult with your lady wife."

"Quite," the doctor said, stonily. Brandon got the distinct impression that Dr. Healdstone had taken an instant dislike to Mr. Smedley. The doctor reached into his inside jacket pocket, and pulled out a small wallet, from which he removed two business cards. He handed one to Smedley, and one to Brandon, who put it in his pocket.

Smedley promised the doctor he would call him the next day, but Brandon, with sinking heart, realized that he was probably lying.

As soon as Smedley had once again disappeared behind his newspaper, the doctor said quietly, "George, if I can be of any assistance, don't hesitate to write or telephone. This is an odd thing, but you remind me very much of a boy I once knew. His name was George, too."

The train was slowing as it approached a station, and the doctor stood and gathered his hat, raincoat and briefcase. The train shuddered to a halt, and he lowered the window, reaching outside to open the door by the exterior handle. As the door swung open, he gave a small wave before stepping down to the platform.

Brandon smiled at him, and mouthed, "I'll call."

Brandon was gazing out of the train window, and, with increasing interest, watched the countryside go by. In all the panic over trying to reunite with the Diases, not to mention worrying about how he would get home, this was the first chance he had had to appreciate where he was.

The England of 1940 paraded gently before his eyes. He occasionally caught glimpses of wonderfully clunky cars—although not many of those, he realized. Very few people owned cars even before the war, and gas rationing ruled out most car journeys in 1940. All the same, as the train chuffed through the countryside, stopping from time to time in towns and villages, Brandon found it hard to believe that this was a country at war.

Everything was so peaceful. The landscape was like a gently rolling patchwork quilt, laced together with hedgerows and dotted with small copses of trees and the occasional house. Brandon was fascinated to see the people: Two old men in flat caps, suits and ties, standing on the street, talking animatedly… A woman in a hat and dress riding a rickety old bicycle with a wicker basket in front, rattling down a hill… Two small girls wrapped up in wool coats, hats, and scarves, walking hand in hand along a road, with a small dog following behind them. Brandon was entranced. But soon it was dark, and he could see no more. He settled back in his seat.

Brandon was napping when the train began to slow down, and he found Smedley shaking his shoulder to wake him: "Come on, it's Kings Cross." He took Brandon's case from the luggage rack, and handed it to him. Brandon rubbed his eyes, and groggily clambered to his feet. Smedley was already standing on the platform, impatiently holding open the door.

Gingerly, Brandon jumped down onto the platform, and excitedly noticed the number posted on a pillar above him. "It's nine! We're at platform nine at Kings Cross Station! I never knew it was a real place!" Smedley looked at him as if he was mad.

"What's the matter?" Brandon asked him. "You've never heard of Harry Potter?"

"Stop talking rubbish and come on," Smedley snapped. They were in a small building, with only three rail lines, a ticket collector's booth, and a newsstand, but as Brandon followed Smedley, he realized that this was not the main part of the station. Smedley led him down a short passageway with ornate trellis-patterned tiles in browns and beiges. Brandon found himself in another, much larger building, bustling with trains and people, that had a huge glass and iron ceiling curving overhead.

All along the platforms were soldiers in uniform, policemen, nurses, uniformed railway porters, and women in the outfits of the WVS. There were old people, middle-aged people, and teenagers but, Brandon noticed, there were no children. "Sten-ad!" yelled a man in a cloth cap and muffler, as he stood behind a huge pile of newspapers. Passing him, Brandon could see that he was wearing war medals hanging from what had once been brightly colored ribbons, and that he was not standing after all: He had no legs, and he was perched on a stool. Glancing at the bundled newspapers, Brandon glimpsed the name *Evening Standard*, and the headline, FIGHTS OVER CITY TO-DAY.

Smedley seized Brandon's arm and ordered him to hurry. Ahead of them was a flight of steps leading downstairs, and a red and white sign shaped like a lollipop that read LONDON UNDERGROUND. They trotted down two short flights of stairs, and waited in a line to buy tickets for the subway train from a woman sitting behind a small glass window in the side of the concourse. They handed the same tickets to a collector, before stepping onto an escalator.

Brandon almost fainted when he looked down. It was easily the longest escalator drop he had ever seen in his life. He felt like he was standing on the precipice of a mountain. He glanced at the step beneath his feet, which was made, not of metal, but of narrow wooden slats. To keep his mind off the height, Brandon looked to either side of him on the moving escalator, through the haze of cigarette smoke. Two more escalators, one going up, and the other down, paralleled the one on which he stood with Smedley behind him. Hanging on the walls on both sides of the escalators were small posters, advertising theatre plays, cigarettes, department stores, and instructions from the Ministries of Food and Information: Colorful pictures delivered stern messages against wasting food and urged people to obey their Air Raid Wardens.

Separating the escalators were wide strips of metal sheeting. Brandon thought what fun it would be to slide all the way down them—but, apparently, someone else had had the same idea, because lamps were strategically fixed on the sheets at regular intervals.

Brandon and Smedley had just reached the foot of the escalator when they heard a loud and sinister wailing from overhead.

"Oh, blimey," said Smedley. "It's the bleedin' Jerries."

"Jerries?" said Brandon, "You mean the Germans?"

"No, clever dick, I mean Vera Lynn… Of course I mean the ruddy Germans! It's an air raid, you stupid boy," he shouted.

As the sirens wailed, Brandon followed Smedley through the tunnel to another escalator, which took them even further beneath the dangers on London's surface. Everything in the subway station was covered in a thin, drab layer of sooty grime. To steady himself and his nerves, Brandon had been clutching the handrail the whole way down, standing on the right as dozens of people hurried past on his left. When he stepped off, he looked at his palm, and saw that it was covered in dirt.

"Alright," Smedley said, as they emerged from walking through a short tunnel onto the crowded narrow platform, "we'd better stop here until the All Clear."

Brandon figured out that he meant that they should wait for a signal that the attack was over. As the muffled sound of bombs began an irregular drumbeat on the city surface far above, he followed Smedley to the far end of the platform. Smedley, with obvious distaste, laid out his overcoat on the grimy floor, and sat down against the curving wall.

Spotting a colorful map of the London Underground on the wall above Smedley's head, Brandon stepped forward for a closer look. He traced the rainbow spaghetti of the various lines with his finger for a while, marveling at the strange, ancient names of the stations: Aldwych, Chancery Lane, Charing Cross, Holborn, Piccadilly Circus, Moorgate, Lambeth, Blackfriars, Dollis Hill. "Never thought a map of the Tube would provide an evening's entertainment," Smedley remarked sourly.

After a while, Brandon sat on the ground next to Smedley, being careful not to sit on the man's overcoat, and wiped his hands on his own jacket. He looked around him. To his left, the platform ended in a wall. In front of him, the track disappeared into a round dark hole, and he could just see where it did the same at the other end of the curving platform. A blast of warm air, followed by a whooshing sound and a smell of brakes, announced the arrival of a train, which suddenly burst from the tunnel like a caterpillar from an egg. To Brandon's eyes, the train looked tiny.

The carriages were packed, and people tumbled off as soon as the double doors slid open. Some made their way to an exit, but the rest scanned the dirty and increasingly packed platform for somewhere to sit. Once the train had departed, Brandon began to read the huge advertisements pasted to the tunnel walls, for newspapers, whiskey, and theater plays. When there were no more to read, he gazed down the platform as people continued to trickle in. Whole families staked out spots on the platform with blankets and lawn chairs as soon as they arrived.

A uniformed subway official approached one family, wagging a finger at them. The grandmother responded by pulling out a handful of small cardboard tickets, and waving them angrily at him. When the man tried to pursue the argument, she waved her hand over the small kids sitting sleepily on the blanket, yelling something about "her rights," and then put her hands on her hips. Finally, the official threw up his hands, and stalked away with a furious look on his face.

"Why was he giving them a hard time?" Brandon asked Smedley.

"Nobody's supposed to take shelter down here." Smedley said. "The government are concerned that people will never come up from below to do their jobs. And quite right, too."

"But you work for the government and you're down here," Brandon pointed out.

"Shut up, boy," Smedley grumbled, but he did look a little embarrassed.

The noise overhead grew louder, and the "crump" sounds made by falling bombs became more frequent. "Are we safe here?" Brandon asked nervously.

"Safe as we can be in a war," mumbled Smedley. He had pulled his hat over his eyes. "Now be quiet. I'm trying to get forty winks."

Good luck, Brandon thought, as babies cried and people talked loudly, even more loudly than his mom and Aunt Morticia when they were gossiping. One family was singing, and others gradually joined in with them. Brandon managed to pick out the words of the chorus, which ran "Pack up your troubles in your old kit bag, and smile, smile, smile." He noticed that almost nobody singing was actually smiling, but he wanted to join in to keep his mind off the bombs dropping overhead. He didn't think Smedley would tolerate it, however. So he lay down, arranging his suitcase as best he could to make a pillow.

Mr. Archer was a kindly man, who was evidently much older than his wife. He was also a little deaf, and Hannah and Alex quickly learned that they had to speak up around him. Mrs. Archer was more self-consciously proper than her husband, and Hannah found her rather distant and snobbish. She proudly explained to Alex and Hannah several times that they were lucky children. Most people, she said, wouldn't have room for a brother and sister, who in her view required separate rooms. But, it just so happened, she said, that their house had three bedrooms, even though they did not have children, only two cats. She showed Hannah into a large bedroom, and Alex into a tiny one.

Hannah's twin bed was covered in a blanket, sheet and plain salmon-colored quilt, and the room was otherwise quite bare. Hanging on the wall was a painting of yellow tulips, and on the dresser there was a small china figurine of a girl in a large blue hoop-skirted dress. The room smelled clean, but dusty and airless, as if it had not been used in a long time. It was breathtakingly cold.

That evening, Hannah sat on the bed, and for the first time, tears sprang into her eyes. She wept as quietly as she could, because she hated people to see her cry. Then she heard sobbing from next door, and followed the sound to Alex's room, to find that he was crying as hard as she was. She sat and put her arm around him.

"What are we going to do?" Alex asked between sobs. "I want to go home." Hannah had no answer, but she hugged him tightly.

Downstairs, the doorbell rang, and Hannah heard Mrs. Archer bustling to answer it, while complaining that she couldn't imagine who would be calling at this time of day.

Alex was still sniffling when Mrs. Archer shouted up to them. "Children? Come downstairs, please. There's a lady to see you. From the WVS."

Alex bolted upright, and looked at Hannah. "Brandon! Maybe they've found him!" he said excitedly. They both hurriedly wiped their eyes, and dashed down the stairs, ignoring Mrs. Archer's pleas that they take their time and not slip.

But there was no Brandon. The visitor had come alone. She was Miss Tatchell, otherwise known as the Professor.

Miss Tatchell asked Mrs. Archer if she could meet with the children in the front room. Mrs. Archer reluctantly volunteered that she had work to do in the kitchen before her husband came home, and she left Alex and Hannah alone with the visitor, who now perched on the edge of the sofa where the kids were sitting.

As soon as the door closed behind her, Hannah and Alex began talking at once. "Where's Brandon?" Hannah asked urgently.

"How do we get home?" piped up Alex, his face creased with worry. "Are we stuck here?"

The Professor smiled, reached over and grabbed Hannah's hand.

"Kids! It's okay, I promise!"

"How is it okay?" Hannah scowled, roughly withdrawing her hand from the Professor's clasp. "Let me get this straight. We're in England, it's World War Two, we're living with strangers, and our new friend just vanished. And we're supposed to be okay with that?"

"Don't worry about your friend…" said the Professor breezily, but Hannah was not going to be put off so easily.

"Why not?"

The Professor ignored the interruption and gestured around the room, "…or all of this, or getting home. The important thing is to find George Braithwaite."

Hannah's jaw dropped. "Say what?"

The Professor repeated slowly, "Find George Braithwaite. I promise you that I'm quite sure everything else will sort itself out, by and by."

"How?" Hannah shot back. The Professor ignored her again. "And how can we find George Braithwaite if we can't find Brandon? I mean, they're the same person, right?"

The Professor touched Alex's cheek, and smiled at him. "Everything will be alright, darling. There's nothing to worry about. You will all get home, and in one piece."

"Oh, really?" Hannah said angrily, and turned her back on the Professor. She heard the door close quietly, and when she turned, the Professor was gone.

Mrs. Archer bustled back into the room. "Did that woman leave?"

"Yes," Hannah said, in a remote voice.

"Well, she might have said goodbye. I was just making her a cup of tea."

"Didn't she come through the kitchen, then?" asked Hannah.

Mrs. Archer just shook her head, and left. However, almost immediately, she reappeared, with a cheery smile. "Well, this is something! That woman left your ration books on the hall table. How you two managed to lose them, I do not know. I wouldn't have been able to buy food for you without them. But now I can go to the grocer's for eggs."

Early the next morning, Brandon awoke to loud noise, but this time, it wasn't bombs, but voices. He also woke to a revolting smell. It took him a moment to realize that the stench filling his nostrils was stale urine. Up and down the platform, people were gathering their belongings, wiping the sleep from their eyes, and putting their children's coats on. In the background, Brandon could hear another siren, this one a constant tone, instead of the up and down wail of the first. That must be the All Clear, he thought: The air raid was over.

Smedley was still asleep on the platform. Brandon needed to find somewhere to pee, and that gave him another idea. As quietly as possible, he got to his feet, and gently lifted up his gas mask box and his case. He looked nervously at Smedley one last time, and turned for the exit.

Quick as a flash, a hand grabbed his left ankle.

"Not so fast, you," Smedley said, pushing back his hat, and looking up at Brandon. Desperate, Brandon lifted his right leg, and kicked Smedley sharply in the side. He knew those tae kwon do lessons would come in handy eventually…It was the only useful sport he had ever taken up.

Immediately, with a roar, Smedley let go, and Brandon ran for it. By the time he got to the nearest platform exit, Smedley was tearing after him, his thin hair blowing about without his hat, which had fallen to the ground.

Running fast, Brandon saw a short tunnel straight ahead of him, and through it, a train stopped on another platform. He ran toward it, and, with a sudden inspiration, turned right, then sprinted past two carriages, jumping onto the third. Smedley arrived in time to watch the doors close, and the train pull quickly from the station. Brandon blew a kiss to the furious man, then laughed with relief, as he saw him recede into the distance, before disappearing into blackness as the train sped into the tunnel. The few other bleary-eyed passengers in the carriage either stared, or looked away, pretending not to see him.

Brandon exited the Piccadilly Line subway train he had boarded just two stations after King's Cross. There, he boarded a train on a different platform, which took him on the Northern Line. He got off at the very next stop, Charing Cross, which was also home to a main railway station, just like Kings Cross. All that hopping around, he hoped, would be enough to put Smedley off the trail for a while. Now, he emerged onto the front forecourt of Charing Cross Railway Station, where a line of black taxis waited for passengers.

Perhaps, Brandon reckoned, he could lie low for a few hours, then catch a train from Charing Cross or—better—a bus back to Balesworth. There, he could call the kind doctor he had met on the train, reunite with Alex and Hannah, and then…What? He shivered. That "what" was what terrified him.

Walking between the brick gateposts at the entrance to the station forecourt, Brandon found himself in the Strand, one of the busiest streets in London. Two ambulances and a fire engine flew past him, with bells ringing, headed eastward. Glancing around him in an effort to get his bearings, Brandon suddenly realized he was still wearing the luggage tag that identified him as George Braithwaite. Snatching it from his jacket, he crammed the piece of cardboard into his pocket.

He had been hungry for hours, and he now scanned the street for a place to eat. But there was no fast food joint in sight, nor even any obvious restaurants at all. Ahead of him, across the Strand, he spotted a grey-haired man of about fifty, in a cloth cap, scarf, and coat, standing over what looked like a cylindrical barbecue grill, with wisps of smoke rising from it, and coals glowing beneath. As Brandon approached, the man scooped some blackened round objects from the top of the grill into a brown paper bag, and handed it to a customer in exchange for coins. "'Ot chestnuts!" the man yelled as his customer walked off. "Get yer 'ot chestnuts!"

"How much?" Brandon asked.

"Haypny a poke," the man said cheerfully.

Brandon had no idea what that meant, but he pulled out a large bronze penny, and hoped that would do the trick. The man took his coin, returned a smaller, halfpenny coin, and then, with a scoop, filled a bag full of chestnuts. Brandon suddenly noticed that the right sleeve of the man's coat was pinned to his chest, and just like the newspaper seller Brandon had seen at King's Cross, he was wearing medals.

"Hope you don't mind my asking, but what are your medals for, sir?"

The man smiled at him. "All from the Great War, my son. I was at the first battle of the Somme, you know, but then I took a Blighty," he indicated his empty sleeve with his remaining hand, "and got sent 'ome. I miss my arm, course, but I'm a lot better off than a lot of my old mates, I'm telling you. Five of 'em are dead. One of them lost 'is marbles with shell shock, and he's still in an 'ospital up in Scotland. Been there for more than 25 years, he has."

Brandon realized with a glow of excitement that he was talking to a veteran of the First World War.

Brandon carried his bag of chestnuts in one hand, his case in the other, and his gas mask box hung around his shoulders. He wandered for a while in search of a bathroom. Finally, he couldn't wait, and he had to make do with a doorway in a deserted alley, although judging from the smell, he certainly wasn't the first.

He travelled farther in search of a place to rest and eat his chestnuts, and was rewarded for his trouble with a bench in a small, quiet park. It took Brandon four burned fingers to eat his chestnuts, but they were delicious, and he eagerly gobbled them all, even though they made him very thirsty. They reminded him of the nut that Alex had found on the country lane, and he wondered if they were the same thing. Soon, all he had left was a bag full of empty shell fragments, and he looked around for a trash can. There was quite a lot of trash along the ground, but no bin, and Brandon reluctantly concluded that most Londoners simply dropped their litter. He couldn't quite bring himself to do that, so he shoved the empty bag into his already bulging pocket.

As he did so, a loud wail exploded all around him, making him jump.

It was the air raid sirens again. Brandon swallowed hard, and immediately decided that the safest thing was to make his way back to Charing Cross Station. He rushed out of the park, past an ornate stone arch, and found himself on a narrow footpath that seemed to be gated at both ends, making it impossible to return to Villiers Street and Charing Cross Station. His heart racing, he hurtled up a small stone staircase onto Buckingham Street, and ran toward the Strand, only to find his way blocked again.

But now, sooner than he thought possible, Brandon heard the ominous buzz of planes approaching overhead, and hideously loud booms as the first bombs began to drop. Panicking now, he ducked down a tiny lane, and looking up, saw a small sign that read *Of Alley*. As he did so, a loud whistling sound approached from overhead. To his horror, Brandon watched as a bomb fell from the sky, like a giant bullet. The closer it got, the more it seemed to be headed directly toward him. He froze in terror, and the last thing he heard was the loudest noise he had ever heard in his life.

Chapter 7
SPLiTTiNG TiME

Lying in bed that morning, Hannah tried hard not to open her eyes. That way she could continue to pretend that she was home. But she couldn't ignore the unfamiliar feel of the coarse sheet, rough blanket, and thinly padded pink quilt, or the freezing cold, or the peculiar smell of the house she was in, or the virtual silence all around her.

Finally, sighing, she opened her eyes, and climbed out of bed, wincing as her feet landed on the cold linoleum floor. She opened her suitcase, and, with a grimace, removed a plain navy blue skirt, white blouse, thin sweater, and some comically large underwear. At least, it was comic if you weren't Hannah, and didn't actually have to wear it.

Dressed, but still bleary-eyed, she opened the door and tentatively stepped onto the landing, from where she could hear Alex's voice downstairs.

Breakfast, in the dining room, was white toast with margarine and jam, accompanied by scaldingly hot tea poured from a pot into cups and saucers for the adults, and milk for Hannah and Alex. Hannah hated milk, and asked for tea. Mrs. Archer looked at her peculiarly, and tutted, but she took away the milk and brought out a cup and saucer from the buffet.

Alex began to help himself to a good-sized spoonful of raspberry jam, but Mr. Archer tapped sharply on the table next to his hand, and said, "Go easy, young fellow. That's got to last us." He only seemed satisfied when Alex finally reduced his claim on the jam to what looked like a half-teaspoonful. Frustrated, Alex started carefully scraping his tiny allotment of jam across his toast.

Mr. Archer resumed reading the newspaper, and Mrs. Archer returned to the kitchen for a moment. Hannah, with a devious grin, stuck the spoon into the jam, and dropped a large dollop onto Alex's toast. He gave it a quick slathering spread, and gulped it down.

When Mrs. Archer came back, her husband said from behind his newspaper, "Terrible bombing raid that was yesterday."

"What's that, dear?" asked Mrs. Archer, putting down the teapot.

"The East End got it badly again, but, listen, the swine bombed up West, too. Hit Regent Street and the Strand. You should see the photographs. Look, here… Absolutely shocking. And I reckon we're not hearing the half of it."

He continued to read in silence. Then suddenly he sat up, and examined the newspaper more closely. He tapped his wife's arm, and pointed out something to her. Mrs. Archer's hand flew to her mouth.

"Children," Mr. Archer said, as casually as he could, "What did you say your friend's Christian name was?"

"His what name?" asked Hannah, confused and irritated.

"His Christian name," said Mr. Archer loudly, as if Hannah were an idiot. "His first name."

The paragraph appeared at the end of the story on the bombings.

> A further unidentified person is believed dead, and it is feared that the victim is a child. In one bomb crater in an alley just off the Strand, a suitcase filled with schoolboy's clothing and a fragment of a ration book has been found, with only the Christian name "George" to identify the owner.

The kids looked at each other in horror.

Brandon opened his eyes. The sun was shining overhead, and he felt oddly peaceful. Above him, he saw the sign for Of Alley swim into view, then come into focus.

He was not dead. That was something. He ran his hands down his sides, and determined that every limb was intact. He vaguely wondered how long he had been lying there.

Carefully climbing to his feet, Brandon realized he had somehow lost his suitcase. He was puzzled, but relieved, to see no evidence of a bomb blast. Cautiously, he emerged from Of Alley onto Villiers Street, and made his way toward the front of Charing Cross Station. As he reached the Strand, he glanced across the road, and caught sight of a chestnut seller, but it wasn't the same man he had met before. Suddenly Brandon halted, and, for the first time, *really* looked around him.

He was in the Strand, true. He was standing on the same street where he had been before, and yet he was not. Red, white, and blue British flags hung from windows all down the road. He didn't recall seeing these before. Perhaps he hadn't noticed? He spotted two horse-drawn wagons, a horse-drawn bus with an open top and a spiral staircase in back…and the very few cars on the road were different…. The people were different: Women wore large hats and long dresses, men wore suits that were styled differently than anything he had seen before the bomb…. He looked down, and saw with shock that he was dressed differently, too. He was wearing a heavy brown wool jacket, shirt, tie, and knickers that ended at his knees, with long socks below.

A newspaper seller was standing before the gates to Charing Cross Station. Brandon dashed over, grabbed a paper from the man's hands, and started to read. German airships, Zeppelins, had dropped bombs on London the day before. Today was September 9, 1915. But that was the last bit of information he registered. As the newspaper seller demanded that he pay for his paper, Brandon dropped to the ground, unconscious.

Some 25 years in the future, Hannah and Alex were sitting at the Archers' kitchen table. Mrs. Archer had asked Hannah to peel potatoes. Hannah hacked at them fiercely with a small knife, taking off half the potatoes along with the skins. Mrs. Archer, alarmed by the violence, not to mention the waste of vegetables, brought her peapods to shell instead. She was highly amused when Hannah had to ask her how to do it.

"That woman," Hannah spat to Alex, shortly after Mrs. Archer left. She ripped open a peapod, and forced the helpless peas into the white enamel basin.

Alex looked up in surprise from the book Mrs. Archer had brought him from the library.

"Who, Mrs. Archer?"

"No," said Hannah impatiently, "not her. That Professor, or Miss Tatchell, or whatever she calls herself. She is totally jerking us around."

"What makes you think that?" Alex asked without enthusiasm, returning to his book.

Hannah slit open another peapod and viciously gutted it.

"She brought us here, right?"

"She did?"

Hannah groaned at how slow her brother could be sometimes. "Duhh! She must have. She appears out of nowhere right before we time travel, and she shows up when we get here. Then she, like, takes off and leaves us here. I think she's evil: She told us not to worry about Brandon, and now he's dead…"

"We don't know that," protested Alex. "There wasn't a body, and the case might not have been his."

Hannah ignored him. "Of course, that's if Brandon ever existed. She probably made him up, too."

"You're crazy," Alex said. "Anyway, okay, if you're right, and she brought us here somehow, that means that she can get us home again. I don't think she's trying to hurt us. I think she's nice. I think we should trust her."

"Wha…?" Hannah was incredulous, and the peas rattled into the basin like machine-gun fire. "And do what?"

"Like try to find George Braithwaite, which I guess means finding Brandon. But it might not." He looked at Hannah steadily. "I don't care what you say, I think Brandon is real, and I don't think he's dead."

"Why?" said Hannah, as she shredded an empty pea pod.

"Like I said, there was no body, was there? Maybe he dropped all his stuff so he didn't have to carry it, or so people couldn't tell he was a runaway. Maybe he's on his way back here right now. We should get on the Web and start searching blogs. Everybody we've seen in England is white, so somebody would notice a black kid."

Hannah laughed at him. "Web? Blogs? Hello? Uh, computers not invented yet?"

Alex slapped his forehead. "Oh, wow. Right." He thought for a second, and said, "Then we do research on foot, I guess. We're gonna have to ask around."

"That's if we can get any of these people to take us seriously," grumbled Hannah. "Anyway, come help me with the veggies, Alex."

"No," he said, with a mischievous grin, "I'll bet it's not a boys' job in 1940. I reckon girls have special pea-pod shelling genes."

Just then, Mrs. Archer came in, pulling on her gloves.

"Alex, please help Hannah. We all have to do our bit for the war, don't we, even if it means doing things we're not used to doing."

Hannah quietly sang "Na-na-na-na-na-naa" so that only Alex could hear.

Mrs. Archer continued, "I shall be starting work in the office at the parachute factory tomorrow. I haven't worked in a long, long time, but we all have to do our bit for the war, don't we? And I think we had better arrange to put you two to our local school."

"What about our friend?"

"Your what…? Oh, dear, I am sorry, Alexander, but I'm simply too busy to worry about that. I don't mean to sound unkind, but there's nothing we can do, really, is there? And he's probably alright. Hurry along and get your coats on, now."

"So much for that idea," muttered Hannah to Alex, as Mrs. Archer bustled from the room.

"Never mind," Alex said confidently, "We can figure out a way. But we are gonna need to find another grownup to help us."

Brandon woke up in 1915 to a smell that was like a combination of cough drops and the powerful bleach his mom used to clean the bathroom. Feeling the soft rustle of a bedsheet beneath him, he opened his eyes, and found that he was indeed in bed, and that he was looking up at a very high ceiling. Turning his head, he saw another bed next to his. Looking in the opposite direction, he saw yet another on the other side, and another after that. In fact the whole room seemed filled with row after row of identical iron beds with white sheets and grey blankets, each holding a patient. He was in a hospital.

Nurses bustled between the rows. In their white dresses and headdresses, they looked, he thought, more like old-fashioned nuns than modern hospital nurses in their colorful scrubs and sneakers.

A young blonde nurse suddenly appeared at the end of his bed.

"Awake, are we?" she said brightly. "Jolly good. I'm sure Sister will be pleased."

As Brandon tried to process what she had said, the harried young nurse began to tuck him in even more firmly. He felt as though he was being bundled into a sweaty cocoon. "Hey, please don't do that, ma'am," he protested. "I'm too warm as it is. I want to sit on top of the sheets, if that's okay."

"It most certainly is not alright," she said indignantly, as she carried on tucking the bed ever tighter. "Sister would have my ears for breakfast…and yours. Now you be a good boy and try to get more sleep. You've had a nasty shock."

"What happened?" he asked.

She looked impatiently to the next bed. "Concussion, if you know what that means. We think you must have been standing too close when one of those frightful Zeppelins dropped a bomb by the Strand. You had a lucky escape, young man. Now, hush. Sister will be here shortly. And she has an important visitor for us. Won't that be a treat?"

"I guess," said Brandon uncertainly.

As the arrival of Sister drew near, nurses rushed about, straightening beds, administering medicines, and clearing tables. Brandon had no idea who Sister was, but she had to be someone pretty scary to throw all these women into a panic. She turned out to be a small but stiff and imposing figure in a long dark headdress. Sister was accompanied by another older woman who wore a long blue dress, an enormous hat, a fur around her neck, and was carrying a large purse. This lady, Brandon guessed, was the special guest.

Sister clapped her hands. The nurses immediately straightened up and looked apprehensively at the two women. "Everyone, your attention please. We are most fortunate today to have a distinguished visitor. Lady Smyth-Howlington is here on behalf of the Ladies' Hospital Aid Society, and she has graciously offered to speak with some of you." Brandon watched with mild interest as Sister began her inspection, stopping here and there to straighten beds or admonish some hapless young nurse, while Lady Smyth-Howlington chatted with patients.

Brandon's interest turned to concern as the two women began to move in his direction. What would Lady Whats-her-name ask him? What would he tell her? He decided to fake sleep. As Lady Smyth-Howlington arrived at Brandon's bed, she paused at his head. He screwed up his eyes tightly, but she didn't seem to be taking the hint. Eventually, he allowed his eyelids to flutter open, and found himself looking directly at a dead fox's face, inches from his nose. His head jerked backward.

"Good morning, Brandon. I trust you slept well?" It was a familiar voice.

His eyes widened at the mention of his real name.

He looked up, into the eyes of the Professor. She was Lady Smyth-Howlington.

"Whoa," was all he could bring himself to say, and then his face cracked into a broad grin.

"Whoa yourself," she said quietly with a smile, then more loudly, "Apparently, I hear you gave us quite a scare, my dear." She leaned down, and whispered, "Next time a bomb is headed straight at you, would you please run?"

"Hey, what can I say? It missed. Everything's cool."

She looked at him skeptically. "I'm glad you think so. Look at where…and when…you are now."

He looked around. "Yeah, a hospital, London, 1915. Any idea how I got here?"

She gave a small shake of her head, briefly bit her lip, and changed the subject. "Anything you want to know about this place?"

"Yes," he said, "I have a question. Are English hospitals always like this?"

She looked around, and saw that Sister was busy, telling off yet another nurse. "It can be hard to tell, can't it, what's old and what's English?"

Brandon nodded.

"Most of what you see is old," she continued, "but some things are the same in our time. Patients altogether in public wards instead of private rooms? That's English, well, except for wealthy people, of course. Calling the head nurse Sister, that's English, or at least, not something we do in America. Disgusting food… that's certainly English." Brandon laughed. "Well, to be fair, that's hospital food wherever and whenever you are. Just be grateful that you don't need a shot—the needles look like drinking straws."

"Of course," she added as she plumped his pillow, "in modern England, most healthcare will be free. In 1915, the poor things have to pay for their hospital stay."

"Why don't they have to pay now? I mean, in the twenty-first century?"

"That's a long story, love. Not for now, I think. But do rest assured that your bill has been settled. By the Ladies' Hospital Aid Society, naturally." She winked at him.

She was already looking back at the door.

"Wait a second." Brandon said quickly. "Are Hannah and Alex in 1915, too?" She shook her head.

"Oh, man…Well, why am I here? I mean, I know a little bit about World War Two, but—this is World War One, right?—I tell you, I don't know anything about World War One."

"Exactly," she said, her eyes twinkling, and then she added, mysteriously, "Perhaps, once you feel better, you will start all over again, where you first began. All you have to do is keep your eyes and ears open."

Brandon wasn't sure he understood all that, but he had a more pressing matter to discuss with her. "How do I get home?" he asked.

"But that's what I'm trying to tell you. Don't worry," she said. "Just make the most of your time here. Use that splendid brain of yours. That's what it's for, after all."

Brandon smiled uncertainly at her as she straightened up, and she waved a finger at him, saying loudly, "I can tell that you'll be right as rain in no time at all, young man. Carry on."

As she left, she winked, and whispered, "Have fun!"

Soon afterward, a nurse brought Brandon a pile of hardcover books (presents from Lady Smyth-Howlington, she said.) Brandon admired the covers, on which were printed gilded letters and elaborate illustrations in bright colors. He opened up *The Cannibal Islands*, by R.M. Ballantyne. But the book inside had nothing to do with the title on the cover. It was instead a modern history of Britain during World War I, with lots of color pictures and cartoons.

Brandon enjoyed the rest of his day, most of which he spent reading and getting up to speed on life in 1915. In the afternoon, a man in a neighboring bed challenged him to a game of chess, and Brandon won, to his opponent's chagrin.

"So where you from, then, George?" the man asked as he put the chess pieces and board back into their box.

"Yorkshire," Brandon said shyly. He was still trying to get used to being addressed by his assumed name.

"Blimey, that's well up north, innit? Never been there myself." The man shook his head.

"Are you from London?"

"Yerr, lived in Clapham most me life. Come to London as a young man, but I was born in Hertfordshire." He pronounced it "Hartferdshirr." "Littletown called Balesworth."

"Hey," said Brandon excitedly, "I've been there!"

"Well, I never!" said the man. "Recently, like?"

Brandon hesitated. "Yeah, I guess you could say that."

"So, how is the old place?"

"Very nice. I met some good people there…Like Dr. Healdstone, I don't expect you would know…

The man smiled at a warm memory. "Dr. Healdstone! Strewth, that takes me back a bit, that does. I used to know him. My mum was in service with his family, years ago, doin' a bit of cooking and that, you know. So how'd you know him, then? A patient, was you?"

Brandon was thoroughly confused. His visit to Balesworth and meeting with Dr. Healdstone had taken place a quarter century in the future.

The man didn't seem to notice Brandon's consternation.

"Shame about what happened to him, wasn't it? My sister wrote me about it. Tragic, a man of his age."

Brandon agreed that whatever had happened to Dr. Healdstone was indeed a shame, testing his theory that if you agreed with them and waited long enough, adults would always explain the answers to their own questions. But, this time, Brandon's theory failed him. The man just shook his head and tutted, then picked up his book from the table at the side of the bed, leaving Brandon none the wiser.

It was a grey, rainy Saturday. Hannah was depressed, and complained of boredom. Mrs. Archer responded by bringing from upstairs an armful of board and card games. Hannah felt herself slipping into an even deeper catatonic state at the sight of them, but Alex was excited, and he immediately pulled the lid from a large plain dark red box.

"Hannah, it's Monopoly! We haven't played that for ages. Come on, I bet I grab Boardwalk and Park Place before you do."

He opened the board on the hearthrug before the fire, and Hannah glanced at it without interest. Then she did a double-take.

"Hey, Alex, check it out. No Park Place."

"No way!" But she was right. In place of the familiar names of the two most expensive "properties" on the board, were "Park Lane" and "Mayfair." Alex read off the names of the railway stations, and said, "I think these are all places in London. This is so cool!"

Hannah smiled. For once, her kid brother was right. It was cool. It had never occurred to her that Monopoly wouldn't be the same the world over.

Mrs. Archer rose from her chair, and suggested hot cocoa for everyone. "Geoffrey, would you care for tea or cocoa?"

"I think I'll have something a little bit stronger," he replied, clapping his hands and standing up. "Don't worry, dear, I'll get it." He poured out a measure of whisky from the bottle on the corner table.

Soon, Mrs. Archer reappeared from the kitchen with hot cocoa and a plate of plain round buns. "It's a treat," she explained, "so drink up while it lasts, children."

"Better turn on the wireless," said Mr. Archer, glancing at the clock on the mantel over the fireplace. "Time for the prime minister's speech." He walked over and switched on the enormous radio, which was so large that it was a separate piece of furniture.

"Why don't you guys have a TV?" Hannah asked, to Alex's embarrassment.

"Hannah," he said with annoyance, "Philo Farnsworth only just invented it."

The Archers looked astonished. Mr. Archer said, "Philo who?"

"Farnsworth," said Alex. "In America."

"Nonsense," said Mr. Archer. "Everyone knows that John Logie Baird invented television. He's an Englishman."

"A Scot, actually, Geoffrey," corrected Mrs. Archer.

"Yes, yes," said Mr. Archer impatiently. "Well, regardless, even if we were wealthy enough to own a television receiver, I'm sure you know that the BBC have suspended broadcasts from Alexandra Palace for the duration of the war. Now, quiet, everybody. Here's Mr. Churchill."

Hannah noticed that the Archers were staring at the radio while they listened, which she thought was very odd. And she found it hard to listen to Winston Churchill, the prime minister. He said so many words strangely, even by English standards in 1940: He pronounced "Nazi" without the usual "T" sound in the middle of the word, and he seemed to have a sort of lisp. She couldn't imagine how he was ever elected, because he looked as funny as he sounded. He was really ugly in the photographs she had seen. Hannah gazed out of the window, and let her mind drift off, until Mr. Archer said pointedly to her, "Hannah, this is the gravest crisis to happen to England in your lifetime, perhaps ever. The least you could do is pay attention to what our prime minister has to say."

The next morning was sunny and not too cold, so Mrs. Archer suggested the two kids go for a walk in the country.

"By ourselves?" Alex asked incredulously. Mrs. Archer replied that she had too much work to do about the house, and that Mr. Archer had to put in extra hours at the office during the emergency. However, she saw no reason why Alex and Hannah could not go. Hannah quietly pointed out to Alex that it might be a good chance to get out of the house and do some investigating.

And so, three hours later, following Mrs. Archer's directions for a "nice walk," Hannah found herself picking her way along a muddy trail—what Mrs. Archer had described as a footpath—through an otherwise grassy meadow. She carefully edged around a quagmire of mud and water, noting the bootprint that someone had earlier sunk into it several inches deep. She still managed to get her feet sucked into the edge of the muck, and the mud almost seeped over the top of her right shoe.

"Ughhh, that is disgusting!" she yelled, and lurched to her left. Suddenly, she gave a yelp as her hand brushed against the foliage at the side of the trail, and immediately began to hurt as if it had been stung by a swarm of bees the size of gnats. "It's those plants again! The ones that attacked Brandon. Yow, that so hurts."

Alex looked knowingly at her. "Stinging nettles. Mrs. Archer warned me that there were a lot of them. She said we should look for dock leaves, and that there are always some nearby. Look, I think this is one." From the ground, he plucked a large, oval leaf, and handed it to his sister. "Try it. Just rub this hard where it hurts."

Hannah looked doubtfully at him, but she did what he said, and rubbed it vigorously on her hand. The leaf soon began to spindle, turn dark green, and leave a green mark on her skin, but the stinging sensation was quickly disappearing. She exclaimed, "I don't believe it, it works! Good job, bro!"

Alex smiled, pleased with himself.

"I know this is weird, but, even with the nettles, I really like it here," he said cheerily, looking out over the countryside, with its small fields surrounded by hedges, and its tiny areas of woodland.

"In the English countryside, or in England in 1940?" asked Hannah.

"Both, I guess. It's just so amazing to be here. Kind of like being the first man on the moon."

"But the food is gross," complained Hannah.

"I like it," said Alex. "I just wish there was more of it. The portions are too small. I guess that's because of the war, because I heard Mr. Archer complain, too."

"But it's just so… heavy. I'm sick of bread and pastry and canned stuff and vegetables boiled to death. I want fruit juice!" cried Hannah, "Salads! Raw vegetables! How did these people manage to beat Hitler eating this stuff? I can feel my skin totally breaking out from the crud they are feeding us. And I so don't wanna think what's in here."

She held up the wicker basket, with its picnic blanket tucked over the food.

"Well, we could find out," said Alex. "We can sit over there." He pointed to a tree stump in the meadow.

They decided to lay out their picnic on the stump. As Hannah looked on with distaste, Alex first tested the thick grass for damp, cow patties, and other hazards before sitting down.

Hannah tutted as she sat down crosslegged on the cold ground, and placed the picnic basket next to her. "I just hope we don't get food poisoning. Mrs. Archer doesn't even have a refrigerator. I can't believe she keeps the food in a cupboard."

"The larder, you mean? It's no problem. It's not like it's hot here," said Alex, reasonably.

Hannah carefully peeled open a paper packet, and sniffed at the contents before pulling a face, and holding her fingers to her nose. "Urgh! These must be the fish paste sandwiches she was talking about. They smell like barf."

She handed the sandwich to Alex, who immediately took a bite and chewed thoughtfully. "Yeah, they do smell kinda yuk," he said, "But they taste okay. You should try one."

But Hannah was now solemnly holding up another item from the basket for his inspection.

"What is *this* supposed to be?" she asked in disgust.

"An… egg?" said Alex.

"And?" said Hannah, raising an eyebrow.

"A boiled egg? So?"

"So? Haven't these people heard of egg salad? Like, why not smoosh this up with some mayo, I mean, is that hard? Am I just supposed to eat this as is, or what?"

Alex took another bite of his sandwich.

Hannah pulled out two glass bottles filled with clear liquid. "She said she packed lemonade. What's this? It has a marble and a –I think it's a plastic ring in it. Yuk."

She couldn't pull out the marble, but she found she could push it in, and that opened the bottle. She took a swig, and shrugged her shoulders. "It's just lemon-lime soda. I don't think it's diet, but it's not very sweet. I wish we could have had Coke, but I bet they don't even know what that is."

"They probably do," said Alex.

Finally, Hannah pulled out two slices of plain cake, wrapped in a cloth napkin. She took one tentative bite, and chewed several times before starting to cough. She took a long draft of soda to wash it down. "It's gross! It's like sand!" she gasped. "It's like somebody sucked all the moisture out of it."

"You'd better eat something," Alex said reproachfully.

"You're right," Hannah said. "But not this crap. Let's go back to town and see if that café is open."

Alex protested, but Hannah was already packing away the food. "Alex, go dump this somewhere."

He looked around. "No trash cans. We'll have to take it with us, and drop it off in town. Hey, I don't mind eating it later."

"Whatever," said Hannah, dismissively. "But let's see if I can buy a cheese sandwich, or something edible."

They walked on in silence, until they saw saw an odd wooden structure with steps, built into the hedgerow. Alex was first to realize that it was to allow walkers to get past the hedge, without allowing wandering animals in or out of the field. Stepping down, he found he was on a road near the edge of town. Ahead, he saw a cottage, where a tall woman with an untidy shock of grey hair was working in the garden with a rake, vigorously clearing out the remains of the summer flower beds.

"Hannah?"

"Yeah?" she said in a bored voice as she carefully negotiated the wooden stile.

"We could ask that lady over there. And maybe we could talk to her about Brandon, if she's friendly."

As the children walked up the otherwise deserted country road, the woman put down her rake, and came to greet them. She walked quickly up the garden path while wiping the soil from her hands onto the floral apron tied over her dark blue skirt. Three brown hens followed, pecking at her legs, until she shooed them away.

"Hallo, children, and how are you two settling into your billets?"

Hannah and Alex looked at her in surprise.

"Well, you are evacuees, aren't you? I met you both at the church hall. It's Alexander and Hannah, isn't it?"

Suddenly, Alex recognized her. "You're the WVS lady!"

Hannah jabbed him with an elbow, saying, "She's not Miss Tatchell."

"I know that!" Alex said. "She's the other one...with the food."

Now Hannah recognized her. She was the tall, bossy old lady who had made her take that disgusting sausage roll.

"That's right!" said the woman. "I'm Mrs. Devenish." She pronounced it

"Deh-ven-ish", with equal emphasis on each syllable.

"What's the WVS?" asked Alex. Hannah turned to shush him, but Mrs. Devenish didn't seem surprised to be asked.

"Women's Voluntary Service, my dear. We're in charge of assisting the evacuees. That's why you met us when you arrived in Balesworth, and I expect you saw some of us on the journey from London." This woman is totally boring, Hannah thought with annoyance.

"Um, we don't want to keep you," said Hannah, putting on the polite fake face she found was most effective with adults, "We've been for a long walk, and we finished up our picnic, but there wasn't much food, and we're starving." Alex looked at her with shock at this total fib, but she continued, undaunted. "We don't want to hurt our host family's feelings by asking for more to eat. Do you know when the café in the main street is open today?"

"The Tudor Tearoom? Well, it's not open at all, not on a Sunday. In any event, it's a pretty dreadful place, too many flies for my liking. Look, why don't the two of you come inside, and you can meet Eric? He's my evacuee. I shall make all of us a nice cup of tea and something to eat. I'm a little peckish myself."

Hannah was horrified. More sausage rolls? Something else disgusting? But Mrs. Devenish was already halfway back down the garden path to her front door, with an enthusiastic Alex happily trotting beside her.

Eric was a short, chatty kid of about ten, with large teeth, a thick London accent, and a keen interest in stamp collecting, which he was happy to explain to Alex. Mrs. Devenish frequently interrupted Eric to tell him to take his elbows off the enormous oak kitchen table, sit up straight, and remember to pronounce the "H"s at the beginning of words. He took her running commentary on his manners and accent good-naturedly, and rolled his eyes at Hannah and Alex as soon as her back was turned. Soon, Mrs. Devenish produced thick slices of bread, smothered in a delicious butter unlike anything Hannah or Alex had ever tasted, and a jar of home-made jam.

"Damson," she announced loudly as she plunked the glass jar on the table.

"Excuse me?" said Hannah, smirking.

"The jam," said Mrs. Devenish. "It's damson, from the garden." Seeing the kids' blank looks, she gave a small smile, and said "They're rather like plums. I don't expect they're commonly found in London."

Next came glasses of milk for Alex and Eric, followed by a round-bellied brown teapot, steam streaming from its spout, a jug of milk covered in a tiny cloth to keep out flies, and a jar of honey.

"I have tried jolly hard to wean myself off sugar in my tea," Mrs. Devenish said, "But it is hopeless. However, my daughter, the younger one who works at the Ministry of Defence in London, suggested I might try honey, since I keep bees. She was quite right, of course. It's certainly better than nothing."

She pulled off her apron, flopped into a chair, and to Hannah's horror, lit up a cigarette, with a match from the large box that sat on the table. Seeing Hannah's face, she said, "I took up cigarettes while I was a nurse, during the last war. My younger daughter says I'm very fashionable, now that all the girls working in London are smoking."

"That's so awful!"

"I don't see why," Mrs. Devenish said indignantly. "As my daughter says, you need something to calm your nerves when old Adolf is trying to kill you on a daily basis. Oh…let me pick this up before someone trips over it." She leaned down, and before Hannah could stop her, lifted the basket that was sitting at their feet.

"That's just trash," said Hannah quickly. "Tell me where you keep your garbage, and I'll toss it."

But it was already too late. Mrs. Devenish, feeling the basket's weight, paused with a puzzled look, pulled it onto her lap, and yanked back the cover. She pulled out a sandwich and an egg, then another, and another, and in silence, piled the uneaten food on the table.

She looked severely at Hannah and Alex. "You told me that you two had eaten your picnic. Would you care to explain yourselves?"

"Don't blame Alex, it's my fault," admitted Hannah. "The food, it's not what we're used to. Alex is okay with it, but I didn't want to eat it. I told Alex we should go to the café instead. We didn't plan on you inviting us in."

Her temper rising, Mrs. Devenish spoke sharply to her. "In case it has escaped your attention, this is a war. Hitler is bombarding London with everything he's got, and we are expecting the Nazis to try to invade us any day now. German submarines are sinking the ships that bring us food, drowning the sailors who risk their lives every day to keep us fed. And I would bet a pound to a penny that you are looking at your foster parents' egg ration for the week. But you, Hannah, you, a spoilt, silly little girl, don't care for this food or that food, and so into the bin it must go." She glared at Hannah.

Hannah felt her own anger rapidly welling up during the speech. As soon as Mrs. Devenish had had her say, Hannah jumped to her feet. "Hey, lady, you know what? Here's a newsflash: Hitler's not coming. You're gonna win the war, whether or not I eat the stinky sandwiches. So why don't you mind your own stupid business?" With that, she ran through the kitchen door, and into the back garden.

"Hormones," said Alex knowingly, to Mrs. Devenish's even greater astonishment, and Eric's total confusion.

For five very long minutes, Hannah sat all alone on the high-backed wooden bench on the lawn, her knees hunched up to her chest, her arms wrapped around her legs, and her face pink with anger and shame. She was feeling a bit sick, and very stupid. She really wished she hadn't said all that, especially that part about Hitler not coming. Oh, duhhhh…

Suppose this Mrs. Devenish lady thought she was a German spy? Or that she was totally nuts? She certainly wouldn't believe the truth. Anyway, was it honestly such a big deal to toss that gross food that Mrs. Archer had given them? It wouldn't really make a difference to those sailors. And why did this woman care what she did? Just the same, Hannah had a queasy feeling in her stomach, one that felt suspiciously like guilt. She fought it down, and focused on getting angrier instead. Who does this woman think she is, she thought furiously, talking to me like I'm a little kid?

She raised her head at the sound of footsteps marching briskly up the path, and, with a stab of uneasiness, saw the imposing figure of Mrs. Devenish headed straight toward her. Looking sternly at Hannah, she sat down next to her on the bench.

"Now listen to me, Hannah Day," she said ominously, "I have a good mind to put you across my knee and tan your backside."

Hannah sat up straight in horrified amazement, gawping at her. "But… What? No… No, you can't! You've got no right…I just met you!"

"You are a child, and I am your elder," Mrs. Devenish said, fixing Hannah with the steely glare that her grown daughters knew all too well. "You lied to me about wasting food, and abused my generosity. That was wicked. Then, when I took you to task, as it was my right and duty to do, you had the impudence to shout at me, and in my own house. So, contrary to what you suppose, I believe I have every right."

She paused to let the threat sink in.

Hannah certainly was taking it in: Her stomach had done a triple axel and dropped through her knees.

There was a long and tense pause, during which Hannah did her best to look cool and unfazed, as she desperately planned an escape route across the lawn and through the bushes to the road. Mrs. Devenish, meanwhile, seemed to gaze thoughtfully into the middle distance. In fact, she was shrewdly watching Hannah from the corner of her eye.

Finally, after what seemed to Hannah like the longest moment of her life, Mrs. Devenish broke the silence. She said gently, "However...Although I am very cross with you, I do understand that this is a difficult time for you children. I imagine that you have endured a great deal in the last few days."

Right at that moment, Hannah was so incredibly relieved that she would not have to choose between a frantic escape attempt and hideous humiliation, she almost began to tell this woman everything. But she realized immediately that this would be a mistake. And, anyway, her gratitude rapidly turned to resentment. Mrs. Devenish had put her through the wringer. What a total hag.

She mulled over for a moment about what she really needed to get out of the woman.

She said: "Our friend who came with us from...from London. He's missing, and we're scared he's dead. Please, can you help us?"

For a talker, Mrs. Devenish turned out to be a very good listener.

When Hannah had finished her edited version of Brandon's disappearance, Mrs. Devenish began to think aloud. "This man you saw in the Tudor Tea Room, the chap with the moustache? You're not talking about the billeting officer, Mr. Simmons, are you? He is the gentleman with a pipe and spectacles who was registering everyone as they arrived." Hannah shook her head.

"Then it must be the older man from London."

"That's him. His name started with an "S" too, but I can't remember what it was."

"Didn't he come with you?" asked Mrs. Devenish. "I thought I saw him bring you in."

"He caught us having tea in the café," Hannah said, "and told us we had to go to the church hall. Then Miss Tatchell said she would take us, and she was the one who brought us. We saw the man in the hall after Brandon disappeared, so he couldn't have gone with him."

"It seems to me," said Mrs, Devenish decisively, "that I must make some enquiries. You have come to the right person, Hannah. I am one of the few lady magistrates in the county."

"What does that mean?" Hannah asked.

"I'm a J.P., Hannah, a Justice of the Peace, otherwise known as a magistrate. It means, in a small way, that I'm a judge. I have the power to try minor cases in court, and to make enquiries that serve the good of the community. I shall pay a call on Mr. Simmons, and that will almost certainly resolve the matter. He has the list of where all the children are billeted."

"But before we left the hall with the Archers, he told us that Br…George had run off," said Hannah.

"Nonetheless, he would have whatever information may be available on George's whereabouts. Now, what is George's surname?"

Hannah guessed that she meant last name. "Braithwaite," she said.

Mrs. Devenish looked surprised. "That name is familiar… I wonder…What an odd coincidence that would be," she said to herself.

"What?" asked Hannah. "What coincidence?"

"That's none of your business, Hannah," said Mrs. Devenish shortly. "Now, in the very unlikely event that your friend truly is missing, I promise I shall contact the WVS in London."

Seeing Hannah look downcast, Mrs. Devenish tried to cheer her up. "I really don't think there's anything to worry about. The evacuation was bound to be a bit of a muddle, but I'm sure we'll find your friend is as right as rain. Now, why don't we fetch Alex and Eric before they make themselves sick gorging on bread and jam, and I'll show you both my greenhouse?"

"Okay," said Hannah. She added grudgingly, "Sorry about, you know, what happened."

She waited for Mrs. Devenish to reply with reassurance and an apology of her own. It didn't happen.

Mrs. Devenish merely gave a curt nod, stood up, and said, "Are your foster family on the telephone?"

"Yeah, they have a phone," she said reluctantly.

"Splendid. Then I shall call them to let them know where you are, and to tell them that I shall send both you and Alexander home later on. This afternoon, I have decided, you shall have your picnic for tea. I put it in the larder to keep while you were out here sulking."

"But…" said Hannah, appalled. She had said she was sorry. What more did this woman want?

"No buts, young woman," Mrs. Devenish said firmly. "Did you really think that I would let you go scot-free after that dreadful exhibition? My word, you are quite the optimist. Perhaps you would prefer that I return you to your foster mother with a smacked bottom and the tale of what almost became of the picnic she packed for you. No? I thought not. Now, if you will tell the boys that we are going out to the greenhouse, I shall ring up your foster family. What is their name?"

Stepping into Mrs. Devenish's large greenhouse was to step into a green sea of plants. There were plants standing in large pots in corners, and plants hanging from baskets hooked to the ceiling. There were plants in small pots arranged like soldiers in rows on wooden benches, and empty pots, awaiting occupants, stacked haphazardly underneath. The children splashed across the wet floors, breathing in a heady smell of moist garden soil. Mrs. Devenish paused in front of a bench. "Now, Hannah, you are probably wondering what an old widow like me needs with such an enormous greenhouse."

Peevishly, Hannah thought, Not really, you witch, I mean, who cares? Whatever. She said nothing.

"Well," Mrs. Devenish continued regardless, in a hushed voice and with a twinkle in her eye, "I need this for my top secret research."

Alex remembered one of the posters he had seen hanging in the church hall. "Careless talk costs lives," he said solemnly. Eric laughed.

"Quite right, too, Alexander," Mrs. Devenish said, with a wink to a sour-faced Hannah. "However, I must confess that perhaps I exaggerate just a little. I am a researcher, but it's hardly top secret, since I will soon broadcast my findings on the wireless."

"You have your own radio show?" Hannah said in surprise.

"Good Lord, no!" laughed Mrs. Devenish. "But I've been asked by a friend at the Ministry of Food to contribute something for the BBC about how people can add more vegetables and herbs to their diets. It is a bit of a challenge, frankly. So many people don't like to change how they eat, do they?" She looked at Hannah knowingly. Hannah turned away from her, and took out her annoyance on a stray leaf she had just decided should be named "Devenish," grinding it to pulp underfoot.

Oblivious to the female drama playing out in front of him, Alex was very impressed. "You're gonna be famous! Can I have your autograph?" Mrs. Devenish told him not to be so silly, but Hannah could tell she was flattered, which made her hate the woman even more. She picked up another leaf, which she silently dubbed "Devenish Two," and shredded it into tiny pieces in her fingers.

Alex was overjoyed when Mrs. Devenish nudged him, handed him an enamel bowl, and rattled off a list of plants she wanted him to pick, then began helping him to find them. She sent Hannah and Eric to walk back to the house ahead of them.

"Mrs. D. threaten you with a good 'iding, then, did she?" asked Eric cheerfully, as they crossed the lawn.

"Get lost, creep," said Hannah stonily, not looking at him.

"Thought so, 'cos you been po-faced ever since you come in the green'ouse. If it makes you feel better, she threatens me all the time, but she's not laid an 'and on me yet. It's just her way of putting the fear of God into us. I reckon her bark is a lot worse than her bite. Mrs. D's not such a nasty old bag as she wants us to think..."

He held open the kitchen door for Hannah, and added, with a grin,

"Mind you, that was a right little performance you gave, wasn't it? I wouldn't be so daft as to push her as far as you did, 'cos there's always a first time for everything, i'n't there?"

"Yeah, I guess there is," said Hannah. "Hey, you don't mind if I tell her you called her an old bag, right? I'm sure she'll get the joke."

Eric's grin vanished. "Don't you dare," he squealed.

"Thought so," said Hannah smugly.

Later that afternoon in the large kitchen, Hannah and Alex sat at the table near a glowing coal fire, helping Mrs. Devenish to recycle the remains of the picnic. Eric had already set off for a friend's house, having been invited to tea.

Mrs. Devenish whisked together a home-made mayonnaise using eggs from her hens, and Hannah, after peeling and mashing the hard-boiled picnic eggs with a fork, stirred in some of the mayo and a sprinkling of fresh chives. Alex then spread the mixture onto freshly buttered bread for sandwiches.

Then Mrs. Devenish carefully opened the salmon paste sandwiches, and Alex artfully arranged upon them crisp fresh slices of cucumber, which she had first showed him how to salt and dry on a kitchen towel to draw out the excess water.

She had even found a way to improve and extend the cake: She broke up the slices, placed them in a bowl, and, to the children's surprise and Hannah's delight, she sprinkled the cake pieces with sherry wine. She added a thin layer of damson jam and some canned peaches, and then, using some of her precious sugar ration, she made a custard sauce on the old stove, pouring it onto the cake when it had cooled a little.

"Not my best trifle," she sighed, "but it will certainly do. There is a war on, after all."

The table was completed with a thin slice of ham on each of their plates, accompanied by a solitary lettuce leaf and a slice of tomato. Mrs. Devenish declared that this was a ham salad, to Hannah's silent amusement. In fact, when they sat down to eat, the meal, although simple, was delicious, especially the trifle. Hannah even drank the last bottle of picnic soda without complaining. By the end of the afternoon, she was beginning to think that, as well as being useful, the Devenish woman had her good points. Well, one or two, maybe.

Because it was growing late, Mrs. Devenish decided to walk Alex and Hannah home. Alex happily chatted with Mrs. Devenish about the plants they passed on the way into town. She assumed that he didn't recognize them because he was a city child. Hannah, still embarrassed to be in the woman's company, trailed behind.

As they arrived outside the Archers' house, Mrs. Devenish said, "You know, I have an idea. My granddaughter is having a birthday party on Tuesday. Why don't you two come along with Eric and me? It's really not far, but I thought I might give my car a run to keep her working, and it's a better excuse for using my petrol ration if there are four of us. I'm sure neither Verity nor her mother would mind my bringing you along. In fact, I rather think Verity and you, Hannah, would find you have a great deal in common. And Alexander, you simply must see the monkey puzzle tree in my daughter's garden. It's a real treat."

"Dinosaur food!" exclaimed Alex in delight. "Dinosaurs used to eat them," he explained to an uninterested Hannah.

When they knocked, Mrs. Archer opened the door and smiled at the children. But when she looked at Mrs. Devenish, her smile faltered. Mrs. Devenish stepped forward and offered a handshake.

"Elizabeth Devenish," she said.

"Margaret Archer," said Mrs. Archer primly. "Thank you for having them, and bringing them home. I hope they didn't make a nuisance of themselves. Say thank you, children."

As Alex and Hannah did so, she quickly began to usher them into the house. But Mrs. Devenish wasn't finished. "Just one more question I must ask you, Mrs. Archer, if you don't mind?"

Hannah could see that Mrs. Archer looked flustered, even afraid, and that Mrs. Devenish was puzzled, and a little thrown by her reaction.

"Would it…ah…Would it be convenient if I were to drive the children to my granddaughter's birthday party on Tuesday? If they will come to me after school, we shall leave from my house… I say, are you all right? You look as if you've seen a ghost."

Mrs. Archer seemed to recover herself. "Quite all right, thank you. And yes… Yes, that would be fine. Good night."

After she closed the door, Mrs. Archer ordered Alex and Hannah into the living room, and told them to sit down. She remained standing. "Children, I will allow you to go to the party, but I must insist that you not discuss Mr. Archer's and my affairs with that woman."

Alex and Hannah, sitting together on the sofa, looked at each other, baffled.

Mrs. Archer shifted uneasily on the spot, and spoke in a voice that was both anxious and angry. "I didn't hear her name properly when she rang me on the telephone, but I certainly recognized her. You mustn't be fooled by her grand manner. That woman is a terrible gossip, and anything she hears from you will be repeated all over Balesworth. If you accompany her, then I must ask that you inform me immediately if she says anything at all about Mr. Archer or myself. Do you understand?"

"No," said Hannah determinedly. "I don't know what you're talking about."

"Me neither," piped up Alex. "She was really nice to both of us, especially after what happened with the…"

Hannah kicked Alex hard, and the sentence ended with an ouch and a whimper.

Mrs. Archer's face hardened. "Very well, then, let me be plain. Whatever it is that you get up to around the Devenish woman, you will not be party to any gossip. If I even suspect otherwise, I shall punish you both, and you will not be allowed any further contact with her."

That, Hannah thought, would be bad. Mrs. Devenish, however difficult she was, was their best chance yet for finding Brandon.

"I understand," Hannah said calmly, "and I'll make sure Alex does, too."

When Mrs. Archer had left, Hannah turned to Alex and said. "Sorry about that last thing I said. It's just, I wanted to shut her up. This situation we're in is getting seriously weird. I think we better speed up our research on Brandon."

Just then, Mrs. Archer returned. "By the way, I've washed your uniforms, so you can wear them to school tomorrow."

"School?" said Hannah blankly.

"Balesworth Primary for Alexander, and it'll be Balesworth Girls' High for you."

As soon as she had left, the two kids looked at each other and grimaced.

"Man, I forgot about that," Hannah grumbled.

Brandon was quite enjoying the hospital, even though sharing a ward with twenty other men and boys had its downside, as did struggling to eat the food, which was mostly mystery meat stews and boiled potatoes with cabbage. He read and re-read his history book, and chatted with the nurses, who doted on him. Not a bad way to spend his day, he thought. His stay certainly gave him time to absorb the atmosphere of the new year in which he had found himself.

But suddenly, Brandon's unusual vacation came to a rude ending, when a nurse abruptly dumped a suitcase on the end of his bed.

"Your belongings, George," she said. "Sister said you can put your clothes on. You're being discharged. We can't have malingerers like you taking beds from our brave soldiers now, can we?"

Brandon opened the case. Inside were his 1915 clothes, and an envelope that read, "Open this NOW." The envelope contained coins and a note: "Don't forget to take the history book with you!" He immediately dropped the book into the case, and began to dress.

On his way out of the hospital, Brandon passed another ward, and casually glanced in. What he saw shocked him. The room was full of men with bandaged eyes and missing limbs. One man seemed to have lost all but one leg. Some of the injured soldiers were playing cards, some reading, but most were lying in bed, staring into space.

Catching sight of Brandon, a nurse marched right up to him. "Stop staring," she hissed. "They're just back from the Front, and the last thing they need is people gawping at them. Now be off with you."

Brandon didn't need telling twice. He hurried down the hall, and through the swinging wooden doors, which banged shut behind him.

Brandon found himself on a busy street. The steady clopping of horses' hooves and the heavy fall of footsteps filled his ears, along with the shouts of street vendors, and the occasional putt-putt of a car engine. He reached in his pocket for money, and felt a card, which he pulled out.

It was a postcard on which someone had written, "You are now George Clark."

"Good deal!" he said aloud. He had dreaded being asked to spell Braithwaite, and it was nice to have at least one of his real names back again. But what did his new name mean? He looked again, and there was an address, too: "Go to 57, High Street, Balesworth, Herts.," he read aloud.

Now that, he thought, is very interesting. He asked a passing man in a bowler hat to direct him to the nearest Tube station.

Chapter 8
MEETINGS AND MESSAGES

As they walked home from their first day at school, Hannah asked Alex, "How was it?"

"Not bad," he said. "Kind of strict. But our teacher is pretty nice. At least we had no stupid worksheets or textbooks. We got to go into town, and sketch an old pub, and we learned a song, and I got to write a story."

"What did you write about?" she asked, curious.

"The future," he said. "I wrote about computer games, cell phones, iPods. Stuff like that. My teacher liked it. She said it was very imaginative, and she read it to the class."

"You're lucky," grimaced Hannah. "My school is all girls, and all the teachers are women, too, but I haven't met any nice ones. They have a million rules, and they yell at you every time you break one. Like, you have to walk on the left in the hall, and you aren't allowed to move in class."

"Like walk around? Come on, Hannah, we weren't even allowed to do that in our school at home."

"No," said Hannah, "I mean move a muscle. My math teacher was totally mean. She kept on telling me to stop fidgeting, like it was a big deal because I was playing with these stupid things." She tugged at one of her braids, which Mrs. Archer had helped her to plait that morning.

"Did you tell her it wasn't a big deal?" Alex asked.

Hannah stopped short and narrowed her eyes at her brother. "Do I look like I have a death wish? She made one girl cry just because she forgot to bring her homework, and she told me the only reason she didn't send me to the head-mistress for looking at her the wrong way was that I'm a 'new girl.' One of the others told me that she once picked a girl up by her hair. Listen, I'm just keeping my head down until we get out of here. The good news is it's totally over-crowded, because they have another girls' school from London billeted there. So we're going to have to take turns using the building. Starting tomorrow, I only have to go to school in the morning."

"Sweet," said Alex. "Hey, did you find out anything about Brandon?"

She shrugged. "Nothing. I talked to some of the girls, but nobody knew anything about a black kid. How about you?"

"Same," said Alex. "I guess we're going to have to keep on at Mrs. Devenish to help us out."

"Great. My buddy," said Hannah mirthlessly, kicking at a stone that got in her way on the road.

"Oh, get over it, Hannah," Alex shot back. "I don't know why you can't believe that she was cheesed off. I think she's pretty cool."

"Shut up," shouted Hannah, and she walked more quickly so she wouldn't have to walk next to him.

As Mrs. Devenish's black Austin Seven car careened along the perilously narrow country lane on the short journey to her daughter's house, Hannah enjoyed the luxury of sitting in the front seat. Still, she was a little alarmed at having no seatbelt, especially when Mrs. Devenish sped around blind corners along the single-track road, sounding her horn to warn any traffic that might be headed straight at them. Alex loved sitting in the back of the old car with Eric. He loved how the back doors opened backwards, and how the steering wheel was on the wrong side, and the fact that he didn't have to wear a seatbelt, because there wasn't one. He was entertained to hear Mrs. Devenish call the car "Maisy," and refer to it as "she", as if it were a person.

A tall and cheerful girl with bobbed dark brown hair answered the door, dressed in her best white party dress with a sash around the waist.

"Hallo, Granny, hallo, Eric. Hallo, who's this?"

"For heaven's sake, Verity, do let us in, and then we can have proper introductions," Mrs. Devenish grumbled as she barged through the door, thrusting an awkwardly-wrapped birthday present at her granddaughter, who took it with an excited cry.

Just then, Mrs. Devenish's daughter, a tall, elegant woman in her early thirties who looked like a younger version of her mother, came to greet them. Mrs. Devenish said simply, and very formally to the kids' ears, "Good evening, Edwina."

"Hallo, Mother, hallo, Eric. And you must be the evacuees. Alexander and Hannah, isn't it? I'm Verity's mother, Mrs. Powell. Go through to the drawing room, children. We're just starting a game of pass the parcel."

Alex paused, however, and said to Mrs. Powell and Mrs. Devenish, "Hey, I have a question, you guys. How come you don't hug when you see each other? You're family, right?"

He heard Mrs. Powell exclaim disapprovingly, "What an extraordinary little boy…" just as Hannah dragged him off, growling, "We're not in Kansas anymore, Toto, got it?" Alex opened his mouth to say that, no, he didn't get it, but Hannah was already walking ahead of him.

Verity introduced them to everyone. Hannah felt awkward and underdressed in her school uniform. Verity and the other girls were all in fancy dresses. The only boys at the party were Alex and Eric. Eric had suspected as much before-hand, and had griped in the car about having to go to a girls' party, until Mrs. Devenish had silenced him with a look.

But soon, all the children were happily playing a round of Pass the Parcel. Mrs. Powell provided the music on an old-fashioned record player, as the children sat in a circle, passing around a newspaper-wrapped package. Every time Mrs. Powell paused the music, whichever kid was holding the parcel could unwrap one layer of newspaper. Finally, Alex unwrapped the last layer, and found a home-made wooden toy car inside. Hannah was afraid he might blow it by comparing his prize unfavorably with the dozens of mass-produced cars he had at home, but fortunately, he was thrilled to be the winner.

Afterward, Verity dashed up to Hannah with a friendly smile. "Hannah, Granny says that you're even more of a pest than I am."

Hannah looked sour. "I'm guessing that's her idea of a compliment, right?"

Verity laughed sympathetically. "Oh, dear. I see you already know her quite well. I hope she's not been too hard on you. She is a bit of a dragon, isn't she?"

Hannah immediately warmed to Verity, who continued, "Still, she does seem to have taken rather a shine to you two, so you can't have blotted your copybooks too badly. You know, she doesn't let on, but I think she quite likes the company of us young 'uns. She nags Eric dreadfully, but she is quite dotty about him, and he's virtually one of the family now. None of us had ever met a proper East Ender before. That's the funny thing about this war, isn't it? Class doesn't matter quite so much, does it? I can't believe I share so many experiences with Eric, considering the differences in our class backgrounds."

Hannah thought this was a bit patronizing, but she let it go. She very much wanted Verity as a friend and ally.

"Class?" said Alex, who, along with Eric, had suddenly popped up next to the girls. "Like math class?"

"No, silly," laughed Verity, "Working-class people like Eric, because he comes from the East End of London, and middle-class people like you and me.

"I say, you go to the grammar school, don't you? I'm at St. Edward's myself, it's mostly a boarding school, but I'm a day girl, because Mummy wants me at home. Honestly, though, I think it would be more fun to board. Oh, before I forget, do tell me about this missing friend of yours. Granny says that he's a Negro."

Hannah tried not to look shocked. What a thing to say, she thought, and then had to remind herself of Brandon's advice to her, about doing as the Romans do when in Rome. "Well, yes, he is black," she said hesitantly, "but that's not the most important thing about him."

"Oh, I'm sure it's not," said Verity, hurriedly. "I don't mean to be rude. It's just that I've never met a colored person."

Eric said, "Come on then, give us the whole story about this mate of yours. From the beginning."

Verity looked sideways at Eric. "Don't mind Eric. He spends far too much time at the pictures, watching American detective films. He fancies himself as Humphrey Bogart."

"Shut your face, birthday girl," said Eric, elbowing Verity in the ribs.

"Our friend's name is Br...Braithwaite. George Braithwaite," said Hannah. "He ran off, so he could be anywhere. Your Grandma says she's going to talk with the billeting officer, but she hasn't got ahold of him yet. Anything you guys hear, could you let us know?"

"Well, there's always the Ghost Evacuee," Eric laughed.

"Oh, that," said Verity, rolling her eyes. To Hannah she said, "It's a stupid tale that somebody made up to scare the evacuees. The story goes that when some boy was evacuated to Balesworth last year, an evil couple threw him into a dungeon in their house, and that they still keep him there in chains."

"Just a story, you reckon?" said Eric. "Fink again. My mate Fred says he heard him crying one day, when he was walking to school."

"Your mate Fred," said Verity coolly, "is an absolute idiot."

"It's an urban legend," said Hannah. The others looked confused, so she explained. "That means it's a story that people swear is true, but nobody ever knows it first-hand."

"Fred says he does," said Eric, stubbornly.

"Oh, shut up, Eric," said Verity, hitting him on the arm.

"Well, I gotta admit, that doesn't sound like much of a lead," Hannah said.

"I'll tell you what," said Verity, "Let's ask everyone we can if they have seen a colored boy, and we'll see what we come up with. And meanwhile, I'll see if I can't persuade Granny to get a move on with her enquiries. She can't refuse. It is my birthday, after all."

Brandon stepped from the train at Balesworth, and was surprised to see how little the station had changed from 1940. But walking into town was a strangely disorienting experience. Balesworth in 1915 was even more sleepy than it would be a quarter-century in the future. Brandon distinctly remembered a row of houses in 1940 that had apparently not yet been built in 1915, and the auto mechanic's shop was now a blacksmith's shop that also sold bicycles. A few stores certainly looked smarter than they would during World War II: They boasted gleaming paint and elaborate displays of goods in the windows. The pubs were unchanged, but when he walked to the Tudor Tea Rooms in search of a snack, he found that it was not yet a café. It was two separate adjoined cottages in which families lived.

Brandon noticed that people stared hard at him, more than in London, and even more than in Balesworth in 1940. But then he remembered from the book he had read at the hospital that black people were more unusual in England in 1915 than they would be later. As Brandon stood on the sidewalk, a horse and cart rumbled by, carrying great churns of milk, and a delivery boy on a bicycle rattled past him, headed in the opposite direction on the road. Looking at the boy, Brandon thought to himself of the mysterious George Braithwaite. It was time, he decided, to check out the address on the postcard in his pocket.

Brandon paused in front of a building he remembered seeing in 1940, a tall row house on the High Street with a brass plaque on the gate. The plaque still read *R. Gordon, D.D.S., Dental Surgery*, but the brass was now brightly polished. He checked the house number against the address on his postcard. Sure enough, it was 57, High Street. Walking up the steps, Brandon was incredibly nervous. He kept trying to tell himself that he did, after all, have a perfectly innocent question to ask: Does anyone know a family called Braithwaite? He pressed the large button at the door, and heard a distant bell ringing. Almost immediately, footsteps approached, and suddenly the door was opened halfway by a young woman in a long white apron and frilly cap.

At first, she appeared stunned by the sight of Brandon, but she quickly collected herself. "Can I help you?"

Brandon was as daunted as she was. "Um, yeah, I think so, I just wondered, like…"

"Oh, wait, I know why you're here," she exclaimed. "But you should have come round the back door," she added reprovingly. "Come in anyway, and I'll tell Mr. Gordon. And for heaven's sake, take your hat off."

Brandon snatched off his cap. He was about to explain that there had been a mistake, but then realized that he was curious to know for whom he had been mistaken. The maid had already hurried off upstairs, leaving him standing in the hallway.

Looking around, he saw that he was not standing in what he would recognize as a dentist's office, but in a private house. To his right was a living room, and he could just see the edge of a small dining table covered in a white lace cloth, and an upright piano on which sat an enormous potted plant with large, dark green, and glossy leaves.

There was a conversation going on upstairs, and it grew louder as the maid and a man approached. "That's splendid, Mary," said the man in what Brandon guessed was a Scottish accent. "I'll speak with the lad right away."

Down the stairs walked a man in his mid-forties, with thin combed-over hair and the huge bushy moustache typical of those that Brandon had seen other men wearing in 1915. The man gave him a warm smile. "I'm Mr. Gordon, and your name will be....?"

Brandon had been ready for that question.

"Clark, sir. George Clark."

Mr. Gordon looked him up and down. "Not from these parts, are you?"

Brandon shook his head. "No, sir."

"Never mind, laddie, neither am I. Is your family in the town?"

Brandon again shook his head, and Mr. Gordon seemed pleased. "Well, that's just as well. If you live in, you'll learn your trade all the more quickly. Now come away upstairs to my study, and you can tell me why you want to apprentice to a dentist."

Brandon almost confessed right then to a case of mistaken identity, but something stopped him. A free place to stay? A job? That sounded kind of cool. And it would give him a base while he tried to figure out the mystery of George Braithwaite. Anyway, the postcard had told him to come to this house.

Upstairs, Mr. Gordon sat down at his desk, and invited Brandon to take the upright chair across from him. Then he leaned his elbows on the desk, and held his hands together at the fingertips.

"So, you would like to learn the art and mystery of dentistry, eh?" he said, pausing significantly.

Brandon immediately realized that a simple "Yes" would not work as an answer.

"Yes. Totally," he said, hoping that this would sound sufficiently enthusiastic. "Teeth. It's all I think about. I love 'em. Especially when they're all.. erm...white and straight." He suddenly noticed that Mr. Gordon's own teeth were somewhat crooked and a little on the yellow side. He rushed on.

"Um, yeah, and I think gum disease is bad. Real bad. Plaque, wow, that's yuk, for sure." He tried to think what else he could say, and suddenly remembered the one cavity he had gotten. "And pain! Yeah, pain in your teeth, man, that's the worst. I want to cure the pain in people's teeth."

Mr. Gordon had been barely succeeding in suppressing a smile, when suddenly he gave a long, loud laugh, and bashed his fist on the table. "George, you are a character. I'm not sure I entirely believe in your apparently newfound enthusiasm for dentistry, but I do believe you'll do. Now, you'll be fourteen, of course?"

"Sorry?" said Brandon, confused.

"Fourteen years old. You'll have the school leaving certificate?"

Seeing Brandon's blank face, he said hurriedly, "Well, we can't stand on formalities these days. With the war, there's too few likely boys about, so unless you tell me otherwise, we shall agree, I think, that you are fourteen and have left school."

Brandon said, on cue, "Yes, sir. That's right."

Mr. Gordon gave him a broad smile. "Very well. I shall have your indentures drawn up forthwith."

"I have to have dentures?" Brandon squawked, to renewed mirth from Mr. Gordon. "What a laddie," he chuckled. "Your apprenticeship indentures, as I think you know quite well. We will agree that you will assist me in my work, and I will provide you with a room, your meals, some pocket money, and clothing, as well, of course, as good a training in dentistry as I know how."

Brandon agreed with a nod.

"Now, there are, of course, some rules," the dentist continued. "You'll be in the house by ten each night, or there will be hell to pay. There will be no leniency from me where alehouses are concerned: I don't hold with strong drink myself, and some of my patients would be scandalized if I allowed my apprentice to lurk around our local hostelries. It will be enough of a difficulty to persuade a few of my patients to accept a Negro as my assistant, and so your conduct must always be unexceptionable. And, of course, no lady friends until your indentures are completed in four years."

Brandon thought that he wasn't likely to spend his spare time in pubs drinking beer anyway, and he agreed that he was a bit young for girlfriends.

"Very well. I'll have Mary show you the house, and your room. After dinner, we'll make a start."

He leaned over and pressed a button on the wall, and a bell rang distantly downstairs. Very shortly, Mary, the maid, appeared in the doorway.

"Yes, Mr. Gordon?"

"This is George Clark, and he is to serve as my apprentice. I want you to show him to his room, and then acquaint him with the house and introduce him to Mrs. Gordon."

"She's gone up to town on the train, sir," said Mary.

"Oh, and so she has, although I must say, these Zeppelin raids worry me. Never mind, she'll meet you by and by. Very well, then, introduce him to my daughter."

"Miss Peggy's out riding on her bicycle to meet her friend for tea, sir."

"That infernal machine," complained Mr. Gordon. "Every time I turn around, she's away out gallivanting. Well, just show George the house, then, Mary, and bring him back by and by. Off you go, both of you. I have work to do."

Brandon's room was a tiny attic nook on the third floor of the house. They had to climb a narrow flight of stairs to reach it, with only a rope to serve as a banister. "It's really the maid's room," said Mary. "But I live out, so you get it. Soon as I turn eighteen, I'm going to work in the munitions factory. Wages is a lot better there. But don't tell the Gordons, or I'll never hear the end of it. All the girls has started working in the factory since the war broke out, and they'll never find anyone to replace me."

The room, with its sloping ceiling and solitary window overlooking the High Street, was barely furnished. Aside from the bed, there was only a small dresser, and a jug and bowl on the washstand. Brandon asked Mary, "Where's the bathroom?"

She looked askance at him. "Downstairs. Your bath night will be Tuesday. The lavatory's separate, and it's on the second floor, too. You'll find the jerry under your bed."

Brandon impulsively looked under the bed, half-expecting to see a German soldier. Instead, he pulled out a large pot with a handle, covered in a cloth. The horrible truth dawned. "When am I supposed to use this?"

Mary blushed. "In the night, like everyone else. Now hurry up."

In the upstairs hallway, she whispered, "Mr. Gordon's son, Master James, is with the Army in France, but he has a daughter, Miss Peggy, and his nephew, Oliver lives here, too." She lowered her voice, and said conspiratorially, "The little boy's mother was Mr. Gordon's sister, but she died when Master Oliver was born, and he came to live with the Gordons when his father died last year."

"That's sad," Brandon said.

"Yes, you can say that again," agreed Mary. "And he's a lovely little fellow, too, make no mistake."

Oliver was sitting in the kitchen, eating a large slice of cake. "Hallo," he said to Brandon. "Are you from Africa?"

"I'm from Yorkshire," said Brandon.

"But that's not in Africa."

Brandon shook his head and smiled. "No."

"Shush, Master Oliver," said Mary. "Not so many questions. This is George. He's your uncle's new apprentice."

"Oh," Oliver said, and solemnly extended his hand to Brandon. "I'm Oliver, and I'm seven and a half. I go to The Grange School, and my school has a proper library."

"You like books?" said Brandon, eagerly.

"Yes," said Oliver. "Heaps. Do you know Jules Verne?"

Brandon had to think. "*20,000 Leagues Under the Sea?*"

"And *Around the World in Eighty Days*, of course," added Oliver. "Imagine being able to travel round the whole world in eighty days!"

Brandon smiled. "Yeah, imagine that."

"Do you like H.G. Wells' books?" Oliver asked.

Brandon was truly stumped.

"He wrote *The Time Machine*," Oliver informed him.

"Oh, yeah! I saw that...I mean, I did read that once. Way cool."

"I would give anything to travel in time," said Oliver.

"You'll be lucky," said a young woman's voice. A girl of about sixteen entered the room, through the back door that led to the garden. She was wearing a light blue blouse with puffy sleeves, a long straight pinstriped skirt, and a large hat, which she now unpinned from her hair.

"Who's this?" she said to Mary, inclining her head toward Brandon.

"New apprentice, miss. His name's George Clark."

"Hello, George. I'm Peggy Gordon. You must call me Miss Gordon."

The words sounded snotty, Brandon thought, but her tone didn't. It was more a statement of fact.

Her accent was English, and not at all the same as her father's. He asked, "Are you from here?"

"Of course," she said. "Father's from Scotland, but we're all English through and through, born and raised in Balesworth."

Brandon asked eagerly, "Do you know a family called Braithwaite?"

Miss Gordon paused for a moment and stared at him. Then she said, "You do ask a lot of questions, rather. Why? Do you?"

"No...Yes...Well, I might. I don't know."

"Well, I certainly don't. Do you, Mary? Oliver, do you have any boys at school by the name of Braithwaite?"

Nobody could help. Then a bell rang from upstairs. "That'll be Mr. Gordon," said Mary, looking at a row of bells near the kitchen ceiling, where one was swinging and rattling. "I expect he wants you in the surgery, George."

Brandon didn't mind most of his visits to the dentist in Snipesville. Soft lights, large framed pictures of hunting and football scenes on the walls, and music playing quietly were all part of the experience. Everyone in the office smiled with perfect white teeth. Brandon's dentist, Dr. McCready, was nice, although he hardly ever saw him for more than a minute or two. Mostly, he spent time with the hygienist, Miss Melba, who had been cleaning his teeth since he was tiny. Sometimes she would nag Brandon about flossing, and make him watch a demonstration on a large fake set of teeth. True, he also hated the fluoride foam treatments: Miss Melba always offered him a choice of good-sounding flavors like lemon-lime or cherry, but they all tasted about the same, which was gross.

But, for the most part, his visits to the dentist's office had been okay, and he always went home with a free toothbrush, sugar-free gum, and some stickers for his collection.

Mr. Gordon's surgery, as he called it, was not pleasant. It was seriously scary, a bit like Brandon imagined a medieval dungeon would be. The only light came from the windows and, on a day like today, when the sky was overcast, a hissing gas lamp on the wall. Mr. Gordon also kept a supply of candles for when he needed to illuminate the patient's mouth.

There was definitely no music playing in the background, and the only picture was a gloomy scene of Scottish mountains in the rain, which Mr. Gordon said was painted near to his hometown. The dentist's chair was not a comfortable cushiony chair with a big squashy leg rest, but something like a cross between a desk chair and an instrument of torture. Its thin cushions were made of dark-red velvet. Brandon wondered if the color was intended to disguise any blood.

Worse yet were the instruments Mr. Gordon showed him: Small but nasty mallets for finishing fillings, terrifying scrapers and syringes, and a huge drill. Brandon's primary job, Mr. Gordon said, would be to observe him work, while pumping the foot pedal that operated the drill. "Perhaps after a week or two, you can hold up the candle for me, and begin to pass me the instruments. Until then, we shall manage."

The hours, he told Brandon, would be long, from eight in the morning to six at night during the week, with an hour off for dinner, which seemed to mean lunch. He would also have to work from 8 a.m. to 1 p.m. on Saturdays, and attend church with the family on Sundays. Sometimes, Mr. Gordon would visit a patient's house on Sunday morning, when he would extract a molar while the patient was made unconscious with chloroform.

"Otherwise, we do try to keep the Sabbath in this house," said Mr. Gordon. "That means no books, games, or sports." Brandon thought a Sunday in

Snipesville was a bit of a drag at times. But even though the services at the Authentic Original First African Baptist Church were long, he could at least hang with his friends at fellowship time, and he enjoyed the singing. He had never even been to white people's church before, but one of his friends had told him it was boring. Still, Brandon reckoned, his stay in 1915 England would be an adventure. And earning money at a real job sounded pretty exciting, even if it was only room, board and a small allowance, rather than proper wages.

It was a crisp and cold but very clear day in 1940, with no wind. Walking home alone, after her school ended lessons at mid-day, Hannah decided to take a detour through the town. It was hard to enjoy being in England when she wasn't sure if she would ever get home, but she felt a need to get outside into the fresh air.

Hannah's walk took her all the way up the High Street. A long line of women, many with babies and small children, waited outside the greengrocers. Hannah stopped to look in the window to see what the fuss was about, but all she could see were the usual potatoes and carrots.

"Why's everyone waiting?" she asked the young woman closest to the door.

"We're queuing for bananas, love," the woman said cheerfully. "He just got them this morning. Hopefully, they'll last until it's my turn, and I'll get some in for tea. Won't that be a treat, now?" She smiled kindly at Hannah, who briefly thought about joining the slow-moving queue, but then decided against it. It seemed like a lot of work for a banana.

She was just slouching away down the sidewalk, awkwardly slinging her satchel over her shoulder, when a car pulled up alongside her. Hannah thought nothing of it, and kept walking. But suddenly she heard someone calling to her. "Hannah? Hannah Day?" She turned, and, in dismay, saw Mrs. Devenish, who had stepped out of the car. "Where are you off to? Would you like a lift?"

"No, thanks," said Hannah. "I want to walk." SThe last thing she felt like doing was making polite conversation with the scary lady.

"The thing is, I want a word with you. I assume that you can spare me a few minutes?" It wasn't said as a question, really, but as a command. Hannah couldn't figure out how to refuse. Instead, she said "whatever," under her breath and, without another word, got in on the passenger side.

"So where have you been on your walk?" Mrs. Devenish asked pleasantly.

"Just around town, I guess," said Hannah. There was a brief pause.

"I say, have you been to see the old church?" asked Mrs. Devenish. "It's fourteenth century, you know, and it has the most marvelous tower."

"No," said Hannah. She felt as unenthusiastic as she looked and sounded, and she gazed out of the window. She didn't see Mrs. Devenish narrow her eyes at her.

"In that case, let's go and have a look. You can see the whole of Balesworth from the top. Are you expected back soon?"

"No," said Hannah, indifferently. "It's cool."

The church was small, bitterly cold, and smelled of damp stone. Hannah looked around her, but saw nothing interesting in the rows of wooden pews, the plain altar with cross and altar cloth, and the various memorials to dead people that lined the walls. Mrs. Devenish asked the verger, a silent man in a long black cassock, to open the small wooden door to the tower. "Take care, Mrs. Devenish," he said quietly, handing her a flashlight. "The banister is almost gone, but we've run a rope down the center column for climbers to hold onto, and it seems to do the trick."

"Thank you very much, Mr. Cooper," said Mrs. Devenish with a nod. To Hannah, she said, "Let's make a start, shall we? You can leave your satchel here. Watch your step now."

Hannah peered anxiously after her into the dark doorway. She saw Mrs. Devenish and the flashlight disappear around the first turn in the spiral staircase. The staircase smelled even more damp and musty than the rest of the church. Hannah reached automatically to her left for a rail, and her hand touched a narrow, carved stone ledge. She held on to it, grabbed the dark-colored thick braided rope dangling on her right, and stepped up. The narrow stairs were wedge-shaped, which she had expected, and crumbling at the edges, which she had not. Moving toward the light cast by the flashlight, she felt the rail suddenly vanish under her left hand, and she paused, then placed her palm on the stone wall to steady herself as she picked her way up.

"Are you alright, Hannah? Take your time."

"Yeah, fine," said Hannah, although she was incredibly stressed, and her pulse was racing, as were her thoughts. Is this the crazy old Englishwoman's idea of fun? What am I doing here? I mean, what's the point?

After what seemed like forever, there was a blast of bright light at the top, as a doorway opened onto the tower roof. The last step was up about two feet, and Mrs. Devenish, who somehow had already negotiated this, was offering down her hand for Hannah to grasp. Hannah took it.

Mrs. Devenish was right, of course. The view was amazing. Hannah could see the whole of Balesworth, its red brick houses and shops clumped tightly together, in a sea of tiny fields of many colors, dotted with green hedges, trees, houses, cows and sheep. A car wound along one of the twisting roads. Up here at the top of the tower, there was a slight breeze, and Hannah's few unbraided hairs ruffled up. There was no safety rail of any kind, and the drop to the ground looked pretty lethal as she carefully craned her neck from a safe distance to peer over the edge.

"Magnificent, isn't it?" said Mrs. Devenish, standing at her side. "It's remarkable to think that people stood where we are standing now six hundred years ago. People used this church as a refuge during the time of the Black Death, you know."

"What was that?" Hannah asked, without much interest.

"The Black Death? Have you never taken a history lesson at your school in London?"

"Sure. I just never heard much about that. It was some big disease thing, right?"

"Yes, you might put it like that, I suppose," said Mrs. Devenish, rolling her eyes. "The Black Death was an epidemic of bubonic plague in the mid-fourteenth century, and it wiped out at least one-third of the population.... You know, I need to find you a copy of *1066 and All That*, Hannah, unless you already own it."

Hannah shook her head. "Never heard of it. Is it a book?"

"Good grief... Yes, it is a book, and a very funny one. It's all about the history of this country, and it might just help you to find a little more enthusiasm for the subject."

Hannah leaned forward just slightly, and considered that it was, indeed, a long way down. She idly daydreamed about how it might be possible to push an old lady from the tower without stumbling over the edge herself.

Mrs. Devenish brought her back to reality with a bump. "I hope you're not thinking of shoving me off, young woman," she said dryly.

Hannah panicked a little. She well remembered how a boy at her school in California had been expelled for writing a story in which his main character plotted horrible deaths for his teachers.

"No, of course not," she said, a little too quickly.

"Good. In that case, I shall restrain myself from similar thoughts about you."

Hannah looked at her with alarm, and realized that Mrs. Devenish was no more serious about murder than she had been.

"I did have that chat with Mr. Simmons, the billeting officer," said Mrs. Devenish, "and I am sorry to say that he has no idea what has become of your friend. Mr. Simmons took the trouble to contact someone he knows at the Ministry, I believe it's the same man we saw at the church hall, and I'm afraid that it appears that your friend ran away from him in London, while he was taking him elsewhere to be billeted."

"But why would he take Br... George to London? What's that about?" asked Hannah.

"I have no idea. Perhaps, when the moment is right, I shall put that question to Mr. Simmons. But I'm afraid that, for now, there is little more I can do. Hopefully, your friend will turn up. I have asked my friend at the WVS head office to keep an eye out for his name and description in reports. We shall just have to wait and see... Come on, I'd better take you home."

When Hannah got to the doorway leading off the roof, she realized that she was terrified of the journey back down the crumbling staircase. "I can't do it," she said, pale-faced. "I have major issues with heights."

Mrs. Devenish was already on the top step. "Yes, you can, Hannah. Come on, take my hand."

All the way down, Mrs. Devenish walked just ahead of Hannah, and coaxed her forward. By the time Hannah reached the bottom of the steps, and emerged blinking into the light, her heart was thumping hard, and her knees had turned to jelly.

Mrs. Devenish switched off the flashlight, and put it back onto the table by the door. "You see, Hannah? You managed it alright. And aren't you glad you did?"

"I guess," muttered Hannah, unconvinced.

As they got back into the car, Hannah said, as offhandedly as she could manage, "Mrs. D.? It's okay if I call you that, right?" She added hurriedly, "I mean, Eric does."

"Yes, of course, Hannah. My last name is a bit of a mouthful, I admit."

"Okay, look, let me ask you something, okay? This isn't really about anyone I know, it's just, let's suppose."

"Alright," said Mrs. Devenish cautiously, turning the key in the ignition.

"Suppose somebody you knew told you that someone else you knew was kind of a bad person?"

"How so?"

"Well, they say the other person is a total backstabber, and goes around saying mean things about everyone she knows, and that I... I mean, you, anyone, shouldn't say much in front of her."

"Yes..." said Mrs. Devenish slowly, accelerating up the road back toward the center of Balesworth.

"And you haven't actually seen this person behave like that. And nobody else seems to think it about this person."

"And we're not talking about anyone in particular?" asked Mrs. Devenish, intrigued.

"No, no, of course not," Hannah said quickly.

"Then, I suppose, I should wonder one or two things. First, whether the person making the accusation is not in fact speaking of herself. And, second, if that is not the case, whether the accuser has something to hide… Hannah, is there something you're trying to tell me?"

"No," said Hannah crossly, wishing she had never brought up the subject. "It's just supposing."

"I see," said Mrs. Devenish shortly. Hannah wondered if she really did.

Just as the car pulled up, Hannah saw with a sinking feeling that Mrs. Archer was outside the front door, putting out empty milk bottles on the doorstep for the milkman to collect on his next round. She said goodbye to Mrs. Devenish, who waved to Mrs. Archer. Mrs. Archer returned a small wave and gave a wan smile before the car pulled away.

As soon as they walked into the house, Hannah began to climb upstairs.

"Wait a moment," said Mrs. Archer, closing the door. She said suspiciously, "Where have you been with that woman?"

Hannah didn't like to lie, but she decided that the less information Mrs. Archer had, the better.

"Nowhere. She saw me walking, and gave me a ride home."

"You were gone rather a long time." It was a question.

Hannah shrugged. "No, I took a walk around town before I saw her."

"What I don't understand," said Mrs. Archer, "is why you would wish to befriend any woman of that age, and especially that one. What on earth would you have to say to her?"

"Not much," said Hannah, truthfully.

"I thought so," said Mrs. Archer. "I imagine that she does most of the talking. At least, I hope so. Remember what I told you about her and her gossip. In any event, I think your time would be much better spent here. I could use a lot more help around the house than I'm getting from you, especially now that I'm working at the factory part-time."

"Are you telling me I can't talk to her?"

"No, of course not, but I do have some authority in this house, you know, and you should respect it. I'm just saying that I want you spending more time at home, and that if you are going out, it's with children of your own age. That's all."

Hannah carried on up the stairs. "I have to do my homework, then I'll help you, okay?"

By the middle of his first week, Brandon was already much less enthusiastic about dentistry. He slept very little in his freezing cold attic bedroom, and even used the chamberpot under his bed one night, rather than go downstairs to the bathroom. In the morning, he had tried to sneak the pot downstairs to empty it, but he ran into Mary on the stairs. She told him it was her job, and took it from him, to his embarrassment.

Breakfast was with the whole family, with Mary acting as cook and server. It was at breakfast that Brandon met Mrs. Gordon for the first time, if "meeting" can be used to describe their encounter. She stared coldly at him when he entered the dining room, and pointed to the seat next to Oliver at the very end of the table. Indeed, she never spoke to him at all, and even avoided looking at him. The meal was eaten mainly in silence, except for the scrape of knives and forks on plates, the ticking of the clock on the mantel over the fireplace, where coal crackled and spat, and the sound of Mr. Gordon's newspaper, as he shook it out and turned the pages.

Breakfast was huge, with lots of eggs and toast, as well as what Mary called bacon, but which Brandon thought was more like thin ham. He enjoyed it very much, although the strip of fat around the edge worried him, until he realized that nobody else was eating that part. At first, he had picked up his fork in his right hand to eat his eggs, but Peggy looked at him aghast, and coughed to warn him. He was confused until he saw how everyone else was eating: They piled the eggs onto the backs of their forks, then balanced them carefully all the way to their mouths. And they never changed hands. Brandon watched and did his best to copy, although it made eggs slow going, as they kept dropping off his fork back onto his plate, and occasionally into his lap.

After breakfast, Brandon went to the kitchen to wash off his hands. As he was passing the dining room afterward, he overheard Mr. Gordon speaking angrily. When he heard his own name mentioned, he stopped to listen.

"And what, pray tell, does it matter if George is a Negro, so long as he does his work and minds his manners?"

Brandon couldn't quite catch everything Mrs. Gordon was saying in reply, but he could make out that she was not pleased to have a black person living in her house.

"Woman," said Mr. Gordon in barely-suppressed fury, "Need I remind you that some of those same people objected to dealing with Scots when I first set up practice? In any case, the employment of my apprentice is none of your concern. My decision in the matter is final."

Hearing Mr. Gordon move across the room, Brandon abandoned his eavesdropping and hurried down the hall, turning into the parlor. As Mr. Gordon passed on his way to the staircase, he caught sight of his apprentice.

"George, what the blazes are you doing in here? Upstairs, now, and let us make a start to the day." As Mr. Gordon disappeared onto the upstairs landing, Brandon stepped onto the staircase.

Just then, Peggy Gordon came hurrying down the hall from the dining room. "George," she whispered quickly, "I'm sorry about what my mother said. I know you heard her. She just hasn't had any acquaintance with colored people, that's all."

"Hey, round here, who has?" Brandon said ruefully. She opened her mouth to say something, but Mr. Gordon roared "George!" from the surgery, and Mrs. Gordon shouted "Peggy!" from the dining room.

"Later," said Brandon, as Peggy retraced her steps down the hall.

The very first patient in Mr. Gordon's surgery that day was a middle-aged man with a major toothache. He held a cloth handkerchief to his cheek, and Brandon thought he looked incredibly nervous. Beads of sweat were forming on his forehead, and his hands were visibly shaking. Mr. Gordon, pretending not to notice the man's distress, was very businesslike toward him. Feeling sorry for the patient, Brandon said reassuringly to him, "It'll be all right."

The patient lifted his head from the headrest, and both he and Mr. Gordon glared at Brandon. Brandon decided that it would be best to keep his mouth shut from now on.

After a careful examination of the man's teeth, Mr. Gordon declared that his patient would need a filling. He gave the man a shot in the inner cheek with an enormous needle, and Brandon flinched seeing the man struggling desperately not to cry out. Once the patient said that he could feel some numbness, Mr. Gordon showed Brandon how to use the footpump that operated the drill.

But as soon as the drill touched the man's tooth, he cringed.

"I don't think he's totally numbed up," said Brandon.

"That's the best we can do," said Mr. Gordon shortly.

Within a few minutes of operating the pump, Brandon's leg muscles began to cramp, but when he tried to take a break to shift to the other leg, Mr. Gordon barked at him to keep going.

"Can't you get one of these that uses electricity?" puffed Brandon. Mr. Gordon laughed. "An electric-powered drill, eh? That's an expensive extravagance, laddie, and why would I need one when I've got you, eh?"

That night, an exhausted Brandon again lay wide awake in his attic room. Wrapped in the thin sheet, blanket, and quilt, he shivered from the cold. His legs ached, and especially his right foot. Worse, so did one of his teeth. He wondered if he was imagining things, and certainly hoped so: He had no wish to have Mr. Gordon do his dental work.

But the worst thing was that he was frightened. It seemed a long time since the Professor had visited him in the hospital. He wasn't making any progress on finding George Braithwaite. Supposing he had misunderstood what he was supposed to be doing in Balesworth in 1915?

And just suppose he was stuck forever in early twentieth-century England? It would be another 25 years before he would catch up with Hannah and Alex, and by then he would be –he quickly added it up—37 years old! He could end up serving in the British Army in World War II. He might get killed fighting Hitler before his own birth… Finally, after hours of tossing and turning, Brandon dozed off into an uneasy sleep.

The next day was Saturday, and because no patients were scheduled, Brandon had the morning off. He was soon bored, and wandered into the front parlor, but Mary shooed him out. "I 'ave to clean, and anyway, you're not supposed to be in here. This is only for visitors and patients at this time of day."

As he left, Brandon picked up the copy of *The Times* newspaper from the table, and took it back to the kitchen with him. Settling into a chair by the fireplace and unfolding the newspaper, he was surprised to see that the whole front page was given over to classified ads.

It was then that he had an idea. He ran upstairs to Mr. Gordon's study, and asked for a pen and paper.

"Writing a letter, eh?" asked Mr. Gordon.

"Yes, sir," Brandon said. "It's to a friend of mine. I want to send him money, you know, for his birthday. How do I do that?"

"That's very generous of you, George. Well, I could draw a check on my account, and dock the sum from your pocket money."

"Oh…ah… I don't want to put you to the trouble, sir. Is there some other way?"

"It wouldn't be any trouble, George, but if you prefer, you could always get a postal order from the post office. You look as though you could use a walk in the fresh air."

"Yes, sir. Thank you, sir."

Brandon decided he would do just that. When he returned with the small certificate he had purchased from the post office on the High Street, he wrote out his letter to accompany it. It was tough going, writing with a real ink pen. He had to dip the nib into the inkwell often, and there were spots and splashes of ink all over the finished letter. Brandon just hoped that the people at the newspaper would be able to read his scrawl. Enclosing his postal order for five shillings, he sealed the envelope.

The reply came on Monday, to Brandon's surprise. He had expected mail to be much slower in 1915, but postal deliveries to the house were amazingly frequent— so much so, that it would seem silly to call it snail mail. He supposed that without email, faxes, or even phones, most people depended on the post office. He opened the envelope.

```
Dear Mr. Clark:

In reference to your letter of the fourth inst.,
we are pleased to accept your payment for an
advertisement to appear on October 15, 1940. We
trust you will understand that this is an un-
usual requirement, and so we hope we are not re-
miss in deciding to file it among the In Memoriam
notices, which we hope will preclude it from
becoming lost during the intervening years.

We appreciate your understanding that we do not
normally accept notices more than ten years in
advance. However, since you are willing to ac-
cept a degree of risk that the notice may not
appear, we are pleased to be of service in this
unusual instance.

Your obedient servant,

a.m., pp. JHRO
J.H.R. Osgood
Advertising Department
```

Reading that day's copy of *The Times*, Brandon realized that with all the men now being killed in the war in France, the In Memoriam column was in no danger of going out of business before 1940. Now he just had to wait, and hope.

A crunching noise was resonating behind Mr. Archer's newspaper, as he munched on his second slice of toast. "Anything interesting in the paper today, dear?" asked Mrs. Archer, as she poured him a cup of tea.

He flipped back to the front page, scanned the classified ads, and said, "Here's something queer that I need to show you." He handed over the newspaper to Mrs. Archer, who put on her glasses, and looked to where his finger was pointing on the page.

"You're right, Geoffrey. That is very odd. What on earth can that mean? You don't think…" She jerked her head toward Hannah.

"What?" said Hannah through a mouthful of toast.

Mrs. Archer frowned at her. "Don't talk with your mouth full, Hannah. It's common." But she took the newspaper to Hannah and showed her.

It read:

Message from Balesworth to Balesworth: Hannah, Alex: Amen 19. 15 Brandon.

"It seems to be for you two," Mrs. Archer said expectantly. Hannah passed it to Alex.

"It's from Brandon!" he exclaimed.

"Who is this Brandon?" asked Mrs. Archer. "You've never mentioned this boy before."

"Oh, he's a friend of ours, from London," Hannah said hurriedly. "But I honestly don't know why he's sending us a message through the newspaper. I don't even know what this is supposed to mean."

"Perhaps you two ought to reply," said Mr. Archer.

"There's no post office box given, Geoffrey," said Mrs. Archer. "Do you children know his address?"

They shook their heads.

"Well, then, perhaps you should place your own advertisement, eh?" Mr. Archer chuckled. "It's all a bit mysterious, isn't it? You lot aren't German spies, I hope?"

Once she figured out how much it would cost for an ad, Hannah wrote out a few words, and had Mr. Archer write out a check. The next day, on the way to school, the kids dropped their letter to the newspaper in a red pillar mailbox.

Just as Hannah pushed the letter through the slot, Alex said, "Wait!"

"Too late," Hannah said, annoyed. "What's wrong?"

"Brandon will never see our reply," he said excitedly. "They got all the punctuation and one of the words wrong. It said "Am in 1915, comma, Brandon."

Hannah looked blankly at her brother.

"Hannah, don't you get it? Brandon's here, he's in Balesworth…But 25 years ago!"

Chapter 9

MYSTERIES AND MESSAGES

Brandon yawned loudly as he dragged himself into the surgery, tying on his apron. Mr. Gordon was looking over the calendar on his desk, reading the appointments that were recorded in Mary's hesitant handwriting.

"I see we have a lady patient," he said with delight. Brandon couldn't see why this was a big deal, since they had already treated several women patients that week, and said so.

"No, no, George," Mr. Gordon said impatiently, "I mean a Lady with a capital 'L', one of the aristocracy, no less. But blast Mary, I cannae read the name." He stuck his head out the door, and yelled, "Mary, what is the name of our next patient?"

She called back up the stairs, "I'm sorry, Mr. Gordon. She told me on the telephone, but we had a bad line, and I couldn't quite hear what she said. I did my best."

"Give me strength, girl, could you not..."

But just then the doorbell rang, and Mary went to answer it. Mr. Gordon retreated to the surgery. "Aye well, we'll know soon enough," he said to Brandon. "Make sure all my instruments are in order, George."

Brandon began to count all the dental tools lying on the table by the window.

Footsteps echoed up the stairs, and a middle-aged woman in a long skirt and blouse grandly entered the room, her hair slightly disheveled by the removal of her hat.

Mr. Gordon introduced himself and asked her name, apologizing for having to do so. She replied imperiously, "How do you do, Mr. Gordon. I am Lady Smyth-Howlington."

Brandon whirled around, and gave a huge grin.

The Professor sat in the dentist's chair, while Brandon carefully held a candle near her face so that Mr. Gordon could see clearly. Suddenly the dentist paused, and tapped on one tooth. "What have we here?"

He removed his probe so she could answer.

"Oh, my crown? My London dentist's work."

Mr. Gordon said, "It's the finest I think I have ever seen. And these fillings. Extraordinary. Forgive me, Lady, ah, Smyth-Howlington, but I should be much obliged if you would give me the name of your dentist in town. His work is absolutely superb, and I do, I assure you, take great pride in remaining abreast of advances in my profession."

She smiled. "I'm sure you do, Mr. Gordon. I shall have my lady's maid call on you with his name and address."

Brandon winked at the Professor over Mr. Gordon's shoulder.

Downstairs, the telephone rang, and Mary came to tell Mr. Gordon that he was wanted for what she called "a trunk call from Scotland." Confused, Brandon thought of elephants. With more apologies to the Professor, Mr. Gordon washed his hands, and rushed downstairs.

The Professor sat up in the rickety dental chair. "A trunk call," she said quietly to Brandon, "is a long-distance phone call. It has nothing to do with elephants." Brandon laughed as though such a ridiculous thought had never occurred to him.

"So how are you?" the Professor asked. "Sorry to pop in like this, but I thought you might need a bit of encouragement."

"You got that right," he said. "What am I supposed to be doing here?"

"Exactly what you are doing," she said. "Keeping your eyes and ears open. I know that time travel is not as exciting as you expected, but just think, you'll have a head start if you decide on a career in dentistry." She laughed, but Brandon was not amused.

"Can't you help me out more? Like, what am I looking for?"

"George Braithwaite, for one thing," she said. "If you hear that name, you should ask about it, quick as you can. And you also have a mission of your own, by the way. It's not as mysterious or thrilling, but it's just as important for George and your friends."

Brandon said cautiously, "Oh, and what's that?"

"Well, actually, you're already doing it, I suspect. It is your job to be kind to Peggy and, especially, little Oliver. It is far more important than it sounds."

"Okay," said Brandon slowly. "I'll do my best."

"I'm sure you will, dear. Oh, and do watch yourself around Mrs. Gordon. She's not very keen on black people, I'm afraid."

"Yeah, I kind of got that impression…Tell you what," he said, as Mr. Gordon's footsteps sounded on the staircase, "I'll keep my eyes and ears open, if you keep your mouth open. I'm looking forward to seeing this guy fix your teeth."

"You have got to be joking, kiddo," she laughed.

Sure enough, when Mr. Gordon suggested to the Professor that she have a tooth filled, she said that today would not be convenient. He agreed to make an appointment for the following week, and reminded her to bring the details of her London dentist. Brandon seriously doubted that Mr. Gordon would see Lady Smyth-Howlington again.

On Saturday afternoon, Peggy was once again out on her bicycle, taking her watercolor paints with her, Mr. and Mrs. Gordon had gone by train to London to visit Mrs. Gordon's aunt, and it was Mary's half-day off. Lacking any better ideas, Brandon asked Oliver if he wanted to go for a walk. Oliver asked excitedly, "Can we go and look for conkers, George?"
"I guess," Brandon said, "What are they?"
Oliver was astounded. "Conkers, George. You know."
"Nope, sorry," Brandon said. "I guess we don't have them in Yorkshire."
Oliver looked sad. "That's a shame. Well, I can show you them. They grow on trees, and then we find the biggest ones, and Uncle Bob drills a hole in them for me, and then I can try to beat you. See?"
Brandon was none the wiser. "I guess this will make more sense when you show me."

Conkers, it turned out, were the seeds of the horse chestnut tree, and they were the same round brown nut-like objects that Brandon and Alex had examined when they first arrived in England. On a shady avenue lined with horse chestnut trees, Oliver showed Brandon how to peel off the spiky green skins, and pointed out the attributes of the most desirable conkers.
"This one is splendid. You see how big this one is, George," he said, holding up a shiny chestnut, "and how round it is, and no cracks?"
"Uh-huh," said Brandon, "and how do we cook 'em?"
"Cook them?" asked Oliver, blinking rapidly. "You mean bake them in the oven to make them harder? That's quite a good idea, actually."
"Uh, no," said Brandon, confused.
"Why else would we cook them?"
"So's we can eat them," said Brandon.
"Oh, you can't eat horse chestnuts, silly," laughed Oliver. "We get Uncle Bob to drill holes in them, then we put strings through the middles, then you hold up your conker…"
He mimed holding a conker aloft.
"…and I pull mine back like this," he said, continuing to mime a conker attack, "and I smash yours to bits."
"Hey, dream on," said Brandon, grinning. "Bet mine's the toughest one."
They started filling their pockets with conkers. Suddenly, Oliver stood up straight and said suspiciously, "Wait a minute, George! I have a schoolfriend

who spent a holiday with his aunt in Yorkshire, and he came home with loads of enormous conkers."

Brandon considered various ways he could spin out the lie. But then he realized it would do no harm to tell Oliver the truth. Who would believe Oliver, after all?

"Oliver," he said, "I'm not from Yorkshire. I'm a time-traveler from America, from the twenty-first century. "

He expected Oliver to be skeptical, but, the little boy was delighted.

"I knew it! You seem so terribly different from everyone, and half the time you don't understand what's going on. Mary said you didn't even know what a chamberpot was! This is frightfully exciting, George! Why have you come back in time?"

"I'm looking for someone," Brandon said. "At least, I think I am. His name is George, too, George Braithwaite."

"Gosh, how jolly exciting. Well, I'd like to help."

"I'm not sure you can. I don't know if he's here. But thanks, Oliver. Now, promise you won't tell anyone, and I'll tell you about the real future. It's better than that H.G. Wells stuff you read."

"Alright," said Oliver. "I'm very good at keeping secrets, you know. I've never even told anyone that Peggy has a gentleman friend."

"Uh, Oliver? You just told me."

Oliver looked downcast. "Oh, gosh, so I have. Promise you won't tell Peggy, will you?"

Brandon said, "I think we got mutually assured destruction goin', kid."

"What does that mean?"

"It means I'll keep your secret, and you keep mine. So she's got a boyfriend, eh? That explains why she's always riding around town on that bike. What's he look like?"

"I don't know," said Oliver. "I just found a letter from him the other day. He's a soldier, and his name is Edward. I think he's going off to France soon."

As Brandon mulled over Oliver's gossip in 1915, Hannah and Alex were about to learn what had become of their effort to contact him from 1940. Breakfast in the Archer household was never an especially chatty time, but Hannah noticed that there was a distinct chill in the air when Mrs. Archer entered the room.

"I was just showing my wife," Mr. Archer said. "Here's your advertisement in The Times—"Colored boy, age 12, answering to Brandon Clark or George Braithwaite. Box 11." I hope you hear something."

After Mr. Archer had left for work, and before Hannah and Alex were ready to leave for school, Mrs. Archer stopped Hannah in the hall, and grabbed her by the arm.

"Why didn't you tell me?" she hissed.

"Tell you what?" said Hannah in alarm, shaking her arm free. "Let go of me!"

"Why didn't you tell me who your friend was?"

"What does it matter to you?" Hannah sputtered.

"Oh, how dare you!" Mrs. Archer yelled back. "You horrid little girl."

"What's wrong with asking a question?" Hannah asked in genuine outrage.

Suddenly, Mrs. Archer seemed at a loss for words. "He's...colored, isn't he?"

"So?" asked Hannah, sensing she had the advantage.

"My husband wouldn't want colored people in the house..." said Mrs. Archer, stiffly. "I hope you're not expecting to have this friend of yours for a visit."

Hannah was astonished. "How come Mr. Archer never said anything like that when he read our ad?"

Mrs. Archer looked flustered. "Stop answering me back, madam. I'll have no more of your questions. I'm just telling you, we won't have that boy in the house."

With that, she turned and stormed into the kitchen, leaving Hannah agog.

Hannah reluctantly dragged herself down the hallway to her first class of the day. She was finally getting the hang of how the school worked, with its bewildering hierarchy of prefects, form mistresses, housemistresses, head girls, school captains, and many more, all of whom seemed to have the right to yell at her.

Most of the girls found Hannah a little strange, but they did not dislike her. Her cool attitude toward school scored points with many, and they liked her sense of humor. She, in turn, was fascinated by the absence of the kinds of cliques that she had heard about in American high schools, like the jocks, the nerds, and the "popular" kids whom nobody seemed to like. She had befriended Jean and Katie, a couple of evacuee girls in her class, and they, persuaded by Hannah that things had been run very differently at her previous school, had helped her adjust.

First class of the day was mathematics. Hannah had always thought she was good at math, but the work was harder than anything she had done. Even basic arithmetic was tricky, especially when it involved problems with money. All money had to be counted in three columns: pounds, shillings, and pence, with twelve pence to the shilling, and twenty shillings to the pound. There were also halfpennies and farthings, or quarter-pennies, to deal with. Hannah's brain hurt in math class, and the experience wasn't made easier by the fact that her teacher, one of the most notoriously strict in the school, scared her rigid.

Hannah arrived in the classroom and settled next to Jean, who was rummaging in her leather satchel for her protractor and compasses in anticipation of geometry.

Jean gave her a quick smile. "The only good thing about Tuesday is that we get this out of the way first thing in the morning, then it's on to double English, art, music and history in the afternoon, all the best subjects. I can't wait to move up next year. I have my fingers crossed that we'll get anyone else for maths apart from this old dragon. Isn't she frightful?"

Just then, chairs scraped back, as the girls stood to attention with the arrival of their teacher. Sitting in the back, Hannah quickly pulled out her math exercise book, and dumped it onto the desk as she rose to her feet.

"Good morning, girls," said an unfamiliar voice.

"Good morning, Miss," the girls responded uncertainly.

"I am Miss Tatchell, and I shall be taking you for mathematics this morning, in Miss Hobbs' absence. You may be seated."

The chairs scraped again, as all the girls returned to their seats. All, that is, except for one girl who was staring at the new teacher, a short woman with glasses in a skirt suit.

Everyone turned to look at Hannah, and started giggling as she remained on her feet.

"You may be seated," the Professor repeated.

Hannah sat down.

"Now, perhaps one of you girls would care to tell me what you've been working on?"

Jean raised her hand, and stood when she was acknowledged. "Geometry, Miss Tatchell."

"I see," said the Professor evenly. "Perhaps you would be so good as to come to the board and show me an example from your exercise book?" She offered a piece of chalk.

Jean walked to the chalkboard, took the chalk from the Professor's outstretched hand, and began to draw the problem on the board.

When she had finished, the Professor invited girls to come to the front, one by one, and devise problems for the class to solve together.

Then she pointed to Hannah. "You, in the back, what's your name?"

Hannah stood and looked at her cynically. "Oh, I think you already know my name," she said.

The Professor's face grew very serious. "Come with me. The rest of you, get on with your work."

As Hannah walked from the classroom, nobody could understand why she didn't look afraid. They were impressed: They certainly would have been, if they had been her.

Hannah followed the Professor down the hall, and into an empty classroom nearby.

"Hannah, please drop the attitude," the Professor said despairingly, as she closed the door behind them. "You almost blew my cover. It's hard enough to pretend I know anything at all about math. It was always my worst subject at school. I used to hide in the back of the classroom and pray for the bell to ring."

Hannah gazed coldly at her. "Whatever. Why should I care? I don't even care if these people find out you kidnapped us from twenty-first century America."

"Well, actually," said the Professor, perching on the edge of the teacher's desk, "I didn't. But that's beside the point."

"Not to me," said Hannah, sitting down on one of the student desks. "I think you must be totally crazy. Maybe you're some kind of evil genius. It's so not fair to get us involved in this stuff that has nothing to do with us."

"Hold it," the Professor said, holding up her hand. "How do you know it has nothing to do with you?"

Hannah looked at her with loathing. "I'm not from England, get it? I don't know any of these people, and they're all probably dead by the time I was born. What difference does it make if I'm here? And now it looks like poor Brandon isn't even in the same time period."

"Well," said the Professor, lifting the lid on one of the desks, and abruptly dropping it closed with a bang. "That's what I have come to tell you. Brandon and George Braithwaite are not one and the same, but you can't find one without finding the other."

"What does that mean?"

"It means what it says. The only thing I can tell you is not to worry about Brandon, because there's nothing you can do right now, and he's fine. But George needs your help. Let Mrs. Devenish help you, because she can and she will, so long as you keep in touch. And please understand that whatever it is that you need to do, and whatever might happen to you, no matter how unpleasant, you are doing a good thing."

"Suppose I don't care?" said Hannah. It wasn't really a question.

"You would," said the Professor firmly. "You would care if you really knew what was happening. And you must care, because finding George is your ticket home."

"Why are you doing this to me?" Hannah cried.

"I'm not," said the Professor. "Now let's go back to class. The other girls think I have been scolding you, so try to look upset and angry. Oh, I see you already do. That's helpful."

A letter arrived from Eric in the afternoon mail that day, inviting Hannah and Alex to Mrs. Devenish's house on Sunday, and instructing them to arrive no earlier than half past ten, after church. Mrs. Archer wasn't pleased, but she reluctantly allowed them to go.

"It's not as though I can say no to the likes of that Devenish woman, is it?" she grumbled. "She thinks she's better than the rest of us, just because she's a magistrate and goes to church every Sunday."

"The invite is from Eric, not her, so I wouldn't worry about it, yeah?"

And with that, Hannah walked away, as Mrs. Archer gave an outraged "Well!" behind her. Hannah realized then what a relief it would be to get out of the Archers' house, if only for an afternoon, and if only in the company of Eric and Mrs. Devenish.

Alex complained of a sore throat and sniffles on Sunday morning, but he insisted on coming along, because he really wanted to hang out with Eric. When they arrived, Eric met them at the gate. He was equally excited to see Alex, and he told Hannah that she could join Verity in the garden.

"She's here? Cool. But can't we go inside?" Hannah asked, "It's kind of cold out here."

He snorted. "You must be joking. Mrs. D. doesn't let us inside in anyfing less than gale-force wind."

Hannah found Verity, who was muffled in scarf, gloves and hat, and sitting huddled on the garden bench.

"Hi, Verity, good to see you," said Hannah. "Eric didn't say you were coming."

Verity dabbed at her nose with her handkerchief before she answered. "Oh, didn't he mention it? I'm living here. Mummy has gone to work with my aunt in London," she explained. "So I'm boarding at school during the week, and I live with Granny at the weekends."

"Where's your dad, anyway?" asked Hannah.

"Daddy's with the Army, somewhere in Scotland."

Hannah looked over to where Alex and Eric were playing at gangsters, shooting each other with their fingers.

"So how, exactly, did Eric become your grandma's evacuee?"

Verity shrugged. "No great mystery. He arrived with the first lot when the war started last year, and she took him in. Most of those kids went home during the phoney war, you know, when there weren't any bombs, but not Eric.

"Actually, come to think of it, there is a bit of a mystery about Eric. He has never had any visits from his parents, although, of course, that's hardly unusual. So at first, nobody suspected anything, because all the grown-ups have their noses to the grindstone, haven't they, and what with the restrictions on travel…. But the thing is, Eric never gets any letters, or postcards, or anything. He never complains, but Granny noticed. And most working-class evacuees get terribly homesick, but Eric just doesn't seem that bothered, even with the bombings going on. Well, Granny made enquiries, and she's discovered that his parents have moved, with no forwarding address."

"Did their house get bombed, or something?" Hannah asked.

"No, that's what's so odd. Granny says the WVS told her it's happening everywhere: Parents are losing their children in the evacuation, and, what's worse, some of them want to."

"But that's horrible!" gasped Hannah.

"I should say so," Verity agreed. "Don't say anything, though. Eric doesn't know. I'm not supposed to know either: I just overheard Mummy and Granny talking about it. Granny doesn't want to tell him until she's quite sure they can't be found. Honestly, though, I doubt he'll be that upset. From what he's said to me, he isn't surprised not to hear from them. And he would hate me for saying this, but he absolutely adores Granny, you know. My guess is that he's hoping she'll let him stay with her after the war is over. I'm sure she will."

Hannah watched as Alex walked across the garden and into the house. Must be going to the bathroom, she thought.

A few minutes later, Mrs. Devenish called Eric, Verity, and Hannah to the kitchen door. She had changed into her WVS uniform and hat, and was pulling on her gloves. "A large group of evacuee families have arrived. Those poor people have been bombed out of their houses in London, and somehow managed to get themselves here. We're getting them settled and fed in the church hall until it's decided what to do with them, so I may be gone for some time. I shall be taking Maisy, because I'm also going to run Alexander home."

"Why?" Hannah asked in surprise.

"He's feeling poorly. I told him it's only a cold, and the fresh air will do him good, but he insists that he's not well. And he's running a temperature. Will the Archers be at home?"

"Probably Mrs. Archer," Hannah said.

"Well, if not, have you a key in case the door is locked?"

"Alex has ours. But isn't he too young to be home by himself?"

"Nonsense, of course he isn't," Mrs. Devenish said briskly.

"Verity, Eric, look after Hannah. I want all of you to stay outside until at least one o'clock, and then you may have the soup and bread for lunch. We shall have Sunday lunch for supper. If for some reason I'm not back by six o'clock, I want you to make a start on preparing the meal. There is a joint of beef in the larder--you can put it in the oven, Verity-- and some potatoes and carrots that you can take turns peeling. And all of you, behave yourselves."

A few minutes later, the kids watched with relief as Maisy accelerated up the lane. Then they snuck back into the house through the kitchen door.

"Thank goodness," said Verity, taking off her hat and shaking out her hair. "Granny's a great believer in children having fresh air, but it's perishing out there."

"I know," Eric said, "but I don't much fancy just sitting round the 'ouse with you two gossiping. I've got an idea. Girls, have you ever seen where they say the Ghost Evacuee lives?"

"Get real, Eric," Hannah said.

"I don't care what you fink. I fink it's true." He made ghostly noises and waved his fingers in Hannah's face.

"Get out of my face, weirdo," she said huffily, pushing him away.

But Verity said, "Come on, Hannah, what harm would it do to have a look? Except, of course, that I'd have to go outside again."

"Yeah, but fink of this," said Eric, "When's the next time we'll 'ave a chance to go 'ave a butcher's together?"

"A butcher's?" asked Hannah, frowning.

"Oh, that's just Eric's colorful Cockney rhyming slang," Verity said, as Eric stuck his tongue out at her. "It means to have a look. Butcher's hook, rhymes with look, you see?"

"Thrill city," said Hannah in a bored voice.

Verity turned to Eric, "All right, cleverclogs, where is it?"

"Not too far," Eric said, "Should only take us about quarter of an hour."

They arrived in front of a run-down small house some way outside of Balesworth. Its only neighbor was another larger and smarter house some distance from it.

"This is it," said Eric.

Verity said, "It looks creepy, like something from…I don't know…Dracula or Frankenstein."

For the next fifteen minutes, the kids tried to look like they were playing, while they watched the house. "I don't think anyone's in," said Hannah.

But just then, the door opened. Startled, the kids quickly tried to pretend they were not interested in the house at all. A woman in an apron and turban, like so many of the women Hannah had seen, stepped outside and stood on the front step, her hands on her hips.

"You lot! I seen you watching this house, and I don't like it. Now be off with you!" She glared at them, and closed the door. A few seconds later, they saw her again, shaking her fist at them through a small downstairs window. The kids walked quickly down the lane, but as they left, Hannah caught sight of the woman sitting down in the front room with what looked like a magazine.

"Well, that's that, then," said Verity.

Eric said, "I dunno 'bout you, but I think that's suspicious behavior. C'mon."

"Where are we going?" demanded Hannah.

Eric was already on his way. "You saw her! She sat down in the front room. That means there's a good chance she won't see us going round the back."

Hannah stopped. "No. No way."

"Oh, come on, Hannah," said Verity. "Where's your sense of adventure?"

"Don't you guys worry that she will tell the police we're stalking her, or something?"

"You mean that we're casing the joint?" asked Eric.

"Eric watches too many American gangster films," Verity explained. "Don't be silly, Hannah. And I do hate to say it, but I think Eric's right. Why does that woman seem so nervous about us?"

"Look, we could tell an adult."

"Honestly, Hannah, what grown-up would listen to us?" said Verity, exasperated. "We haven't any proof."

"Just follow me," Eric yelled back, as he led them through the fields in a large arc to the back of the house. Hannah had a very bad feeling about this, but she followed him anyway, caught up in the excitement. The kids stood on the edge of the yard, and began to keep watch on the back of the house.

For the next ten minutes or so, they saw absolutely nothing happen. Then the rain started. It was a light drizzle, but enough for Verity to suggest to the others that it was time to go.

"I still say someone's in there," Eric said. He leaned down, grabbed a handful of gravel from the dirt, and moved closer to the house.

"What are you doing, you moron?" hissed Hannah.

"Watch this," Eric mouthed at her, and started tossing individual pieces of gravel at the upper windows. Hannah was growing very anxious.

"C'mon, Eric, get on with it," she hissed at him. "Use something a bit bigger."

The girls watched as, again, Eric looked around on the ground. Before either girl could warn him against it, he had picked up a small rock, and hurled it a little harder.

The window broke, with a resounding crash.

For a second, all three kids stood transfixed by the sight of the smashed glass. Hannah turned to say something to Verity, and realized she was talking to air: Verity was already tearing off across the fields. Hannah turned back to look at Eric, and he was hurtling toward her. He suddenly tripped and fell, skidding on his knees. Without hesitation, he jumped up again, and started to run, his knees streaming blood, and raced past Hannah. She was soon sprinting behind him. As they turned the corner, they heard the woman screaming and swearing, and the sound of her dog barking loudly as it ran after them.

Only when the barking receded into the distance did the kids slow down and turn to look back. "It's only a Jack Russell," laughed Verity, as she tried to catch her breath, pointing to the tiny dog that was trotting back to the woman's house. "I thought it was a great big fierce Alsatian."

All three kids were clutching their sides and stomachs.

"I saw..." Eric wheezed, stopping and spitting. "I saw... someone."

"What?" puffed Hannah.

"I saw someone... Come to the window. A kid. I think. I'm not sure. I think he was colored. Maybe. Look, I dunno. But I saw someone."

It began to rain during the walk home. When the kids arrived back at Mrs. Devenish's house shortly before four, they took off their wet coats, and Verity warmed some milk and made cocoa. She also offered bread and dripping, which Eric eagerly accepted.

"What's that?" asked Hannah.

"You're joking!" said Verity. "Bread and dripping? You know, the fat from the Sunday roast?"

"Oh, bread and *dripping*. I thought you said something else. No, thanks." Hannah shuddered, thinking to herself, *Gross*.

Eric lit the fire, after watching Hannah's foundering attempts with great amusement, and Hannah fetched blankets for everyone from the hall closet. The kids settled into the cushioned chairs next to the fireplace, wrapped in blankets, with their hands clasped around mugs of cocoa, sweetened with honey, and their feet warming by the fireside. Conversation gradually shifted from what Eric might have seen, to worried discussion of whether *they* had been seen.

Hannah, to Verity and Eric's surprise, was by far the least concerned of the three of them.

"Who would have seen us out there? I mean, there was only the one other house, and I bet nobody was home."

But Verity was growing fretful. "I didn't recognize the big house next door at first, because I've only been there once, after dark. Granny sometimes visits the old lady who lives there, and she took me with her last year. The old woman is a bit of a busybody. I know she's on the telephone, so if she saw us, she might well have called the police."

Eric also looked increasingly unhappy, and he shifted uncomfortably in his chair, as he stared into the fireplace. "Your gran will 'ave my guts for garters if she finds out. And I don't want to wind up shipped off to some new billet."

"Eric, I really don't think Granny would get rid of you," Verity said kindly. "But, yes, you might very well be right about the first bit, even if you did use that rather vulgar expression. Of course, she would be absolutely furious with me, too. Oh, gosh." She now looked very worried.

Hannah was fed up with their wallowing in angst. "Look, worst case, alright, guys? So Mrs. D. finds out, right? Well, whatever. If Eric saw something, she'll know we had a right to be concerned, yeah? People need to know, yeah? Anyway, it's no big. It's just a window."

"That's hardly the point, Hannah," Verity snapped. "Granny's a magistrate. She's got her position to think of."

Hannah bridled at the rebuff. "That's kind of shallow, isn't it? I mean, worrying about what people think about her? And it's nothing to do with her if we accidentally broke a window."

"Don't you know anything, Hannah?" said Verity, frustrated. "It's not just about what other people think. Granny says middle-class people like us—and that goes for you, too, Eric, because you live with us--have no right to enjoy privilege unless we deserve it. She won't approve of us acting like common hooligans. Even Eric."

"Fanks a lot, I don't fink," said Eric, taking a swig of his cocoa.

"Eric, there is a 'T' and an 'H' at the beginning of both "thanks" and "think." Not an 'F'," said Verity, superciliously.

"Oh, belt up. I get enough of the flippin' elocution lessons from your gran, *th*ank you."

"Anyway," Verity said with forced jollity, "With a bit of luck, Hannah's right. Nobody recognized us, and nothing will come of this. Granny will be none the wiser, and we'll just have to think of some way to interest her in that house."

But Hannah was silent. She was thinking, how did I get myself into this situation? What was I doing when I agreed to this totally stupid, childish plan? Why didn't I take off when Eric started throwing rocks? And what, exactly, *is* the big deal about a broken window? It's not like it costs that much to replace.

When Mrs. Devenish returned about ten minutes later, she found the three kids sitting silently in the chairs next to the kitchen fireplace, still wrapped in blankets and drinking the last of their cocoas.

She looked very tired, and had a lit cigarette between her lips. Taking off her hat and jacket, she hung them on the hooks on the back of the kitchen door. Only Hannah greeted her, with a wary "Hi, Mrs. D."

"Good evening to you, Hannah. Is everyone else feeling quite well? Cat got your tongues? I don't know what you three have been up to while I was out, but I must say, I do find the quiet rather unnerving."

Eric gulped, Verity shivered, and Hannah, suddenly made uneasy by the tension in the room, took a sip of her cocoa to hide her discomfort.

Mrs. Devenish looked oddly at them for a moment, and then caught sight of Eric's bloodied knees. "Take a tumble, did you? Never mind. Did you give those knees a good wash with soap and water?" Eric muttered that he had. She said, irritably, "Don't mumble, Eric. Speak up. A simple yes or no will suffice."

Just then, someone rapped on the front door. Mrs. Devenish pinched off the end of her cigarette and went to answer, closing the kitchen door behind her. The children looked at each other, alarmed. They heard voices in the hall: Mrs. Devenish was talking with someone who spoke in a low rumble.

Shortly afterward, she returned with a stony face and a police officer, his bobby's helmet tucked under his arm.

"Constable Ellsworth," she said frostily, "has received a report of three children pestering a householder, one Mrs. Smith, and throwing a stone through her window. Was it you?"

There was a long silence. Hearing the tone of her voice, nobody wanted to confess.

The constable held up a small printed booklet. It was Eric's identity card. "Yours, I believe. Apparently, you dropped it," he said, handing it to Eric, who reluctantly took it with a shaking hand.

The kids all looked at the ground.

As if it were possible, Mrs. Devenish's expression darkened even more.

"I see," she said grimly.

Verity said, "Granny…"

"Hold your tongue!" snapped her grandmother, turning on her. She turned back to the policeman, and said calmly, "Thank you for bringing this to my attention, Constable Ellsworth."

"Not at all, Mrs. Devenish. What with you being a lady magistrate and all, I reckoned you would want to handle this yourself…"

"Quite," she said swiftly. "Naturally, I appreciate your discretion, and please rest assured that I regard this matter with the utmost seriousness. But we need not trouble you further. I will see to it that Mrs. Smith is compensated."

Mrs. Devenish left the room with the policeman. The kids heard further muffled discussion, and Hannah was sure her name was mentioned. Then Mrs. Devenish bade the constable good evening, and closed the front door. The kids heard her footsteps going up the stairs. Eric gazed wretchedly at his grazed knees.

"We're for it," mumbled Verity, looking very pale.

"Busted. Totally," Hannah agreed glumly. "But don't worry, you guys, it's cool. I'll pay for the window. When she's done chewing us out, I'll tell her I have enough money to cover it…"

Verity was staring at her in amazement. "Shut up, Hannah. You can be so dense."

A moment later, they heard heavy footsteps coming back downstairs, and Mrs. Devenish walked in, her face now set in stone. She was carrying a fearsome leather belt, and she dropped it with a thud onto the kitchen table.

All three kids stared at it.

Only Hannah spoke, and she made a noise that sounded like "Ahk."

Mrs. Devenish looked directly at Hannah, whose heart skipped a beat. "Hannah, I shall deal with you first. Eric, Verity, you will wait your turn in the hall."

As Eric and Verity sheepishly made their way out of the kitchen, Mrs. Devenish reached over, and pulled out a chair from under the table. Hannah remained frozen in shock. Through the doorway, Verity looked back and gave her a sympathetic look, before her grandmother closed the door.

Out in the hallway, Eric immediately kneeled down on the wood floor to listen at the keyhole in the heavy door.

"Sounds like she's trying to talk your gran out of it," he hissed to Verity, who was sitting despondently on the stairs. "Fink she'll manage?"

"Hope so," said Verity, in a less than optimistic voice, as she examined her fingernails.

"Blimey, I wouldn't lay odds in her favor," said Eric, shaking his head.

"Nor me, honestly," said Verity, with a heavy sigh. "I've never seen Granny so livid."

Eric listened at the door again, and frowned. He came over and slumped down next to Verity on the stairs. "You won't flamin' believe it. She's only gone and told your gran it was all our fault."

Verity was shocked. "That's absolutely vile. How *could* she? What a simply beastly thing to do. Well, I know Granny, and she won't be the least bit impressed."

Seconds later, Verity was proved right. The kids heard Hannah erupt in a long howl of outraged protest. They both cringed at the unmistakable sound of the first whack, followed by Hannah's anguished yell.

"Ow, gosh, I bet that hurts," said Verity nervously. "Granny's never given me more than a smack, you know. Neither has anyone else, actually."

Eric had tears welling up in his eyes. "I'm sorry, Verity. I've let you and your gran down, 'aven't I?"

"Chin up, Eric," Verity tried to sound braver than she felt, and she nudged him affectionately with an elbow. "It's not the end of the world, silly."

"It don't 'alf sound like it, though, dunnit?" Eric said morosely, jerking his head in the direction of the cries echoing from the kitchen.

Then, suddenly, it was over, and Hannah's wails trailed off into piteous weeping. Verity was not sympathetic. "Imagine Hannah trying to weasel out of it, leaving us to face the music. I'm glad Granny walloped the daylights out of her, the rotten little sneak."

The kitchen door opened, and both kids jumped up in anxious anticipation. Hannah walked unsteadily into the hall, her eyes fixed on the floor, and she wiped fiercely at her tear-streaked face. Behind her stood a grim-faced Mrs. Devenish, who beckoned to Eric and said tersely, "You're next."

At a snail's pace, Eric miserably shuffled after her into the kitchen. The door closed once again. In silence, Verity sullenly watched Hannah, who now stood holding onto her bottom with both hands. Her face was screwed up in pain, her eyes were shut, and her forehead was pressed against the wall.

"Stop staring at me," said Hannah, irritably, opening one eye and returning Verity's gaze. "That was total torture. And I've never been so embarrassed in my whole life."

"Don't expect me to feel sorry for you," said Verity furiously. "At least you got it over with first. And we heard what you said to Granny. That was a disgusting thing to do."

"I don't care," Hannah shouted. "It was Eric's idea, and you guys made me go. I kept telling you it was a totally dumb idea. I hate you, I hate Eric, and I totally *hate her*. I'm going home." Stiffly, and with as much dignity as she could muster, Hannah took her coat and hat from the hooks in the hall, and left the house through the front door.

Slowly and painfully, Hannah was walking along the road into the center of Balesworth, when a car pulled up alongside her. Startled, she stepped well away, looking at it suspiciously. She was afraid that it was a stranger, and even more afraid that it was Mrs. Devenish. But another familiar face and voice called to her.

"Hannah, it's me!" said the driver.

It was the Professor.

"Hop in, and I'll give you a ride home."

"No, thanks, I'm walking," said Hannah haughtily.

"Why? Whatever's the matter?" the Professor asked innocently, as she slowly drove alongside.

"What's the matter?" Hannah said through clenched teeth, then raised her voice to be heard over the car engine. "Okay, lady, I'll tell you what the matter is. You know what? I can't sit down. You know why? Because, thanks to you, I'm in England, it's 1940, and the scariest woman who ever walked the planet just took a belt to my bare butt. Have you got any idea how I feel right now?"

"Rather sore, I imagine," said the Professor with an amused smile.

Hannah stared at her. "Are you actually enjoying this? God, you are so mean. And you told me and Alex we wouldn't get hurt."

The Professor waved a finger at her. "No, not so. I told you that I know you'll all go home, and in one piece. Well, probably in one piece."

"Great," scowled Hannah. "Any more good news ?"

"Since you asked, yes. I suspect that you are very close to finding George Braithwaite. If I were you, I would keep in close contact with your Mrs. Devenish over the next week or so."

"You have *got* to be kidding," said Hannah, fuming. "Don't you get what I'm saying? Do you really think I could look that woman in the face again?"

But the Professor was smiling and shaking her head. She stopped the car. "Come on, get in. Look, you can sit on this. It's nice and soft."

She held up a sheepskin, which she folded onto the passenger seat. Hannah thought about it for a second, and then opened the car door. Carefully, she sat down, wincing, and was surprised to discover that the sheepskin did help. The Professor started the car again.

"Hannah, try to understand. Mrs. D. didn't want to spank all of you. And I am quite certain she had to pour herself a stiff drink afterwards. But you must realize that she thinks what you kids did today was hugely damaging, to her and to you. She believes she had a duty to see that you're punished, and she wants to save all of you from worse fates than anything she could inflict."

"Oh, please," said Hannah disparagingly, as she looked out of the window, her arms folded in front of her.

"Listen. This is England in the fall of 1940. Despite the war, people are hoping and planning that life will go on, and this is a place where respectability is still terribly important. Mrs. D. worries that Eric, a working-class boy with so much potential, will get a bad reputation and even a criminal record. That could harm his chances of gaining admission to the boys' grammar school next year. If he doesn't go there, she believes, he doesn't stand a chance of a decent life. And Verity could be expelled from her private school if it were ever found out that she had been involved in vandalism, which might ruin her chances of going to Cambridge University. Mrs. D. knows that would be a huge disappointment to her granddaughter."

"Fine, whatever, but what about me? I'm not her kid," said Hannah, sticking out her lower lip.

"Well, Mrs. D. either had to punish you herself, or she had to inform the Archers," said the Professor, swerving to avoid running over a little hedgehog crossing the road. "She believes that the Archers would have been outraged if the police were called to their home on account of you, and I think she's right. A lot of people are looking for an excuse to get rid of their evacuees. You quite likely would be sent to a hostel for misbehaving kids. Oh, yes, there is such a thing. It would not, I assure you, be a pleasant place to live."

"But it's not fair," Hannah grumbled, her chin trembling. "It was Eric's idea to go to the house, Eric broke the window, and they both made me go along with them."

"Made you?" asked the Professor, with a knowing smile. "How exactly did they do that?"

The sun was setting, and Hannah stared at the passing hedgerows. The Professor continued.

"You know, what the three of you did will also make it awkward for Mrs. D. to investigate George's whereabouts. Not to mention that she now feels obliged to a very annoying local policeman, because he offered to keep quiet about what you guys got up to."

"But why didn't she just tell us?" said Hannah, with feeling. "She could have explained. We would have got it. She didn't have to whip us."

"Mrs. D. doesn't think like the adults in your world, or at least like the adults in your world tell you that they think. In her world, unlike ours, almost everyone says it's fine to spank children now and then, but it is not considered a good idea to burden kids with grown-up worries. So Mrs. D. reckons that kids are kids, and her two only needed a simple lesson today: If they misbehave to the extent that the police are called, she will whip them. She hopes they will learn their lesson so she never has to repeat it. As for you... well, actually, you're right in one way. You are a different case... Look, I'll tell you the whole truth, but I'm warning you, you might not like it.

"As I said, Mrs. Devenish was worried about what would happen if your misbehavior was reported to the Archers. Even so, since your upbringing is not really her responsibility, she figured she would just give you a bit of a scare, tell you off, and send you home. It didn't work out that way, as you know. She was tired and stressed, and when you whined, and tried to lay all the blame on Verity and Eric, she lost her temper. Big time."

Hannah was scandalized. "So I got whipped because she was in a bad mood? That is so wrong. I mean... Just who does this woman think she is?"

She was taken aback when the Professor replied angrily, her voice rising. "Mrs. Devenish is a grown-up in England in 1940, an important member of her community, and an ordinary human being. That's who she thinks she is, Hannah. And I hate to tell you this, kid, but, no, this didn't happen just because she was angry at that one moment. She is really fed up to the back teeth with your snotty attitude. She tried to let you off with a scolding this afternoon, but you wouldn't let her get a word in. You prattled on, making excuses and ducking blame, until she suddenly realized that if she didn't teach you a lesson, nobody would. Mrs. D., like most women of this time, thinks differently from the adults who have raised you: She doesn't hold much with trying to analyze the causes of your bad behavior, or with questioning her own judgments. And her judgment was that you're a spoiled brat who's long over-due for a spanking..." The Professor added quickly, "In her opinion, that is. Not necessarily mine, of course."

Hannah scowled, but she was surprised to realize that she was very hurt by this news. She thought: That's it? Mrs. D. just thinks I'm a brat? She stared out of the window, and tried not to cry.

"Sorry, Hannah. That was a little harsh of me," said the Professor quietly, looking uncomfortable. She patted Hannah's hand. "I understand why you're confused, dear," she said carefully. "Nothing in your life has prepared you for being in England in 1940. So let me ask you something that might help: You may not care for Mrs. D's values or her way with children, but do you really hate her? Truth?"

Hannah sighed heavily, and stared at the dashboard for several seconds. Then she shook her head. "No," she said reluctantly, with a cross look.

"Well, now, you've said it. Doesn't that feel better? I know it's difficult for you to deal with the fact that you've become fond of this complicated woman who is not at all demonstrative with her affections, and who is all too demonstrative when she's angry. But she has her own way of showing her concern, and I think it's worth your while to try to understand her. I mean, I don't know if you have thought about this, but Mrs. D. has been trying to help you find George, and, not incidentally, to reach out to you, despite your behavior. Oh, and when she decided to punish you along with her own kids, it wasn't all bad."

Hannah snorted in disbelief, but the Professor continued. "No, it wasn't, I'm serious. That's because, you see, at that moment, she was also deciding to take you under her wing. Despite her anger and frustration, Mrs. D. does care what happens to you, Hannah."

The rain began to fall heavily, and the Professor pulled over into a wide spot at the side of the road, switching off the engine, which ground into silence. Hannah stared at the water running down the windshield, as it threw shadows onto her legs. At the same time, tears were trickling down her cheeks.

"It might surprise you to know," the Professor said slowly, "that most of the time, Mrs. D.'s thoughts are not on you, or Eric or Verity, or her daughters in London. She is preoccupied with the war. The adults all across Britain are putting on a brave face for the children, but the stress is tremendous. Mrs. D's horrified by the Blitz, by all those bombs dropping on London, and she's frightened that the Germans will invade any day now. We all know in our own time exactly what happened to the countries that Germany invaded, all the people murdered and imprisoned and tortured in concentration camps, but even in 1940, everyone in Britain knows that it would be horrific.

"The British would like to believe their prime minister, when Mr. Churchill tells them they will fight German soldiers in the streets if it comes to that.

"But most adults know, deep inside, that they have no idea, really, what they will do if Nazi soldiers come to their front doors. Mrs. D. is doing her best to stay calm, and to do everything she can for you children.

"You know, Hannah, Mrs. D. is quite a remarkable woman. She is very well regarded in Balesworth, even though people find her a bit daunting. She's tough because she's had to be. She has had a hard life, you know. She lost her husband to the fighting in the First World War. She was a widow when she was not yet thirty, with two daughters to raise alone. But she moved in with her mother so she could reduce her expenses and volunteer as a nurse. Don't be embarrassed that you like and respect her, even after what happened today. Even though she's prickly, she has a good heart, and lots of people admire her for it. I mean, just look at Eric! He's devoted to her, isn't he? He's like a little puppy, following her around."

Hannah gave a short laugh through her tears, wiped her nose on her sleeve, and nodded with a watery smile.

"Of course he adores her," said the Professor gently. "Mrs. D. has made Eric feel loved for the first time in his life. And you like her, Hannah, despite everything, because you can tell that she's brave, and caring, and trustworthy. She has her faults, and she's unlike anyone you know in our world, but she is kind and decent. I'm right, aren't I?"

Hannah sighed, and gave a rueful half-smile. "Why do the Brits need an army to fight the Nazis? They could have saved themselves a whole lot of trouble, and just sent her to Berlin instead. If Mrs. D. took Hitler over her knee, the war would be over...."

"That's the spirit," said the Professor, laughing. She turned the key in the ignition, and they set off again. "You know, I just might borrow that joke... I'm glad to see you cheer up, because you need a sense of humor when you're in another time and place, Hannah. Time travel is like ordinary travel, only more so: It tends to turn our ideas of what is right and usual completely upside down. Believe me, I do know."

"Okay, but I still don't get something. If Mrs. D. is so nice and all, why doesn't she care that she hurt my feelings?"

The Professor groaned. "I have said all that I'm going to say. You must form your own opinions. But I hope you'll think carefully about everything I've told you."

They pulled up outside the Archers' house. The Professor said, "Life's complicated, isn't it? And time only makes it more so."

"I guess," said Hannah uncertainly, as she stepped carefully out of the car, grimacing. But then, she paused, and turned to look curiously at the Professor. "How do you know all this stuff, anyway? Like, what Mrs. D. is thinking?"

"I told you," said the Professor. "I'm an historian. Good night, now." And with that, she drove off.

Hannah dragged herself slowly upstairs to her brother's room, flinching with every step. Alex was having a nap, but she woke him, tugging at his shoulder. He struggled to sit up, pulling the sheets and blankets around him. Gingerly,

Hannah sat on the bed, and immediately turned, lying down on her side. In tragic tones, she described to Alex what had happened since his departure, with special emphasis on her own indignity and suffering. She chose not to mention ninety percent of her conversation with the Professor.

Finally, Alex shook his head, and said, through his stuffy nose, "Hannah, I've been listening to the radio. Do you know that World War Two is happening? It's happening right now, and it's about thirty miles away, okay? Bombs are falling on London. People are dying. Everyone's afraid. So, excuse me if I don't care that Mrs. D. flipped out and spanked you. No permanent scars, right?"

"She totally damaged my self-esteem!" exclaimed an indignant Hannah.

"Wow, did she? Did she really?" said Alex in a voice laden with sarcasm. "Hey, is that a new name you gave to your butt?"

Hannah gasped.

"Look, sis, I'm sorry, but it's no big deal. Everyone will get over it. Don't be such a drama queen."

"No wonder I have issues," Hannah raged, "when my little brother is such an insensitive jerk." Suddenly forgetting her delicate state, she stormed from the room.

When school ended on Wednesday, Hannah found Eric waiting for her at the gate.

"Eric, are you okay?" she asked anxiously.

He was puzzled. "Yes, of course, why wouldn't I be? Why? Has somefing happened?"

"You know...Sunday."

"Oh, that," he said with a wan smile. "Nah, 'course I'm alright. Mind you, when the old girl's on the warpath, her bite is a damn sight worse than her bark, innit?"

"She shouldn't have whipped us," said Hannah, shaking her head. "I mean, no offense to Mrs. D., but that's child abuse."

Eric scoffed at her. "Don't be so soft. What did you think she would do, give us all a medal? I'm just happy she's not going to pack me off to another billet. Mind you, Verity said I was daft even to fink she would do that to me." He smiled happily at Hannah, and looked at his wristwatch. "Look, I can't 'ang about," he said, "but I 'ave got some good news: Mrs. D. wants you and Alex to come round the 'ouse on Friday afternoon. Verity's got an 'alf-day 'oliday off school, so she'll be 'ome, too."

Hannah was amazed. "Mrs. D. wants to see me? So soon?"

He laughed. "Of course she does. Verity's right. She's a big believer in by-gones being bygones, is Mrs. D. And, anyway, she wants to talk to you. You see, after me and Verity stopped 'opping up and down the hall clutching our bums, we got her to listen to us about what I reckon I saw at that woman's 'ouse. And 'ere's what else, and you'll never believe it. Mrs. D. got a letter yes-terday, the WVS in London thought she ought to see it. It's from some bloke, name of George Braithwaite."

Chapter 10
MESSAGES AND MYSTERIES

It was a late afternoon, not long after the Balesworth Arms pub had opened, and customers were already trickling in. A strong smell of stale beer and a fog of tobacco smoke hung in the air. A woman and two couples sat at the small tables and the cushioned benches that lined the walls beneath the frosted windows. Only three men stood at the bar, each of them resting a foot on the brass rail that ran along its base.

Among them were Constable Ellsworth, the billeting officer Mr. Simmons, and, newly arrived, Mr. Smedley, who was digging in his pocket for change.

"My round, I think. You're both having a pint of best, right?" Smedley said to the others. To the middle-aged woman behind the bar, he said, "Same again, love."

"No more pints, boys. Only halves of bitter for the rest of the night, Betty," said the pub landlord, edging past his wife. "Same goes for the mild, too."

"Old Adolf's got a lot to answer for," said the constable. "But a shortage of beer, I mean to say, Ernie, what's the world coming to?"

The landlord shrugged his shoulders. "There's a war on, in't there?"

While Betty pulled the handle to dispense beer into a dimpled half-pint glass, Smedley turned back to the other two men.

"So, how's tricks, then? Evacuees all settling in alright?"

"Seem to be," said Mr. Simmons the billeting officer, taking a sip of beer. "No complaints from my end. Mind you, I mostly let the WVS keep an eye on them. I think it needs a woman's touch, dealing with all the domestic arrangements. What about you? Did you ever find that little Negro kid who ran off?"

Smedley let a cigarette and shook his head. "No. Vanished into thin air. We reckon a bomb might've got 'im, poor mite."

Exhaling smoke, Smedley turned to Constable Ellsworth. "No nicking from the shops, then, or scrumping apples from some farmer's orchards? These evacuees can be a right tough lot of little so-and-sos."

Ellsworth said, "Well, we did have the one incident, just this past Sunday as it so happens: Two evacuees and a local girl, bothering some woman and breaking her window."

"I didn't hear about that, Jim," said Simmons.

"You wouldn't, would you," said Ellsworth, taking a drag from his cigarette, "because I haven't said anything to anyone about it. The local kid was only Mrs. Devenish's granddaughter, and one of the evacuees was hers, too."

"Oh, I see," said Simmons, significantly. He lit a cigarette, and blew out a great puff of smoke.

Seeing Smedley's bafflement, Ellsworth explained. "Mrs. Devenish is one of our local magistrates. She's a bit of a tartar, between you and me, so I left her to deal with the three kids. I'll bet those little blighters won't sit down for a week."

Simmons said, "I say, Mrs. Devenish should know better than that. There was some edict came down from London, said that you can clip the evacuees round the ear and so forth, but that they shouldn't be beaten. At least, I think that's what it said. I don't always read these things too closely."

"Yeah, well, good luck to that," said Ellsworth, with a snort. "I mean, it's one thing when people are treating the kids like dogs, that's when I'll take steps if I get wind of it, I promise you. But it's another thing altogether when they treat them like their own kids. I've no objections if they give them a hiding when it's warranted. And would you want to be the one who tells off Mrs. Devenish?"

"Well…er…no…" admitted Mr. Simmons.

"It is the law," grumbled Smedley.

"Well," said Simmons, "with apologies to Charles Dickens, there are times when the law is an ass. No offense, Constable."

Ellsworth laughed. "None taken, mate," he said. "Anyway, the end of the story is that I ended up in Mrs. D.'s good books, because I kept it on the QT about what the kids got up to." He tapped the side of his nose with his finger.

"Except for telling us about it," Simmons interrupted with a short laugh. "Careless talk costs lives, eh?"

"Yes, well, obviously, I'd be much obliged if it didn't go any further," said Ellsworth, flustered. "Having Mrs. Devenish in my corner should make my life easier next time I go to give evidence in magistrate's court. Usually, she's far too much concerned for the rights of the accused, that one. That's the trouble with having some of these ladies on the magistrates' bench. Last time I was in court, Mrs. Devenish questioned my evidence about an old widow woman who had pinched two tins of beef from the grocer's. What do you reckon to that, eh? She said the old dear probably just forgot to pay, and that it wouldn't be right to punish her. I mean, I ask you, what a blinkin' waste of police time."

"You said two of the kids were hers, but what about the other evacuee you mentioned?" asked Smedley.

"Yes, who is it, anyhow?" asked Simmons.

Ellsworth tapped his chin with his fingers. "Oh, let me think…I'm sure she told me…Day's the name. Hannah Day."

"I remember her!" Simmons said. He turned to Smedley. "She was a cheeky little madam. Came in with a brother, and that colored boy of yours. Odd thing, really. Some WVS woman from London brought them, and then went off in a hurry. They weren't with the rest of the children that day, but we got the girl and her brother settled with Geoffrey Archer and his wife. Nice enough couple, although I heard my wife say that Archer's missis isn't very happy with the kids. Nothing too urgent, I gather, but she's asking around, trying to find them another billet. I'm not surprised, now I know what the little beggars have been up to."

"Is she now?" said Smedley thoughtfully. "Maybe I can help? Look, give me an address for these people, and I'll see if I can't sort something out. It's a bit late tonight, but I'll be back up this way in a few days.…"

"I say, that's very good of you," said Mr. Simmons. "Saves me the trouble, and, to be honest, while I don't mind the old pencil-pushing, I'm a bit at sea when it comes to that sort of thing." He asked the landlady for a pencil and paper.

It was a quiet evening in the fall of 1915, when Brandon plunked himself down in a chair in the parlor. Too late, he saw that Mrs. Gordon was already seated in a corner of the room, working on a piece of embroidery. He had always managed to avoid being alone with her before.

She looked up and stared at him sourly, reminding Brandon of his Aunt Morticia, who could screw up her face until she looked like a prune.

"I would really prefer that you not sit in this room," Mrs. Gordon snapped. "The kitchen is a more proper place for you…assuming that any place in this house, or in this country, might be described as proper for one of your kind."

Brandon felt his anger rise, and he decided that while he would not lose his temper, neither would he try to please her. As casually as he could, he picked up a book at random from the table. Within minutes, he was tempted to give up on it, because it was very boring. But suddenly he realized, to his shock, that the author was arguing that non-white people were inferior to white people. He glanced at the cover, which read *The Science of Eugenics*. Flipping through the chapters, he saw that the author had also written that white English people, whom he called Anglo-Saxons, were far superior to other Europeans, such as the French and Germans. The author also seemed to have a special dislike of Jewish people. It was all very disturbing.

Just then, Oliver entered the room, clutching *The Time Machine*, one of his favorite books, and gave Brandon a quick smile.

"I trust you find that informative?" said Mrs. Gordon to Brandon, nodding pointedly at the book on eugenics.

"Very much so," said Brandon, staring hard at her.

"I'm surprised you can understand it," she retorted.

"What's that supposed to mean?" asked Brandon, angrily.

"What that means," she said, laying down her embroidery in her lap, "is that Negroes such as yourself are among the many alien races weakening the purity and strength of the English people. I don't know where you came from, but I do wish that you would go back there."

"Yorkshire?" said Brandon, raising an eyebrow at her.

"You know what I mean. Whichever savage country your family came from. Not long down from the trees, I imagine."

Brandon's struggle with his temper was usually successful, but not this time.

"You are a stuck-up, ignorant racist," he seethed. "I bet you've never even been out of Balesworth more than half a dozen times in your life. You don't know anything."

"How dare you, you…you *nigger*," she hissed at him. "How dare you speak like that to a white woman?"

"How dare you use that word to me?" shouted Brandon.

Oliver had been observing this exchange with alarm, but now he jumped to his feet.

"Leave him alone, Aunt Sarah!" he yelled. "George is jolly clever, and really nice too. And he talks to me, and you never do."

"And you," she said, rising to her feet, and staring down her little nephew, "ought to be flogged. I shall have a word with your uncle."

But Oliver knew better. "Uncle Bob would never beat me, if he knew what you were saying to George. You're a nasty old witch, and I hate you." He stamped his foot.

His aunt glared at him. Then she said quietly, "I didn't want you in this house, you know. We shall be glad to see the back of you when you go to boarding school next year."

Brandon could see that Oliver was devastated, and was struggling not to cry. Suddenly, the child threw down his book onto the floor, and ran from the room, sobbing.

Brandon looked at Mrs. Gordon in wonderment. "What the hell is the matter with you? What kind of woman would do that to a little boy? I'm going to pray for you, Mrs. Gordon, because it seems to me like you need all the help you can get."

She was unmoved. "Don't bother making any prayers on my behalf to your heathen god," she said stonily.

Without another word, Brandon left the room to go and look for Oliver.

In the kitchen, Mary and Brandon comforted Oliver, soaking up his tears with cloth handkerchiefs, and tried to persuade him to eat some of his favorite cake. Suddenly, one of the service bells rang.

"It's the study," Mary said, looking up. "Back in a minute." She hurried toward the stairs. A minute later, she returned. "It's Mr. Gordon, George. He wants to see you."

"Can you tell him I'll be up in a couple of minutes?" Brandon said, glancing anxiously at the inconsolable Oliver.

"Sorry, George," she said, giving him a sympathetic look. "He said he wants you upstairs straightaway."

Brandon had expected to be in trouble, and he was.

"I cannot allow my apprentice to speak like that to my wife," fumed Mr. Gordon, as he paced about the study in front of Brandon, who was standing to attention before the desk, "or to any member of the family. What on earth were you thinking, George?"

"She... Mrs. Gordon...said that black people live in trees, and she was really mean to Oliver... Sir."

Mr. Gordon paused. "What prompted that?" he asked curiously. Brandon told him as politely as he could, and Mr. Gordon looked both thoughtful and angry at the same time.

Finally, he said, "My wife has demanded that I rescind your indentures, or, failing that, that I beat you. I have told her that I cannot afford to lose you, that your work is satisfactory, and that the shortage of workers would make it difficult for me to replace you. That, of course, would appear to leave me no choice in resolving the matter."

Brandon nervously wondered which part of the apprenticeship contract he had apparently not read closely enough, as he watched Mr. Gordon take off his belt. But immediately, Mr. Gordon put his finger to his lips and handed the belt to Brandon.

"George," he whispered conspiratorially, "she'll be listening. Just go and thrash the armchair, would you, lad? Gie it laldy....That means hit it hard."

After Brandon did as he was told, enthusiastically bashing the armchair and throwing in an occasional yell for effect, he handed back Mr. Gordon's belt to him with a smile.

"Ach, just man to man, I'll tell you, she's not a bad woman, in her way," said Mr. Gordon, pouring out a whisky for each of them, to Brandon's amusement. "But she has always had some funny ideas, and the war has made her worse. She reads all this eugenics nonsense, even though my late brother-in-law was a medical man, and he used to tell her it was absolute tripe."

Brandon sipped his whisky, and immediately regretted it. He tried to disguise the fact that he was gasping and shivering from the burning in his throat.

Mr. Gordon didn't notice Brandon's distress: "And now, nothing will persuade her otherwise. There are so many of the English who think that the Germans will invade, and commit all the dreadful outrages they are supposed to have committed in Belgium, although my son tells me that the soldiers take all those stories of German atrocities with a pinch of salt. If the Germans invade, my wife thinks, the English race will be lost. The irony, George, is that all these proud sassenachs…" and here he chuckled.

Brandon was confused. "I'm sorry, Mr. Gordon, but what are sassen.. sass… That word you used?"

"Oh, aye, I'm sorry. That's sassenachs. It's an auld Scotch word, George. It means foreigners, and especially the English. Look, the thing is, George, the English are always blethering about their damn racial purity. And what are they? They're Germans. They're all damn Germans. They're descended from the Jutes, and the Angles, and the Saxons, and what have you, all the German tribes that invaded England when the Romans left. If there were actually any purely British people, and, mind you, I hae me doots, it would be the Welsh and the Scots." With that, he laughed, and Brandon laughed with him. "Anyway," Mr. Gordon added, "in the words of the immortal Robert Burns, the finest poet in Christendom, a man's a man, for a' that, eh?"

Brandon had never liked Mr. Gordon more.

On a cold and wet Saturday afternoon, Brandon was at the kitchen table, playing chess with Oliver, and occasionally allowing him to win. Mary had brought them glasses of milk and what she called toasted tea cakes. These were warm, slightly sweet pastries, like puffy saucers. The boys split them in half, and spread them with melting butter.

There was a knock at the front door. Mary wiped her hands on her apron, and adjusted her cap in the mirror, before going to answer it. But Peggy was already at the door.

Seeing her there, Mary stood stock still in the kitchen doorway.

"What's up, Mary?" asked Brandon, as his rook captured Oliver's knight, and Oliver pouted.

"It's a telegram," she whispered.

Oliver looked up in alarm, as Mary hurried to Peggy at the door. "Oliver, help me out here. What's the big deal about a telegram?" whispered Brandon.

Oliver looked scared. "It's…like a letter. Only it goes by telegraph wire, so it comes very quickly… Rather like, what did you call it? Email."

"Yes, but why is everyone nervous?" asked Brandon.

Oliver turned and looked at him desperately. "Most people only get telegrams when somebody is hurt or killed. It must be Cousin James."

But seconds later, Mary returned to the kitchen with a smile. "It's all right, whatever it is. It was for Miss Peggy, and she looked happy enough with whatever it said. Not that she told me, mind."

Everyone gave a sigh of relief, and Brandon and Oliver resumed their chess and their teacakes. Mary returned to washing the dishes. The only sound was the loud ticking of the kitchen clock. Suddenly, a bell rang, summoning Mary upstairs to Mr. Gordon's study. She let out a sigh of annoyance, before setting off upstairs.

There was another knock at the door, and Brandon, realizing that Peggy might not have heard it, decided to answer it himself. "No cheating," he said to Oliver, before turning toward the door.

He opened it, and there stood a young boy with a bicycle.

"Telegram for you," the boy said, handing a small envelope to Brandon. Brandon had no sooner taken it from him than it was snatched from his hands.

"Mine, I think," said Peggy Gordon excitedly. "I have a gentleman friend who's a soldier at the front," she whispered to Brandon, "and he's just sent me a telegram to say he's coming home on leave soon. Don't tell my parents, whatever you do! He said he would send me another telegram to let me know when he's due to arrive in Balesworth. Gosh, that was fast!" She ran into the parlor and closed the door behind her.

Brandon shrugged, and turned toward the kitchen. He was only halfway down the hall when he heard a loud scream, followed by a long wail. He dashed back, hearing Mr. Gordon tearing down the stairs shortly afterward. Brandon threw open the door, but Mr. Gordon pushed past him.

"For the love of God, Peggy, what's the…."

She was on her knees on the rug, her hand over her mouth, the telegram dropped beside her.

"It's James…" she said.

Shaking, Mr. Gordon leaned over, and picked up the fallen telegram. As he read it, his face crumpled, and he let out an anguished cry that chilled Brandon to the core.

Brandon stood open-mouthed, unsure of what to do.

"George, it's my brother," said Peggy, starting to sob. "He's dead. He's dead...."

"George, look after Oliver," said Mr. Gordon, fighting to stay in control. "And not a word to my wife until I have seen her, I beg of you."

"Of course, sir," said Brandon.

He put a hand on Mr. Gordon's shoulder, and Mr. Gordon, with tears in his eyes, patted his hand, and then waved him away. By the time Brandon got to the kitchen, he found Mary and Oliver in tears. Oliver was bawling helplessly. Brandon picked him up, and sat him in his lap, and let him cry all he wanted. At once, Brandon felt very sick, and very grown up.

While the agony of the First World War made itself felt in the Gordons' house in 1915, Verity and Eric were playing with marbles on the dirt patch under the oak tree in Mrs. Devenish's garden in 1940. As Hannah and Alex arrived, Eric was explaining to Verity a complicated new version of the game that he had invented. Alex volunteered to learn it, too. Hannah stood awkwardly to the side while the others played, and she and Verity carefully ignored each other. Finally, at a loss for what to do with herself, she retreated to the garden bench, and picked up some pieces of grass, which she busied herself by pulling apart.

It was Verity who broke the ice. She left the boys to their game of marbles, and walked over to sit on the opposite end of the bench from Hannah.

"Come on, Hannah, let's be friends," she said, matter-of-factly.

Hannah looked apprehensively at Verity. "I'm sorry about trying to blame everything on you guys. I was just scared, I guess. Nobody ever whipped me before. So I, like, totally freaked when I figured out what your Grandma was gonna do to me. I have, like, big issues with violence, you know? I guess that the adults I know are just less mean. They don't hit kids..."

"I've never been beaten before, either, Hannah," said Verity, so icily that for a moment, Hannah was reminded of Mrs. Devenish.

"You haven't?" Hannah was astonished.

"No," Verity said curtly, "so it wasn't any easier for me than it was for you." She paused and then said, emphatically, "And whatever you choose to think, Hannah, my grandmother is not a cruel woman. I don't deny that she is a bit strict...Well, very formidable, really... Yes, alright, she's an absolute fire-breathing dragon at times. But I have never known her to be deliberately unfair or unkind."

There was an awkward silence.

"Look, I am sorry, Verity, I don't mean to disrespect your family...." Hannah tried to figure out how to explain. "But I still don't think you understand. I know it was bad for you and Eric, but the whole thing was super-awful for me. You see, I have lots of issues already, and your grandma has really hurt my self-esteem."

Verity smirked. "She hurt your what? Tell me something, Hannah. Is that usually what you call your bottom?"

Hannah pouted, but Verity refused to show her any sympathy.

"I say, Hannah, buck up. We can all agree that it was horrid, but it's over now, isn't it? No point in dwelling on it, is there? The less said, the better, I think."

This was news to Hannah, whose family had always hashed out problems and feelings at length, turning them over and over until everyone was quite exhausted.

There was another uneasy silence, and then Verity spoke up. "You know, did Eric tell you, Granny got a letter from George Braithwaite! Isn't it exciting?"

"Yeah. I guess so," said Hannah, guardedly. She was amazed by the speed and determination with which Verity had changed the subject. "What does it say?"

"I have no idea," Verity said, "I only heard about it when I arrived home last night, and Granny hasn't said much to either of us. She does want to talk to you, though. I expect it's because you were the one looking for him."

"I guess. I'm kind of nervous about talking to her. I have major issues with scary old women who use violence on kids. Is she still mad at me?"

Verity exploded. "Hannah, for heaven's sake, would you please, *please* stop going on about it! You are an absolute fusspot. Anyone would think you'd survived a bomb blast, not just a smacked bum... Er, as Eric would say... Oh, golly, please don't tell Granny I used that word, or she'll think he's a bad influence."

Hannah smiled despite herself, and Verity smiled right back. Hannah didn't always understand Verity, but she did like her.

A moment later, Mrs. Devenish called to her from the kitchen door. "Hannah Day? I want a word with you. Come into the drawing room." Then she disappeared back inside.

"Oh, great," said Hannah with a groan.

Verity squeezed her hand. "Go on, don't be daft. You'll be as right as rain."

Mrs. Devenish was in an armchair next to the fireplace, holding a pencil, and peering through her reading glasses at a newspaper. Emmeline, the spaniel, was snoozing in her lap.

Mrs. Devenish didn't look up when she heard Hannah enter the drawing room, but said, "An ocean vessel far astray, nine letters."

Hannah said, "Huh?" She threw herself down in the chair on the opposite side of the fireplace, and sprawled, staring into the hissing and crackling coals. Mrs. Devenish looked at her over her glasses and said dryly, "Yes, you may be seated, Hannah. I assume that your extraordinary exclamation meant 'Excuse me?'"

Hannah sat up a little straighter, and finally looked Mrs. Devenish in the eye. "Sorry, yeah, I meant excuse me."

"I was hoping you could help me with the crossword."

Hannah looked blank. Mrs. Devenish sighed in a long-suffering sort of way, and returned her newspaper to the rack beside her chair.

"Oh, never mind. I shall finish it later. Now, there's a matter I must discuss with you."

Hannah nodded, her brow furrowed.

Mrs. Devenish took off her glasses and addressed Hannah directly, wagging a finger at her. "First, let me be clear about something: I have by no means revised my opinion of your inexcusable behavior towards Mrs. Smith. It was a very stupid thing to do, and it was quite right that you should all be severely punished."

No surprise that you would think that, thought Hannah. Why rub it in?

Mrs. Devenish almost seemed to know what she was thinking. "I want to be absolutely sure you understand that, before I tell you that it seems that there is a silver lining to this particular cloud. I am still not convinced that Eric saw what he thinks he saw. However, I do think, on reflection, that it would be wise and proper for me to pursue the matter, and I hope to have ample opportunity to do just that when we visit Mrs. Smith to pay for her window. I have already written to her, asking for a convenient day when we may call. The cost, incidentally, is one I have decided that you three will bear by taking my place assisting Mrs. Roberts, the vicar's wife, with the cleaning of the church brasses next week."

Hannah said, shrugging, "Actually, if it's all the same to you, Mrs. D., I'd rather just give you the money..."

Mrs. Devenish looked at her as though she had lost her mind. "In all my life," she said through gritted teeth, "I don't believe that I have ever met such a sublimely witless girl as you, Hannah Day. You take my breath away. Allow me to spell it out for you, since you obviously have far more money than sense. If you simply hand me a few bob for your share, that won't help you learn your lesson, now, will it? Really... I ought to write to your mother and give her a piece of my mind about your upbringing."

Hannah shot back angrily, "Fine, okay, I get it. Whatever. Now what about the letter?"

"Don't be impertinent, young woman," Mrs. Devenish said firmly, squashing her with a look. "I was coming to that. The WVS in London received a letter through the Red Cross, from a Corporal George Braithwaite. He was taken prisoner at Dunkirk, and is now imprisoned at a Nazi P.O.W. camp in Germany."

Hannah gasped, but Mrs. Devenish continued. "A copy of the letter was passed along to me, because a friend of mine at head office recalled my writing to them about the boy of the same name. Corporal Braithwaite writes that he is very concerned about his son. The boy was evacuated last year from his home in London, to Bedfordshire. Then, sadly, the child's mother died. She was killed by a car while she was walking in the blackout."

Hannah's eyes filled with tears. "That's sort of how my Mom died," she said suddenly. "She had a car accident."

Mrs. Devenish looked absolutely taken aback, but then her eyes grew sad and kind. "I'm very sorry to hear that, my dear," she said softly. There was a brief silence as Hannah fought not to cry, and Mrs. Devenish pretended not to notice.

Then she resumed, briskly, "Well... Afterwards, the father kept in touch with the son. But the boy stopped replying, and then Corporal Braithwaite's letters began to be returned to him. Soon afterwards, he was captured by the Germans. But here's what is interesting, Hannah: The child is colored. And his name, it seems, is the same as the father's. Could this child be your friend?"

"Yes," said Hannah, nodding thoughtfully. "Yes, Mrs. D. He totally could be who we're looking for."

"Well, there is one further mystery," Mrs. Devenish said, as she stood, picked up a pair of tongs, and added another lump of coal to the fireplace. "And that is that I may know Corporal George Braithwaite myself."

"You do?" said Hannah, astounded.

"Yes," said Mrs. Devenish. "I believe I do. But I had better say no more until I am quite sure that he is the same man."

When Hannah and Alex returned to the Archers' later that afternoon, Alex realized just a few hundred yards from home that he couldn't find his house key. "Well, I don't have one," said Hannah, impatiently. "I hope Mrs. Archer's home, or they left the key by the door. Mr. Archer isn't due back for ages. People in this country sure work long hours."

"It's the war," said Alex, turning out his pockets. "I hear that people work up to seven days a week, sometimes fourteen hours a day, to make stuff for the troops."

"What does Mr. Archer make?" asked Hannah. "I thought he worked in an office."

"He does," said Alex. "But I guess they need people to do all the government paperwork, from what he says. He's a manager at a factory in the next town. They used to make ladies' underwear."

Hannah laughed.

"You know, like silk stockings," said Alex. "Now they make parachutes."

"Wow, that's a huge change," said Hannah, as they reached the front door-step.

"Not really," said Alex. "A parachute is kinda just a giant silk stocking, when you think about it. Where the heck is that key?" He had emptied his pockets, and found nothing.

Suddenly, a voice from behind them made the kids jump.

"Yours, I believe?"

It was Miss Tatchell, the Professor, holding out a key on a string.

"You dropped it on the road."

Alex gratefully took the key.

"That's so weird," Hannah said. "Are you following us, or what?"

The Professor ignored her. "Useful things, keys, aren't they?" she said. "Always handy when we don't feel like breaking windows to get in."

Hannah peered at her through narrowed eyes. "Is that supposed to be some kind of sick joke?"

The Professor smiled at her. "Not at all. It's simply an observation. Of course, not all window-breaking is done out of necessity. Or out of mischief. Sometimes, it's done to make a point. Did you know that Mrs. Devenish was once a suffragist?"

"What? What are you talking about? She was a whose-a-what?" said Hannah impatiently.

"She was a suffragist. In the years before the First World War, Mrs. D. campaigned for women's right to vote. She wrote hundreds of letters. But, you know, she didn't entirely approve of some of the more militant members of her movement, the so-called suffragettes. To draw attention to the need for women's suffrage, they smashed windows…"

Hannah smirked despite herself. "No, I bet she didn't like that."

"But she understood that what they did was for a cause in which she and many others believed passionately. It was not a method she thought effective, but nor was it a piece of childish foolishness. When the suffragettes were sent to prison, they refused to eat in protest, and were horribly forcibly fed through a rubber tube. Mrs. D. was only in her early twenties, but she agitated very hard for their humane treatment and release, you know."

"Well, isn't that special," said Hannah, sarcastically. "I'm sorry, did I miss something? Is there anything we can help you with? Or have you just come to tell us useless stuff?"

The Professor stared hard at her. "Speaking of suffrage, you really are an insufferable girl, Hannah Dias. I'm sorry I bother to tell you anything. Take care, Alex."

Alex called after her as she strode back up the street. "Hey, I'm sorry about...."

But she had turned a corner.

Alex rounded angrily on his sister. "Do you always have to do that?"

"What?" said Hannah, her face burning.

"Push people away like that. She was being nice, and she was trying to tell us something."

Hannah stared up the road, and said nothing.

Alex walked silently alongside her for a moment. Then he said, "Are you okay, sis?"

"I have no clue," said Hannah distantly.

Alex opened the door.

The kids were about to head upstairs, when Mrs. Archer called to them. "Children, come here. We have a visitor."

Hannah raised her eyebrows at Alex, and said, "Sure."

They followed her into the front room, where a man with a moustache was sitting. He wore a grey suit, and his hat lay on the sofa beside him. Mrs. Archer cleared her throat.

"Alex, Hannah, this is Mr. Smedley. He's with the government," she said importantly. "Sit down, children."

Hannah took the only available armchair, while Alex, reluctant to sit next to Smedley, sat on the floor at his sister's feet. The man looked keenly at the two of them. "I have a few questions to ask you both. Don't you remember me?"

"I do," said Alex slowly. "You're the man we met in the café, when we first came to Balesworth."

"That's right," said Smedley, unsmiling, with a nod.

"Have you come to tell us what happened to our friend, George?" asked Hannah.

"No. I have not. I'm here on different business. As I have just told Mrs. Archer, I've learned that you, Hannah, were mixed up in an incident that concerned the police."

Hannah's heart sank. Alex grimaced and dropped his head.

"Why didn't you tell me?" asked Mrs. Archer, sharply.

Hannah said, "I'm sorry. I feel really bad about it, but it won't happen again, I promise."

Alex nodded vigorously. "Yeah, I saw her that day, Mrs. Archer. She felt really, really bad. But you know, you don't need to punish her. Mrs…" Hannah kicked him in the back, and he stopped.

"What were you going to say, sonny?" asked Smedley. "I saw your sister kick you."

"Nothing."

"Perhaps you would like to come over here. Or you can tell me in the next room, away from her. A bit of a bad 'un, your sister, is she?"

"No," shouted Alex. "She's not! She's totally the best big sister, and she just did something stupid, and all I was going to say was that Mrs. Devenish already punished her, so there's no reason for anyone to punish her again, okay?"

Hannah was amazed. Alex had never defended her like this before. She suddenly felt a wave of sisterly love.

"Right, alright," said Smedley, trying to calm Alex down. "No need for that. Now, the thing is, Mrs. Archer is concerned, and I am too, that this may not be the most suitable billet for the two of you. Might be, you two will need to move on to other accommodations."

"Is this what you want?" Hannah asked Mrs. Archer sharply, but she wouldn't look at the kids.

Smedley spoke placatingly, as if trying to sound as reasonable as possible. "You know, there are three million evacuated persons, at least, most of them children. This evacuation was smoother than last year, but difficulties still arise. Some children get lost…"

"Like George Braithwaite," interrupted Alex.

"No, not exactly," Smedley said. "I'm talking about youngsters who are separated from their brothers and sisters, or who aren't properly reported to London, and kids whose parents lose them. Mrs. Archer tells me that neither of you has ever had any letters from home, and that concerns both of us. Now, if you would just give me your father's name…"

"William Di.. Day," said Hannah. Smedley wrote it down in his notebook as "William D. Day"

"And his address?"

Hannah realized with horror that she would have to make something up. She looked at the picture on the wall above Smedley's head. "Three hundred and forty seven Tulip Street."

"Three hundred and forty seven?" Smedley said suspiciously.

"Hannah…" said Alex quickly, knowing full well that no house numbers on residential streets that he had seen in Balesworth ever climbed beyond 99. He turned to Smedley. "My sister means thirty-seven. I think she's just upset. Maybe she's annoyed by all your questions."

Smedley stared at them both, then wrote it down.

"And what area of London is that, then?"

"Cricklewood."

"That's a fairly rough part of north London, isn't it?"

The kids said nothing.

"Are they on the telephone, your parents?"

"No," both kids said quickly.

Smedley dropped his notepad back into his inside jacket pocket. "That will be all, children." He nodded to Mrs. Archer, who said, "Go to your rooms, please."

Alex and Hannah climbed the stairs, both of them feeling deeply uneasy. When they got to the top, Hannah signaled to Alex to wait silently on the landing. She opened then closed her bedroom door with a bang, quietly removed her shoes, and tiptoed to the top of the staircase, carefully avoiding the creaky spot halfway along the landing. She paused at the top of the stairs, and listened intently. Fortunately, Mrs. Archer had left the door of the front room open.

"I can see your problem," Hannah heard Smedley say. "The girl's an incorrigible troublemaker, and a bad influence. I could leave him and take her, if you like…" Mrs. Archer's voice was fainter than Smedley's, but it was clear to Hannah that she was not keen on that idea. "Well," Smedley said. "If you wouldn't mind waiting, I'll see if I can get in touch with the parents, shall I?"

Mrs. Archer apparently agreed, then said something that included the word "husband."

"Of course, madam, I will certainly respect your wishes in the matter," Smedley said. "I can remove them tomorrow with a minimum of fuss, and your husband need not be told about the..ah…police incident. And you may be sure that the children won't be removed to anywhere in Balesworth. I have in mind a hostel in Norfolk, in fact. A very efficient place, and, of course, far from here."

Mrs. Archer moved closer to the door, and Hannah could now clearly hear what she was saying. "They will be treated well?" asked Mrs. Archer anxiously. "It's just that I would much rather they go to a private home."

"That, madam, is a matter for the proper authorities," said Smedley, as Hannah heard him getting to his feet. By "the proper authorities," Hannah thought, he probably means himself. Quickly, she ducked back along the landing as they came out into the hall.

As Mrs. Archer brought Smedley his raincoat, Hannah dragged Alex into his room. Standing with her back to the door, she said, "We have a problem."

Downstairs, as soon as the door had closed on Smedley, the telephone rang in the hall. Mrs. Archer answered it, and then called upstairs to Hannah.

"It's the telephone for you. Apparently, it's urgent. It's some woman who says she is your maths teacher."

Rushing downstairs, Hannah picked up the receiver. Mrs. Archer stood next to her, ignoring Hannah's glanced hints to leave her alone.

Over the phone line, Hannah could hear what sounded like a railway station. There were steam trains, hissing, puffing, and chugging along tracks, and the hum of dozens of passing voices.

"Sorry, dear, can't chat for long. Can you speak freely?" asked the Professor.

"No, not at all," Hannah told her.

"Well, that's alright. I just rang to let you know that I do think things are starting to work out."

Hannah chose her words carefully, for she was only too aware that Mrs. Archer stood right behind her. "I don't think so, actually. I don't think my... homework is going well at all. In fact, since I saw you, it's all gone wrong. It's a bit of a disaster. I'm sorry, but I need your help."

"Sorry, dear, what was that? Can't hear you, all this noise—oops, excuse me, sir...I say, madam, be a little more careful with that case, there...Anyway, Hannah, I'm sure you will do whatever you need to. Can't stop! Bye!" And then she hung up.

Feeling very alone, Hannah replaced the heavy black telephone receiver on its cradle.

"Why didn't you tell me about the window?" Mrs. Archer asked quietly from behind her.

"I didn't want to get in more trouble," said Hannah, shrugging.

"But why were you throwing stones through people's windows? It doesn't seem like you."

Hannah thought of explaining to Mrs. Archer what Eric claimed to have seen, but then she realized that she didn't want to tell her anything more. She looked into Mrs. Archer's eyes. "Yes, well, we can't always tell from first impressions what people are really like, can we?" With that, she retreated upstairs to talk with Alex, leaving a silent Mrs. Archer with her arms folded, looking troubled.

That night, Hannah waited until the Archers had gone to bed. The house soon descended into silence. She lifted the blackout curtain a short way, and held her watch up to the moonlight. It was midnight. Sitting silently on the bed, she thought about everything that had happened, and what she now had to do.

Time went by very slowly, but Hannah was not worried that she would drift off to sleep. She was too nervous and excited for that. When her watch told her that it was 2 a.m., she tiptoed next door, and woke Alex. Quietly, carrying their packed cases and school satchels, they slowly made their way downstairs. Hannah felt sick, and full of dread as well as hope. She was taking a huge leap of faith. She hoped she had made the right decision, or everything was about to fall apart.

It was around 2:45 a.m. when Verity was woken by the loud knocking on the front door over the sound of the heavy rain pelting the roof. She didn't hear Eric or her grandmother stir, so she threw back the thin quilt, blanket, and sheet, got out of bed, and put on her robe and slippers. Shivering in the freezing cold house, she felt her way along the walls down the pitch-dark hall to her grandmother's room. She knocked, and when Mrs. Devenish sleepily called out, "What is it?" Verity entered.

"Granny, there's someone at the door," she said into the darkness.

Her grandmother switched on the bedside lamp, rubbed her eyes, and then peered at her alarm clock. "But it's almost three in the morning…" she yawned. "It must be some sort of emergency."

"Shall I answer it?" asked Verity.

Mrs. Devenish sat up, ran her fingers through her hair, rubbed her face with both hands, and snapped out of sleep.

"You will do no such thing. Back to bed with you this instant."

Climbing out of bed, she put her robe on over her nightdress, before putting on her slippers. To her annoyance, her granddaughter waited for her.

"I said, go back to bed. Verity, for once, would you do as you are told?"

Verity scowled, but she reluctantly made her way back down the hallway, and hid in the bathroom. As soon as she heard Mrs. Devenish reach the front door, she tiptoed back to the top of the stairs, and listened.

Carefully, Mrs. Devenish cracked open the door. There, on the doorstep, stood a scared, sleepy, wet, and shivering Hannah and Alex, carrying their bags.

"What the...?"

She threw open the door.

"What is the meaning of this? What are you two doing here?" she demanded, flabbergasted.

Alex swayed slightly, and looked befuddled.

Her lower lip trembling, Hannah said, "Mrs. Archer was going to send us away tomorrow. Because of the window, you know, the lady's window. That man, the one who took away our friend, he's supposed to come and collect us and take us to a hostel, in somewhere called Norfolk. Please don't send us away, Mrs. D. Please, please don't."

Hannah made that speech with every last bit of energy she had. Everything that had happened to her suddenly seemed to fall upon her shoulders at once, and the weight of it was unbearable. Her face crumpled, she doubled over, and she started to cry in great, helpless sobs.

Immediately, Mrs. Devenish ushered the two children inside. She put a hand on Alex's back and steered him toward the drawing room, as she reached around Hannah's shoulders, and gently led her behind her brother.

Listening from the upstairs landing, Verity decided to risk her grandmother's ire, and slowly started downstairs.

"Alexander, take that wet blazer off before you fall asleep, or you'll catch your death," Mrs. Devenish ordered, pointing to Alex's soggy wool school jacket. She still had her arm around an exhausted and sobbing Hannah, who was hanging onto her as if her life depended on it. When she saw her granddaughter standing awkwardly in the doorway, she gave her an exasperated look. "Verity, it was very naughty of you to disobey me, but since you're here now, at least make yourself useful. Please take Alexander upstairs to Eric's room, and try to make sure that he leaves his wet clothes on the landing."

Verity moved toward Alex, who was sitting on the sofa looking completely out of it. Mrs. Devenish looked down at Hannah, who was bitterly weeping by her side, and said quietly to her granddaughter, "Before you go, Verity, could you please put a record on the gramophone? Something calming, I think. I should imagine a little Grieg would do the trick."

Mrs. Devenish lowered herself into her armchair by the fireplace, pulling the distraught girl onto her lap as she did so. Verity dropped to her knees by the record player, and sorted through the stack of stiff black discs in their beige paper sleeves. Soon, with a happy smile, she held up a record to her grandmother.

"How about Gracie Fields? I mean, I know you got it as a present and you don't care for her, but I rather like her, myself. It's *Sally*, so it won't be too loud or jolly."

With a roll of her eyes and wave of her hand, Mrs. Devenish indicated that it would do in a pinch. Verity cautiously removed the record from its sleeve, and placed it on the turntable, then carefully lowered the arm onto the spinning record. There was a burst of orchestral music, and then a woman's soprano voice began a sweet and gentle song in which a man begged a girl called Sally to marry him, and never to leave the street on which they both lived.

As Verity walked Alex upstairs, Mrs. Devenish gazed into the last glowing embers in the fireplace, and, without saying a word, gently rocked Hannah. Hiccupping, Hannah sank her head into Mrs. Devenish's shoulder, and, soon, was asleep.

When Verity returned, she said, "I've got Alex settled, and I've put his wet things on the clotheshorse." She yawned, and then smiled at her grandmother. "Are you all right there, Granny? I bet she's heavy."

"Just a little, and she is absolutely soaking," said Mrs. Devenish. "Verity, be a dear. Run upstairs and fetch your spare nightdress, and let's see if we can't get her into it and into bed. At least she's quietened down."

As Verity left the room, she heard her grandmother murmur to the sleeping girl in her lap, "Just look at you, you poor, poor little thing."

The next morning was Saturday. Hannah woke to the patter of rain on the windows of Verity's room, and the smell of toast. She dressed in some old clothes of Verity's, a skirt and blouse that had been laid out for her on the end of the bed, and came downstairs to find that her own clothes were still drying on the rack in front of the fire, as were Alex's. Her brother was in his pajamas and Eric's robe. Verity and Eric were very quiet, and everyone seemed anxious, except for Mrs. Devenish, who efficiently served them all oatmeal and toast.

"Not for me, thanks, Mrs. D." said Hannah as a steaming bowl of oatmeal was placed in front of her.

"Why ever not?" asked Mrs. Devenish with a frown. "I make rather good porridge, if I say so myself."

"I just don't like oatmeal," said Hannah. "It's kind of like the stuff my dad uses to spackle the walls…"

"That's enough," said Mrs. Devenish with irritation, taking Hannah's plate and putting it in front of Eric, who happily added it to his own helping.

"I don't mind that you don't care for it," she said quietly to Hannah, "but you really don't have to insult my food."

Hannah's brow creased. She didn't want to hurt Mrs. Devenish's feelings, not after she had been so kind. "I'm sorry, Mrs. D. My bad," she said remorsefully.

"It's alright, my dear," said Mrs. Devenish softly, not looking at her.

"Mrs. D.?" asked Alex, "Are we going to have to go with that Smedley guy?"

"I don't know," she said curtly, to Hannah's dismay. "We shall have to see."

"Don't worry," Verity whispered to Hannah. "That means, 'Over my dead body.'"

"Don't whisper, Verity," chided her grandmother, leaning over and tapping her hand.

"Mrs. D," asked Alex again. "How long will it take the Archers to find out where we are?"

"They already know. I telephoned them this morning."

"*What?*" Hannah blurted out.

"Calm down, Hannah. They won't be coming. I spoke with Mrs. Archer, and she said that they had decided it would be better for you to seek a billet elsewhere. I don't know why she is so determined that this should be so, but nothing I said seemed to persuade her otherwise. She also said that she will inform Mr…What was his name?... Mr. Smedley of the circumstances."

"But he'll send us away," Hannah yelled, leaping to her feet.

"I said, calm down," barked Mrs. Devenish. "I will speak with this Mr. Smedley, if and when he contacts me. Now, either stop this silly panicking this minute, Hannah Day, or you can go and sit upstairs. It does you no good at all, and it gives me a headache."

As it turned out, they did not have long to wait. Eric and Alex were playing chess, while Verity read a book, and Hannah helped Mrs. Devenish polish the silverware. There was a knock at the door. Mrs. Devenish was in the dining room, replacing the forks in their drawer in the buffet, when she saw a taxi pull up in front of the house. Immediately, she returned to the kitchen.

"Children, go to your rooms," she ordered, pointing to the stairs. "And I'm warning you: If I see so much as a toenail peeping over the landing, there will be sore bottoms."

Once the kids were safely upstairs, she opened the door to Mr. Smedley and invited him in. Hannah and Verity, who were by now leaning as far over the landing rail as they could, were dismayed to hear Mrs. Devenish close the door to the drawing room behind her.

"Oh, bloody hell," said Verity in a disappointed whisper.

"Verity!" exclaimed Hannah in delight. "You swore!"

"So? I'm not an absolute goody-goody, you know…Just don't tell Granny."

Soon, they heard the sound of the front door closing. Verity and Hannah glanced at each other nervously, and tiptoed into Verity's room. From there, with the door open, they could hear Mrs. Devenish speaking to someone on the telephone, but they couldn't make out what she was saying. Shortly afterward, she hung and came up to Verity's room. "It's alright, girls, you can come downstairs," she said. "He's gone, and I daresay he won't be back."

"How…?" said Hannah delightedly.

"Did you give him a fright, Granny?" asked Verity with a cheeky grin.

"I don't know what you mean by that, Verity," she said severely, as Alex and Eric joined her at the door. "I simply pointed out to Mr. Smedley that I am a magistrate, and that I have decided that the best course of action is for Alex and Hannah to be billeted with me."

Alex and Hannah beamed at each other, and both of them felt an enormous wave of relief. Eric and Verity cheered excitedly. Mrs. Devenish continued, "I also told him that if he had objections, he would need to take them up with the proper authorities, but he assured me that there would be no need for the matter to go further. I have rung the billeting officer, Mr. Simmons, to inform him of your removal. So that's that."

She looked at the four happy faces around her, and rolled her eyes. "I must have taken leave of my senses," she said. "Now, let me be quite clear about this. I want all of you on your best behavior. I'm not having any nonsense. Do you hear me, Hannah?"

"Me?" exclaimed Hannah with a tone of injured innocence. "Why pick on me?"

"Quite," said Mrs. Devenish. "Oh, and before I forget, I took the opportunity to ask Mr. Simmons about Mrs. Smith. It seems that no evacuee has been billeted to her, to his knowledge. However, he says he doesn't know her at all, so it's possible she has a child of her own. This assumes, of course, that you saw anything at all to begin with, Eric." She looked piercingly at him, and he quailed under the onslaught.

Chapter 11

ARRIVALS AND DEPARTURES

It was Sunday afternoon at the Gordons' house, and a week since the news of James' death on the battlefield in France. Black crepe hung in the windows, and the whole family dressed in black every day, except for Brandon, who had almost no black clothes. Mr. Gordon had solemnly presented him with an armband to wear.

"What's all this for?" he quietly asked Oliver, gesturing to the crepe in the front hall. Oliver was confused by the question. "Well, because James died, of course."

"Well, yeah, but…Why?"

Oliver looked lost. "I suppose…" and then he remembered what his cousin Peggy had told him when he had asked her the same question about a house on the next street. "I suppose because then everyone will know we're in mourning, and not say anything to upset us."

"Oh, I get it," said Brandon. "I'll have to pass that idea along to my Aunt Morticia…I mean, Marcia. She runs a funeral home… You know what?" he suddenly asked, "Shall we go check out the park?"

"Oh, we can't do that," Oliver said. "We're in mourning, and it's Sunday."

"Okay, okay, but let's find something to do outside. I'm going totally stir crazy in here. We could go for a walk. Where's your cousin?"

"I think she's out."

"Right. Well, hey, two guys together…How about we go look at the trains. They run on Sundays, yeah?"

"Only a Sunday service," said Oliver. "Do you really think there will be many trains, George?"

"Sure," Brandon said. "Balesworth's on the main line to the north, there's always plenty of trains, even on Sundays."

"We could collect engine numbers…" said Oliver, thoughtfully.

Brandon couldn't think of a better idea. "Sure."

"…but not on a Sunday," Oliver added. "Uncle Bob wouldn't approve."

"Oliver, would you please live a little? I mean, come on, what Mr. Gordon doesn't know won't hurt him. It's not like we're out smashing windows."

At Balesworth Station, blazing fires were lit in the waiting rooms, and the station café was doing a brisk trade in pots of tea and buttered toast. A few people waited on the platform, among them a young woman in an enormous hat and elegant laced boots, carrying an umbrella, who soon boarded the next train, entering a ladies-only carriage, along with two small boys in sailor suits. A young man with an empty sleeve pinned to his jacket stood with a friend on crutches, who was missing his right leg below the knee.

A group of soldiers in battle uniform were moping around, their kit lying on the platform. Most of the men were smoking cigarettes. A passing civilian-stopped and said, "Back to France, eh, lads? Doing your King and Country proud, you are." But the men stared at him, and he quickly walked away, embarrassed, his head down. One of the soldiers began to sing, and the rest slowly joined in:

"Pack up your troubles in your old kit bag, and smile, smile, smile…
While there's a Lucifer to light your fag, smile, boys, that's the style…
What's the use of worrying? It never was worthwhile, so…
Pack up your troubles in your old kit bag, and smile, smile, smile."

Brandon had heard the song before, in the air raid shelter in 1940. None of the singers had smiled then, either.

Brandon and Oliver took up a position on the covered bridge between the platforms, and Oliver retrieved his notebook and pencil from his jacket pocket. Brandon scanned the platforms, and almost immediately spotted a familiar face.

"Hey, Oliver?"

"Yes, George?" Oliver was opening his notebook.

"Is that your cousin down there?" He nodded toward a young woman in a black dress and hat.

"Might be…Yes, actually, I think it is. I wonder where she's going?"

"Should we go say 'hi'?" asked Brandon.

"If you care to," said Oliver politely. He was about to redeposit his notebook in his pocket, when suddenly he said "Look!" and pointed down the line toward London. A plume of white smoke announced the imminent arrival of a train.

As the engine pulled in, it hid the platform from sight. Brandon supposed that Peggy must have boarded the train. Meanwhile, Oliver was fussing beside him, because he couldn't read the engine name and number, since the train had pulled too far up the platform.

"Come on, George. Let's go and look before the train departs."

He dashed down the iron staircase, and Brandon followed at his leisure. Reaching the base of the steps, he gazed along the length of the platform ahead of him. At the far end, Peggy stood talking with a soldier. As Brandon came closer, he was astonished to realize that the soldier was black.

Oliver had already rushed up to his cousin. "Peggy! It's him, isn't it? It's your friend, isn't it?"

Peggy Gordon looked horrified, and she tried to shush Oliver as Brandon joined them.

"Er, is this, like, a bad time?" he asked, standing next to Oliver.

The shy-looking soldier with a trim moustache smiled kindly at the boys.

"You must be Oliver," he said, in an accent that Brandon couldn't quite place. "And this must be George," he said, shaking Brandon's hand.

Peggy covered her eyes briefly, then looked resigned. "Well, I suppose now is as good a time as any. I say, could we go into a waiting room? That one looks empty."

They entered the waiting room. Peggy hesitated until the door had closed, looked about, and then took the soldier's arm in hers.

"This," she announced, "is Captain Edward Braithwaite. He has asked me to marry him, and I have accepted." She gave a great smile.

Brandon was stunned by the name he had just heard.

"Is there anyone in your family called George?" he abruptly asked Captain Braithwaite.

The Captain was baffled. "No, not that I know of. Why?"

"No matter," said Brandon. "Just wondered."

On the journey back to the house, Brandon walked with Captain Braithwaite, eager to learn more about him.

He told Brandon that he was born and raised in Kingston, on the island of Jamaica. Although Jamaica was thousands of miles from England and, indeed, was close to the United States, it was part of the British Empire. When war broke out in August, 1914, Captain Braithwaite had volunteered to fight. But the War Office in London had refused, at first, to allow black people into the British army.

"But why?" asked Brandon.

"They're concerned that the Germans will think us weak for relying on so-called 'inferior' races to fight," Captain Braithwaite said sadly. "This is the sort of nonsense we're all up against, George. Have you heard of the NAACP?"

"Sure I have," Brandon said without thinking. "My dad is former branch president."

"I would like to believe that," said Braithwaite, "but you must be mistaken. The National Association for the Advancement of Colored People? In America?"

"Oh, um, *that* NAACP," said Brandon. "No, you're right, he's in the other one, you know, the National Association for...um...Art, Crafts and Painting."

"Don't think I've heard of that one, George," said Captain Braithwaite, suppressing a smile. "The National Association for the Advancement of Colored People, was founded just three years ago in America. But we need a British Empire NAACP. At least I've been allowed into the Army, although they won't send me to France. Still, it's a start."

"You want to be in the war?" said Brandon, wide-eyed. There was a long pause.

"I thought I did," said Captain Braithwaite carefully. "But I don't anymore. George, I shouldn't say this, and I won't tell Miss Gordon, of course, but..." He looked about him to be sure nobody was listening. "It's a disaster."

"Are you... Are we losing?" Brandon asked.

Captain Braithwaite gave a short, mirthless laugh. "It's probably more accurate to say that nobody is winning. Listen, I've been talking to some of the officers, back from France. The damn generals are sending infantry, even cavalry—horses, George!—against machine guns and barbed wire. We can't move, and we're dug down in deep trenches of mud. Once in a while, the orders come from behind the lines, and we send another group of brave young men to die. Men lose their faces, George. A shell hits a man, and the next thing, he's vanished, blown to bits. And we don't even know why we're there. All those stories we heard at the start of the war, about German soldiers bayoneting babies? The officers told me it's rubbish. The government and newspapers made it up."

"But suppose..." said Brandon. "I mean, suppose the Germans really did something awful. Like, like try to kill all the Jewish people? Just as an example."

"That's a little far-fetched, George. But, since you ask, I wouldn't believe anything the government or the papers told me about Germany. Not now."

Brandon had a horrible cold chill running down his back. He seemed to remember seeing something on TV about how British and American people heard that Hitler was murdering millions of Jews during World War Two, but they refused to believe it...

Oliver was now skipping ahead with Captain Braithwaite, and Brandon was walking with Peggy.

"We met in the park," said Peggy happily. "But I have waited to tell Mother and Father about him until we're sure we will be married."

"You think they're gonna be happy about this?" asked Brandon, nervously.

"Mother won't," she said. "There will be the most terrible row. Perhaps my father will be more understanding. It wasn't easy for them when they got married. My mother's family didn't want her marrying a Scotsman, you see. I suppose we hope they will both come around. Anyway, there won't be much they can do. We plan to run away to Gretna Green on Edward's next leave."

"What's that?" asked Brandon.

"Oh, it's the first village over the Scottish border. We can get married in Scotland without my parents' consent. Otherwise, of course, we would have to wait until I'm twenty-one."

"You have this all figured out, huh?" said Brandon.

"I hope so," she said uncertainly.

"But what about the war?" asked Brandon. He thought of all the returned soldiers he had seen at the hospital, with their missing limbs, and bandaged eyes, not to mention the soldiers who had never returned at all, like James.

Peggy thought for a moment and then said, with certainty, "I can't think about that, George."

Their reception at the house was worse than Brandon had feared. He heard Mrs. Gordon and her daughter arguing, with ever-rising voices, and Mr. Gordon trying, without success, to intervene. Finally, he heard Mrs. Gordon clearly announce that she would throw her daughter out of the house if she had anything to do with a colored man. Mr. Gordon again tried to add a reasonable voice, but the women ignored him. He had not been the same since James' death. He rarely said more than he had to, and spent many hours alone in his study. At meals, he barely spoke. Now, the will to argue with his wife seemed to have left him.

Brandon heard the commotion as Captain Braithwaite left the house, and Peggy Gordon ran upstairs, bursting into noisy tears. "We must get married," she was crying hysterically. "We have to."

Her mother followed her.

Brandon didn't plan to eavesdrop, but he had work to do in the anteroom next to the surgery, checking inventories and filling out orders for supplies. Peggy's room was next door, and he could hear most of the discussion, not least because, neither woman having realized he was there, they had not lowered their voices.

"You always were childish and irresponsible," shouted Mrs. Gordon. "Always thinking of yourself first, and never considering your father or me. Your brother was always dutiful, and he was a good son to us. But you...You disgust me. I wish you had never been born."

Peggy had been weeping loudly, but now she suddenly turned on her mother. "I hate you. And you can't stop me, you know. We're going to Gretna Green."

There was a pause, and Brandon imagined that Peggy already regretted what she had said. Mrs. Gordon shrieked at her, "You will do no such thing, you stupid girl...Do you really think you will be here when and if that creature returns for you? You have only one choice to make. I will find you somewhere to stay where nobody will know you, or..."

"Or what?" said Peggy.

Mrs. Gordon's voice now grew chillingly quiet. "Or I shall regard your behavior as a sign of mental deficiency and instability. I will speak to your father about having you committed to an asylum where you can be cared for properly."

Peggy gasped so loudly that Brandon could hear her. "You wouldn't...Father would never allow it."

Her mother paused, and said quietly in a voice filled with foreboding, "I could persuade him. It would be for your own good...and for ours."

The next day, Peggy was sitting in the front parlor, dressed to go out, and with an enormous traveling trunk at her side.

Brandon knocked on the door, and entered. "You alright?"

She shrugged. "I suppose so."

Brandon sat down across from her. "I heard what your mom said yesterday. I'm sorry, I know I wasn't supposed to, but I was working, and I couldn't help overhearing y'all. Was she seriously threatening to send you to a mental hospital?"

"Yes," said Peggy, not looking at him.

"Wow," said Brandon, shaking his head. "That's not where you're going, is it?"

"No," she said. "It's not. I just hope that where I am going is not just as bad."

"I'm really sorry," said Brandon, "I don't understand any of this. It's not like anything I've ever seen in...Yorkshire. I hope it all works out in the end."

Peggy gave him a grateful half-smile. "George, I may be gone for a few months. If I write to you, will you write back?"

It was an odd request, but Brandon saw no reason to refuse. "Sure. I guess. I mean, I'll try."

"Thank you," she said simply.

Ten minutes later, the taxi driver rang the doorbell, and then she was gone.

In the coming weeks, Brandon heard nothing from Peggy Gordon, or the Professor, and he began to wonder what he would do if he never made it home to Snipesville in the twenty-first century. One afternoon, he was mulling over his uncertain future while he tidied the surgery near the end of a dreadful day. There had been two extractions, four fillings, and a hideous scene with a small boy who was terrified of going to the dentist. Mary tried to tug the screaming boy up the stairs by the arm, while his mother sat in the parlor, wringing her hands. Finally, Brandon couldn't stand listening anymore, and ran downstairs.

"Mary, let me try," he said.

"Good idea. You're stronger than me, I reckon."

But Brandon had no intention of dragging the boy anywhere.

He sat down on the stairs, and spoke to him.

"Hello, I'm George. What's your name?"

"Freddy," said the boy, looking at him suspiciously.

"Have you ever been to a dentist before?" Brandon asked.

"N..n…no," the boy hiccupped.

"So why are you here?"

"My tooth hurts."

"A lot?"

The boy nodded miserably.

"If I promise not to hurt you, will you come with me?"

The boy looked skeptical, so Brandon tried again.

"I promise, we'll just look at your tooth. And if it needs to be fixed, we'll use our special fairy gas to put you to sleep. Do you know, it gives you the best dreams, just like in Peter Pan."

"Honest?" asked the boy.

"Honest," said Brandon.

"How much does gas cost?" asked the mother.

"Two shillings and sixpence," said Brandon.

"I can't afford that," said Freddy's anxious mother. "I just told him, if he's a good boy and gets it over with, I'll buy him some sweeties later."

Brandon figured that Freddy had already had enough "sweeties," judging from the state of his teeth. And he didn't feel like extracting a child's tooth without anesthetics.

He said, "Look, we have a special today: Free gas with every tooth extraction for all children under 11." He reckoned Mr. Gordon wouldn't mind so long as he took the money from his own allowance. Freddy and his mother both looked very relieved.

"And first, if you like, I will show you how our special chair works. It can go up and down."

"And round and round?" the boy asked.

"Yes, that's right. Wanna come see?" He offered a hand, and Freddy took it.

Freddy's tooth was in bad shape, but the nitrous oxide helped. He turned out to be remarkably calm once he was in the dentist's chair. Now, Brandon swept the surgery, and turned out the gas lamp. The last patient had left, and Mr. Gordon had gone to town on business.

"Letter for you, George," came Mary's call from downstairs.

The writing on the envelope was unfamiliar, and there was no return address, but that, he had learned, was normal in England. He opened it, and was surprised to see that the writing on the letter was different from that on the envelope.

It was from Peggy. She was staying at an address in Bedfordshire, the next county. There was, she wrote, no need to reply, and she begged him not to tell anyone, including Oliver, about the letter. Her message was brief. She wrote, "Captain Braithwaite was killed in action two weeks ago."

Chapter 12
REUNIONS AND REVELATIONS

Now that Alex and Hannah were members of Mrs. Devenish's household, they were expected to accompany her to church every Sunday.

The Friday before their first church service, Mrs. Devenish took both kids to pick out some clothes from a collection of used garments assembled by the ladies of the WVS and the Women's Institute. Hannah was shocked to be offered only secondhand clothes, and said so. Taking her firmly by the arm, Mrs. Devenish pulled her aside. She sternly lectured Hannah on the need for sacrifice in wartime, and the government's campaign to "make do and mend" clothes. Most clothing factories, she said, were now making supplies for the troops, not pretty dresses for little girls.

Hannah sulked a little, but she managed to find an acceptable dress in light blue. It was very plain-looking, she thought, and rather drab, but that was true of all the clothes, and at least it didn't look totally sad.

Alex, on the other hand, was happy to accept whatever Mrs. Devenish could find to fit him, even though there were several holes in the shorts which she darned later that evening. All the same, as the kids walked to church, Hannah thought her brother looked smart in his blue pants, white shirt, and matching blue sweater.

"What I don't understand," said Hannah quietly to Alex, as they walked behind Eric and Verity, who in turn walked behind Mrs. Devenish, "is why Mrs. D. bothers to go to church every Sunday. I mean, the Archers never did, and lots of girls at school say they only go at Christmas."

"Maybe Mrs. D. goes to keep an eye on God. She can't much like the competition." Alex laughed at his own joke.

"Yeah," said Hannah, who hadn't listened. "But most Christians I know in California talk about Jesus all the time. Mrs. D. never even mentions him. I've never seen her open a Bible. There's no religious stuff in the house, like crosses. She smokes, and she drinks…"

"She does?" said Alex, astonished.

"Well, sometimes. There's a whisky bottle in the kitchen, you know, and the level is slowly going down."

"Slowly, yeah, but that makes sense. Kind of like Grandma and Grandpa, or Dad…They all like a drink, but they're not drunks."

"You know," continued Hannah, still not listening to her brother, "I told her we don't usually go to church at home, and that we have to lipsync the hymns and prayers at our school assemblies every morning, because we don't know them. She's all," and here Hannah gave a passable imitation of Mrs. Devenish, looking over imaginary glasses and wagging her finger at Alex, "'As Christians, you children must take your religious education more seriously.' So I go, how do you know we're Christians? I mean, we could be Muslims, or Wiccans, or whatever…"

"Yeah, well, I bet that set her off," said Alex with a smile. "You know, I don't think we know what counts as Christian here. I guess it's kind of like the difference between the Masses that Grandma and Dad sometimes drag us to, and that wacky religious stuff that your friend Britney's mom is into, and all the no alcohol stuff that Brandon's church preaches. From what I can figure out at school, everyone here assumes you're a Christian unless your parents say otherwise."

"Yeah, maybe," said Hannah, but she didn't sound convinced.

"Why is this church so new?" Hannah asked Mrs. Devenish as they drew near to the building. "I kind of like the other church better, you know, with the stained glass and tower, and stuff."

"Balesworth has grown a great deal in recent years," said Mrs. Devenish. "It's much larger than it was when my husband and I moved into our house in 1907. The old parish church became quite unsuitable for a large congregation, and the parish was divided in two. But, you know, I rather like this new church. It's very modern, isn't it?"

"Yes, but that's the problem," said Hannah, "That's kind of boring. What's the point of an English church if it isn't cute?"

"I doubt very much that God sees it that way," said Mrs. Devenish wryly. "In any case, you should know that St. Swithins Church, while beautiful, is not terribly comfortable. There are no lavatories…"

"You mean toilets?" interrupted Hannah.

"I do," she continued, "and it's absolutely freezing in the pews, especially in the winter. I don't like to complain, of course, but I didn't object when I learned I was to belong to the new parish…"

Just then, Verity, who had been walking with the boys, rushed up on Mrs. Devenish's right, and took her grandmother's gloved hand.

"Mind if I join you two?" she asked cheerily. "The boys are talking about aeroplanes." She pulled a face, and Mrs. Devenish smiled at her.

Suddenly, to Hannah's surprise, Mrs. Devenish grasped her hand, too. Hannah was torn between feeling a bit silly to be holding hands with an old lady and being rather pleased. The three of them walked hand in hand to the church, where the vicar, dressed in his vestments, greeted them at the door.

The Church of England service was surprisingly like the Catholic Masses they had attended: Alex and Hannah simply copied the others as they kneeled, sat up, and stood. The service lasted about an hour, and they might have found it extremely boring, but Mrs. Devenish never once allowed them to become bored: She nagged the kids constantly.

"Do stop fidgeting, Hannah," she murmured, as Hannah played with her cloth handkerchief. When Hannah resumed folding it into a smaller and smaller lump, she suddenly found it taken from her, and deposited in Mrs. Devenish's substantial purse.

Glancing to her left, Hannah saw Eric and Verity sitting bolt upright in the pew, gazing intently at the pulpit while the vicar gave his sermon. Hannah giggled, as she realized that Eric was actually staring into space, daydreaming. Suddenly a gloved hand gently but firmly grabbed the top of her head, and turned her face forward again. Hannah almost protested, but then she saw several adults glaring at her, and she changed her mind.

Alex fared no better. He gradually slid down the hard wooden pew, until Mrs. Devenish hissed "Sit up!' at him, and yanked him straight up by the collar, almost throttling him. When he began to make up his own words during the singing of *Bread of Heaven*, she smartly slapped the back of his head, without lifting her eyes from the hymnal or missing a note.

But when time came for communion, Mrs. Devenish was shocked to see Alex and Hannah get to their feet. "Neither of you is confirmed," she whispered urgently. "Sit down at once." They gladly did as they were told.

As Mrs. Devenish was returning from the altar, Hannah noticed her give a sudden surprised look of recognition to someone in the congregation, followed by a small smile. Hannah tried to see who it was, but she couldn't figure it out.

After the service ended, Mrs. Devenish and the kids paused at the church door to greet the vicar. He was a young man, in his late thirties, with a receding hairline and a gentle smile.

"And who might you be, eh?" he asked Alex and Hannah kindly.

"These children are Alexander and Hannah Day, Vicar," said Mrs. Devenish, before they had a chance to answer for themselves. "They are my new evacuees, but I've known them since they arrived at their first billet in Balesworth, and we have become friends. Haven't we, children?"

Hannah looked at her with amused disbelief. "Well, yeah, I guess that kind of describes it. Sort of."

Mrs. Devenish glanced at her warningly and said under her breath, "That will do, Hannah."

"Now, Vicar," she said more loudly. "About that sermon of yours."

The vicar blenched. "Yes, Mrs. Devenish?"

"It's all very well for you to twitter on about the need to raise funds for the diocese to replace the church roof over at St. Swithin's, but I must say that I find it in remarkably poor taste... Run along, children, I'll catch up with you...Vicar, don't you think that in the middle of a war, the money would be better spent on our Spitfire fund?"

"Good old Granny," said Verity, laughing, as the kids walked away. "The poor vicar is terrified of her. I've seen him run a mile in the other direction when he sees her coming up the High Street."

"You two," was her opening salvo from the front door.

"You two, Alexander and Hannah Day, simply must learn to behave properly, and especially in church. I feel like poor Professor Higgins, what with Eric and now the pair of you."

"What does that mean?" asked Alex casually, as he and Hannah stepped into the hall to see what Mrs. Devenish was fussing about.

"What it means, Alexander, is that I feel rather like a character in a play by George Bernard Shaw, who lives not too far from here, by the way. The play is called *Pygmalion*, and it is about a professor who trains a Cockney guttersnipe to speak and act like a lady."

"Oh, you mean *My Fair Lady*," said Hannah. "That was an awesome movie. I saw it on DVD with my Grandma once." She began to sing the song to a hip-hop beat, "I coulda danced all night, I coulda danced all night..."

Mrs. Devenish shook her head. "Hannah, that's ridiculous. I don't know what you are talking about. Indeed, that pretty much sums up my experience with you two. Anyone would think you had just arrived with Flash Gordon in a spaceship from the planet Mars."

"Hey, Mrs. D.," laughed Alex, "how do you know we didn't, huh? Did Hannah tell you where she stores her antennae when she's out in public?" Hannah giggled.

"Oh, good grief, what a lot of bosh you two talk," said Mrs. Devenish. She pushed past them into the kitchen, but Hannah saw her suppressing a smile. "Come on, I have to finish making the lunch, and I need all of you to help."

Lunch was roasted pork, with roasted potatoes that were crisp, buttery and golden on the outside, white and fluffy on the inside. Mrs. Devenish also made sliced boiled carrots, and chunky, tart applesauce with apples from the old tree in the garden. And there were Brussels sprouts.

Hannah tasted one of those at Mrs. Devenish's insistence, and loudly declared it to be disgusting. Mrs. Devenish responded by adding two more to her plate. "And I expect to see that plate cleaned before you leave the table," she said.

Shortly after the meal began, Mrs. Devenish got up to check the oven, where an apple crumble was baking for dessert. Hannah thought she wasn't looking, and quickly lifted the sprouts off her own plate, stuffing them in the pocket of her dress. The other kids saw her, and started giggling. They soon stopped when Mrs. Devenish turned to look at them suspiciously. Grabbing a spoon, she took two more sprouts from the tureen, and dropped them onto Hannah's plate.

"Go and empty your pockets, young woman, before you get a stain on your dress. You can put them in the bucket I keep for Mr. Johnson's pigs."

"How did you know?" said Hannah, agog, as she stood up.

"I didn't," Mrs. Devenish replied with a wry smile.

Alex looked at Hannah and mimed "Duh…"

"That will do, Alexander," Mrs. Devenish said. "I haven't seen you eat your Brussels sprouts yet, either." Alex looked appalled. The other kids smirked, until Mrs. Devenish said, "All of you can wipe those silly smiles off your faces. Each and every one of you is fussy about some food or other. You are all pests."

After lunch, during which Hannah managed to finish the sprouts with the aid of the potatoes and several glasses of water, Mrs. Devenish pulled out a letter from the pocket of her apron, which was hanging on a hook on the kitchen door.

"I received a letter yesterday that concerns all of you except Alex," she said, sitting down at the kitchen table, and putting on her reading glasses. "It's from Mrs. Smith. Let me refresh your memory: She is the unfortunate woman whose window you broke, and for whom you caused so much trouble. She insists that she does not wish the three of you to make a personal apology, but would prefer I simply send her a postal order for the amount of eleven shillings, sixpence ha'penny, which is apparently the payment she requires."

"Cool!" said Hannah. "That's nice of her. See, I told you guys it was no big…"

She was suddenly silenced by one of the looks from Mrs. Devenish that Alex had named "the death rays from hell."

"I, however, have begged to differ," said Mrs. Devenish, "I've written back to Mrs. Smith to ask her to reconsider. The three of you will apologize to her, and, as far as I am concerned, that is final."

She tucked the letter back in the envelope, and placed it on the table in front of her. "Now, I have some rather more pleasant news for everyone. I ran into old Mrs. Lewis at church today. I was surprised to see her there, but she said," and here she coughed, "she said that the roof is leaking too badly at St. Swithins for her to attend communion there." Verity gave a small smile, remembering the conversation between her grandmother and the Vicar.

"And Mrs. Lewis would be....?" asked Hannah in her attitudey voice.

"I beg your pardon?" sputtered an offended Mrs. Devenish.

"You never learn," breathed Alex in a singsong to his sister.

"Um, sorry," Hannah said. "Who is Mrs. Lewis....please?"

"That's better," Mrs. Devenish said with a nod. "Mrs. Lewis is an old lady to whom I pay occasional visits. She lives on the outskirts of the town. In fact," she added casually, as though it were an afterthought, "she just happens to be the next door neighbor of Mrs. Smith. She has kindly invited me to afternoon tea today, along with Hannah and Verity."

"Oh, joy," Hannah muttered, sarcastically. "Joyous occasion," she corrected herself to say, seeing a flash of annoyance cross Mrs. Devenish's face.

"You, my girl, are pushing your luck," said Mrs. Devenish with a sour look, as she got to her feet, and pulled on her apron. "Come and help me with the washing up. You can dry." With that, she handed Hannah a dish towel.

At the same time, but on a very different Sunday, in 1915, Brandon had reached his destination. After a ten minute walk from the railway station in the small town in Bedfordshire, and three stops to ask passersby for directions, he had found the address in Peggy Gordon's letter. It was a large house, two stories, with a window on each side of the door, above and below, and a gravel drive-way. Brandon hesitantly knocked at the door, which was opened by an elderly maid, whose grey hair flew out from under her cap. "Oh," she said in surprise, looking him up and down.

"Er, good afternoon. I'm here to see Miss Gordon?"

"May I tell her who's calling?"

"My name's George Clark." He handed her one of the visiting cards he had had printed in a shop on Balesworth High Street. This seemed to impress her.

"Very good, sir. Please come in, and I'll let Mrs. Hughes know you're here."

"Hey, um... Mrs. Hughes? I'm sorry, it's Miss Gordon I'm here to see."

"Yes, sir. This is her house, and Miss Gordon's her guest."

"Oh, okay," said Brandon, uneasily.

He waited awkwardly in the hall of the house, until the maid returned to inform him that Mrs. Hughes would receive him in the drawing room.

Brandon hadn't counted on this. He suddenly felt an attack of nerves, as he followed the maid through to the living room.

An old lady, wearing elaborately-arranged hair and a long dark green dress, sat stiffly on the sofa. She looked Brandon up and down as he entered the room. "Master Clark, is it? I'm Mrs. Hughes. Please state your business," she said, without inviting him to sit down.

"I'm an apprentice to Mr. Gordon, a dentist in Balesworth, ma'am."

The woman's eyes crinkled, and he thought she would smile, but she seemed to catch herself.

"No, Master Clark, I did not ask your profession. What I meant was, what is your business here?"

Brandon was speechless.

She finally said with the barest trace of a smile, "Cat got your tongue, Master Clark?"

Now he was even more confused. But he suddenly felt courageous, or possibly desperate.

"Ma'am, I'm just here to see Miss Gordon. I can come back if she's out, or something, but I took a train from Balesworth and it cost me a ton of money, so I'd like to see her today if I can. I'm a friend of hers."

"I'm afraid that Miss Gordon has not mentioned that you would be calling."

"Well," said Brandon, "It's kind of a surprise, my being here."

Mrs. Hughes looked at him with piercing blue eyes. She said, slowly, "You say you are a friend of Miss Gordon's?"

"Yes, ma'am." Brandon thought he had made that clear, but adults always seemed to take forever to hear answers, even when you do give them.

"Forgive my asking, but are you a relation to her?"

"Nooo…" said Brandon, wondering where this was leading.

Suddenly, he heard a woman's laughter from behind him, and he whirled around, expecting to see Peggy.

Instead, standing in the doorway was a tall woman of about thirty, with bobbed brown hair. She was wearing a white nurse's dress that ended at mid-calf, with a broad white belt around the middle, and a red cross on the breast.

"I'm sorry," the younger woman said to Brandon with a smile. "My mother assumes that all colored people must be related to one another."

"*Really*, Elizabeth!" Mrs. Hughes looked very annoyed with her daughter.

"Well, honestly, it's true, Mother. Poor young Master Clark must be wondering what on earth he's walked into."

She offered a hand to Brandon to shake. "I'm Mrs. Devenish. Miss Gordon is one of my patients, and she is staying here as our guest until she can be admitted."

"Patient?" asked Brandon, with alarm. "Is she okay?"

"Well, of course she is," said Mrs. Devenish. "It's perfectly natural, you know."

Mrs. Hughes interrupted with a cough. "Elizabeth, please. *Pas devant le garçon.*"

"Mother…" said Mrs. Devenish in a warning voice. Brandon was confused. That was French, he was sure of it, but what did the old lady say?

"Mother, why don't I make some tea, and then Master Clark and I can leave you in peace? We can sit out in the garden while we wait for Miss Gordon." She turned to Brandon. "She's taking a walk to the park with my daughter, and I'm afraid they may be some time. It's a lovely day today, and, you know, I could use some fresh air myself before I return to work this evening."

Mrs. Hughes looked slightly shocked, and said to her daughter, in a voice laden with concern, "Elizabeth, is that really wise?"

"My mother," said Mrs. Devenish, looking at Mrs. Hughes, but speaking to Brandon, "is rather old fashioned, and thinks that tongues will wag if an attractive widow like me is seen in the exclusive company of a handsome young chap like you." She gave him a wink. Brandon was so mortified, he didn't know where to look, but he also took an instant liking to young Mrs. Devenish.

Mrs. Devenish turned back to her mother. "Honestly, Mother, this lad is young enough to be my son. Aren't you, George?"

Brandon laughed. "Yep, I'm twelve. But please don't tell Miss Gordon. Her dad thinks I'm old enough to be an apprentice."

"I'll bet he doesn't, actually," Mrs. Devenish said with an impish smile. "You don't look anything like fourteen to me. He must just have been desperate for the help. Come on, George, let's go and make tea. We'll leave you in peace, Mother."

Mrs. Hughes gave an exasperated sigh, and shook her head in despair.

The maid tried to argue with Mrs. Devenish that she ought to be making the tea, but the younger woman dismissed her with a wave of her hand. "I am quite capable of boiling water, Flora. For heaven's sake, stop fussing."

Brandon stood by while she filled the kettle, and set it on the huge, black-leaded kitchen range in the fireplace. "Aren't you going to give me a hand, George?" she scolded in jest. "Come on, there's the teapot and the tea caddy.

Put in one spoonful for each of us, and one for the pot." Brandon happily did as he was told.

"A man who can make tea! Well, that's one for the books," she joked.

"Oh, hey, give me a break" said Brandon, mildly offended. "I help my mom make sweet tea all the time."

"Sweet tea? What on earth do you mean?" asked Mrs. Devenish.

"We mix hot tea with a whole heap of sugar, then we pour cold water and ice into it. It's great on a hot day."

"Ice? Good gracious, where does your mother find ice?"

"Oh, we've got an icemaker at home…" he said, his voice suddenly trailing off as he saw her face.

"George, now I know you're just pulling my leg. An ice-maker indeed."

"No, really," he protested. "Look, I'll give you the recipe, in case you want to try it sometime."

"Where on earth would I get ice? Unless I snap off some icicles from the front of the house in January."

"Hey, that would work," said Brandon.

"Well, perhaps, but, George, who would want a drink with ice in it, especially in January? My teeth are freezing just thinking about it."

Someone rang at the front door, and Flora answered it. Suddenly, Mrs. Devenish's head jerked up, as she heard the voice of whoever had just arrived.

"Oh, Good God," she exhaled with a frown. "Surely not…"

She hurriedly grabbed the tea tray. "Come on, George, let's go outside," she said, hustling him into the garden. Whoever it was who had turned up, Brandon reckoned, it most likely wasn't Miss Gordon, and it certainly wasn't a welcome visitor.

A few minutes later, as Brandon and Mrs. Devenish sat at the garden table sipping tea, Flora appeared at the kitchen door. "Begging your pardon, Miss Elizabeth? Your mother asked me to let you know that Mrs. Lewis has called to see you, and would you please come into the drawing room?"

Mrs. Devenish looked unimpressed. "Kindly remind my mother, Flora, that I already have a guest, and that I'm entertaining *him* in the garden." She gave a rather naughty smile, Brandon thought. "But if Mrs. Lewis would care to come here, I will receive her."

As Mrs. Devenish leaned forward to sip her tea, Brandon was sure he heard her mutter something to herself. It sounded like "What a bloody nuisance." Surely he was mistaken?

"Very good, Miss Elizabeth," said Flora in long-suffering tones that clearly said she didn't think it was very good at all.

The woman who soon entered the garden was small, thin, and had grey hair swept up under a grand purple hat decorated with long feathers.

"There you are, Elizabeth," she announced as she made her way toward Brandon and Mrs. Devenish. "I haven't heard from you in a very long time."

"Yes, here I am,' Mrs. Devenish sang sarcastically under her breath. More loudly, she said, "Good afternoon, Mrs. Lewis. What brings you here? Oh, let me introduce this young man. This is Master George Clark. George, this is Mrs. Lewis. She is a friend of my mother's."

"And a friend of yours, too, I hope, Elizabeth," said Mrs. Lewis, taking a seat at the table. Mrs. Devenish didn't say anything, and there was an awkward silence.

"So, nice day today, huh?" said Brandon, trying to lighten up the mood. He was ignored.

"Well now, Elizabeth," said Mrs. Lewis, "I was passing on my way home to Balesworth from a meeting of our Board, and I thought I would pay you a call to see if I might enlist your help. As you know, the Women's Suffrage Association has, in common with all like-minded societies, decided to suspend our political activities for the cause of votes for women for the duration of the war. Even Mrs. Pankhurst and the Women's Social and Political Union have ceased their ridiculous campaign of wanton destruction of property…"

"Yes," said Mrs. Devenish impatiently, "I think we're all well aware of that." Brandon wasn't, but he kept quiet.

"No need to snap, Elizabeth," Mrs. Lewis rebuked her with a glare. Mrs. Devenish seemed a little abashed, and she looked away to gaze into the distance.

"Now, as I was saying….We have decided that our energies should instead be expended on the war effort. Women are now taking the places of our brave men serving their country in France, serving capably in hundreds of positions of responsibility, as bus conductors, clerks, shop assistants, and in so many other walks of life. We show our patriotism thereby, while establishing the rightness of the cause of women's equality."

Mrs. Devenish stared at her. "Again, Mrs. Lewis, there is no cause to exhaust yourself with long speeches. I am well aware of that, too."

Mrs. Lewis looked at her coldly. "Perhaps, Elizabeth, but why don't you allow me to tell you why I am here?"

Brandon thought Mrs. Devenish was about to say "because life is too short," but then decided against it.

Looking coolly at the older woman, Mrs. Devenish casually reached into the pocket of her nurse's uniform, and pulled out cigarettes and matches. Brandon couldn't help noticing that she was carefully watching Mrs. Lewis' reaction. On cue, Mrs. Lewis looked stunned, as the younger woman lit a cigarette. Noting Mrs. Lewis' shock with a satisfied expression, Mrs. Devenish exhaled a large cloud of smoke, shaking out her match and dropping it onto the lawn. With some effort, Mrs. Lewis recovered herself.

"I am here today, Elizabeth, because it seems that too many young women still need encouragement to put their efforts into the cause of victory over Germany. I would like you to work with me on a new campaign, to urge young women to commit themselves absolutely to working for victory."

"No," said Mrs. Devenish flatly, exhaling another cloud of cigarette smoke from the side of her mouth.

"I beg your pardon?" gasped Mrs. Lewis, recoiling as if she had been slapped.

"George," said Mrs. Devenish to Brandon, "I'm sorry to have to ask this of you, but would you mind terribly making yourself scarce for a few minutes? There's a very comfortable seat over there. I'll join you shortly."

From his vantage point across the lawn, Brandon tried to look like he wasn't eavesdropping, while trying hard to catch every word. It soon became easy for him to listen in, as the conversation quickly grew very heated.

Mrs. Devenish, it seemed, was not at all interested in helping with the war effort. Brandon heard her say "pointless bloodbath," and Mrs. Lewis, horrified, reply with "patriotic duty."

Soon, both women were on their feet, and Mrs. Devenish was shouting at Mrs. Lewis so loudly that not only could Brandon hear every word, but, he reckoned, so could the entire street.

"May I remind you that I am no longer, if indeed I ever was, some flibbertigibbet to be ordered about by my mother, or by you. I am the widow of a soldier killed in battle, a nurse, and the mother of two daughters. And I am telling you that this war is shameful. I won't take any part in any ridiculous scheme to assist the slaughter in France, and neither should you."

Mrs. Lewis drew herself up. Brandon thought she looked quite formidable, even though her head barely reached Mrs. Devenish's shoulder. "How *dare* you speak to me like this? I'm sorry for your loss, Elizabeth, and I am also sorry that you have reached this conclusion. I shall take your refusal as final. But know that I am very angry with you for your discourtesy toward me. You have given me great offense, and you may be sure that I will tell your mother of your conduct."

"I can't imagine why you would do any such thing," said Mrs. Devenish furiously. "My conduct is my own affair. I'm a grown woman."

"Is that so? In that case, you would do well to act as one," said Mrs. Lewis. "All I see before me is the same spoilt, silly little girl who caused me so much trouble ten years ago. However, since you wish me to leave you be, I shall do so. I shall not trouble you from this day forward. Good day to you." And with that, she swept away.

As soon as Mrs. Lewis had stormed into the house, Mrs. Devenish sank into her seat and put her head in her hands. Brandon came to join her. "She's kind of a pill, isn't she?" he said sympathetically.

Mrs. Devenish's head snapped up and she gave him a withering look. "George, I will thank you to keep your opinion of my visitor to yourself."

He shrank back from her, but he couldn't help noticing, to his embarrassment and surprise, that she was crying.

To Brandon's relief, Peggy Gordon chose that moment to enter the garden, accompanied by a little girl of about eight.

"Hello, Mrs. Devenish…. And George! What are you doing here?"

"Thought I'd come to visit," said Brandon, shyly. He couldn't help noticing how fat Peggy had become since he had last seen her, especially around the middle.

"You're a colored boy," announced the little girl.

Mrs. Devenish had discreetly recovered her composure, and she now spoke severely to her daughter. "Edwina, I think that's obvious to everyone, but it's extremely rude of you to mention it. George, this is my eldest child, Edwina. Edwina, this is Master George Clark."

Brandon nodded to the little girl, who quickly lost interest in him, and rushed off to find her grandmother.

On a tray in the kitchen, Mrs. Devenish quickly placed clean cups, saucers, plates, teapot, and all the other paraphernalia of tea-making, as well as two slices of something she called seed cake. It was a dry-looking vanilla cake with tiny caraway seeds dotted throughout. She handed the tray to Brandon. "Why don't you and Miss Gordon take tea outside? I should probably wake my other daughter from her nap before I leave for work."

In the garden, Peggy poured out tea for Brandon.

"Thanks for coming, George. How's my father?"

"Not too good," Brandon admitted. "He doesn't say much more to me than he has to. Do you think I offended him?"

"I shouldn't think so," said Peggy. "He's just upset about James, I expect. It's broken his heart, what with James being the boy. And," she paused, and swallowed hard, "with me gone."

"Why did you leave? I mean, if you're sick, like that lady said, shouldn't you come home, so we can look after you?"

"Sick? What made you think I'm sick?" she asked in surprise.

"That lady said you were one of her patients," said Brandon, furrowing his brow.

Peggy looked at him with something like pity. "You mean you haven't already guessed what I'm doing here? You're not that young, surely? "

Brandon honestly didn't have a clue. And then he looked across the table, and thought again how.. fat... she... was... Oh.

"You know now, I see," she said. "Mrs. Devenish tells me that all over England, young women are having babies without husbands. They're soldiers' babies. I'm not alone, George. Well, actually, I am alone. That's the problem. My baby will be an illegitimate child, and it will be colored. I can't keep it, of course. It will probably be sent to an orphanage. I've already signed the papers. Just as well, really, I mean, I don't feel much like a mother."

"But..." Brandon was shocked. "But, why can't you keep the baby?"

"Surely you must understand why? My parents are horrified. My mother cannot, she says, accept a colored grandchild."

"What about your father?" He was thinking of kindly, tolerant Mr. Gordon.

"Father doesn't mind as much about the baby being colored, I reckon. But he takes a dim view of it being born out of wedlock. I don't know why that's more important to him, but there it is."

"What about you?" he asked.

"They're paying for me to stay here with Mrs. Hughes, and then for the nursing home, where Mrs. Devenish works. And after that, Mother has arranged for me to take a secretarial course in London, to keep me out of Balesworth for a year or two more."

"But is that what you want?" asked Brandon.

"Don't be stupid. What do you think?" she asked angrily, her eyes full of tears. "Do you really think I have any choice? My parents would cut me off, and nobody wants to give a job to a girl with a baby and no education or training to speak of. I certainly would never find a good husband. I would be lucky to find a husband at all. George, I can't believe you think it's that easy."

"I'm sorry," said Brandon. "It's just...Man, that is so unfair."

"Well," said Peggy, "Life is unfair, as Mrs. Devenish likes to say. She should know: She has lost her husband in the war. George, I see how life is in this house, and I can't imagine how she manages to live with her mother. Mrs. Hughes is a kind lady in her own way, but she is disgusted by everything that's happened to England since the death of Queen Victoria. I can only imagine what it would be like if I came back to Balesworth with a baby and tried to make a home with my parents. And how would my mother treat her grand-child? This way, at least I get to make a fresh start. And so does the baby.

"So you see," she said, "It's probably all for the best. I really don't want a baby, you know. It's Edward I want. And I can't have him." Her chin trembled.

Suddenly, she put her head in her hands. "Oh, everything's a mess because of this stupid, stupid war. Everyone acts as though it's something to be proud of, with their silly flags and songs. Nobody seems to care that half the boys who go never come back, and the ones who do, have lost arms, and legs, and eyes, and faces, and sometimes their minds. We act as though nothing is wrong, and everything's wrong. Everything's wrong." And with that, she broke into sobs. Brandon was embarrassed. What had he done to deserve two weeping women in one afternoon? But then he remembered what the Professor had told him about his mission. Quietly, he got up, walked around the table, and put his arm around Peggy.

From the dining room window, Mrs. Hughes was watching. She called to her daughter, who was standing in front of the hall mirror, adjusting her nurse's cap with bobby pins. "Elizabeth? Elizabeth! Come quickly…. I told you she was a girl of low moral character…Look at this."

Mrs. Devenish wearily joined her mother at the window.

"There, you see?" said Mrs. Hughes triumphantly. "That's how she got her-self into trouble in the first place."

"Oh, for heaven's sake, Mother," said Mrs. Devenish. "Don't be absurd, and come away from that window at once."

Her mother said stiffly, "I'll thank you not to shout at me in my own house, Elizabeth Hughes. If your father were alive…"

"Yes, Mother," Mrs. Devenish interrupted in a bored tone, as she moved toward the door. "So you're always telling me."

"And I will thank you not to use that tone of voice with me, young woman!" Mrs. Hughes said loudly to her daughter's departing back.

In the garden, Brandon returned to his seat.

"Do you know what Edward and I were going to call the baby if he's a boy?" Peggy asked him, wiping her eyes. "Well, it's a coincidence, but we planned to call him 'George.' Just like you."

Brandon tried to wrap his head around this.

"George Braithwaite, huh? Yeah. I like that."

"Not Braithwaite, I'm afraid," she said. "Illegitimate children always have the name of the mother."

"I wouldn't be so sure of that," said a firm voice from behind them. It was Mrs. Devenish, who had come to wish them goodbye. "It depends upon who registers the birth. And as it happens, that job at the hospital often falls to me."

Later on that Sunday afternoon in 1940, led by Mrs. Devenish, Verity and Hannah walked well beyond the other side of town to visit Mrs. Lewis. As they walked, Hannah quietly asked her friend, "So exactly who is this lady we're going to see?"

"Some old bat," Verity whispered. "She and Granny knew each other in the women's suffrage days, from when Granny was only about sixteen, I think, maybe younger. Mrs. Lewis was important in the Women's Suffrage Association for years, practically since the Stone Age. Mummy told me once that she and Granny were close at one time. But there was some sort of falling out between them, and Granny won't say what. Granny still pays a call on Mrs. Lewis once in a while for old time's sake, but they really don't get on. When I went along last year, I had the impression that Granny's quite afraid of her."

Hannah laughed delightedly. "This, I have to see!"

"I thought she was rather sweet, actually, but Granny says that's because old age softens people. But, oh, Hannah, I do hate this sort of thing. Having to get dressed up, and minding my manners, it's all such a frightful nuisance. And it's not as though anyone will say anything to us, it's all 'children should be seen and not heard.' We can only hope that the grub is decent. She had some rather nice cream cakes for us last year, but what with the war and it being Sunday, I don't expect we'll have anything like that."

She was right. They soon found themselves sitting silently and awkwardly on a very upright sofa, with cups and saucers balanced on their knees, being presented with slices of crumbly seed cake.

"No, thank you," said Verity primly, when Mrs. Lewis offered her a piece.

"Just a small slice for Verity, please," said her grandmother, shooting Verity a warning look.

Seeing the death rays aimed at Verity, Hannah hurriedly said, "Same for me, please." The cake turned out to have a very pleasant if rather odd flavor, vanilla lightly scented with caraway seeds. But the texture, as with all the cakes she had eaten in England, was dry as dust, and it would take Hannah two cups of tea to choke it down.

"I trust you are keeping well?" Mrs. Devenish asked Mrs. Lewis. "Mrs. Miller at the Women's Institute often speaks of you."

"Oh, yes," said Mrs. Lewis, who appeared to be in her mid-eighties. "She is very kind to me. She often comes with flowers from her garden, or some of her scones."

"I expect you enjoy her visits."

"I certainly do enjoy having visitors," said Mrs. Lewis. "And I would have no objections to seeing *you* a little more often than I do, Elizabeth."

Mrs. Devenish looked uncomfortable, and muttered something about her pressing duties. The two girls exchanged amused glances.

"I'm quite sure that having three evacuees on your hands, not to mention Verity on the weekends, must not leave you a great deal of time," said Mrs. Lewis. "Although these girls don't seem to be any trouble at all, I must say. You behave quite splendidly, don't you, my dears?"

Verity and Hannah smiled ingratiatingly.

"Yes, quite unlike the dreadful hooligans I saw breaking Mrs. Smith's window, as I mentioned to you after church," Mrs. Lewis added, to the immediate discomfort of her three visitors. "I told that young constable who came after I telephoned the police, one wonders about young people nowadays, doesn't one? I never approved of the suffragettes, as you know, because I thought they lowered standards of decent and polite behavior, and now the chickens have come home to roost. Have you ever had those three window-breakers come up before you in magistrate's court?"

"Oh, believe me, Mrs. Lewis," said Mrs. Devenish, glancing dourly at Hannah and Verity, who were desperately trying not to catch her eye, "they really wouldn't want to come to my attention."

"Well, I should hope not," Mrs. Lewis said. "Did I mention that two of those wicked children were girls? What on earth is the world coming to? When I used to march for the vote, I never dreamed that we…"

And then she looked at the girls again.

"It was you two," she pronounced heavily.

There was an appalled silence.

"Yes," said Mrs. Devenish, embarrassed. "I'm sorry to say it was."

"Well, really!" said Mrs. Lewis in a voice so shocked that it made Hannah want to curl up under the tea table and die. "Elizabeth, is there an explanation for this? You're a magistrate, for heavens sake, and you know how hard we had to fight for women to be appointed to the bench. Can't you control the young people in your own care?"

"Not all the time," said Mrs. Devenish. "Nor would I want to. After all, Mrs. Lewis, surely that's the thing we're fighting against when we fight the Nazis? All that conformity and constant surveillance of everyone's behavior, it's so…Well,

I fail to see how it is in accordance with our great British commitment to freedom."

"Please don't make speeches at me, Elizabeth," said Mrs. Lewis quietly.

"Well….Be that as it may, I do assure you, Mrs. Lewis, that this won't happen again. As you know, these girls and my evacuee boy were caught red-handed. I daresay they have learned their lesson. Constable Ellsworth brought the matter directly to me, and I gave all three of them a good hiding. They have all helped to polish the church brasses to pay for the cost of replacing the window, and we shall pay a visit to Mrs. Smith as soon as it proves convenient for her, for the children to make their apology."

"I am glad to hear it," said Mrs. Lewis sternly, with a look at the girls, who were staring at the floor, mortified by the turn the conversation had taken. "You deserved to be severely punished for such wickedness, both of you."

Then she paused thoughtfully. "I must say, Elizabeth, that I really expected better from you than to keep this quiet because it was your children who were the culprits. You ought to have had them brought up before your court, yes, even Verity. You should never have shown favoritism like that, but made an example of them instead…."

While Mrs. Lewis told her off, Mrs. Devenish stared into space, looking extremely chastened. Hannah felt terrible, especially knowing that Mrs. Devenish had acted to protect her and the others. When Mrs. Lewis had had her say, there was a long and very awkward pause. Hannah kept trying to tell herself that it didn't matter what this old lady thought, but it wasn't working. She began to wish that there was a polite way to run screaming from the room.

Then suddenly, Mrs. Devenish's eyes grew wide, and she looked slyly at Mrs. Lewis. "I seem to recall you shielding a young person who broke a window. Back in nineteen hundred and five or thereabouts. Do you remember?"

"Of course I remember," said Mrs. Lewis, tutting. "But that was different. I acted for the greater good. Your childish behavior almost caused the Women's Suffrage Association a great deal of embarrassment."

Hannah opened her mouth to ask what they were talking about, but Verity grabbed her arm and shook her to silence her. When Hannah turned to look at Verity, she could see that she was fascinated by the conversation.

"Of course, if you hadn't kept it quiet," said Mrs. Devenish, "I might very well have acquired a taste for militancy, and I quite likely would have gone to prison with all the others. I certainly would never have become a magistrate, for better or for worse." She had seemed to forget all about the girls, who were both now sitting open-mouthed.

"I might," she added, "have gone on hunger strike in prison, and ended up like some of those poor women, unable to smell or taste anything because of the forcible feeding."

"I don't doubt you would have," said Mrs. Lewis, gruffly. "You always did have a flair for the dramatic."

"Jolly good thing some of us did," shot back Mrs. Devenish. "Because someone needed to push the fight for the vote harder."

"Perhaps," said Mrs. Lewis, firmly, "but not you. You knew better. You knew as well as I did that all that stone-throwing and vandalism was utter foolishness. The vote would come without it, as indeed it did in time, and you were well aware of it. I thought you had momentarily taken leave of your senses. As far as I was concerned, yours was a petulant act, as I seem to remember I told your parents at the time, Elizabeth."

"Yes," said Mrs. Devenish, glaring at her. "Believe me, I have *never* forgotten what you said to my mother that day."

There was a hostile silence. Then the two women suddenly seemed to remember Hannah and Verity's presence in the room.

"To return to the subject of naughty children," Mrs. Devenish said, with forced calm, "Mrs. Smith doesn't want them to apologize to her in person, whereas I rather think they ought to."

"As do I," Mrs. Lewis replied carefully, again glancing with disapproval at the two girls, who were both gazing longingly at the door. "I can't imagine why she is so reluctant. She was very upset at the time, you know. She came and spoke with me about it after the constable left....In fact, she was perhaps a little more upset than is warranted. Not that I am in any way suggesting she ought to absolve them from blame so easily, but..." and here she seemed to struggle with whether to say something. "It just seemed rather odd."

Everyone sipped tea, then Mrs. Lewis said, "She's my housekeeper, you know."

"Who is?" asked Mrs. Devenish.

"Mrs. Smith," interrupted Hannah brightly, forgetting herself. Both women looked at her angrily for speaking out of turn.

"Sorry," Hannah said to nobody in particular. "My bad. Shutting up now."

"As I was about to say," said Mrs. Lewis, "Mrs. Smith does for me just once a week, which is as much as I need at my age. The rest I manage myself. Sometimes, she brings along her evacuee boy to help her. He's..."

"Evacuee?" said Mrs. Devenish, astounded. "I'm sorry, but you must be mistaken. I have checked with Mr. Simmons, and there is no evacuee billeted with Mrs. Smith."

"Oh, I assure you," said Mrs. Lewis, "there is. A little boy, by the name of Thomas. She tells me he's too delicate to go to school, but he never seems to have any trouble helping her with the work in this house. And, you know, Elizabeth, it's very curious, but he's colored, apparently part Negro. Imagine that!"

They were only a few yards down the road, when Mrs. Devenish stopped and turned to Hannah and Verity.

"Right, girls, what do you think we should do?"

"You want *our* opinions?" said Hannah in amazement.

"Obviously that's what I'm asking of you, Hannah. I'm not in the habit of asking questions I do not mean to have answered. Now, I'm not saying I'll follow your suggestions, but I will listen to them."

"Let's go apologize," Hannah said. "It will get us in the house. Sound like a plan?"

"Alright," said Mrs. Devenish evenly. "Verity? What do you think?"

Verity nodded emphatically.

Mrs. Devenish wagged a finger at them. "Now, I am prepared to do just that, but on certain conditions. Neither of you will do anything hasty or improper. You will follow my lead. Is that clear?"

Mrs. Smith answered the door, opening it only partway. She was a hard-faced woman in her mid-forties, wearing the usual turban over her scraped-back hair, and the same style of apron worn by most of the British housewives Hannah had seen.

"Yes?" said Mrs. Smith. She greeted them, Hannah thought, as if she suspected them of having come to her door to sell drugs.

Mrs. Devenish stepped forward. "Good afternoon, Mrs. Smith," she said briskly. "I'm sorry to disturb you, but I'm Elizabeth Devenish. I wonder if we might step inside to discuss the matter of the broken window?"

"No," said the woman. "I told you in my letter. No apologies. Just let me have the money, and be off with you. You only got two of the kids with you, anyway, so a fat lot of good that would do."

Mrs. Devenish paused, and Hannah thought she was counting to three to avoid losing her temper.

"I must insist, nonetheless, that I have a brief word with you. May I come in?"

"Have you got the money?" demanded Mrs. Smith.

"Not at present, but…"

"Well, come back when you do," she said, and closed the door. Mrs. Devenish pressed the doorbell, but nobody answered.

"Granny?" said Verity hesitantly. "Perhaps we ought to leave before she tells the police that we're pestering her."

"Oh, very well," spluttered Mrs. Devenish, as she walked away. Not realizing how well the kids could hear her, she muttered, "That bloody woman is an absolute battleaxe."

The two girls almost burst into giggles. "It takes one to know one," Verity whispered to Hannah, who stifled a laugh with her hand.

On the way home, Verity lost the coin toss, and posed the question to Mrs. Devenish that the girls had been dying to ask ever since they had left Mrs. Lewis.

"Granny? Were you actually a suffragette?"

"Well, not as such," said Mrs. Devenish, looking uncomfortable.

"What's that supposed to mean?" asked Hannah, with a devious grin, taking her hand.

"Well...I...I wasn't a member of the Women's Social and Political Union, and they were the only real suffragettes. And I really didn't subscribe to their methods...Really."

"*Really?*" said Hannah, wickedly.

"But you said to Mrs. Lewis that you threw a stone through a window," Verity persisted.

There was a pause.

"Actually," Mrs. Devenish said slowly, "It was half a brick."

The two girls gasped in delight. Hannah leaned in front of Mrs. Devenish and tried to give Verity a high-five, but Verity didn't understand, so she gave her a thumbs up instead.

Half-proud, half-embarrassed, Mrs. Devenish told the girls the story. "I wrapped it in a piece of paper on which I had written 'Votes For Women.' I'd been reading in the newspapers about the WSPU's militant campaign, and I suppose I just...I just got carried away. I didn't mean to get caught, you know. I wasn't as brave as the real suffragettes. So I waited until my parents and sisters were out, and I thought nobody was looking, and I chucked it.... through the, er, front window of our house, actually. My mother was opposed to women being given the vote, you see..."

The kids laughed, then Hannah said excitedly, "Someone saw you do it, didn't they?"

"Yes, yes they did," admitted Mrs. Devenish. "Our maid, and several of the neighbors, as a matter of fact. I have no idea now what I was thinking. It was a

Sunday afternoon, and broad daylight, and absolutely everyone was home, sitting in their front parlors. They heard the glass break, and they all saw me tear off down the street. My mother and Mrs. Lewis told everyone afterwards that I'd locked myself out of the house, and had broken a window to get in. I'm not sure anyone believed that."

Hannah couldn't help herself. "So, did you get spanked?"

"Oh, good heavens, no, I was almost twenty years old at the time....Mind you, not that Mrs. Lewis didn't suggest it to my mother ... I've never forgiven her for that."

She suddenly realized that she was walking alone, and she turned around to see Hannah and Verity hanging onto each other, doubled up with laughter.

"I have only one thing to say to you two on this subject," said Mrs. Devenish with great dignity. She turned to face the girls and drew herself up to her full height. "And it is this: Do as I say, girls, and not as I do."

Wiping her eyes, Hannah said with a giggle, "Isn't that kind of hypocritical of you?"

"Perhaps it is, Hannah," said Mrs. Devenish with a rueful smile. "But it's also good advice. If we decide to disregard it, we all of us must live with the consequences.

"Of course, I don't think you lot would be half as amusing if you were always perfectly behaved. And if you or Eric or Alexander or anyone else *ever* asks me whether I actually said that, I shall deny it categorically." And with that, she turned on her heel.

Chapter 13
REVELATIONS AND REUNIONS

Two days later, Hannah returned from school in the afternoon to find Mrs. Devenish writing at her desk at the drawing room.

"In light of our encounter with Mrs. Smith, I have decided that it is not practical for you three to make her an apology," she said, without looking round at Hannah.

"Are you going to mail the money to her?" asked Hannah, dropping her school satchel on the floor in the corner next to the bookcase. Mrs. Devenish turned sharply at the sound.

"Pick that up at once, Hannah… No, I'm going to take it to her myself, and see if I can persuade her to let me in. I have reported my information and suspicions to Mr. Simmons, and he has agreed to meet me at Mrs. Smith's house later this afternoon."

"Is he going to be there when you arrive?" asked Hannah with concern.

"I have no idea. Why?"

"I want to come with you," said Hannah decisively. Mrs. D. is ancient, she thought. This Smith woman gives off bad vibes. She shouldn't be alone with her.

"No, Hannah, that will not be necessary. Go and do your homework."

"But…"

"Homework, Hannah."

Even Hannah knew that further argument was pointless, and possibly hazardous to her health. She now had to think of another way to handle the situation, and fast.

Once Mrs. Devenish returned in the car, having picked up Verity at school, all the kids were home. While she went to change into her WVS uniform, the kids gathered for an emergency conference around the garden bench. The boys stood, Alex leaning against the oak tree, as Hannah explained her concern to the others.

"We could tell Mrs. D. she needs to have at least one of us along," suggested Alex.

"Tell her?" said Verity, incredulously.

"What are you thinking?" Hannah asked her brother.

"Okay, cool," said Alex. "Well, what do you guys have in mind?"

There was silence.

"Okay, then," said Alex. "Hannah, do you remember how Grandpa always says it's easier to get forgiveness than permission?"

"Yeah, and I also remember how Mom and Dad would tell him not to say that."

Verity looked at Alex with renewed interest. "Are you suggesting that we go anyway?"

There was a brief silence while everyone considered the awful implications of this proposal.

"Yeah," said Alex, matter-of-factly. "And I think this visit can do double duty. We can check out the house for the kid while we keep an eye on Mrs. D. But we're gonna have to think fast, because we're not gonna have much of a head start on her."

Eric was looking at everyone, from face to face. He was panicking. "I dunno, you lot, I dunno...I dunno if I can do this."

Verity said, "Come on, scaredy-cat. It will be an adventure."

"Yeah, right, Verity," Hannah said cynically. "That's what you said to me last time."

"And look what 'appened," blurted out a now visibly terrified Eric.

Verity looked at him sternly, and Hannah thought once again how she could bear a startling resemblance to her grandmother. "Sometimes, Eric, we have to do what's right, regardless of the risks. And this time, if it makes you happy, I promise that I shall own up as the ringleader."

"No, actually, Verity, that doesn't make me 'appy. Not one bit," said Eric, firmly. He suddenly seemed to come to a decision. "Alright, I'm in." Then he added, mostly to himself, "I must be mad."

The taxi bumped along the pot-holed road, splashing up a sheet of water that just missed Mrs. Devenish, as she walked toward Mrs. Smith's house. Smedley was sitting in the back of the cab, looking over some papers from his briefcase, and didn't notice her. He was feeling thoroughly put out, and a little worried. Mrs. Smith had written to tell him that she wanted the boy moved along. Now Smedley would have to collect him, and he was already thinking of a story to tell that hostel in Norfolk. Not, he reflected, that the man in charge cared much one way or the other. He was far too busy to care enough to dispute what he was told about the children who were placed with him.

As the kids crossed the fields, Verity sank ankle deep into a puddle, while the soles of everyone's shoes became thickly coated in mud. As they drew closer to the house, the kids also grew more wary. They took a break in a meadow, behind a tall hedge, and wiped the mud from their shoes on the long grass, scraping off the worst of it with rocks and twigs.

"Right, then," said Verity. "We might as well make our base here. I suppose we should send Alex first. Got the biscuits for Mrs. Smith's terrier?"

Alex patted his pocket. "Yep, got them. I'll bring the dog back as fast as I can."

The driver pulled up outside Mrs. Smith's house, pulled on the handbrake, and shut off the engine. Smedley got out and said to the driver, "Shouldn't be more than a few minutes, I reckon."

The driver, who was muffled in a flat cap, scarf, and woolen gloves, clapped and rubbed his hands together. "Hope not, guv," he grumbled. "It's blinkin' freezing out 'ere."

"Yeah, well, no fear, I'll make it worth your while."

As soon as Smedley knocked, Mrs. Smith opened the door.

"The boy's upstairs, packing," she said, stepping back to allow him to enter.

She showed him into the sparsely furnished front room. The largest piece of furniture was a buffet, with a couple of cheap ornaments on top, along with a photograph of Mrs. Smith's late husband as a soldier in World War I. Mrs. Smith and Smedley both sat down.

"I'm sorry for the short notice, Mr. Smedley, but this palaver is more trouble than it's worth. My nerves are in tatters, worrying about prying eyes, especially some of those busybodies in the WVS. I been thinking, I might as well just ask Mr. Simmons for an ordinary evacuee. This farmer up the road, he gets lots of work out of his two, especially because they're only in school for half the day now. And it wouldn't cost me anything, not like it has with you."

"Well, do whatever suits you," said Smedley, curtly. "There's plenty more people interested in finding an extra pair of hands, not too many questions asked. And we got plenty of riff-raff kids like this one," he jerked his head at the stairs, "who nobody is likely to ask questions about. I've got lots of takers, believe me."

Alex had returned with Mrs. Smith's Jack Russell terrier, which he had carried most of the way. It had enjoyed the dog biscuits he had offered it. The kids now tied it to the bush with the piece of washing line they had brought, and gave it the last of the dog biscuits as compensation.

"Alex, this may or may not be a problem," said Verity. "We just saw a car come to the front of the house, and we're pretty sure it's a taxi cab. So either she's going out, or she has a visitor. What should we do?"

Alex considered this calmly, and said, "Let's keep going. Maybe the visitor will distract her, and we can try our first plan, yeah?"

The kids ran as fast as they could toward the back of the house, slowing only as they approached the yard. Now came the biggest risk of the adventure. Her heart pounding, Hannah pushed open the back door. They were in luck. It was already partly open, and it did not creak. Looking ahead, she could see the door that led to the hall, and heard voices. She beckoned all the kids forward, and they took off their shoes, laying them outside, upside down in case of rain. Verity, whose socks were wet, removed those too.

As they hesitated in the kitchen, Hannah, standing in the doorway, suddenly heard someone in the living room stand up, and she heard Mrs. Smith say, "There's a bit of a draft." Hannah froze, holding her breath. But Mrs. Smith only closed the door that led from the front room to the hall. Hannah let out a silent sigh of relief. She gave the kids the thumbs up, and they filed into the hall on tiptoe. Going up the stairs took some time, as all four of them tested every step for creakiness before they put their weight on it, but finally they all arrived on the second floor. Hannah dropped slowly to her knees, and began to crawl along the landing. The others followed suit.

By good luck, Hannah could hear someone moving about behind one of the bedroom doors. Silently, she retrieved from her pocket the note that Verity had written. She glanced at it:

"Hello! Do you need to be rescued? Please reply on this paper. We are friends." With trembling hands, Hannah shoved the note and the pencil through the gap below the door and waited. She signaled to the others when she heard the note being picked up. A minute later, the paper came back.

"Thank you. Yes please. I'm locked in."

Mrs. Devenish arrived at the front door, took a deep breath, and knocked with three sharp raps. There was a small pause. Then the door opened.

"Oh, it's you again, is it?" said Mrs. Smith with distaste. "Brought the money, have you?"

"Good afternoon, Mrs. Smith," said Mrs. Devenish smoothly. "I have indeed, but I would like to come inside. I have something I wish to discuss with you."

"I got nothing to say to you. So just hand it over, won't you?"

When Mrs. Devenish did not move, Mrs. Smith said, "Well, if that's 'ow it is, you can just stick it in the post."

She began to close the door, but Mrs. Devenish was ready for her. She jabbed her umbrella through the doorway to stop the door from closing, and then leaned forward and shoved it open. She advanced on Mrs. Smith, who was backing down the hall, yelling at her with indignation, "Who do you think you are, you..."

"I have reason to believe you may have a child here who is an unregistered evacuee. I'm not leaving until I am absolutely sure one way or the other."

"What?" shrieked the woman. She looked up into Mrs. Devenish's determined face, and something snapped. She screamed, "Get out of my house, you interfering old cow!" and lunged at the older woman, fists flying.

Mrs. Devenish held up her arms to protect herself. Suddenly, Hannah ran between the two women, and gave a fast sharp low front kick to Mrs. Smith's shin, yelling, "Get your hands off my...my friend!" As the woman gave a cry of pain and doubled over, Hannah clapped both of her ears hard with the flats of her hands, just as Eric gave Mrs. Smith a hard kick up the backside. Verity leaned past him and pulled hard on Mrs. Smith's hair, and then all the kids piled on her. As she groaned, Eric, who was proud of the knot-tying skills he had learned in Boy Scouts, took off his tie and quickly began to restrain the woman's hands with it, while Alex extracted her keys from her apron pocket, and ran upstairs. It all happened in seconds.

Smedley was standing open-mouthed in the doorway of the front room. "What the blazes do you think you're doing?"

Shaken, Mrs. Devenish was adjusting her hat, straightening out her jacket, and trying to disguise exactly how impressed and furious she was with the kids. "Children, would you kindly escort Mrs. Smith into her front room? Mr. Smedley, I want a word with you."

The kids helped up a struggling, angry Mrs. Smith, and pushed her into an armchair, her hands still firmly tied behind her back.

"This is disgusting," she screamed. "You're not above the law, Mrs. High-and-Mighty! I'll have the law on you and this lot, and don't you think I won't."

Mrs. Devenish ignored her and looked at Smedley.

"Where is the boy?" she demanded.

"I don't know what you're talking about." Smedley protested angrily.

"Oh, I think you do," Mrs. Devenish said with quiet determination. "Now, once again, where is he?"

The answer came in the form of a gangly, light-skinned black kid of seven years old, who stood awkwardly in the doorway with Alex.

"Everyone?" said Alex. "Meet George Braithwaite."

George looked at the ground most of the time, and could not bring himself to look at Mrs. Smith at all, even as she spoke to him.

"Tell them, Thomas. Tell them you're my son, and this is all a mistake," she ordered.

He remained silent, and everyone's eyes turned to him.

Mrs. Devenish put a hand on his shoulder. "George, is this your mother? Now tell me the truth," she said, not unkindly. "I want you to trust me. Nothing can happen to you." He looked up at her, and gazed into her eyes for several seconds before he said "No...No, Miss, she's not. She just makes me work in her house." And then he looked down again. Mrs. Devenish patted his shoulder gently. Hannah looked at Eric, and, with surprise, saw that he was crying.

Just then, Mr. Simmons and Constable Ellsworth entered through the open front door, and came straight into the front room.

"What's going on?" asked a shocked Mr. Simmons, as he looked around the room. A red-faced Mrs. Smith was collapsed in an armchair with her hands behind her back, while Smedley and Mrs. Devenish were facing off against each other like wrestlers, as all the children stood at the ready.

It was Hannah who replied. "This is George Braithwaite. This total witch, the Smith lady, locked him up here, and she's using him as slave labor."

"That's right. And I've come to collect him," said Smedley, abruptly. "I will be taking him to a hostel until I can find him a new billet."

Mrs. Smith took a sharp and indignant intake of breath. "Don't you dare blame this on me!" She turned to plead with Ellsworth and Simmons. "He took money off me, he did. He said I could have a kid what'd earn his keep, no questions asked, and I didn't need to send him to school."

"This woman's lost her marbles," said Smedley. "Another reason we have to remove the boy for his own good."

Mrs. Smith gave an indignant "Oh!"

"Mrs. Devenish," said Mr. Simmons, trying to understand, "do you have any idea what is going on?"

Smedley, still looking at Mrs. Devenish, was thinking quickly, Hannah realized. He said, "Well, funny she should turn up here. That's the other matter I needed to attend to in Balesworth today. I'm investigating a report that this lady gave a beating to two evacuees, including this girl here. And her a magistrate, too…" He tutted.

"Are you threatening me?" Mrs. Devenish asked, in a cold fury. "How dare…"

Constable Ellsworth had been quiet to this point, but now he stepped forward and held up a finger to shush her. "Tell me, Mr. Smedley, do you have evidence for this charge against Mrs. Devenish?"

"But you said… to me and him in the pub," said Smedley, aghast.

"I said nothing of the sort. Do you recall me saying such a thing, Mr. Simmons?" Ellsworth said, turning to the billeting officer.

"Oh, no, this doesn't ring a bell at all, Constable Ellsworth. And you," Mr. Simmons said to Hannah, "You're one of the evacuees in question. Has Mrs. Devenish beaten you, or otherwise mistreated you?"

It took a great deal of self-control, but Hannah somehow managed it. "Me? Mrs. D. treats me just like she treats her own granddaughter," she said, and flashed a smile at Mrs. Devenish, who ignored it. Verity allowed herself a sly grin at Hannah's cleverness.

Mrs. Devenish demanded (and got) the money from Smedley to pay off the taxi driver, and then rang the police station from Mrs. Lewis' phone. Alex walked back across the fields and retrieved the dog from the bush. Constable Ellsworth's sergeant arrived in a police car soon afterward, and the two officers removed Smedley and Mrs. Smith for questioning.

"What do you reckon he'll be charged with?" Simmons asked Mrs. Devenish afterward, as they sat in Mrs. Smith's front room.

"I should imagine some charge of abusing his official powers to sell children into servitude," she replied. "I hope they throw the book at him."

"What I don't understand," said Simmons, shaking his head, "is Mrs. Smith. Her conduct seems so unwomanly to me."

"Not all women are motherly, Mr. Simmons, especially when they have no children of their own. I suppose she thought she would need the help," said Mrs. Devenish. "She must have had a jolly hard life as a widow of limited means." She walked over to the window and gazed out thoughtfully for a moment, before turning back to Simmons. "But that's not an excuse. There is no excuse for this ghastly cruelty, and especially not to children."

As George Braithwaite sat quietly on the sofa next to Hannah, she wondered briefly how Smedley could ever have confused him with Brandon. But then she realized that he had probably not seen George for over a year, and that in a place where there were so few black people, he probably saw blackness first, and individual people second.

George told them of how Smedley had removed him from his last billet in Bedfordshire, telling him that he was a bad kid, a troublemaker.

"He said that to us, too," said Hannah, thoughtfully. "I guess he thinks you're less likely to argue that way."

George continued, explaining that Smedley had brought him to Mrs. Smith, and told him that he would have to stay with her until he had redeemed himself for his bad behavior. He was not allowed to go to school, and the only time he was permitted to leave the house was to help Mrs. Smith with cleaning Mrs. Lewis' house.

"Didn't you think that was kind of weird?" Hannah asked him.

"No," said George, shaking his head. "My dad always says I should do as adults tell me."

"Wow," said Hannah, looking meaningfully at Mrs. Devenish. "Maybe that isn't such good advice. Right, Mrs. D?"

"Don't you dare take that tone with me, Hannah Day," said Mrs. Devenish sternly. "What has been done to George is evil. And you would do well to learn why that makes a difference."

Simmons, sitting with his knees apart, and hands clasped in front of him, slowly shook his head. "I can't tell you how sorry I am, Mrs. Devenish," he said sorrowfully. "I should have paid more attention."

"Mr. Simmons, this was not our doing. Anyone could say that we at the WVS could have been more assiduous, and that the government could have paid closer attention to Mr. Smedley's activities. But there is a war on, and these things will happen. I receive reports from a friend at WVS in London, and she has made it very plain to me that we cannot keep up with every evacuee. We can but try. I am only glad that we found George before things deteriorated even further."

"All thanks to us meddling kids!" said Hannah cheerfully, to blank looks from everyone except Alex, who put his hands over his eyes.

"Hannah, do be quiet," said Mrs. Devenish irritably.

After some discussion, Mr. Simmons agreed that George would stay with Mrs. Devenish until a suitable new billet was found. As they left the house, Mrs. Devenish walked silently ahead, holding George's hand, while the others trailed behind, Alex walking the happy terrier on its improvised leash.

"Has Granny said anything to any of you about what we were doing in Mrs. Smith's house?" asked Verity, worried.

"No," said Hannah, perplexed. "She's kinda quiet, isn't she? Not even the usual threats. That's a good sign, huh?"

"You must be jokin'," said Eric, kicking disconsolately at a stone in the road.

"Eric's right. Quite the reverse, in fact," Verity said. "It's a very, very bad sign. I think we had all better prepare ourselves for the worst. Well, no, Eric, not your idea of the worst, which is just silly. And Hannah, this time, no matter what, would you please do all of us a favor and take whatever Granny doles out with a bit less fuss?"

"I'll try," said Hannah, uncertainly. "But it's not fair…"

"Shut up, Hannah," they all said simultaneously.

They entered the house after Mrs. Devenish, who sent the rest of the children into the kitchen while she took George upstairs to get him settled in Eric and Alex's room.

When she came downstairs alone, she found all four kids standing in front of the kitchen fireplace, watching her intently. They relaxed a little as they observed that she had not come armed.

Silently, she removed her hat and jacket, and then closed the door behind her. She looked at all the kids with a serious face.

"We have some unfinished business from this afternoon, children," she said gravely.

The kids looked uneasily at one another. Suddenly, Mrs. Devenish marched up to Hannah's side, put her left hand on Hannah's left shoulder, and extended the other arm behind her. Hannah had closed her eyes and was steeling herself, waiting for the blow to fall. But instead, she felt the right arm reach around her shoulders. Mrs. Devenish, standing beside her, gave her a brief squeeze.

"Where did you learn to do that, when you did such a splendid job of defending me from Mrs. Smith?" she said with a smile, her hands still on Hannah's shoulders.

"Oh, I did two years of karate," said Hannah modestly. "Kind of been a while, but I guess I still got it."

"Good Lord," said Mrs. Devenish in wonderment, looking down at her. "You never cease to amaze me, Hannah Day. Well, thank you. I don't know what I would have done without you, my dear. And the same goes for the rest of you. Thank you." She beamed at the children, who smiled back proudly. Hannah couldn't remember feeling this happy or pleased with herself in a very long time.

"In light of the circumstances, I am prepared this once to overlook the fact that you entered Mrs. Smith's house without permission. But mark my words, children," said Mrs. Devenish quietly, with a definite air of menace, "if you ever attempt a little stunt like that again, I will skin you all alive. Do I make myself clear?" Her eyes glinted dangerously.

There was a subdued chorus of "Yes, Mrs. D," and, from Verity, "Yes, Granny."

"Now, one of you boys, go and invite George downstairs. Hannah, you and I have an errand to run."

"Where are we going?" asked Hannah, putting on her shoes in the hall.

"To pay a visit to Mrs. Archer," said Mrs. Devenish. "I think it's high time."

"But why?" asked Hannah, who stopped still. "We don't live there anymore. They're nothing to do with us."

"What an odd attitude, Hannah. The Archers took care of both of you for several weeks, at no small trouble or expense. And they haven't ceased to exist simply because you no longer live with them. I do think that Mrs. Archer needs to know what has taken place. Now, come along, don't dawdle. We shall take Maisy, because I need to stop at the butcher's before they close, to pick up some sausages for our supper, now that there's another mouth to feed."

Mrs. Archer's eyes grew wide when she opened the door and saw Hannah and Mrs. Devenish standing on her doorstep.

"Good afternoon, Mrs. Archer," said Mrs. Devenish. "May we come in?" It wasn't a question. Mrs. Archer meekly held open the door, and showed them into the front room.

"Would you like a cup of tea?" she asked.

"No, thank you," said Mrs. Devenish briskly. "That won't be necessary. Sit down, Hannah. And you, Peggy."

Hannah was surprised. "Hey, um, Mrs. D? Her first name? It's Margaret."

"Don't be stupid, Hannah," said Mrs. Devenish, "Peggy is a short form of Margaret."

"When did you realize who I was?" Mrs. Archer asked forlornly.

"This afternoon, finally. I didn't recognize you before. You have got quite fat." Hannah cringed at Mrs. Devenish's tactlessness. "And I don't remember your wearing spectacles. I'm not surprised nobody recognized you as old Mr. Gordon's daughter, even here. Of course, I never knew you in Balesworth, so it's hardly surprising that it took me so long to put two and two together, until now."

"Hello?" said Hannah. "Would someone please tell me what this is about?"

"Hannah Day, speak when you are spoken to," said Mrs. Devenish abruptly. Then she continued. "What I don't understand, Peggy, is why all the subterfuge? I realized that you had told Hannah that I was a gossip, and I couldn't understand it, until now. You just didn't want me to find out who you were, did you? You were afraid that she would somehow get wind of it, and tell me."

"Nobody in Balesworth knows about the baby, you know," said Mrs. Archer quietly. "My little cousin doesn't even remember me. And I had no idea that you lived in Balesworth until I arrived here. It was my husband's job that brought me back. I didn't want to come here, but I could hardly tell him why.

"But then these children arrived, and began talking about their colored friend, George Braithwaite, and I was afraid somebody would find out. I knew he couldn't be my son, but I thought he might be my grandson, and I just didn't want him in the house. I was afraid my husband would somehow work out the truth."

Mrs. Devenish looked at her sadly, and when she spoke, her voice was kindly. "But would it really have been that dreadful? So many young women had soldiers' babies during that war, and it was such a long time ago. And now, it's happening again to lots of young girls. We live in changing times, and there are far greater sins."

Mrs. Archer suddenly looked at Mrs. Devenish with distaste. "Well, I have changed, too, you know. I'm not the naive little girl you remember. I have no interest in a colored grandchild. What would people think? What would they say? You can't trust people with foreign blood, can you?"

Hannah couldn't stop herself. "That's so bizarre. I mean, what color is foreign…"

"Hannah!" snapped Mrs. Devenish, and Hannah fell silent. Mrs. Devenish returned her attention to Mrs. Archer.

"So, in short," she said unsympathetically, "you decided that the most convenient course of action would be to send the children away with Mr. Smedley. You do realize that the man has been arrested?"

Mrs. Archer looked shocked.

Mrs. Devenish continued. "He was collecting children who he thought would not be missed, and billeting them with people who wanted to misuse them, for various and sundry wicked purposes. Your grandson was kept in a locked room for much of the time, and viciously beaten. I have seen the scars running up and down his legs."

Hannah hadn't noticed that, but clearly, Mrs. Devenish had.

"Hannah and Alexander could also have found themselves in the most nightmarish circumstances imaginable for a child."

"I'm sorry," whispered Mrs. Archer. "I didn't know…"

"No, I don't believe you did," said Mrs. Devenish calmly. "But you do now."

"Please," Mrs. Archer pleaded, "for God's sake, please don't tell my husband."

"Peggy, since that is your wish, I will not reveal your secret to anyone. And Hannah, neither will you ever—and I mean, *ever*—repeat what you have heard to anyone, not even to your brother or to Verity. Is that clear?"

"Yes, ma'am," said Hannah.

"I am not Her Majesty the Queen," said Mrs. Devenish, dryly. "But I am glad that you understand me."

She turned back to Mrs. Archer. "Hannah and Alexander are with me, and George will remain until I have found him a suitable billet. We will not trouble you any further this evening, or, indeed, ever again, Mrs. Archer, with the affairs of these children. Good evening. Come along, Hannah."

With that, she shepherded Hannah out of the front door, and out of Peggy Archer's life.

Meanwhile, in another Balesworth, that of 1915, Mr. Gordon was in town, visiting the bank, Mrs. Gordon was visiting friends, and Oliver was at school. Brandon was in the surgery, getting ready for the afternoon's appointments, when the front doorbell rang downstairs. He thought nothing of it, until Mary appeared at the surgery entrance. "It's a patient, a lady," she said. "She insists on seeing you."

"Me?" exclaimed Brandon.

"Yes, well, that was what I said, but it's you she wants."

"Look, tell her that Mr. Gordon will be back this afternoon, and have her make an appointment, unless it's an emergency."

"I'll try," said Mary, without enthusiasm.

Soon afterward, there was another set of footsteps on the stairs, and into the surgery swept the Professor.

Before Brandon could say anything, she said, "It's time. We have found George, and everything is as it should be. We must leave now."

"But, I can't. We have patients, and Mr. Gordon said…"

"Now, Brandon. It can't wait."

"Can't I even leave a note?" he asked desperately. She looked at the clock. "You have one minute. Absolutely no more."

Brandon ran to the desk in the study and grabbed a pencil and the first piece of paper he could find, an invoice from the dental supply company in London. He flipped it over, and scrawled on the back,

Dear Mr. Gordon and Oliver:
I'm sorry. I've been called away on an emergency, and I won't be back. Please forgive me. I wish it didn't have to

happen like this. I will really, really miss you both and I'm sorry for the inconvenience, Mr. Gordon. I won't forget either of you.
Sincerely,
George

Then, even as the Professor hovered behind him, he added,

P.S. If Mrs. Gordon ever starts getting all excited about the ideas of a guy called Adolf Hitler, get her to a psychiatrist. She needs help.

"Time, Brandon," yelled the Professor. "Let's go."

She hurried along the narrow upstairs landing, and Brandon sprinted behind her. He followed her onto the staircase, into a darkness he had never seen there before. And he was gone.

In London in early November, 1940, the British prime minister stood before a collapsing pile of rubble heaped in front of what, just two days before, had been an intact four-story building. Looking up, the people who had gathered around him could see exposed rooms still full of furniture, mirrors on walls, and flowers on dining tables. People's lives had been opened up to view as though by an enormous can opener.

The prime minister, Winston Churchill, stepped forward, broken glass crunching under the soles of his shoes, and looked at the expectant crowd around him. There were housewives, apprentices, shopkeepers, office managers, Air Raid Wardens, and WVS ladies. Bright flashbulbs popped as news photographers took shots. Then he held up his hand, and there was silence. The crowd waited to hang on the every word of this rather ugly, roly-poly man, who was wearing his trademark bowtie and hat, and had an enormous cigar clamped in his mouth. He removed the cigar so that he could address the waiting people.

"Herr Hitler," he bellowed, so everyone could hear, "Herr Hitler underestimates the resolve of this great island nation." A great cheer went up.

Suddenly in the momentary silence that followed, there came a shout from the crowd.

"Crikey," bellowed a man in a butcher's overalls and straw hat, "What's 'e doin' up there?"

The crowd looked up, and there was a collective gasp. At the top of the pile of rubble had suddenly appeared a small figure in grey shorts, shirt, grey sweater and school cap. He looked confused, and he began to slip and slide down the pile, somehow managing not to fall. The prime minister, who was not used to not being the center of attention, turned around too late, just as the boy stumbled off the pile and barreled right into him. Churchill almost dropped his cigar as he awkwardly caught the falling boy. "What the devil...," he said. His bodyguard came to his rescue, but Churchill waved him aside. "What's your name, my boy?" Churchill asked the disheveled kid, who was looking thoroughly disoriented.

"Um, wow, are you who I think you are?" said the boy, rubbing his head.

Churchill and the bodyguard laughed, as did those of the crowd who had heard him. They passed back the joke to those behind, to waves of laughter.

"Well, I certainly hope I am," said Churchill, mock seriously. "And now, may I ask, who might you be?"

"My name's Brandon Clark, sir," he said, bewildered. "I've just survived a Zepp...I mean, an air raid. It was quite a close call, actually."

"Well, now, young Master Brandon-Clark," said the prime minister, patting Brandon on the head. "If you're sure you're quite well, why don't we pose for a picture? Hopefully, it will appear in one of the newspapers, and then you shall have a keepsake of this remarkable day, won't you, my boy?"

Brandon looked up at the man in absolute awe. "Oh, I don't think I'm likely to forget this, Mr. Churchill. Not ever."

Mrs. Devenish returned home with a copy of a newspaper, and called outside to the children. "The vicar has just visited London, and he gave me this," she said, as they came to the kitchen door. "He thought George might be interested to see that a colored boy is on the front page, and with the prime minister, no less. Come in for a minute and you can all take a look."

She unfolded it on the kitchen table, and Alex and George came to see. "Hannah, you won't believe it!" said Alex excitedly, jumping up and down. "It's him! It's Brandon! I mean Braithwaite! The other Braithwaite! Whoever!"

Mrs. Devenish put a restraining hand on his shoulder. "Alexander, calm down. What on earth are you talking about?" But Hannah had already rushed over to look, and she had a delighted smile on her face. "You're right! It is him!"

George, Verity and Mrs. Devenish looked at each other in bewilderment.

"Would one of you please explain this to the rest of us?" said Verity.

They did their best.

Later that afternoon, Brandon arrived at Balesworth Station once again. Walking up the High Street, he stopped in front of Mr. Gordon's house, and hesitated. Finally, he decided to ring the doorbell.

No maid answered this time. The woman who came to the door was smartly dressed, and in her early forties.

"Can I help you?" she asked.

"I was just wondering if I could see Mr. Gordon, please?"

She looked startled. "Mr. Gordon? Oh, he's been dead for years. It's Mr. Hanbury and Mr. Wood who are the dentists, only Mr. Wood is gone for the duration of the war. Air Force, you know. Is this an emergency? Only we just ended surgery, and Mr. Hanbury has already gone home. I could give you his number at the house, if you like."

Brandon felt sick. Of course, 25 years had passed, and so much must have happened.

"No, no emergency. I just stopped by to see Mr. Gordon. How long has he been gone?"

"Since long before you were born, I reckon," said the woman. "I've been the receptionist here for about ten years, and he'd been gone quite a long time before that. We never got around to removing the brass plate from the gate. A lot of our older customers have memories of Mr. Gordon, and it would upset them, so Mr. Hanbury and Mr. Wood thought we should leave it like it is. Look, I'm sorry, but I really must shut up shop. I've got ARP duty tonight, and I have to run home and have my tea first." With that, she gave an apologetic smile, and closed the door.

Because the evening was closing in, and all the shops had closed by 5:30 p.m., Brandon decided to ask in a pub for help finding Alex and Hannah. The Balesworth Arms was noisy and busy when he opened the door. He was also hit by a wall of smoke. He remembered how Hannah had not wanted to enter the pub when they first arrived, and he had never walked through the doors in 1915, either, thanks to Mr. Gordon banning him from alehouses.

As soon as he walked in now, though, Ernie the landlord spotted him, and pointed him back to the door. "Out!" he roared.

"Why?" asked Brandon, "You don't allow black people to ask questions? What?"

A furious Ernie lifted a section of the bar, and walked through, right at Brandon. Taking him by the scruff of the neck, he began to propel him toward the door.

"There's no kids allowed in my pub, I don't care if they're white, colored, or bloody purple, makes no difference. Now, hop it before I give you a good kick up the arse."

But just then, there was a shout from the bar.

"Hang on, Ernie," called over a man with a moustache and glasses. "Let me deal with this."

Brandon peered through the smoke, trying to see the man more clearly. He didn't sound like Smedley, and as the man approached, Brandon was relieved to see that, although he looked familiar, he was not his old captor.

Ernie let go of Brandon, who almost dropped to the ground. "Come outside for a minute," said Mr. Simmons, "I just want a quick word."

They stepped out into the rapidly chilling evening. Mr. Simmons turned to Brandon, "Look, sonny, are you an evacuee?"

"Not exactly," said Brandon, "But I have some friends who are, and I think…"

"Not exactly?" interrupted Mr. Simmons. "What's that supposed to mean?"

Before Brandon could answer, Mr. Simmons looked at him with a shock of recognition. "You're that lad who ran off, aren't you? I know exactly who you need to see."

Brandon turned, and began to sprint down the street, but Mr. Simmons called after him, "Come back! It's all right! It's not Smedley! He's been arrested."

It was the word "arrested" that got Brandon's attention. He came skidding to a halt.

It was eight o'clock in the evening. In the drawing room, Mrs. Devenish was reading *David Copperfield*, Alex and George were playing chess, and Eric was sketching a Spitfire. Hannah and Verity were lying on the floor, listening to the wireless, and laughing at Tommy Handley's radio show, *ITMA*. Hannah was astonished by how well she understood the show: It had made no sense at all to her when she had first tried to listen to it at the Archers'. Now, she thought it was hilarious.

A knock at the door brought no response from the children. "Would one of you get that?" said Mrs. Devenish, turning a page. Nobody moved. She rolled her eyes, sighed heavily and got up to answer it.

When she returned, she said, "That was Mr. Simmons. He brought us a visitor." With that, she held open the door, and in walked Brandon Clark, with an enormous smile.

Hannah was sure she would never forget the giddy feeling of that moment. Brandon, Alex, and Hannah enthusiastically hugged each other while the English people stood by in happy awkwardness. Then Mrs. Devenish sat in her armchair as the children all sat on the floor at her feet. To George and Brandon, she said, "I think it's an extraordinary coincidence that both of you would be named George Braithwaite, and I'm not entirely sure I understand it. I suppose I shall have to call the older of you George Major, and the younger George Minor while you are both staying here."

Brandon thought quickly, "I usually go by my middle name."

"And what is that?" Mrs. Devenish asked.

"Brandon," he said, to smiles from Alex and Hannah.

"An old family name I assume? Very well, Brandon, that is what we shall call you. But you know, I have far too many of you underfoot now." She didn't notice Eric suddenly hugging his knees to his chest, and looking frightened, but Verity did. She whispered to him, "You're not going anywhere. I wish you would believe me. She would never, never get rid of you."

Brandon looked again at Mrs. Devenish and it was then that he recognized her. He couldn't believe how much she had aged,

"Hey, you're...We met, don't you remember me?"

"No, I can't say I do. I certainly think I would remember if I had," she said.

Of course, he thought. Their meeting had taken place 25 years before, and she would never think that a child she met then was still of the same age and appearance. She, on the other hand, looked very different, with gray hair and wrinkles. As Mrs. Devenish stood to poke the fire and add more coal, Brandon, unthinkingly, marveled aloud to himself, "Wow, you got old." Alex and Hannah waved their hands and mouthed "No" at him.

It was too late. "I beg your pardon?" said Mrs. Devenish in a deeply offended voice, as she straightened up and turned to look at him.

Brandon noted how she had perfected the death rays since their first encounter, and he thought fast. "I said, you've got an old house here. Nice...."

"Oh. Oh, I see. Yes, much of it was built in the eighteenth century." She returned her attention to the fireplace. The kids gave Brandon the thumbs up and victory signs. He grinned.

Eric leaned over to him. "You gotta mind your Ps and Qs around Mrs. D.," he advised Brandon in a whisper, "But she's alright."

Verity tried to change the subject, saying brightly, "Isn't this amazing? We must be the only house in Balesworth with not just one colored person, but two!"

Eric muttered to George and Brandon, "If she keeps collecting, she'll soon 'ave the whole set." They laughed, and Verity looked at them suspiciously.

Mrs. Devenish returned her attention to the children. "Now, before I forget, we really must discuss the subject of finding billets for George and Brandon.

And before you say a word, Verity Powell, I am not practicing some hideous form of color segregation as one hears about in America. The fact is, we haven't the room, and it's last in, first out. Brandon and George, I want you to know that I shall be conducting a full and careful inspection of your new billets, whatever they may be, and I will allow you ultimately to decide whether they are suitable."

Brandon suddenly said, "Hey, I have an idea. When I was with Smedley, I met this really decent chap on a train." Hannah noticed how English Brandon's speech sounded these days. "He said he lives in Balesworth, and he said that he and his wife might be willing to billet me. Look, I have his name in my pocket." He pulled out a crumpled slip of paper, and read from it. "It's Dr. Arthur Healdstone."

"Ah yes, I have met Dr. Healdstone," said Mrs. Devenish. "He spoke before the parish council last year. A pleasant enough man, but he's only just now managing to establish his medical practice. Too many older people in Balesworth find it hard to take him seriously, because they remember him as old Mr. Gordon the dentist's little nephew, Oliver. Small wonder he's decided to use his first name again. I think he's hoping that people will associate him with his father, Dr. Arthur Healdstone the elder, who was a wonderful doctor."

Brandon was astounded, but, of course, he could not explain why.

Mrs. Devenish continued. "I don't know whether he and his wife would be prepared to take on two of you, because they have a small son of their own. Nonetheless, Dr. Healdstone would be a most suitable host, and he may be able to manage both of you, since he is rather young."

"By her standards, who isn't?" whispered Verity to Hannah, who giggled.

"I shall give the Healdstones a ring," said Mrs. Devenish as she made her way to the telephone in the hall. "And I heard that, Verity Powell."

Chapter 14
RETURNS

The next morning, Alex, Brandon, George, Verity, Eric, and Hannah were playing tag in the garden when Mrs. Devenish came out of the kitchen. She was not alone. Behind her was Miss Tatchell, the Professor, who was carrying an enormous camera.

Mrs. Devenish spoke slowly, and her voice sounded oddly weak. "This is Miss Tatchell with the WVS… I believe some of you have met her before. She has come to collect you three, Alex, Brandon…and Hannah. Your parents have decided that you should be billeted closer to them." She paused for a moment, seeming at a loss for words, then appeared to collect herself. "She has also very kindly brought some photographic apparatus, so that we will all have a photograph as a memento of your stay in Balesworth. This is a tremendously generous gesture, as I'm sure you will agree. Now come along, let us take our photograph, and then the three of you must pack all of your belongings. Miss Tatchell has very little time before she must leave."

While the Professor set up her camera, Hannah, Alex and Brandon approached her. Brandon was first to ask the question.

"Where are we going?"

The Professor fiddled with the lens, and looked though the viewfinder. "Home, of course. It's over, kids. We all did what we were supposed to do. We did good."

"Thanks," said Alex. "But it does seem weird just to leave like this. It's so sudden."

"That's just how it is during the war. People are thrown together and torn apart at a moment's notice. I know it's hard, but it can't be helped."

Brandon noticed that Hannah was gulping, and trying not to cry. He patted her shoulder, but she shook him off, and turned away.

"Alright, guys, go join your friends," said the Professor, "I'll try to get the best picture I can."

They took the photo in front of the garden bench and the oak tree. Everyone managed a smile, except for Hannah, who was standing between Verity and Mrs. Devenish, and who looked into the camera with a very serious face. If I really do somehow get a copy of this photo, she thought, I will always know that I was thinking at that moment of how I would one day look back at myself in the future.

As the kids brought their cases downstairs, Brandon thought with disappointment that he would never be reunited with grown-up Oliver. But it was good to know from their meeting on the train that Oliver had never forgotten him. Perhaps George would benefit from his generosity.

Alex thought how sad it was that he would never walk down these steps again. He consoled himself with the thought that if he ever traveled to England in his own time, he could once again enjoy walking in the countryside. Hopefully, that would not have changed.

Hannah tried not to think at all.

Now, in the front garden, the boys all shook hands, and Hannah shyly kissed Eric on the cheek, to his huge embarrassment. Verity threw her arms around Hannah, and tried very hard not to cry, which was what Hannah was also doing. Normally, Hannah would have indulged in floods of tears, but Hannah wasn't sure what "normal" was for her anymore.

Finally, Hannah stood before Mrs. Devenish, and found that she didn't know what to do. Mrs. Devenish leaned down, and kissed her cheek. Then she laid her hand gently on Hannah's face and looked into her eyes. "Behave yourself, do you hear me? And don't forget us. I shall expect a letter from time to time." Hannah nodded, tears rolling down her face.

"Goodbye, Hannah Day."

Hannah didn't trust herself to reply, and just shook her head. She followed the Professor and the boys to the car. The last thing she saw as she looked back was Mrs. Devenish and the kids waving. And then they were out of sight.

As the Professor's car left, it passed another on the road. The driver was a man in his early thirties with horn-rimmed glasses and a kindly face. He barely glanced at the car that passed him. But only a second later, when he gave another casual glance in his rear-view mirror, he was astonished to see that the car had vanished. It must, he reflected, have been moving faster than he had realized. Soon, he put all thought of it out of his mind, when he caught sight of the small, sad-looking group gathered in Mrs. Devenish's front garden. They watched him curiously as he pulled on the handbrake, and stepped from the car. Only Mrs. Devenish recognized him, and she walked forward with a hand extended. "Dr. Healdstone? I'm Elizabeth Devenish."

"Yes, good to see you again, Mrs. Devenish," said Dr. Healdstone. "And I assume that this is the second of our two Georges?" He gave a kind smile to George.

"Yes, this is George," said Mrs. Devenish. "But he's the only one who will be returning with you. The second George has just left with one of my colleagues in the WVS, to return to his parents."

Dr. Healdstone looked very disappointed, but he quickly recovered, not wishing to hurt George Braithwaite's feelings. "I see…Well, all the more room in our little house for you, George. Diana, my wife, and our son, Robert, are looking forward to meeting you. They're at home making a chocolate cake right now. Do you like chocolate cake?"

George nodded happily.

"Blimey, so do I," said Eric longingly.

Mrs. Devenish shushed him.

Hannah landed with a bump, and Brandon and Alex were right behind her. One moment they were in the Professor's car, leaving Balesworth, and now, in less than an instant, here they were on the grassy lawn in front of the oldest buildings of Snipesville State College, surrounded by pecan trees. A wall of heat hit them. Alex and Brandon were dressed in baseball uniforms, and Hannah was in T-shirt and shorts, her purse lying at her feet. All three kids looked at each other, bewildered. None of them could think of anything to say.

Hannah remained unusually quiet as they walked across campus. The boys, meanwhile, exchanged phone numbers, email addresses, and promises that they would get together the very next day, so long as they weren't grounded when their parents discovered they had skipped out of camp. They talked excitedly about becoming famous. They even reached the point of speculating about book deals and appearances on Oprah, only to realize that they had no proof that they had traveled in time.

"Would you two shut up?" Hannah snapped. "How do you know if this is even the right year? We might not have been born yet."

The boys agreed that she had a good point. But at that moment, the college clock struck noon, and ahead of them, they saw a line of boys in baseball uniforms walking toward the Union. The assistant coach, who was talking on his cellphone, made a U-turn, and headed back in the direction of the fieldhouse.

Alex and Brandon did not see themselves in the line of boys. "Maybe we should try and catch up," suggested Alex. "See you, sis. Hope you find writing camp. Tell…What was the babysitter's name? Well, whatever. Give her a call and tell to meet us over by the baseball field at four."

The two boys ran off toward the Union, leaving Hannah in the middle of the campus, feeling very angry, and very alone.

Hannah wasn't surprised to learn from the secretary in the history department that there was no Professor named Tatchell at Snipesville State College. Just to be sure, though, she described the Professor's short grey hair, and her odd, almost English accent. The secretary immediately knew who she was talking about. "Oh, you're looking for Dr. Harrower. Her office is just down the hall. I'm not sure she'll be in, though. She just got back from out of town."

Hannah walked determinedly to the end of the hallway. Finding the Professor's door wide open, she walked in without knocking.

The Professor was working at her computer, with her back to the door. The office was desperately untidy. Piles of papers and cardboard boxes were heaped on the floors. Books were stacked two deep in the bookcases. The desk seemed to be divided into geologic layers, and it was littered with old Starbucks cups, some of which still had coffee in them, covered in thick layers of mould. Various dust-covered objects were strewn about, and Hannah recognized some of them from England. Among them were a gas mask, an old black telephone, and she saw, with a great pang of sadness, a WVS hat just like Mrs. Devenish's.

But Hannah had not come to admire the Professor's office, or the Professor herself.

"So, what gives?" Hannah said bluntly.

"Hmm?" The Professor did not stop typing on the keyboard.

"Are you a witch, or what?" said Hannah.

Finally, the Professor turned toward her, and laughed incredulously. "Don't be ridiculous," she said, as if it were the most absurd thing she had ever heard.

"Well, what *are* you then?"

The Professor seemed bewildered. "You know perfectly well what I am. I'm an historian."

Hannah sighed heavily. "Yes, but, like, *time travel?*"

"Oh, that! Well, so far as I understand these things, the past is an odd thing. It never really goes away, I think. It's a bit like energy, you know, it can't be created or destroyed. At least, that's an interesting idea…Can't prove it of course, I'm not a scientist."

Hannah spoke scathingly. "I don't know what you're talking about, and you didn't answer my question. Are you a time traveler?"

"Well, obviously, and so are you, and so are the boys. But really, Hannah, I mean, all these labels! Witch? Time traveler? Do you really find labels helpful? I find the minute I sum up something give it a name, and put it in a box, I've stopped trying to understand it, and that will never do…."

Hannah picked her way through all the stuff lying on the floor, removed a pile of papers from a chair, and sat down. She tried again. "Okay, so you won't tell me that. So how about you tell me this. What's the history lesson?"

"Lesson?" The Professor looked puzzled.

Hannah rephrased her question, as though talking to someone slow. "Yeah. What's the history lesson we're supposed to have learned? I mean, what's your point? I'm guessing you have one. Is there a test? Do we have to fill out a worksheet? Am I supposed to have learned something about myself?"

The Professor smiled. "That assumes that you have had a history lesson, that I gave it, and that I had a point in giving it. Tell me, Hannah, in your view, does everything have to have a creator and a point?"

Hannah hesitated. She didn't even know how to begin to answer that.

The Professor continued, "Really, isn't the experience itself the point?"

"If any of it really happened," said Hannah, as she slumped back in her chair and stared at the ceiling.

"Let me show you something," said the Professor, reaching into her briefcase. She pulled out a clear plastic sleeve containing a yellowed newspaper clipping, and handed it to Hannah. It was the photo of Brandon with Winston Churchill. Next she gave Hannah a stapled wad of photocopies. On the top sheet was the image of the patterned exterior of a small notebook.

"What's this?" Hannah asked.

"Turn the page," instructed the Professor.

Hannah did so and gasped. There, in a neat, beautiful hand, were the words, "Elizabeth Devenish, 1940." She was holding a copy of Mrs. Devenish's diary.

"Verity deposited it at an archive in Hertfordshire," said the Professor, quietly. "That's where I found it, while I was on a research trip. I'm not psychic, you know. Together with books and other papers from the period, it helped me piece together what your Mrs. Devenish had on her mind while you were there."

Hannah was already slowly leafing through the packet. She found the entry for September 15, 1940:

Hannah and Alexander Day, two new evacuees, came to the house today. Eric enjoyed Alexander very much. It was good for him to have the company of a boy of his own age. Hannah is a bright girl and, I believe, at heart a good child, although something of a handful. They had been on a walk, but had not eaten the picnic their foster mother had given them because they found the food unfamiliar, and so we added a few ingredients from larder and greenhouse. The results were apparently satisfactory, because not a crumb was left after tea. I invited the children to Verity's birthday party, and they have accepted.

Very bad news from London. Hundreds of Luftwaffe planes, and tremendous damage. I spoke with Millie Cooke at WVS H2, and everyone is trying to keep spirits up. It cannot be long now before Hitler launches his invasion plans, and then may God help us all.

Hannah read and re-read this entry several times, running her finger along the words "*at heart a good child.*" She felt inexpressibly happy and sad, all at once. Mrs. D. had never spoken of her fears about the war, but of course, she wouldn't, would she? Not to the children.

"I'm not sure you ought to read any more," said the Professor. "It's too soon, and you're too young. Hand it over, please." Hannah felt she had been insulted, but she reluctantly returned the packet. "However, you should have this. Give it to Brandon from me." The Professor handed over George Braithwaite's identity card, which was in another acrylic sleeve. Hannah shoved it into her purse. "Oh," the Professor said, "and he may want this, too." Reaching into a drawer, she pulled out what looked like an enormous old English penny, several inches wide. Hannah saw that it was a bronze medallion. At its center was an embossed relief of a woman wearing a helmet and carrying a spear, with a lion at her feet.

"Is that Lady Liberty?" asked Hannah.

"No," said the Professor, "but I expect Lady Liberty began with her. This is Britannia, symbol of Britain." Hannah read the words *He Died for Freedom and Honour*, which were embossed around the coin's edge. The name *James Robert Gordon* was embossed near the center. Hannah asked the Professor about the small nail hole in the medallion.

"Mrs. Gordon nailed it to the front door, as a memorial to her son. The family of every British soldier who died in the First World War received one of these after the war ended. By then, Mr. Gordon was also dead. He was a victim of the flu epidemic after the war. The poor woman seems to have left Balesworth after that, and I have no idea what became of her."

Thoughtfully, Hannah turned the medallion in her hands. "One for every dead soldier. That's a lot of work. They must have had to make a couple of thousand of these, huh?" said Hannah.

"More like three-quarter of a million."

Hannah's eyes grew wide. "And one of them was Mrs. D.'s husband, right?"

"Right."

There was a long silence.

"What about all that stuff with finding George? So we found him, big whoop."

"It was a big whoop for him, wasn't it?" said the Professor.

"Whatever," Hannah said. "I just don't know what it had to do with us."

"Everything. You found the card, and you changed his life."

"No, you know it's not that simple."

"Isn't it? I told you, I'm an historian. Historians record and interpret the past, don't we? We don't create it."

Hannah looked at her skeptically. Something about what the Professor had said irritated her, but she wasn't sure what. Come to think of it, all of their conversations had been that way.

"Anyway, you still haven't told me. Why us? I mean, what does George have to do with us or this place?"

The Professor leaned down and picked up a copy of the local phone book from the corner where it had been thrown thoughtlessly, next to a dusty unused coffeepot and a box piled high with books. She riffled through it, and then ran her finger down a page. Silently, she turned the book around to face Hannah, and pointed to something.

Hannah leaned forward and took the phone book from her. "What am I supposed to be looking..." She stopped, and stared at the book, and then at the Professor. "Are you serious?"

"Am I?" asked the Professor, raising an eyebrow.

Hannah looked again to be sure, but there it was: *George Braithwaite, M.D.*

"I think you and the boys might want to visit with Dr. Braithwaite," the Professor said, as Hannah continued to stare at the page in the directory. "And I," she paused and took a paper from the pile balanced precariously on her desk. "I have books to read, classes to plan, papers to critique, meetings to attend, programs to organize, students to advise, and lots and lots of very stupid paperwork devised by stupid people to waste my time. I'm going to have to throw you out now."

"But..." said Hannah, as the Professor stood, gently took her arm and smoothly guided her to the door. The door was closed before Hannah could form a sentence.

Hannah stamped her foot, and leaning close to the door, yelled, "I'm going to find out about you. I'm going to report you to someone."

The Professor's distracted voice came through the door. "Are you, dear? That's nice..."

Hannah cried out "AUGHHHHH!!" and marched off to find Brandon and Alex.

Chapter 15
TiME...AND TiME AGAiN

When Kimberly dropped off Hannah and Alex at home, Alex found that he had an email waiting for him. It was from Brandon, who wrote that he had a dentist's appointment in the morning, so he would miss camp. But after Alex relayed what Hannah had told him, Brandon immediately messaged that he could accompany them to Dr. Braithwaite's house at 2 p.m.

Brandon felt foolish when he read what Hannah had learned from the Professor. Dr. Braithwaite did not attend Authentic Original First African Baptist, because he was one of a handful of black Episcopalians in town. But everyone black living in Snipesville knew who he was: He was a Big Shot. Unlike most Big Shots, however, he had moved to Snipesville, not away from it.

Brandon, who had never met the celebrated doctor, never thought about him, and would have assumed that his first name was "Doctor" if he had, had not connected him with George Braithwaite. He wondered how different things might have been if he had, and decided that they would have been far less interesting.

He looked in the bathroom mirror, and realized that he didn't look any different than when he had left. He had spent ten months in Balesworth, growing in height and muscle, especially from the hours spent operating Mr. Gordon's drill. But now he seemed to have shrunk back to normal size. He was disappointed, but he was also relieved that he would not have to explain to his mother how he had expanded in a matter of hours. Giggling to himself, he thought how she might have assumed a miracle had taken place at baseball camp.

The next day, Hannah and Alex had their dad pick them up from the house at lunchtime, and drop them off downtown, before he went back to his job at the bank. The kids had lunch in Zappy Burger. Hannah had always loved their MegaBurgers, but, today, although she finished hers, she wasn't enthusiastic. "I miss real bacon and eggs," she said sadly.

"Me, too," admitted Alex. "The food tasted like food, didn't it? Not like this stuff." He looked over the remains of his lunch, and toyed with the idea of throwing the rest away.

Hannah guessed what he was thinking. "You can toss it if you like," she said carefully. "I don't mind."

Alex looked up at her mournfully. "I guess," he said.

"She wouldn't mind, either. Not knowing how different things are now."

Alex knew who Hannah was talking about, and gave a small laugh. "She bloody would, you know."

With half an hour to kill, the two kids visited the tiny park, where pine trees loomed over a sad selection of playground equipment that all looked at least fifty years old. They played on the swings for a while, then on the carousel, and climbed on the jungle gym. Neither of them said much to the other. After a while, they knew it was time to begin the long trek to Brandon's house in West Snipesville. The journey, Hannah later reflected, was the only part of the day that felt even a little bit normal.

"So how was the checkup?" Alex asked, as they walked up a long country road out of West Snipesville.

"Great!" said Brandon enthusiastically. "You should see the new composite fillings he showed me. Plus he has this great acupressure technique for when he gives you the novocaine. And he told me..."

Hannah interrupted. "Brandon, you are totally obsessing on dentistry. Anyone would think you were there for a year, not two months."

Brandon stopped. "I was there for ten months...Weren't you?"

It began to dawn on them all how different their experiences had been.

"So what was the best part?" Alex asked Brandon.

Brandon looked thoughtful. "I liked the people...Some of them. But you know what I'll really miss? I mean, it sounds silly, I know, but...but I miss being important. That's crazy, I wasn't important at all, I was just an apprentice...But Mr. Gordon counted on me, and he talked to me like I was a real person. I'm gonna miss that. What about you?"

Alex thought a little before answering. "Being in the middle of things, you know, the War. It was neat to know that everything was going to turn out fine for England, but it was still scary and kind of exciting, even if we were in Balesworth. I'll miss Mrs. D., even though she nagged a lot, because she was...well, she was Mrs. D. She reminds me a little of my Grandma, but she's kind of unique, too, you know what I mean? I've never known anybody like her. And I'll miss Eric, of course, because we liked a lot of the same things. And Verity, because she was fun. Now I want to go to England and go walking in the countryside again. I bet it's not the same as it was, though."

Brandon looked over at Hannah, who was unusually quiet. "What will you miss most, Hannah?"

"Nothing," she said. "I'm glad to be back. I just wish we could have landed in California instead of back here in Armpit, Georgia."

Alex was puzzled. "But you'll miss Verity, right?"

Hannah walked ahead of the boys, saying nothing, her shoulders hunched.

As the walk dragged on, Hannah began to lose faith in Brandon's sense of direction. "So, where is Dr. Braithwaite's house, again? Are you sure this is the right way?"

"Of course I am. This time."

They were on one of the few hills in Snipesville, traveling along a road that meandered up a gentle slope. At the very top was a very ordinary white ranch house, surrounded by pine trees, with a line of carefully trimmed bushes in front. As the kids drew closer, they spotted an elderly, tall, thin, light-skinned black man with a neat moustache, who was leaving the house through the carport. He was dressed in a short-sleeved shirt and khakis, and smoking a pipe. Under his arm was tucked a set of small garden clippers. He approached a row of rose bushes down the side of the front lawn, and began to snip off the dead flower heads, his back toward the children.

"That's him, isn't it?" said Hannah. Unexpectedly, she found tears welling up in her eyes. Brandon was nervous, and he could see that Alex was, too.

"Should we do this?" Alex asked, uncertainly.

"Of course," said Hannah. "I mean, we gotta give him back his card." She pulled it out of her purse, and handed it to Brandon. "You do it."

"Me? Why me?" said Brandon, "I mean, what if he recognizes us? He might drop dead from the shock."

"He won't," said Hannah firmly. "After all this time, you think he's going to know it's us?"

The two of them were so busy arguing, they didn't notice that Alex had already walked halfway up the drive. Hearing his footsteps, Dr. Braithwaite turned, straightening up, and took his pipe from his mouth.

"And what can I do for you, young man?" he asked.

His accent was a little like an aristocratic Southerner might speak, Alex thought: It was kind of American, but kind of English.

"Are you Dr. Braithwaite?"

"That's right."

Brandon and Hannah now joined Alex, and Brandon held out the card in its plastic sleeve.

"We found this, and we found you," he said.

Dr. Braithwaite took it from him, stared at it, and said, "What in the world...?"

Then he looked at the children's faces, one by one. He dropped the clippers, which fell with a clatter onto the driveway.

He said, awestruck, "My God..."

They could not possibly be the same children. It was inconceivable. But Dr. Braithwaite had no other explanation for the appearance of these children than the one his guardian had given him a half-century before: Time travel is real, and time travelers live among us.

Soon, the kids found themselves seated in Dr. Braithwaite's small, neat living room. He brought out a tray on which were four glasses filled with ice, and a pitcher of chilled sweet tea.

"The last time I saw that card," he said sitting down in an armchair, "was in the summer of 1940. I remember losing it because it disappeared around the time that Smedley brought me to Balesworth. I guess I always assumed he had taken it from me. Mrs. Smith took my ration book, and she changed the name on it to Thomas Smith. Nobody argued if you altered a name. I was always afraid that nobody would ever find me, and that I would never again be able to prove who I really was. Of course, that was little crazy, but it was a little hard for a seven year old boy to think clearly under the circumstances. By the time you kids rescued me, I didn't trust anyone."

"You trusted us to get you out, and you trusted Mrs. D. when she asked you to tell the truth," said Hannah. "Don't you remember? It was only a few days ago..." Then she realized what she had said.

He smiled patiently at her, and said, "Not for me, it wasn't. That was a lifetime ago. But some things I remember like they were yesterday, and I remember a lot about that day. I remember looking into Mrs. D.'s eyes, and that was when I knew things would be all right. She had the kindest eyes I ever saw, before or since. And, of course, I remember you guys. But none of us could ever have guessed you were time travelers. Not in a million years."

"How do you know we're not imposters?" asked Alex.

Dr. Braithwaite, pouring out the iced tea, smiled at him. "Nobody could make this up. And, Alex, even though you all sound like Americans now, I never forget a face."

He told them what had become of everyone after they left. Dr. Arthur Oliver Healdstone and his wife Diana had adopted him, and Dr. Healdstone, who now went by his first name, Arthur, had told many stories of his brief child-hood friendship with George.

"You might not think that you could have made much of an impression in such a short time," Dr. Braithwaite told Brandon. "But Uncle Arthur would remember you the rest of his life. He was so lonely in that house. Mr. Gordon did his best, but Mrs. Gordon resented having to care for her husband's sister's son, and his cousin, Peggy, vanished from their lives. It broke his heart when you left, too, but he appreciated the note you left for him. As he got older, the more certain he said he was that you had really been a time traveler. I thought he was joking, or maybe losing his marbles." He chuckled.

"What about your dad?" asked Alex.

Dr. Braithwaite shook his head sadly, "My father never made it home. He died in the P.O.W. camp at the very end of the war in Europe. Uncle Arthur told me it was an escape attempt, but I tried to find a record of it years later, and there was nothing. I think Uncle Arthur just wanted me to feel better."

The Archers, he said, had continued to live quietly in Balesworth, until Geof-frey Archer died in the last year of the war, most likely from overwork brought on by all the demands of producing parachutes. After that, Mrs. Archer moved away from Balesworth, and was not heard from again. Brandon found himself feeling so sorry for the young woman in the garden, whose life, it seemed, had never really been happy. He felt a strong need to change the subject.

"So how did you end up in Snipesville, sir?" asked Brandon.

"Now that," Dr. Braithwaite said, lighting his pipe, "is a long story. Hannah, do you want to open a window? I seem to recall Eric saying how much you hated people smoking."

"Yes, I do," said Hannah, "and now I can make a big deal of it, because ev-eryone knows it kills you. And you're a doctor!"

Dr. Braithwaite looked at her and gave her a wise smile. "True enough," he said knowingly, "but don't forget, I am in my own house. Now go open a window."

It was weird, she thought, as she pushed the window open, to be bossed around by an old man who just two days before had been a shy kid.

Dr. Braithwaite told the kids that Dr. Healdstone had helped him gain ad-mission to grammar school, and that he eventually earned a degree in biology from Oxford University. "I taught in a boys' boarding school for a year," he said, "but by then I had already decided I wanted out of England. You have to understand that everything was pretty bad in the years after the war. All the clothes and furniture were shabby, there was a housing shortage because of all the people bombed out of their homes, and the food rationing actually got worse. They even started rationing bread after the war, and they cut many of the other rations. We didn't starve, of course. Mrs. D. even helped us out, because she often stopped by with eggs and vegetables from her garden."

He finally emigrated to New York in 1955, and won a scholarship to study medicine. "By then, the civil rights movement was in full swing in the South, and like a lot of people, I wanted to help. I learned that white doctors wouldn't treat black patients, and that there was a shortage of black doctors. So that's how I came to be the only black doctor in Snipesville. I'm glad to say that's no longer the case!"

"That is so cool!" breathed Brandon. "Well, except for the 'living for forty years in Snipesville' part. That's too bad."

"Well, son...I mean, Brandon, sorry..." he smiled and shook his head. "It's different when you're not from here. This house was paid off a long time ago, and since I retired, I've been able to do a lot of traveling. Whenever Snipesville drives me crazy, I just get on the Web and book another flight."

"You know how to use the Internet?" squeaked Alex.

"I didn't get stuck in 1940, you know," laughed Dr. Braithwaite. "Life moves on, and most of us move with it."

"But what about Eric? What happened to him?" asked Alex.

"Oh, now, there is a story," said Dr. Braithwaite. "Mrs. D. adopted him, although I don't know that anything formal was ever signed, kind of like with me and the Healdstones. It was different back in those days, you see. Mrs. D. got Eric into the grammar school on a scholarship. She didn't pull any strings to get him there, mind. After you guys and I left, and Verity was away at school much of the time, Eric says that Mrs. D. put a lot of energy into nagging him to do his homework. Eventually, he got a degree in civil engineering from the University of London."

"Did Verity make it to college, too?" asked Hannah.

"Sure she did. She graduated from Newnham, which is a women's college at Cambridge University, with a degree in English literature. And then she married Eric."

"She did?" gasped Hannah. All three kids giggled.

"You're all surprised?" Dr. Braithwaite asked with a twinkle in his eye. "I don't know that Eric was given much of a choice, to be honest. You know how Verity is. I was at their wedding, which took place not long before I went to the States. Mrs. D. made a speech at the reception. I remember how she embarrassed poor Eric and Verity when she told everyone that she was the only person present who could say she had spanked both the bride and the groom."

The kids laughed.

"Are Eric and Verity still alive?" asked Alex. Hannah wasn't sure she wanted to know, but Dr. Braithwaite nodded emphatically.

"Oh, very much so. I started going over to England every year when plane fares got cheaper in the Eighties, and they always insist I stay with them for a couple of weeks. Eric and Verity had two children in the end, a boy and a girl, but their daughter wasn't born until Verity was forty, and by then they had pretty much given up hoping for kids. Their daughter, Lizzie, works at a museum in London, and she and her husband just had a baby girl a couple of years back. Eric and Verity's son, well, he's a story for another day." He gave a small tight smile.

To Alex and Hannah's delight, he offered them Eric and Verity's address. When Hannah read the address, she was puzzled. "Eric and Verity Powell? Wasn't Powell Verity's last name?"

"Sure," said Dr. Braithwaite. "You see, Eric had no interest in passing along the name of the parents who'd abandoned him, and he thought Devenish was too hard to say, so he took hers....Now, if you write to them, don't tell them the truth about yourselves. They won't believe it."

"You could tell them," protested Hannah.

Dr. Braithwaite shook his head. "They'll just think I'm losing my mind in my old age. Oh, and by the way?"

He looked mischievously at them.

"I assume you know that we did beat Hitler in the end. We won the war, whether or not...Now, what is it Eric likes to say? Whether or not Hannah ate the stinky sandwiches."

While Dr. Braithwaite was back in the kitchen, fetching Cokes from the refrigerator and a bag of chips to share with them, Alex turned to Hannah, who was reading Dr. Braithwaite's medical degree on the wall.

"Hannah, you haven't asked him about...Hey, Dr. Braithwaite, what happened to Mrs. D.? Was she mad at us when we didn't write?"

Hannah didn't turn around.

Dr. Braithwaite dropped four Coke cans on the coffee table, and emptied a bag of chips into a red bowl. "You know, Mrs. D. wondered what had happened to you guys. She grumbled a bit, but she wasn't really angry. I expect she was disappointed, but, of course, being Mrs. D., she never said anything like that. A lot of people lost touch in the years after the war, and you have to remember that it was hard to trace people before we got the Web. Like most people, I guess, Mrs. D. just let it go, and assumed you had readjusted to being at home. But she never forgot any of us. She always talked about y'all, and especially Hannah. She wouldn't come all the way to America to see me, although I was always asking her over. It was very expensive in those days, but I offered to pay for her ticket, of course. I think she wouldn't come because she was afraid of flying, although she would never admit to such a pitiful thing as a fear of heights."

Hannah thought to herself of Mrs. Devenish at the top of the church tower.

Meanwhile, Dr. Braithwaite continued, "Even so, she wrote letters to me for many years, even when I was young and busy and not very good at writing back. And she did live a wonderful, long life. She lived to be 93 years old. I remember Eric telling me in his letter back in, oh, when was it now...must have been around 1978...He told me that she was working in her garden on the day she died."

Hannah had been watching Dr. Braithwaite with a strange expression on her face. As he finished speaking, she burst into tears. Alex, who wasn't too happy himself, was nonetheless amazed by Hannah's reaction. Mrs. Devenish and his sister had battled so much, and now she was upset because Mrs. D. was long dead?

Dr. Braithwaite immediately crossed the room, and took Hannah's hands in his. "I'm so sorry, honey. I should have realized how this news would affect you.... Look, there's something you should know. Mrs. D. was an English-woman of her time, and, unlike us Americans today, and even many of the Brits these days, she was very reserved. She didn't hold much with showing her feelings, and especially her affections. But I know for a fact that she thought the world of you. If she had known what things would be like today, here and now, I'll bet anything she wouldn't mind my passing something along to you, Hannah. This is from Elizabeth Devenish." With that, he wrapped his arms around Hannah, who bawled into his chest for what seemed to both Alex and Brandon like a very long time.

Brandon, fighting the annoying lump in his throat, felt like crying himself when he thought of Mr. Gordon and Oliver, but he decided that he would wait until he got back to the privacy of his room.

When Hannah and Alex arrived home, their dad noticed a box in the corner of the carport. He picked it up and inspected the label. "Hannah, looks like you got a package from the college. Must be from your writing camp." He handed it to Hannah, who was puzzled, but she brought it inside. She struggled with the heavy box all the way up the stairs to her room, where she opened it up.

Inside were three huge scrapbooks and a note, printed onto the college's letterhead:

> Dear Hannah,
>
> One of these is for you, one is for your brother, and one is for Brandon. You will know which is which. Never lose these photos: Such mementos are irreplaceable. So long as you have these pictures, it is easy to revisit the past anytime you like.
>
> Best,
> Dr. Harrower

Hannah sat on her bed, and opened the album that had her name on it.

On the very first page, she found a huge photo of her in the garden with Alex, Eric, Verity, George, Brandon and Mrs. Devenish. It was dated November 15, 1940. It was hard for Hannah to look at the picture, but she found it even harder to look away.

EPILOGUE

South Kensington, London: Today

The Professor walked briskly through Hyde Park, past well-wrapped-up officeworkers sitting on benches eating sandwiches, dogwalkers, soccer players, children playing tag, inline skaters, picture-snapping tourists, and all the hundreds of other people enjoying the enormous green space at the heart of London. Once upon a time, this had been King Henry VIII's hunting grounds.

The Professor crossed to Exhibition Road. More than 150 years before, this was the gateway to the Great Exhibition, the very first world's fair, which was held in an enormous purpose-built greenhouse called the Crystal Palace. The Victoria and Albert Museum was now to the Professor's left. She glanced at where, in 1940, falling German bombs had taken chunks of stone out of the side of the building. It looked as though a great monster had snacked on the solid wall. Turning left onto Brompton Road, the Professor climbed the great stone steps into the museum.

An hour later, she was seated in the researchers' reading room examining a very odd object with a magnifying glass. It was a tiny rectangular metal plate with holes in it. A smartly-dressed tall woman in her thirties with short dark brown hair walked up next to her.

"Excuse me?" the woman said, "I hope you don't mind my interrupting you, but one of the staff told me about your interest in this artifact, and I would love to chat with you about it. You're Professor Harrower, is that right?" The Professor shook hands with her and smiled, saying "Kate, please."

The younger woman smiled back. "I'm Elizabeth Powell. Lizzie. I'm one of the curators."

"Oh, I know that," said the Professor. "You know, I believe I once met your late great-grandmother while I was doing some research in Balesworth."

"Wow, did you really?" Lizzie laughed. "She was a character, wasn't she?"

"Indeed, she was. A truly remarkable woman."

"But how do you know I'm related to her?" Lizzie asked, puzzled.

"Well, as I like to say, I am an historian. Plus your full name is on the website, and I couldn't help noticing that your middle name is Devenish."

"Oh, right," said Lizzie, uncertainly. "Yes, Mum and Dad named me after her."

The Professor swiftly changed the subject. "Now, I wonder whether there are any manuscript collections related to this thing? It was part of the Great Exhibition, wasn't it?"

"Hmm, so far as I can tell." said Lizzie. "It's a bit of a mystery, actually. It wasn't in the official catalogue, but it arrived here with the rest of the exhibits that were retained after the Exhibition closed in 1851. Apparently, it looked like this when it got here. Nobody knows what it is, and nobody has studied it since the 1920s, from what I've been able to find out. After I came across it, I did some checking in other archives. What's interesting is that it did leave a bit of a paper trail. I've discovered some materials related to it, and I'd be very interested in having you take a look at them. I'm afraid they can't be photo-copied under the rules of that particular archive, but if you're interested, I'd be happy to pop along with you today and see if we can't grease the wheels a little bit..."

The Professor was thinking fast, asking herself questions. Was she ready...? Well, when was she ever?

"I'd appreciate that very much. When can we go?"

The End.

ACKNOWLEDGMENTS

I am a professional historian by trade, but, as Professor Harrower notes in her introduction, this is NOT a work of history. It is a work of art (with a very small 'a'), and I won't sully it with footnotes, bibliographies, and all the other contemporary apparatus of nervous authors.[1] I'm also sure that despite a fair bit of research, not to mention a large amount of background knowledge diligently applied, I have got some things wrong. There is also stuff that I (gasp!) made up. No time traveling kid, to my knowledge, ever crashed into Winston Churchill. Folks, that's why it's called fiction.

If you would like to know more about the actual history behind the book, and especially about what it was really like to be a kid in England during the two World Wars, please visit my website, www.AnnetteLaing.com, where Dr. Harrower has graciously agreed to discuss your queries. If your question is not already answered there, please message her with it, and she'll do her best to help.

My reluctance to use footnotes in a novel doesn't mean that I fail to recognize that I have received a great deal of kind assistance. In fact, I fully realize that any book is a collaborative venture, depending on the time and talents of dozens of helpers.

I would like to thank the following people in England for their prompt and very helpful research in response to my arcane enquiries:

Helen Barker at Beamish, North of England Open Air Museum, for information on Edwardian dentistry and what it might have actually cost to fix that broken window. Thanks also to all the staff and volunteers at Beamish for a delightful and inspiring visit I made with my family one very drizzly day in summer, 2006. It was exciting to visit a town street and mining village from 1913, and what a thoroughly helpful and friendly group of people greeted us!

Barry Attoe at the National Postal Museum, for fielding my enquiries on the frequency of postal delivery in Hertfordshire in 1915, and the terms on which one could buy postal orders during the First World War.

---

1 This is the lone footnote. I owe the Professor's discussion of Dame Irene Ward in the Prologue to Christine Hamilton's *Bumper Book of British Battleaxes* (London, Robson Books, 1997), 160-163. Great book, by the way, although (listen up, Mrs. Hamilton) if there's a sequel, I would like to see more of the good-hearted battleaxes like Dame Irene and Bessie Braddock, rather than the mean-spirited sort, whom I decline to name. So much more inspiring.

Karen Baker at the National Railway Museum in York helped me visualize the interiors of railway carriages in 1940.

Matthew McMurray, archivist of the WRVS (formerly Women's Royal Voluntary Service, and, before that, Women's Voluntary Service), for his cheerful help in tracking down two of the photos and gaining copyright permission, not to mention answering the awkward question, what color was that Hartnell-designed uniform, exactly? I still can't believe it's really green.

The first draft of this book was written almost entirely in my favorite corner of the newly-opened Starbucks in Statesboro in fall, 2006, during my unpaid, self-funded sabbatical. The cheerful baristas diligently kept me caffeinated, and guarded my laptop when I had to go to the loo, which was often, thanks to my drinking too much of the coffee they made. They also supplied me with invaluable consultancy on the vocabulary and behavior of my young characters, and even helped me choreograph scenes so I could be certain that they were physically possible. Most importantly, they cheered me on. What lovely young people you are. Thanks to all of you: Alli, Anna, Ashley, Billy, Chelsy, Drew (1), Drew (2), Emmy, Hayley, Jeff, Jessica (1), Jessica (2), Kathy, Katie, Margo, Michael (1), Michael (2), Miranda, Neal, Q., Raquiyah, Sean, Shay, Stevie, Tovah, and Tina.

Thanks especially to Jessica Richard, a student barista and martial arts trainer, who helped me to understand how kids are taught to use martial arts against adult attackers, and who suggested all the forms of attack that the kids used in rushing to Mrs. D's defense.

I owe an enormous debt of gratitude and affection to the college students who have participated in TimeShop: Wartime England. I thought TimeShop was a daft idea that I just had to get out of my system before I could return to my more "serious" projects as an historian. How silly. TimeShop turned into the most profound and memorable experience of my career, and it was you who made it so. Thank you, TimeShop Team, past and present, for your hard work, enthusiasm, and incredible loyalty. I am so proud of you all. Adam, Aisha, Alexis, Amanda, Angelica, Ashley, Beth, Brandon, Carla, Carmen, Caroline, Christine, Danielle, Don, Eboni, Edward, Heather, Jackie, Jessica (1), Jessica (2), Josh, Karen, Katie, Kim, Kristin, Lauren (1), Lauren (2), Leila, Lelia, Liz, Mark, Martin, Mary (1), Mary (2) Megan, Melanie, Nick, Niki, Noel, Paul, Paulette, Quintel, Reid, Nicole, Shane, Sheridan, Tameka, Tracy, and Vivien.

And thank you, TimeShop kids, for your giddy embrace of our program. You have been an inspiration. There are too many of you to name, but you know who you are.

I owe a huge debt to all who made my sentimental journey back to England this winter such an emotional and pleasurable experience—and thank you all for your part in making my entire life such an adventure. Cheers to Alan, Angela, Mrs. C., Colin, Heather, John (1), John (2), Joyce, Karen, Katy, and Mrs. S. (who demonstrated magnificently during my visit why she remains one of the most extraordinary and influential characters in my life, whether she likes me saying that or not.) Thanks also to all the many kind strangers who became new friends.

I am very grateful to the kids and adults of all ages on both sides of the Atlantic who read and commented on various drafts. Many thanks to the following: Merritt Skidmore-Hess, Ken and Gloria Skidmore, Alec Ogihara, Lauren English, Megan and Summer Taylor, Tovah Shoup, Ashley Stevens, Cate Godley, Ryan Daigneault, Jack and Joyce Howard, Ellie and Miriam Bryant, Christopher Stephens, Jane Hall, Mary Hadley, Kimber Queen, Bethany Caliaro, Roz Goodson, Loretta Brandon, Sharon McMullen, Joanne Newland, Kristin Marzec, Katie Glorieux, Fielding Keeley, Breanne Dykes, Joyce Harper, Angela Hepworth, Deborah Harvey, Hannah Salway, Katy Gardner, and Brandy Baird.

I didn't expect to work on this book in a hospital bed, but there you go. A pulmonary embolism in February 2007 was a dramatic reminder to value every moment and every friend. This episode also made it all the more important to me to see this book into print at the earliest opportunity. Thanks to Drs. Branch, Purves, Jain, Harrison, and Cichelli, and the overworked nursing staff at East Georgia Regional Medical Center, for caring for me during the enforced extension of my sabbatical.

The splendid cover design is by my friend and fellow ex-Californian Deborah Harvey. The layout and prep were expertly executed by my friend and former student, Kelley Callaway, who I am sure never expected that I would want to make quite so many changes in the final stages. Ahem. The able and cheery staff of the Eagle Print Shop, led by the lovely Brenda Aytes and Gloria Joiner, printed the innumerable copies of the manuscript that were delivered to readers. Joanne Newland and kids at Sallie Zetterower Elementary gave me lots of great feedback on the cover. Who knew there were so many talented and cool people in a small town in Georgia? I did. Kudos, guys.

In particular, I want to thank three dear friends and colleagues for their encouragement, support, and brilliantly creative ideas, which they shared with me over everything from burritos to cheesecake, not to mention the odd glass of wine. As ever, they got me out of several fixes. I especially appreciated their urging me, in the words of one of them, "not to worry about the P.C. people." You're right: The past is not politically correct. I send love and gratitude to Michelle Haberland, Laura Shelton, and Cathy Skidmore-Hess, all fine historians and strong women of character.

Finally, much love and thanks to my ever-patient husband Bryan and my ever-impatient son, Alec. My boys—Whatever would I do without them?

A.L.

P.S. It turns out that there is a Snipesville in south Georgia, something I learned only after the book was written! The real Snipesville is a hamlet near Hazlehurst, and it has nothing to do with the fictional college town depicted in this novel. It goes to show that no matter how silly the material that I dream up, Georgia is always one step ahead of me, bless its heart.

Dr. Annette Laing was born in Scotland, raised in England, spent many years in California, and now lives in rural Georgia. She was a professor of early American and British history before resigning in 2008 to concentrate on her work in children's history, as director of Imaginative Journeys, a nonprofit that offers creative kids camps. In 2010, *A Different Day, A Different Destiny*, Annette's second book in The Snipesville Chronicles series, was published by Confusion Press.

To learn more about Annette and her work, visit www.AnnetteLaing.com